THE MEANING OF LUFF
AND OTHER STORIES
BY MATTHEW HUGHES

The Meaning of Luff and Other Stories

Copyright Matthew Hughes 2013

ISBN: 978-0-9881078-6-1

Cover illustration by Ben Baldwin; book design by Bradley W. Schenck

To Bradley W. Schenck,
webpage designer extraordinaire

TABLE OF CONTENTS

INTRODUCTION

Luff Imbry, confidence man, thief, forger extraordinaire, aficionado of a myriad art forms, began life as a supporting character in my novel *Black Brillion*, published by Tor in 2004. He reappeared again in the same role in a companion novel, *The Commons*, published by Robert J. Sawyer Books in 2007.

And that should have been the end of him. In fact, in the original draft of *Black Brillion* that I submitted to Tor, I killed him off in a rather messy fashion near the end of the novel. But my editor, David G. Hartwell, was wise in the ways of science fiction readers and he advised me that it was a mistake to murder the only likeable character in the book. So I rewrote that segment and Luff lived on.

But the tale that he was part of was still over and done with; or so I thought. But around the same time I as I was selling the companion novel to Rob Sawyer, I came to know Nick Gevers, co-editor of the quarterly magazine (now a quarterly anthology) *Postscripts*. Nick had warmly reviewed my first two sf novels, *Fools Errant* and *Fool Me Twice*, in another magazine, and when I got in touch to express my appreciation, he let me know that he'd like me to try my hand at writing something for *Postscripts*.

I thought, *Why not bring Imbry back on stage?* I am a crime writer at heart, and the fat man (modeled on Sydney Greenstreet's characters in *The Maltese Falcon* and *Casablanca*), offered all kinds of possibilities. So I wrote a story called *The Farouche Assemblage* and sent it to Nick. He bought it, and thus encouraged, I wrote more stories, and they each found a market. Luff appeared not only in *Postscripts* but in *The Magazine of Fantasy & Science Fiction* and an anthology of stories entitled *Forbidden Planets* (DAW) that was commissioned to mark the fifitieth anniversary of the iconic science fiction film.

Pete Crowther, who co-edited the anthology and also co-edits *Postscripts*, commissioned three Imbry novellas, two of which are reprinted here. And Victoria Blake, owner of Underland Press, commissioned a Luff Imbry novel, *The Other*, which appeared in 2011. One of these days, I mean to write a sequel to it.

But in the meantime, here are nine adventures of the corpulent master criminal of Old Earth in its penultimate age.

THE MEANING OF LUFF

Welliver Tung had owed Luff Imbry a sum of money for longer than was advisable. The amount was more than five thousand hepts, Imbry's commission on the return to their owner of certain items that had gone astray late one evening when Tung found herself in the objects' presence while passing through the private rooms of the financier Hundegar Abrax while he and his household slept.

Abrax had not wanted the nature of the missing items to become public knowledge. He knew people who knew people who knew Imbry. Overtures were made, inquiries carried out, the items located and a finder's fee agreed upon. Neither Tung nor Imbry had thought it wise to attend at the transfer of the goods to Abrax's agent, in case the Archonate Bureau of Scrutiny had somehow caught a whisper of the doings. They sent a young man experienced in such assignments who did not mind having all of his memories — except for the time, place and terms of the handover — temporarily misplaced. Their restoration was never complete, and always brought on headaches and double vision, but the fellow considered himself adequately paid.

The operation was carried out with smooth precision on a busy corner in the ancient City of Olkney, capital of the incomparably more ancient world of Old Earth. But Welliver Tung did not keep her appointment the next day at Bolly's Snug, a tavern where Imbry often liked to conduct business; its back reaches were a warren of private rooms, some with ingenious exits known only to those who paid the owner, Bashur Bolly, handsomely for that knowledge.

Imbry waited until it was clear that Tung was not coming, then returned to his operations center — a concealed room in a nondescript house in a quiet corner of Olkney — to consult his information retrieval matrix. He soon ascertained that Tung had not been taken up by the scroots overnight, nor had she been fished out of Mornedy Sound with heavy objects fastened to her person — an occasional occupational hazard of her profession.

Imbry placed the tips of his plump fingers together and rested his several chins upon them. He thought through the situation. Tung knew him well enough to understand the danger inherent in pulling him when he expected a push, as the expression went. If she was withholding the fat man's commission it was because she needed the funds. If she needed the funds to pay a debt to someone whose collection methods might be even more appalling than Luff Imbry's, he would have heard of it. Therefore, she required the five thousand hepts to take advantage of some opportunity to earn even more, out of which she would seek to mollify Imbry with a bonus.

He returned to his research matrix and made inquiries that spun off from Welliver Tung's several fictitious identities, which he knew about though she did not know that he knew. Data flowed his way and he soon snapped up a telling mote: under the name Harch Belanye, Tung had that morning placed a deposit on a derelict house in Ombron Square, in a district that had once been fashionable but had now fallen into the disrepute that hangs upon desperate poverty.

He conducted more research, this time centered on the property, and acquired further facts. After careful thought, he decided to equip himself with a needler, a police-issue shocker and an elision suit. The garment was made of a material that bent light around its wearer, making him unnoticeable except to the well trained eye. He retrieved the items from a concealed closet that was well stocked with the tools of his illicit trade, many of them designed by Imbry himself.

Outside, he summoned a public aircar and had it drop him beside an alley two streets from Ombron Square. There he slipped into the elision suit, positioned his weapons for easy deployment and set off to find Welliver Tung. His unseen passage along the debris-strewn streets excited no comment from the few pedestrians he slipped past.

The house that Tung had bought dated from the umpteenth revival of an ornate style of architecture that Imbry considered both finicky and overdone. Its defenses were also standard and he rapidly tickled his way through them, entering the rear of the place on the ground floor. The cleaning systems had cycled down to minimal, and dust hung in the air, along with a faintly sweet mustiness that Imbry recognized as the scent of death, attenuated by the passing of several years.

The odor corroborated what Imbry had gathered from his researches: the former owner of the property, Tib denAarrafol, had been a recluse with few associates and no family. He had not been seen in public for more than a decade, and had most likely died a solitary death here at home, his corpse drying and moldering inconspicuously while the house puttered on about him. At some point, tollsters from the Archonate's fiduciary division had affixed a notice to the door stipulating that unless unpaid taxes were made good, the place would be auctioned. Tib denAarrafol being unable to meet his obligations, the property had gone to the sole bidder: Welliver Tung.

Imbry listened and deduced that the new owner was engaged in moving furniture in one of the front rooms. With his shocker in one hand and the needler in the other, he made his way toward the scraping and bumping. At the end of a dimly lit hall he peered through a doorway and spied his debtor shoving chairs and side tables across the uncarpeted floor, leaving a blank space before a sideboard that stood against the far wall. On its recently dusted surface rested what looked to be a dull black stone the size of Imbry's head, set in an armature of tarnished silver.

The fat man turned his gaze to each corner of the room, determining that Welliver Tung was alone. Then he stepped into the doorway, aimed both weapons and said, "You owe me."

Tung neither squeaked nor jumped. Imbry admired the professionalism that caused her to freeze then turn oh so slowly toward the door, showing her hands empty and well clear of her body. He knew that all she was seeing was a slight shimmer behind a needler and shocker suspended in the air and directed her way. But his voice would have been unmistakable.

"I knew you would show up eventually," she said. "I was hoping to have enough time to ready this for you."

"In situations like this I have found it useful to appear unexpectedly," he said.

"I fully intended to pay you."

"Of course you did. Now explain to me, and be brief, why you haven't, and while you do so I will I weigh the penalty."

She had prepared her story. She had been looking for out-of-the-way premises in which to store various items over the short to medium terms and had canvassed abandoned properties in this district. The denAarrafol house had seemed promising, so she had entered and inspected it, finding the former owner upstairs in bed, where he had quietly expired some years previously.

His faint presence did not disturb Tung, who had then gone through the house carefully, in case there might be objects of value pining away for want of ownership. She had found two secret compartments, one of which contained a number of odd items, including an ancient grimoire whose author assumed that magical spells could be efficacious.

"It seems that denAarrafol dabbled in a thaumaturgery," she said. "He was working on a book of his own when he died. He believed that magic and rationalism alternated over the aeons in a great cycle and that we are approaching a cusp at which the Wheel turns anew and spells and cantrips become operative, while physics and chemistry become unreliable."

"I have heard of the theory," Imbry said. "It can be a useful construct when separating the gullible from their assets."

"It turns out there is something to it," Tung said.

"Oh?"

"Along with the spell book and various paraphernalia, I found that," Tung said, indicating the stone on the sideboard.

"And that is?" Imbry said, stepping into the room for a closer inspection of the black thing, though he kept an eye on Welliver Tung.

"In denAarrafol's book, it was referred to as a 'salience indicator,'" Tung said. "It reveals the purpose of a life."

"Of life in general?"

"No, of a specific life — yours, mine, anyone's."

Imbry peered more closely at the stone. It seemed to be a mere lump of black stuff, dull and unreflective. "And how is this determined?"

"It is difficult to..." Tung broke off. "You're going to think that I am trying to slip a flat one under you."

"You would not want me to think that," Imbry said. He assessed the unconscious messages that came from her face and posture, as well as the tiny beads of perspiration that appeared on her upper lip. "I believe you are about to offer me what you, at least, believe to be the truth."

He saw honest relief wash over her. "I'm waiting," he said.

"DenAaarafol's notes say it is a portion of the consciousness — not an organ like the brain but the 'condition of being aware' was how he put it — of an entity that inhabits another continuum," she said. "This entity comprehends the interlinkages of all life in our continuum. It knows the why of every creature's existence."

"Some sort of god?" Imbry asked.

"No," she said, "for it can do nothing with the information. DenAarrafol likened it to a book on a shelf, though the kind of intelligence that would open such a book and read what is written in it was beyond his comprehension. This lump represents but a single 'page,' a page that nonetheless contains the meaning of every life on Old Earth, and perhaps even all the lives of the trillion inhabitants of the Ten Thousand Worlds."

Several large questions came to mind, but Imbry put them aside for later consideration and chose instead to ask a small and simple one. "Why did you buy the house if all you wanted was the 'salience indicator?'"

"It won't move," she said. She spread her hands in a gesture of bafflement. "Again, I don't understand it, but it seems that the object is not really 'here.'

Instead, an 'impression' of it is reflected into our universe, but a reflection from its continuum manifests itself as a dense and lightless object in ours, though it remains 'connected' in some manner. In short, it would be easier to move the Devenish Range to the other side of the planet than to budge that thing a hairbreadth."

Imbry moved on to another question. "How does it work?" Then he quickly added one more. "And what does it actually do?"

The operation was uncomplicated: touch the black lump with the written name or the image of any person, or even an item that had often been in close proximity to the subject. The effect was also simple, Tung said, and immediate: the meaning of that person's existence appeared in the mind of he who had initiated the operation.

Imbry digested the information. "Then if I write my name on a piece of paper and bring it into contact with the object, it will reveal to me the meaning of my existence?"

"No," said Tung. "It will reveal to you the meaning of anyone else's existence except your own. The thaumaturge found that seeking to know his own salience brought on a blinding headache. He conjectured that persevering would create a feedback resonance that would damage his brain."

"Damage how?"

"Boiling followed by melting, was how he put it."

"You have, of course, tested denAarrafol's surmises?"

"I have. They seem to be correct."

"And thus your plan was to reopen the house as a venue for revealing the meaning of their lives to those who would offer a reasonable fee?" Imbry said.

"At first," Tung said. "Once it became the vogue to discover one's salience, I intended to charge a quite unreasonable fee, out of which I would repay what I owe you, plus a substantial bonus."

"A good plan," Imbry said. "It requires only one small emendation."

Tung stiffened. "I think it is perfect as it is."

"You lack the perspective," said Imbry, "of someone with two weapons."

Her shoulders slumped. "I have made a considerable outlay from my limited resources to acquire this house."

"From *my* resources," Imbry corrected her. "Thus it shall be a joint venture. I shall take eighty parts; you will have twenty. But, out of gratitude, I shall write off the five thousand hepts you owe me."

"This seems unjust."

"It seemed no less unjust to me that my five thousand were put to work without my consent. I know several less indulgent persons who, in the same circumstances, would now be arranging to remove two corpses from these premises."

Tung grumbled but acquiesced. "It was ever thus," she said. "The big teeth take the big bites."

Imbry invested more of his funds in the enterprise, thoroughly refurbishing the house so that its appearance would not startle or dismay persons of advanced social rank. When all was in readiness, he employed his research matrix to identify a dozen persons each of whom met two criteria: they would be intrigued by the concept, and they would spread the word among the refined of Olkney in a manner that would bring those whose lives were governed by fashion to his door, thirsting for knowledge.

He summoned the dozen to a soiree and demonstrated the salience indicator. As he had expected, the meaning of each of the initial batch's lives was confined to the subject's having an effect on style. To Imbry these seemed poor excuses for existence, but the opinion makers were delighted to have their tawdry and ephemeral goals demonstrated.

Word soon spread. Imbry engaged a pair of large, silent attendants and dressed them in suitably impressive costumes. The mutes collected extravagant fees and conducted aristocrats and magnates into the presence. The fat man had determined that he would earn more if he restricted his operation to no more than one hour, every other night. The compressed supply of enlightenment speedily drove up demand, returning his investment many times over in the first week, then lifting his profit into reaches that were enough to make even Imbry blink in surprise.

He fastidiously meted out to Welliver Tung every grimlet that she was owed as a twenty per cent participant in the venture. Her take must have greatly exceeded whatever she might have expected to have received before his entry into the proceedings, Imbry knew. Yet she showed a sour attitude, even as he handed her a valise bulging with pelf.

To cheer her, he said, "Let me put your name to the salience indicator. Free of charge. It will be as if you were a duke or count-margrave."

She signaled a negative. "I decided from the beginning that that was not a knowledge I cared to encompass."

"Why?" Imbry said, in an airy tone. "Did you not wish to discover that the point of your existence was to assist me in my goals?"

Tung's eyes became narrow, glinting with a hard light, but she said nothing. She departed and Imbry prepared to receive the next intake of well heeled punters.

In time, however, a bleakness threatened to descend upon the fat man. He tired of the sameness of the life-meanings he dispensed to the highest echelons of Old Earth society. Too often, he was required to extemporize an answer because he soon discovered that telling the unvarnished truth, as it appeared in his mind when he touched a name or image to the lump, could never satisfy the client.

A young lordling did not welcome being told, "The meaning of your life is that you will father a child who will in turn father a child who will, seventy-three years from now, bump into a man on a street corner, causing that man to miss an appointment."

They preferred to hear, "Because of a remark that you drop into a casual conversation, a brilliant new epoch in appliqued fabric design will sweep the finest salons of Olkney. Unfortunately, it will not become the overpowering vogue until months after your demise, but your genius will be recognized as its inciting spark, and the ages will remember you and bless your name."

He was not surprised that the clients found these patent fantasies much more palatable than the blunt truth. But it continued to wear on Imbry that so many of the lives he touched to the salience indicator were revealed to be of almost no consequence at all. So many people were little more than place-holders, keeping a seat warm until someone of true moment should come along and briefly occupy it.

"But, perhaps," he told himself, "I achieve these tiresome, tawdry results because I am limiting the revelations to the idle rich, who live notoriously unproductive lives. If I sought out saints and savants, I would likely see cheerier visions."

Then he reminded himself that the quality of the visions was not the purpose of the endeavor. The goal was to make wealth flow thickly toward Luff Imbry, and the returns were more than handsome. Imbry used them to indulge his increasingly elevated tastes and fancies — especially those that arose from his gustatory appetites. He devoured dishes that were legendary, including some that could not be created more than once in a century, so rare were the ingredients. From these occasions he derived a grim satisfaction, reveling in the textures and aromas, while saying to himself, *If not I, then who?*

Sometimes, as he lay in his bed, the savors of the evening's feast lingering on his palate, his mind would drift toward the inevitable question. Always, he pushed temptation away. What would it serve to know the salience of Luff Imbry? If he learned the context of his existence, for good or ill (and he did not expect much good), could he summon the strength to go on doing as he did?

He recalled one client whose purpose in life was discharged even before he reached full maturity: by waving a wad of currency under the percepts of an autocab, the young buck had snatched it from a poor young woman already late for an interview with an editor, thus smothering a prospective great literary career in its infancy. The rest of the client's life was an empty afterthought. The young woman's fate was unrecorded.

Suppose Imbry discovered that the point of his being had been unwittingly achieved in his youth. Could he go on filling and voiding his innards, year upon year, knowing that his moment had already come and gone, unmarked, unheeded?

Or suppose, for all his mastery of the arts of peculation and hornswogglery, he turned out to be but a minor player in someone else's grander game — the user used — would his pride withstand the illumination? These were questions best left unanswered.

It would be different if he had someone with whom he could share the burden of such knowledge, but Imbry accepted that solitariness was a necessary condition of the profession he had freely chosen. It would not do to make dear friends only to see them become liabilities that must be disposed of.

Then one evening, he came to the denAarrafol house to discover that Welliver Tung had arrived before him. She was waiting in the now opulent room where the salience indicator sat, wearing an expression that Imbry could only characterize as a mean-hearted sulk.

He sent one of the attendants to retrieve her portion of the week's proceeds: the big man returned lugging two filled satchels, but Tung accepted them with ill grace.

"What is wrong?" Imbry said.

"This should have been all mine."

Imbry formed his plump lips into an arrangement that expressed a sad knowledge. "Be thankful that it wasn't. I have discovered that there is a price to be paid for what that thing reveals, and paid even by one who merely transmits the revelation."

Tung made a wordless sound that indicated she neither shared nor valued his opinion.

Imbry said, "Not everything that passes through pipes is clean and wholesome, thus it is fortunate for many pipes that they are not burdened with awareness." He looked inward for a moment, then said, "I have come to believe that denAarrafol's death may have been self inflicted."

Tung made the same sound as before, only with more emphasis. "Don't try to wax me," she said. "I don't hold a polish."

Imbry was capable of expressing much with a shrug. He now offered her a particularly eloquent one. Her jaw line grew sharp, and she reached into a pocket and withdrew a slip of paper.

"While I was waiting I wrote down your name," she said. Before he could move she leaned back and touched the paper to the dull blackness. Imbry saw the effect of the contact appear in her face: surprise followed by comprehension succeeded by feline satisfaction.

"Do you want to know the point of your existence?" she said. "Such as it is?"

"From your face, I believe I already do," he said.

"Why settle for faith when certainty is at hand?"

There was a needler in his pocket. He thought about using it, then decided that he would not. He stood quietly while she told him the meaning of his life. It did not take long.

When she was finished he remained standing, contemplating the images she had conjured into his mind: his future self, the persons into whose story he would be drawn, the small role he would fulfill — not as the hero, not even as the pivot of fate, but as merely a supporting player in another's drama, there to speak his lines and do his business, then fade away.

After a moment, his eyes came back from the vision to encompass Welliver Tung, saw her flinch at the hardness in his face. Then he smiled a small smile, gave her another shrug and said, "The house is yours. I advise you to close it up and forget its secrets."

He turned and left, took an air car to his favorite club and treated himself to a sumptuous dinner. He paid close attention to every facet of the experience, lingered over each dish, cherished every morsel. Sated, he retired to one of the transients rooms and slept better than he had for some weeks.

Not long after, business took him away — an extended tour of several worlds up and down The Spray, where people could be persuaded to pay remarkable sums for goods that were bedecked with just the right glamor of legend blended with trumpery. He took pleasure in his work, not because it had intrinsic meaning but because it was well wrought.

"It is good to have substance to one's existence," he told his dark reflection in the first class observation port of a space liner, as the stars streamed by. "But if fate denies one substance, one can yet do a lot with style."

When he returned to Olkney he learned that Welliver Tung had leapt from the upper story of the Brelle Tower. He heard nothing of what had happened to the salience indicator, and did not inquire.

THE FAROUCHE ASSEMBLAGE

Having made an immense fortune amid the commercial frenzy that characterized life in the Canton of Zeel, the magnate Paddachau Chin retired to his secluded family estate in the County of Ambrou, where his singular collection of artworks became the chief jewel of his reputation. The incomparability of the Chin Collection was universally agreed, though there could be no certainty as to how many of Chin's wide circle of acquaintances had been permitted the unequalled pleasure of viewing them. Those who whispered that they had been afforded the uncommon privilege would say no more; they had sworn to keep silent.

Luff Imbry's encounters with art centered mainly on its traffic, especially when that trade was diverted through the more ombrous avenues of the ancient city of Olkney. Under Imbry's hand, works passed quietly from their previous owners to their next, inconvenient questions were left unvoiced, and the new possessor was as unlikely to advertise his acquisition as Chin's visitors were to burble about whatever glories they might have seen.

Chin's miserly sequestration of so many exquisite pieces offended Imbry's sense of how things ought to be in a well ordered universe, namely that valuable goods existed to be appreciated by those who could afford to pay Luff Imbry to provide them. His was a rich and comprehensive philosophy, with many corollaries and axioms involving the iniquity of locks and the virtue inherent in weaving ways around watchmen and other obstructions.

He resolved to teach Chin a moral lesson by transferring as many as possible of his possessions to grateful hands. The lesson would be all the more pointed for those hands being connected to some of the magnate's circle who had long and vainly sought an invitation to view them.

Imbry conducted research, conceived an approach and made preparations. He learned that Chin had spoken of a frustrated desire to acquire a new work by Hassol Humbergruff, who worked in multicolored wire figurines. These he assembled in various configurations hung from strings and thin rods so that, as they were moved by currents in the air, they enacted a shifting series of tableaux. The figures might at first glance suggest a ribald joke that as soon as it was understood became an ironic commentary on itself, before transforming into a tragic statement that then plunged all the way into bathos.

New creations by Humbergruff had of late become increasingly difficult to acquire. The artist alternated between short bouts of feverish creativity, followed by long spells of somnolence. The latter were caused by his addiction to blue borrache, a powerful lethetropic drug, the former by his need to acquire the money to buy the dream-swept oblivion he craved. Unfortunately, the addiction was progressive, the drug tending to burn its way through one neural structure after another until there was scarcely enough left to maintain the most elementary functions. Or, as Imbry put it to Humbergruff as he sought to rouse him from a six-day stupor, "It won't be long before you're unable to tell any part of you from any other. The likelihood of unhappy accidents will then approach a certainty."

The artist's reply was somewhere between a word and a moan. He rolled over on the stained pallet that occupied a corner of his studio, pulled bony knees up toward a thin chest, and smacked gummy lips. Imbry sighed and, seizing a hank of the man's greasy hair, pulled him to a semi-sitting position propped against one wall. He squeezed Humbergruff's cheeks in a way that forced open the slack mouth, dodged the puff of foul breath that emerged, and poured another measure of restorative into the cavity.

The artist choked and spluttered but Imbry pinched the man's lips closed and held them until he saw the protuberance in the scrawny throat bob up and down. "There," he said, "now come up out of it. I need you."

Still within the borders of his dream, Humbergruff muttered something unintelligible. Imbry methodically slapped one cheek then the other with carefully measured blows until the artist's eyes opened. Seeing that each eye was looking in a different direction from the other, Imbry continued to rock the man's head from side to side until both red veined orbs were focused on him.

"Are you here?" he asked.

Humbergruff blinked and peered. "Who are you?"

Imbry told him a convenient name. The artist did not even struggle to place it. His allowed his eyes to close and his head to loll.

Imbry delivered another slap. Humbergruff raised an ineffectual hand. "What do you want?" he said.

"Later. First we must make you bearable in a closed room."

Luff Imbry was a figure of pronounced corpulence, so thickly upholstered in layers of fat that some people thought that if he ever fell down he was at risk of rocking himself to sleep trying to get back up. But beneath the sleek exterior was a well concealed musculature and a practiced mobility. Imbry now applied both to raise the artist's spare frame to a standing position before propelling him to the studio's sanitary suite. He secured Humbergruff in its grip then activated the controls for the full cycle. A short time later, the artist emerged shaking and pale, but thoroughly scrubbed, emptied, groomed and polished.

While that process had been in train, Imbry had instructed Humbergruff's integrator to prepare some innocuous food and a pot of strong punge. "Sit and eat," he said, making sure that the man did as he was told. "I have a proposition to make."

He watched the artist lethargically spoon up a sweetened gruel. As the last wisps of blue borrache effervesced from Humbergruff's system, his attention retained a tendency to wander inward. Imbry questioned him, partly to compel a continued awareness of where and when they were, partly to satisfy a curiosity about the drug's attraction. "What draws you to spend your life, indeed to shorten it, in this sorry manner?"

"Dreams," said the ruins of Humbergruff. "I dream of worlds and wonders."

"Starships depart hourly. They can take you to worlds and wonders all up and down The Spray."

The artist's drawn face took on a reflective aspect. "True, but they are not mine."

"You had fame and accolades," Imbry said, "and could have them again."

Humbergruff sighed. "We inhabit an impossibly ancient world. What can be done that has not already been done to perfection? What is there to say when all has already been said? And not just said, but heard and understood? We are naught but a recurring dream. What is the point of all this making and shaping?"

"The world's regard?" said Imbry. "Which translates into fine dinners and a comfortable place to lay one's head, often beside an engaging companion."

"I have done all of that, and now I am done with it," said Humbergruff. "It pales." He touched his brow. "In here, I have found more. I have found everything."

Imbry was no stranger to narcissistic impulse; indeed, he preferred the world to revolve about his own needs. But here he saw the purest form of vanity, a shutting out of all experience but that of the self, rattling down the shutters and sealing the doors of perception, to sit in a darkening solipsism until the essential inner spark dwindled and went out. He shuddered then pushed the image aside and came to business.

"Humbergruff," he said, "I will acquaint you with your situation. It is not a happy one." He explained that the artist had entered a downward spiral, producing haphazardly in order to purchase temporary oblivion, but each visit to limbo lasted longer than the one before, while his productive periods grew correspondingly shorter. At the same time, his tolerance for blue borrache increased, requiring him to make a greater effort to earn its cost, but the drug steadily robbed him of that ability. "Eventually you will have neither the drug nor the capacity to acquire it."

The artist blinked. "I have never been good at grasping the obvious," he said. He turned and regarded a credenza set against the far wall where his few remaining vials and paraphernalia lay scattered. "You have opened a sad vista."

"I will now reveal a more comforting one," Imbry said. "I have purchased a large supply of blue borrache, enough to keep you dreaming until you have passed over into the ineffable."

Hassol Humbergruff's head snapped toward the fat man. His gaze had lost all trace of dreaminess. "Where is it?" he said.

"Close by," Imbry said.

The artist was rising from his seat. "And yet we sit here bandying irrelevancies? Let us go get it," he said.

Imbry reached across the table. The shoulder beneath his plump hand was perilously thin and he easily pressed the man back into his chair. "First let us come to terms."

"You will find me very agreeable," Humbergruff declared.

Imbry quickly outlined his proposal: Humbergruff would produce several works. When Imbry was satisfied with their quality, he would hand over the supply of blue borrache. The artist could then slip into a languorous dream from which he would never emerge.

Despite the fat man's having pointed Humbergruff along the path to sure extinction, the artist displayed a fervent interest in the arrangement. "First, though," he said, "I should sample the merchandise, to be sure that it will meet the test."

"It is the finest product of the Green Circle syndicate," Imbry assured him. "You will not be disappointed."

"Still," Humbergruff said, his pale tongue emerging to lick his lips, "only the taste will tell."

Imbry showed him an unhappy face and mused aloud, "Perhaps there is some other artist with whom I could do business."

And so the bargain was struck. In short order, Imbry removed Humbergruff and his working materials to a secluded location, a remote and rural cottage where there was plenty of light and a complete absence of blue borrache.

The artist suffered pangs and fearsome bouts of nightsweats, ameliorated by liberal doses of Imbry's restorative, and several times tried to call off their agreement. But Luff Imbry displayed an adamant resolve, expressed in stern words backed up by occasional shoves and buffets, until five assemblages of wire figures adorned the air above the workbench. Two of them were minor pieces, produced in the first several days of their association, but the latter period had brought three first-class constructions, as good if not better than anything Humbergruff had produced in his prime.

"These are excellent," Imbry said, watching the hanging shapes dip and rotate to create evolving stories of mythic intensity shot through with subtle subtexts.

"You have driven me cruelly," Humbergruff said. In the last two days he had ceased to eat, spending every hour bent over the bench, plying his crimps and twizzlers to shape the delicate metal fibers into precise alignments. Though his legs trembled as constantly as the leaves of a wystol tree, his fingers were crisp and sure in their judgements.

"Your suffering has raised you to new heights," Imbry said. "You have surpassed yourself."

"It has all been done before, as well or better."

"Not to my knowledge."

Humbergruff made a face that did not speak highly of Imbry's understanding. Imbry dismissed the criticism with a twist of his plump lips and said, "Your views are your own. I am satisfied with the work."

"Then pay me."

Imbry saw that Humbergruff's time away from the spell of blue borrache had not diminished the craving. He made a gesture of acquiescence and summoned the aircar that had brought them to the cottage. It had removed itself to an inaccessible ledge on a cliff face some distance away until Imbry, and only Imbry, should call for it. Now it eased down in the front yard and opened its luggage compartment. From behind a false bulkhead Imbry withdrew a package and handed it to the artist, who tore it open then sighed when he saw the vials and equipment within.

"This place is leased for quite some time," Imbry said. "Or I could take you back to your studio."

"Here will be fine," Humbergruff said. He went inside and sat on one of the beds, lining up the containers of blue borrache on a shelf set into the headboard. It took him only moments to deploy the apparatus that would continuously administer the drug while he sank deeper into the dreamscape. Then he poured the substance into the hopper and lay back. Within moments his eyelids were fluttering and Luff Imbry and all the world became no more than the flimsiest of distant shadows.

The fat man carefully packed up the five pieces and stowed them in the aircar. He locked the door of the cottage and left the key in a safe place. Moments later he was high above the rural landscape, instructing the flyer to set a course for the County of Ambrou.

"What is your purpose in seeking to enter the County of Ambrou?" said the customs inspector. Imbry knew that the man must have asked the question a myriad of times, yet the fellow's elevated nose and suspicious eye suggested that he had yet to receive a truly satisfactory answer.

"I mean to attend Toppling Fair," Imbry said.

"To buy?" said the border man, his manner easing fractionally. Fees and levies collected by the County from the annual fair's revenues probably accounted for a sizeable portion of the officer's salary.

Imbry signed in the negative. "To sell."

The custom inspector's brows drew together, like furry predators coordinating an attack. "To sell? And just what do you propose to sell?"

Imbry waved toward the open hatch of the aircar. "My works," he said.

The inspector came out of his booth and examined the contents of the luggage compartment. He lifted one of Hassol Humbergruff's delicate creations until its various parts dangled from his thumb and forefinger, blew on them gently until they dipped and rotated into different alignments. His gaze softened as he followed their movements and read the changing stories, then hardened as he turned back to Luff Imbry. "Entry denied," he said.

"On what grounds?"

"It is forbidden to import works of art into the County for subsequent sale."

"It is not," said Imbry. "Artists have brought their wares to Toppling Fair since time out of mind."

"And departed to spend the proceeds elsewhere," the customs man said. "Which is why the new Board of Fuglemen has changed the regulations. Now only those works produced within the County may be sold at the fair, though you may import materials."

"That is a recent change."

"Fairly recent," the man agreed.

"You might have let the world know."

"The regulations were proclaimed. You must not have been paying attention."

"Indeed," said Imbry. "I was in seclusion, preparing these." He gestured toward Humbergruff's works and assumed an air of innocent speculation. "I don't suppose if one of them were to remain here, under your guardianship, the others might go to the fair."

The inspector's face became as a dark cloud, and Imbry realized that the man was a captive of narrow views that denied him a creative imagination. "Never mind," he said and packed the goods away. He quickly reversed the aircar and departed in the direction from which he had come.

He returned to the cottage, but as soon as he unlocked the door he knew that there was no hope of reviving the artist and taking him to Ambrou to make new assemblages. Imbry went back to the aircar and sat in the gathering gloom of dusk, as the tired orange sun sank wearily behind the forested Polpol Hills, and thought about the unhappy twist that Ambrou's fuglemen had given to his plans.

Toppling Fair was one of Old Earth's preeminent venues for the buying and selling of art. It drew connoisseurs from all of the still-inhabited parts of the planet as well as persons from the Ten Thousand Worlds for whom this timeworn ball of dust was not irredeemably out of fashion. It was also a social necessity for Ambrou's most prominent citizens. Paddachau Chin had never been known to miss it.

The collector personally toured the fair at least once during the several days of its run, lingering at some booths, merely glancing into others. He had been known to buy on the spot, sometimes elevating a new artist from anonymity to instant fame. Even when he did not purchase, he would often invite those whose works he favored to a private masque whose other guests were the cream of Ambrou.

The masque, on the final night of the fair, was held in the antique formal garden at The Groves. The garden was within the walls of the estate and overlooked by the west wing. In that part of the house sat the treasure rooms that housed the most fabulous pieces in Chin's collection, according to the few who said they had entered its well guarded precincts, though they honored Paddachau Chin's request not to divulge what they had seen.

Luff Imbry intended to make himself one of that few, though he would do so without an invitation. He was sure he could overcome or undercut whatever defenses lay between him and his goal. He would, however, remain as closed-mouthed as any about what he expected to find within the west wing, although his reasons for silence would be his own.

But in order to put his plans into operation, he must first gain entrance to the well guarded formal garden. The easiest way to do that was to be invited to the masque. And to be invited to the masque, he must exhibit at the fair the works of Hassol Humbergruff and pass them off as his own.

But now that carefully planned sequence of events had been roughly truncated by the Board of Fuglemen. He stepped out of the aircar and reentered the cottage. Humbergruff breathed slowly and heavily on the bed. Imbry went to the workbench where the artist's tools and materials lay scattered. The fat man took up one of the shaping boards, a flat surface thickly covered in tiny holes. Into these pock marks Humbergruff would place pins in selected configurations then loop and bend his wires around them, rough-shaping his figures before lifting them free to refine them with crimps, pulls and twisters.

Imbry took a few pins from a flat dish and placed them in some of the board's holes. He looped a piece of green wire from one point to another then to a third and considered the result. During the time he had spent with the artist in the cottage he had often hovered over the man's shoulder, urging him to the work. An observant overseer, Imbry had absorbed the basic techniques of the assembler's art. Now he wondered if he had learned enough to forge a convincing Humbergruff.

On the last day of the Fair Imbry installed himself in a booth in the second tier near the bottom of Deobald Rise. He was far enough away from the fire dancers and the bottle-bell ringers to be undistracted by whiffs of smoke and discordant arpeggios, but he was still unaccustomed to being watched as he worked — though forgery and counterfeiting were two of his greatest strengths, he was unused to practicing them under the public's gaze.

"But it is this very openness," said the official who had showed him to his booth and stamped his hand, "that is now the most attractive aspect of Toppling Fair. The new Fuglemen have swept out the old fustiness and imbued all with a sense of imminence. Virtuosity appears, not as if from behind the curtain of mystery, but moment by moment, before the eye of the beholder. The viewers are greatly entertained."

"Yet I, the author of that entertainment, am not paid for any of it," said Imbry, "but only for the products of my labors, and then only if someone deigns to buy what I make."

"You also breathe and digest your dinner while I stand here and observe you,' said the officer, a crabbed and angular man whose skin hung loose wherever gravity could tug at it. "Should I pay you for those activities?"

"If they entertain you."

"They do not."

"But that is beside the point," said Imbry. "The Fair charges admission to the attendees, many of them mere look-ins who do not buy so much as a smoked-glass button, and you retain one hundred per cent of that fee. But we artisans and crafters, who create the spectacle that draws the crowds, receive nothing."

"Are you saying you will not work unless you are paid?" said the Fair man. "I can assure you that your booth can be let to another artist. There is a queue of them outside the gate."

"No, I am saying that I would prefer to work in solitude. It has ever been my way."

The officer drew himself up and regarded Imbry from the very pinnacle of his nose. "Then go home. But if you wish to exhibit at Toppling Fair, you must do so in public view."

A small collection of fairgoers who had been watching the altercation now burst into a smattering of applause, which quickly died as Luff Imbry glowered at them from beneath lowered brows. But then the fat man took a deep breath and when he let it go he allowed it to carry away his fruitless opposition. He raised both hands in a manner that signaled his surrender, adding a fillip to the gesture that said that the matter was fundamentally beneath his concern then paid no further attention as the official sauntered off.

Now Imbry lifted the rough draft of a wire figure from its armature of pins and regarded it critically. He was copying from memory one of Humbergruff's most successful assemblages, and the form he held between a fleshy thumb and forefinger was that of Farouche. This was the eternally yearning lover, always presented carrying his bardolade, though with its strings broken by long and tearful years of unavailing strumming as he pursued his unrequited courtship of unfeeling Ardyss.

Humbergruff's Farouche had been rendered in two contrasting materials: a heavy-gauge wire of dark purple that showed a sheen of verdigris when the light of the old orange sun struck it obliquely, and a lighter filament of tarnished gold. The bardolade had been a mere sketch in purest silver.

Imbry remembered how the artist had gone at his Farouche with crimps and twizzlers and believed he could emulate the technique. But after he had bent the figure's arm — the one that would hold the bardolade, not the one raised to heaven in a last plea for aid — he held it up to see it in the round. Immediately he knew that he had extended the limb's position farther than Humbergruff had. He returned the figure to the workbench and reached for the number four kinker.

But then he stopped and held up the figure again. The greater length of the arm's line would allow for a more fully realized bardolade, Imbry saw — especially if the broken instrument was rendered uncompromisingly in flat black instead of silver — and that would draw the viewer's eye toward the futility of the lover's quest rather than to the upraised hand of hope.

That was not how Hassol Humbergruff had seen it. And yet, as Imbry regarded the bits of wire dangling by their thread from his pinch, he felt that that was how Farouche ought to be seen.

He allowed his gaze to change focus and saw the faces of several fairgo-ers peering at him from the entrance to his booth. On an impulse he said to them, "The bardolade — in black or silver?"

"Silver," said one of them, a well fleshed matron with an arrangement of fa-cial wrinkles and creases that suggested she had pronounced more disapprov-ing judgements than blessings. Most of the others signed agreement with the woman's dictum, but a man with a lean and corded neck and a more thought-ful aspect said, "Silver is traditional, but black would make a statement."

Imbry set down the Farouche and reached for the black wire. He rapidly fashioned a miniature bardolade, then at the last moment added a filigree of the thinnest silver to represent its forlorn broken strings. He crimped the instrument to the figure's hand and held up the ensemble to the light and the gaze of his audience.

A gasp of insight came from the matron and a knowing nod from the man who had spoken for black. Imbry fastened the figure's thread to a horizontal rod hung from the ceiling as he had seen Humbergruff do in the cottage. He began to bring together the materials for the second major figure in the piece: Goladry, the green and untried youth, innocent as an egg. Already, Imbry had an idea for how he could express the young exemplar's naiveté. The crowd murmured as he set pins in the board and chose a strong platinum wire to be the boy's torso.

There would be nothing new under the old orange sun. It could not be ar-gued otherwise: no fresh, undiscovered stories waited to be told on a world as ancient as Old Earth. Every tale that could be recounted had been, in every possible permutation, a thousand times a thousand times. Heroes of every quality, villains of all shades and persuasions, had strutted and fretted along the mazed paths that led to story's borders, had bounced off and sashayed back again. Every possible beginning, every possible end, and all the myriad middles had been spun and cast and reeled in time after time.

Everyone knew every tale. There could be no grand surprises. And yet there was always the possibility of an unthought-of juxtaposition, or if it was not truly unthought of then perhaps the thought had last occurred so many millennia ago that now it had been forgotten and could be revived, like a shade from the underworld, to be briefly enjoyed before it was allowed to fade anew.

The effect of all these aeons of telling and being told was to create not boredom, but a vast and complex language of symbol and allusion. Farouche and Goladry were universally recognized archetypes; each drew after it a comet's tail, broad and long, of meaning and association. To present one such figure in the context of the other, and then to add a third — like Marrenya, the young maiden poised on the cusp of full adulthood — was to make a subtle and involved statement on the vagaries and cohesions of life.

Imbry fashioned his Marenya in green and red, iridescent and matte. He strung her from the same rod from which Farouche dangled, but on a longer thread so that she would rise and fall between levels of the assemblage. He had turned her head so that sometimes she would be glancing idly away — innocently spurning an unnoticed infatuation — but as her figure rotated she would come to be wistfully gazing over her shoulder.

The arrangement brought a ripple of comment from the crowd that now watched him work. Imbry was conscious of the reaction as background to his own perceptions, but now his thoughts took him in an unexpected direction. In his piece, Hassol Humbergruff had arranged Farouche, Goladry and Marenya thus and so, adding in minor figures — the faithful attendant, the old man who harboured a lifelong guilt, each offering a mutable commentary on the main themes — but letting the central trio dominate the assemblage.

What if I mixed Grond into the trio? he thought. He turned to the shaping board and began placing pins even as his mind was considering types and colors of wire. He found a spool of lead, the wire thick, dull and lifeless, perfect for the old libertine's coarse body. Then he chose a length of brilliant diamontine from which to fashion the roué's signature hat and full length cane. He formed and crimped, joining the accoutrements to the main figure, angling the cane so that from the right perspective it became an obscene expression of the rake's true nature.

He fastened a thread to Grond's wattled neck and tied it to one end of a long rod, putting a globular counterweight at the other end. He positioned the rod in the rest of the assemblage so that Grond would perpetually circle Farouche, Goladry and Marenya, alternately rising above their plane before dipping beneath their view in an endless cycle.

"Ah," said the man with the corded neck, while the woman with the seamed face took on an introspective expression as she relived some experience that the assemblage had conjured from memory into the foreground of her mind.

Imbry quickly made two minor figures: Haft, the true friend; and Shigharee, the reflective older sibling. These he hung at heights that would allow them to intersect the main action of the piece where necessary for narrative purposes. He adjusted relative distances among all the figures until, suddenly, the disparate parts coalesced into a comprehensive whole. Here was a tale of longing, of a road not taken, yet as the figures slowly spun in the ruddy light of the tired sun, it became a cynical commentary on the follies of youth and the calculating guile of age. But scarcely had those sour notes sounded than the arrangement shifted again into a quiet statement of hope amid dignified endurance.

I have a talent for this, Imbry thought. *I have not copied Humbergruff. I have stood upon his shoulders and leapt higher still.* He watched the figures rotate and spin, dip and rise.

"Brilliant," said a deep voice, one that was comfortable in making such pronouncements and expected no contradictions. "I wish I had been here to see the process from the beginning."

Imbry looked away from his creation and found himself under the gaze of a man of mature years, attired in a daygown of embroidered silk with slashed sleeves and the "covert ruffle" motif that was the fashion of the moment. Equally fashionable were the man's split-toe slippers and his complexly folded hat of red patent leather.

"I am Paddachau Chin," said the paragon. "What price the assemblage?"

Imbry looked thoughtful, then quoted a number that would have been fitting for a Humbergruff masterpiece. One thing he knew about the wealthy — and he knew many things about them — was that when they were buying for themselves, the more expensive the object the more they desired it. A high price gratified their desire to spend as much on themselves as they felt their own intrinsic worth deserved.

Paddachau Chin put a finger to his lower lip, looked upwards as if consulting some relevant information written across the sky, and said, "Done. Would you bring it to my estate tonight? The Groves. We're having a masque, if you're free."

"I will make myself free."

"Your work reminds me of that of Hassol Humbergruff. What is your name?"

"Hassol Humbergruff," Imbry said.

Chin peered at him. "You look different from how I remember you."

"It's not something I care to talk about," Imbry said, adding a gesture that indicated the subject was indelicate.

"No matter," said Chin. "It is the work that counts. The who is always less important than the what, certainly less than the why." He made his farewells, employing a mode that signified that Imbry's status had risen, at least temporarily, to the same plane as the magnate's. Imbry responded in kind.

The crowd had watched their interaction with almost as much interest as when they had followed Imbry's assembling of the wire figures. The man with the noticeable neck offered congratulations. "It is no small thing to be invited to Chin's masque," he said.

"No small thing indeed," said Imbry.

The Groves was a well founded estate, although its agricultural surround appeared neglected. The manse had suffered an accretion of styles and enthusiasms of former generations of Chins, but that was not unusual in rural houses. Either by fortunate accident or the efforts of some able architectural syncretizer, the present state of the old building showed an unexpected balance among all the spires, domes, colonnades and air-suspended roofs. Paddachau Chin had apparently added nothing to the mix since inheriting the place. Imbry assumed the magnate preferred to spend his fortune on the art works he sequestered in the west wing.

This was a long, high-ceilinged extension from the main body of the house, clad externally in brushed virentium that had tarnished nicely over the centuries. In the lights strung about the trees and topiary of the garden, the walls gave off the ghostly glow for which the pale metal had once been prized by builders. The tall narrow windows were shuttered in a material that allowed those within to see all without, but denied anyone outside so much as a glimmer of the treasures said to reside in the wing's galleries.

Luff Imbry would have made no attempt to see through the windows even had they allowed an easy perspective. He intended to submit Paddachau Chin's collection to far more than the attentions of his eyes; his program included seizing, stowing and stealing away in his aircar, which hovered somewhere nearby, equipped with devices that rendered it all but invisible to prying energies. Always an inventive thief, Imbry also concealed about his person an apparatus of his own design that he was eager to apply to the virentium walls.

He sauntered among the revelers at Chin's masque, nodding affably and offering the kind of florid gestures that were appropriate to the evening's mood and the elevated rank of the attendees. The garden boasted several marquees and portable stages, the former dispensing food and drink and the latter a variety of entertainments that ranged from the subtle to the gross. Imbry stopped at a bar and accepted a selection of small sausages and chopped vegetables wrapped in stiff paper as well as a flagon of a robust tawny ale made on the estate.

He wandered about, chewing and supping. He could do both without difficulty because he had chosen for a mask a version of the wei-wei bird, with crimson-feathered brow and blunt ocher beak that protruded over his nose, leaving the lower half of his face uncovered. Above the brow the mask became a cowl of gray cloth that encased his head and flowed behind him in a voluminous cape. He had not hired the costume, but had employed yet another of his useful skills to fashion the garment himself, adding a number of pockets and pouches that could transport small but valuable items without drawing attention.

He stopped near one of the stages to watch a performance by several young men and women, all of them healthy and limber and clad in not much more than body paint. Their antics combined gymnastic strength and flexibility with artistic representations similar to those of the assembler's art, except that their tableaux were punctuated by sudden tongues of vertical fire from the back of the stage or explosions of scintillating confetti from the front. While the audience gasped and oohed at these eruptions, the players quickly rearranged themselves for the beginning of the next sequence.

Imbry appreciated the artistry of distraction as a technique. Indeed, many of his career successes had relied on his being able to draw someone's eyes to look *here*, and definitely not *there* at a crucial moment. He swallowed the last of his smoked sausage and downed the lees of his ale and waited for the next arrangement of bodies, letting his gaze drift about the crowded garden.

Some distance off, in a doorway sheltered by a decorated arch, he spied Paddachau Chin. The magnate was not masked, but was splendidly attired as a marshall of Hemistor's Grand Militia. He was deep in conversation with a man whose only concession to the conventions of the masque was a domino across his eyes and the bridge of his nose, the rest of him being attired in nondescript clothing. Yet something about the fellow tickled an association somewhere in the depths of Imbry's mind. He resolved to let it slowly bubble its way to the surface where he would examine it later.

A bulky object wrapped in paper passed from Chin to the man, then a smaller item went the other way. Neither examined what he had received but each tucked his acquisition away and they parted without ceremony. The anonymous man faded into the crowd while Chin stepped openly into the light of an overhead lantern and was immediately noticed and celebrated by a swirl of his guests. After a few moments he extricated himself with smiles and playful gestures then stood looking purposefully about him.

Imbry slid the bird mask upward until it sat above his forehead, leaving his face visible. Moments later his gaze met that of Paddachau Chin. The magnate raise a finger and both eyebrows then began to make his way through the throng, sliding past jolly greetings and attempted embraces until he pitched up beside the fat man.

They exchanged salutes and made the appropriate observations as to the success of the festivities, Imbry's being warm and fulsome, Chin's self-deprecating. The formalities over, the magnate said, "Have you brought the piece?"

"It is here," Imbry said, indicating an inner fold of his cape. "Shall I bring it out?"

"Please."

The assemblage was neatly packaged in fine cloth. Imbry carefully drew it from an inner pocket of his cape, slipped off the covering and allowed the rods and figures to dangle free. The different colors and textures of the wires caught the various hues and intensities of light from around them.

"Very fine," said Chin, his eyes glinting, "It will be a high point of my collection."

"I am honored," Imbry answered then took the opportunity. "I would be delighted to see the works among which my little collation of wires will be set."

A curious expression took possession of Chin's face but was quickly dismissed. He spoke briskly, "Not possible, I'm afraid. I am reordering elements of the collection. Everything is jumbled."

Imbry arranged his face in an expression that conveyed a mellow fatalism. "Some other time, perhaps."

"Indeed," said Chin. "But I almost forgot your fee." He drew from within his bemedalled tunic a compact purse and passed it to Imbry, who pocketed it without further examination.

"If you don't mind, I will go and hang this immediately in the treasure room," the magnate said, holding the glittering work before him. Imbry signaled acquiescence and watched the man go, the crowd parting before him with more oohs and sudden intakes of breath as people caught sight of the assemblage.

The fat man accepted the disappointment. It would have been useful to have toured the collection in advance, but he had a good eye for quality and would be able to choose well when the moment came. In the meantime, he noticed a stand offering seedcakes and a colorful punch. The sausages and ale now but a memory, he made his way through the crowd.

The masque went on all night, the public revelry giving way in time to more private celebrations in the shadows beneath the decorative trees and behind convenient shrubs. Here and there about the gardens clumps of guests wandered, parts of their costumes askew or altogether missing. They hung on each other's shoulders, swaying and singing elegiac ballads or humming quiet songs of melancholic affection that spoke to the Ambrou character.

Imbry waited in a dark corner of the west wing's facade until a nearby choir had passed by. He drew from an inner pocket of his cape a small device of his own manufacture and activated it, then watched as it consulted his immediate surroundings and identified the means by which Paddachau Chin guarded his premises. As he had expected, the wards and got-yous defending the west wing were several and powerful. But Imbry had prepared for them. He now instructed the device to gull and lull the house's defenses.

Within moments, the telltales all showed that he could proceed to the next stage of his plan. He tucked away the inquisitive instrument and brought out another: a short, thin cylinder of metal something like a stylus. He put the point of the object against the wall of virentium, at a height just above his head, and depressed a stud on its base. A shivery sound emanated from the tip, along with a glow of deep purple luminescence.

Virentium was an artificial material, a combination of metals and other substances that ordinarily could not cohere. Imbry had researched the compound and found that its components were induced to bind to each other by a treatment that combined a particular sequence of high energies. The resulting composite would resist the most incisive cutting tools. However, Imbry had discovered that one of the forces that bound the aggregate together could be convinced to reverse its polarity if an energy of the right intensity and frequency were applied to it.

Imbry's instrument now applied that energy at precisely that intensity. He tuned the instrument's control until it reached the indicated frequency. At that point, the purple glow at the stylus's tip deepened until it fell below the range of human vision. A small hole abruptly appeared in the virentium. Imbry drew his hand downward and the hole lengthened into a crevice taller than he was. He smoothly continued along the base of the wall, turned upward then across. He put his fingertips to the top of the oblong shape he had created and tugged. An Imbry-sized slab of virentium leaned out of the wall. He caught it and carefully lowered it to the ground then stepped into the opening.

He found himself standing in the outer wall of a long gallery that ran the length of the wing, its inner wall interrupted by doors at intervals of several paces. The passage was dimly lit by tiny lumens set in the molding just above the carpeted floor and by widely spaced hemispheres of pale glass in the ceiling.

Imbry remained in the opening while he exchanged his cutting stylus for the inquisitive device he had used earlier. It identified three defensive systems in the gallery, infiltrated their decision-making processes, and diverted them into harmless directions. The fat man stepped into the gallery and approached the nearest door.

It was locked, but not for long. He eased the portal open and saw an unlit room. His inquisitor detected no surveillance. Imbry threw back his masque and cowl and brought from another pocket a harness studded with lenses, emitters, and receptors that he fitted over his skull. He touched a control at one temple and the apparatus flooded the chamber with several wavelengths of energy, recaptured their echoes and translated them all into a coherent picture. The image appeared in the air before Imbry's eyes as if he were looking through a hand-sized window into a brightly lit room.

Which turned out to be effectively empty. Imbry turned his head from side to side, scanning the space. Along the walls he saw shelved cabinets with their doors hanging open. Here and there about the floor were truncated columns whose flat tops would have been perfect for displaying objects of beauty and wonder. But the shelves were bare, the plinths supporting nothing but dust-flecked air.

Imbry withdrew and closed the door. He went to the next portal and repeated the procedure that gave him entry and view. Here the walls were lined with shelves that should have held rare books or a collection of small items, perhaps reliquary boxes or the intricately decorated bottles in which the aristocracy of Old Earth kept their baby teeth. But here, too, the shelves were vacant.

He drew back from the doorway. Then a thought touched him. Might this be an illusion rendered by protective systems even more sophisticated than the devices he had built to overcome them? He stepped into the room and advanced to one of the shelves, reached out and touched. But his plump fingers met only emptiness and a fine powder of dust.

Imbry returned to the gallery and pondered. Might the magnate have moved his treasures to another location? But no other part of the manse boasted such security systems. And Imbry trusted his intelligence sources too much to believe that the Chin Collection could have been relocated beyond the walls of The Groves without his having heard of it.

Some would have found in the disappearance of the trove a piquant mystery. Luff Imbry found a source of sharp irritation. He had invested much time and many resources in this operation, and now it seemed he might as profitably have strode down Ekhevry Row, Olkney's main commercial thoroughfare, throwing armloads of currency to the thrusting crowds.

His black mood deepened as he tried the next chamber and the one after that, finding them as bereft of plunderables as the first two. Grimly, he made his way down the concourse, seeing one empty room after another, until he came to the final door. Here he stopped, for his inquisitor told him that within the chamber was life, light and movement.

Imbry removed his surveillance headgear and carefully tried the door's control. It responded to his touch but he eased open the portal no more than a crack. A warm glow of golden luminescence shone through the narrow opening and Imbry put his eye to it. He saw another chamber like the others, full of empty cabinets and display stands, but in the center of this one stood Paddachau Chin beneath a cone of light that shone from a lumen in the ceiling. Also captured by the warm illumination was a gibbet of base metal, of the kind commonly used to display assemblages, and from that dark frame hung the collage of rods, threads, and wires that Imbry had made and sold to the man who now stood enraptured before it.

Finding nothing to steal, a common malefactor might have slunk away, cursing his disappointment, perhaps to kick some blameless shrub on his way through the garden. But Imbry was a proud man. He knew his abilities to be superlative, for all that some might raise certain ethical quibbles. It was a crime that his efforts should have been so egregiously wasted. He required at least the satisfaction of an explanation.

He flung wide the door and stepped into the chamber. "What is the meaning of this?" he said.

Paddachau Chin had just blown a puff of air at the assemblage, causing it to reorient its components into a new gestalt. His lips remained pursed even as his eyes widened and blinked in surprise, putting Imbry in mind of a comical fish. The fat man was, both by necessity and by lifelong study, an expert judge of character. He gauged that this situation required him to continue on the offensive. "What have you done with one of the greatest collections of the age?"

Chin stepped back, his eyes flicking about the room like an errant schoolboy caught in mischief. When he spoke, the words tumbled over each other, "I had no choice! I had severe reverses, financial commitments came due, and there was the upkeep on the estate and the house in town."

Imbry formed his features into the sternest censure. "You sold it all off? Everything? How could you?" he said, advancing on Chin like a small, rotund army. "You've callously dismantled and dispersed a collection the like of which will never be seen again!"

A part of Imbry was genuinely incensed that such wanton destruction had been visited upon the treasures of The Grove, even as another part of him was aware that it had been his intention to commit exactly the same acts. But Imbry had a supple mind, capable of assessing moral situations and discovering clear distinctions between right and wrong that would entirely elude anyone who did not have the good fortune to be Luff Imbry.

Still, the moment's pause it took the thief to dispose of his brief episode of internal disharmony was enough time for Paddachau Chin to come across the obvious question. "What are you doing in my house?" he said, and went on to an equally salient query: "And how did you get in?"

"This is not the time for trivia and superfluous tangents," Imbry said. "The important issue is that you are a fraud. The Chin Collection is a byword for unparalleled taste. People have dined out for years on a hint that they have glimpsed the merest corner of it."

"You're not Hassol Humbergruff," Chin said, his eyes narrowing and the corners of his mouth turning down. Then all three formed circles as a connection was made at some obscure level of his intellectual apparatus. "I know you! You are Luff Imbry! You were pointed out to me once as someone who might be able to sell a piece or two, if my current agents became unavailable."

If my current fence should be taken up by the Bureau of Scrutiny, was how Imbry translated the remark. And now he knew where he had seen the man in the garden from whom Chin had acquired the purse that had been paid over to Imbry. "I might have been interested," he said, though inwardly he felt a faint unhappiness at the thought of being associated with the wanton dissolution of a magnificent collection. *It's one thing to nabble a few bits and pieces and pop them off to the buyers*, he thought. *It's quite a different matter to undo the work of generations.* "But now I do not know what to say."

"You must say nothing!" Chin said.

Imbry saw a desperate flash in the man's eyes that made him quietly reach into a pocket of his cape. He slipped his hand around a powerful shocker and only when he had thumbed its control to stand-by did he reply. "You would be ruined," he said.

The fire went out of Chin. His shoulders declined. "My friends would find me a figure of pity and amusement," he said. "Who would come to my masques?"

Imbry felt a mild twinge of sympathy. But he put it aside and concentrated on what was truly important in this situation: that it should lead to a recoupment of his expenses and a reasonable profit. He released his hold on the shocker so that he could put both his hands in front of him for a vigorous rubbing of palms. "The past is fled. The future lies shapeless before us. The question is: what shape shall we give it?"

"Do not look to me as a fount of income. My resources are limited," Chin said. "I invested too heavily in the Fassblind Bubble. By tonight I had settled my obligations, but that left only one truly worthwhile work in the collection — the Waldolid Tapestry."

Imbry knew of the hanging; who did not? It had been woven over umpteen generations from the hair of a family whose gene plasm had been the venue of a unique mutation. A clan of master weavers had used the incomparable material — it shimmered, changed colors in responses to heat and light, glowed in the dark — to create a masterpiece of masterpieces.

"But it would buy more than five estates like this one," Imbry said.

"True," said Chin, "if I could have sold it openly."

"Ah," said Imbry, because now he saw it. The collection had been precious to Paddachau Chin, but more precious was his reputation as its owner. By selling off the works surreptitiously, he had retained their reflected glory. But he had received only a fraction of their monetary worth. Even Imbry could appreciate the ironic pain of the magnate's situation, and he allowed his face to display it.

"No, no," said Chin, "it has not been so bad. I have long suffered from a creeping case of lapsed ardor, the result of having lived so long in the Canton of Zeel."

Imbry signaled that he understood. The cultural ethos of Zeel demanded constant novelty. Goods retained their allure only as long as they satisfied the unslakeable thirst for freshness; once that faded, the most exquisite work of art was of no more interest to a Zeelot than the box in which it had arrived.

A hapless expression took ownership of Chin's face. "So now I acquire, one by one, the pieces that catch my eye. I enjoy each until it inevitably palls, then quietly sell it on to acquire funds with which to buy the next."

Imbry saw that, like Humbergruff, Chin was trapped within a narrowing, descending spiral. "You pay more for what you buy than you receive when you sell it."

"Yes," said Chin, "the progression worries me. In the end my reputation may suffer."

A spark glowed in the back of Luff Imbry's mind. He allowed it to burgeon until it took on a warm effulgence then became a burst of brilliance. "I have an idea," he said.

The discreet plaque beside the inconspicuous door on Ekhevry Way read, *Vervacity — Works of Creativity for the Discerning.* In smaller type below was, *Exclusive agents for the Chin Collection.*

Through the door came two distinct types of persons. The first were artists who wished to sell their works to Paddachau Chin. These were often surprised at the small prices they were offered; some left throwing harsh words over their shoulders, but most were intrigued enough to stay to learn the rest of the terms. Almost all who heard the proposition agreed to it. They departed Vervacity bearing a purse that contained a sum somewhere between a pittance and trifle, and a short document that entitled them henceforth to decorate their premises and letterhead with the phrase: *By Appointment to Paddachau Chin.* Their popularity, and therefore their incomes, inevitably climbed. As did Chin's reputation as a patron.

The second category of patrons at the exclusive agency slipped quietly through the door after regular hours, having made arrangements to be received without names or identities being needlessly bandied about. These persons came bearing more substantial sums of money and purchased works that had somehow lost their way and strayed from the Chin Collection into the shadier channels of commercial intercourse. Each departed bearing an object of beauty to be enjoyed in strictest privacy, lest anyone pose the kind of inconvenient questions that might draw the attention of the Bureau of Scrutiny.

A third class of person entered the premises, though always by an unmarked door in the rear. These were close confederates of Luff Imbry who toiled in a basement workroom to copy each new purchase, usually producing several quite good forgeries that were then sold to the second class of upstairs visitors. The originals themselves were passed on to The Groves, where Paddachau Chin briefly enjoyed them before sending them back to Vervacity, whose proprietor, Luff Imbry, carefully stored them away, along with the five original Hassol Humbergruffs that were the beginnings of the Imbry Collection.

This arrangement endured for some time, and all the participants were well satisfied. Eventually Chin developed new enthusiasms, involving memorabilia associated with sporting contests, by which time Luff Imbry had also broadened the scope of his appetites and abilities, so that the shop on Ekhevry Way was a mere bagatelle. The two partners wrapped up Vervacity and parted on good terms.

"But you know," said Chin, as they marked the dissolution of their partnership with a dinner at one of the clubs where Imbry always found good food and often encountered persons who would be shaped into participants in his various enterprises, "you could have gone another way."

Imbry paused with a glass of ruby Phalum halfway to his lips. "How so?"

"The piece you made when you were masquerading as Hassol Humbergruff — the Farouche, Goladry, Marrenya — was as good as anything he ever produced. Indeed, it had a unique quality that could only have come from you."

Imbry sipped the wine. "I fail to grasp your point."

"Instead of forging other people's efforts, you could have been creating true works of lasting renown, under your own name," Chin said. "You might have made a legitimate fortune."

To Luff Imbry, the concept was completely novel. He turned it over in his complicated mind, then said, "No."

"But why not?"

Imbry offered a tiny shrug. "I have my reputation to consider."

PASSION PLOY

"What exactly is it?" Luff Imbry said. He walked around the object that occupied the center of the small table in the secluded rear room of the tavern known as Bolly's Snug, viewing it from several angles and blinking at the way it caught the light.

"I took it off Chiz Ramoulian," said Dain Ganche.

"Took it?" Imbry's round, multichinned face showed a mild concern. Provenance could be a contentious issue when buying items of value behind closed doors. Chiz Ramoulian was only a minor hoodlum yet he moved through the back streets of the city of Olkney attended by a reputation for sudden and inventive violence. He had also exhibited a knack for locating those with whom he had business. "Took it how?"

Ganche crossed corded arms across a broad chest. "I found him in an alley near the slider that comes from the spaceport. He was sitting against a wall, blurry eyed and cradling this in his arms. I reminded him that he owed me a substantial sum from a joint enterprise." Like Imbry, Ganche regularly invested in highly profitable ventures whose details were known only to those directly involved in their execution. "I suggested that this object would settle the score. Then I took it."

Imbry's gaze returned to the glittering thing on the table. He was finding it difficult to look away. "And he was content with that?"

Ganche's heavy lips took a reflective bend. "He made a noise or two, but nothing actionable. To put it all in a single word, he seemed... distracted. But, then, he has a fondness for Red Abandon and once he cracks a flask he does not leave it till it's drained. That may account for his mood. In any case, a scroot patrol picked him up shortly after."

"Hmm," said Imbry. He again circled the table and examined the item. "It is inarguably beautiful," he murmured. Indeed, beauty seemed almost too flimsy a word to fling around in its presence. It compelled the eyes.

Imbry turned from the thing and found that it took an increased effort to do so. He took up the dark cloth in which Ganche had brought the object and covered its brightness. He kept seeing a ghost of its outline imprinted on the walls, as if it were the negative image of a bright light.

"I've found it best not to stare at it too long," said the big man. "But what on Old Earth is it?"

"Certainly not *of* Old Earth," Imbry said. "It's of ultraterrene origin. I'd lay a hept to a bent grimlet on that."

"Ramoulian often haunts the spaceport," Ganche said, "in hopes of coming across baggage that is indifferently attended. He has been known to wear a cleaner's uniform. Or he inserts himself into a stream of disembarking passengers, playing the affable traveler. He strikes up a conversation with some off-worlder and offers guidance. Then he leads the mark into a dark and out-of-the-way corner and relieves him of his burdens. Perhaps this was in someone's valise."

"Possibly," said Imbry. "But why was Ramoulian languishing with his prize in an alley when the scroots were on the prowl?"

"Again, Red Abandon?"

"It has an unmistakable odor," Imbry said. "Did he smell of it?"

"Not that I noticed."

"Then I lean toward the notion that this object caused the distraction."

Ganche lifted up a corner of the covering cloth. "It does not affect me that strongly."

"Nor I," said Imbry. "Perhaps Ramoulian was peculiarly susceptible. But the main question is: what is it?"

"No," said the other man, "the main question is: what is it worth? You are more knowledgeable than I in the buying and selling of art."

Imbry stroked his plump earlobe with a meditative finger. "I have no idea," he said. "We will find out by offering it in auction to a carefully chosen group of buyers. My commission will be forty per cent."

"Fifteen," said Ganche with a speed that was reflexive. They haggled a few more moments and settled on thirty per cent, which had been Imbry's intent.

When they had executed the mutual motions of hand and arm by which such bargains were sealed, Imbry said, "I may consult an expert in ultraterrene artifacts."

"Discreetly," Ganche said.

"Of course." There was another brief haggle and a flurry of gestures that decided how the expert's fee would be paid.

"So you think it is, in fact, a manufactured item?" Ganche said. "I thought it might be of natural origin."

Imbry moved his large, round head in a gesture of indecision. He tucked the square of black cloth about the object then lifted it gently and deposited it in the large satchel he had brought with him. The thing was surprisingly heavy — densely packed, he thought. He closed up the bag and activated the fastenings. The room seemed emptier now that the object was out of sight.

Imbry repaired to his operations center, a room in a nondescript house on a quiet street in a modest neighborhood. He traveled carefully, taking detours and laying false trails by entering public buildings that were busy with people, going in by the main doors then immediately departing by rear exits.

Partly, this was habitual caution; a practitioner of Imbry's profession never knew when the scroots might have singled him out for pre-emptive surveillance. Lately, though, he had found himself caught up in a worrisome dispute with Alwinder Mudgeram, a man of blunt opinions and brutal instincts who was convinced that Luff Imbry owed him a substantial sum. The funds had been advanced toward a project that had not come to fruition. Unforeseen disappointments could blight any line of endeavor, Imbry had counseled Mudgeram, advising him to consider his lost capital a failed investment. But the investor preferred to see it as a debt to be repaid, and Mudgeram was renowned for collecting every grimlet due him.

Secure in his operations center, Imbry had his integrator deploy a research and communications matrix that spent most of its time disguised as a piece of battered furniture. He removed the mysterious object from the satchel and unwrapped it, taking care to keep his eyes averted, and let the matrix's percepts scan it. Its effects upon him he found annoying, as if it were a spoiled child who kept tugging at his garment, insistently importuning him with, "Look at me! Look at me!"

As soon as it was scanned he rewrapped and resatcheled the object, then placed it in a concealed locker beneath the floor of a closet that appeared to be stuffed with the kind of items one acquired at jumble sales. Some of the bric-a-brac had artfully concealed functions that would have drawn sharp attention from agents of the Archonate Bureau of Scrutiny.

"Integrator," he said. "Conduct a class-two inquiry as to nature and origins." Imbry had designed his integrator, as he had designed the closet's false kitsch, to answer the special circumstances that often arose in the conduct of his business. What he called a class-two inquiry, for example, was not unlike an information search along Old Earth's connectivity grid that any citizen might undertake, except that Imbry's integrator could ease in and out of public data stores without being noticed. That was important when the whereabouts of an item being researched and valued was of interest to the scroots.

The integrator hummed and fussed for several seconds. As he waited, Imbry was vexed to discover in himself a surprising urge to go to the closet and view the object. He got up and paced until his integrator reported that it had found no matches in publicly accessible records.

"We will try private sources," Imbry said. "Catalogs from dealers in ultraterrene artworks, both here and...," he thought for a moment, then named the four planets along The Spray that were major nexi for trade in nonhuman artifacts and had offices on Old Earth where such catalogs would be found. "Plus any places where curios are discussed."

It took a little longer for his matrix to locate and insert itself unnoticeably into the private data stores, but again it came back with no solid results. "Nothing from the dealers. I have a partial match, though the correspondence is less than ten per cent," his integrator said.

"Show me."

The displayed image appeared in the air before him. It was a curved fragment, dark and stained, of something that had been broken. It superficially resembled the exterior of the object beneath the closet floor, except that its surface was not bright and glittering with points of diamond-hard light, nor did it shimmer with unnamable colors that ravished the eye.

"What is it?" Imbry said.

"It is tentatively identified as a fragment of the husk of a seed pod from an uncataloged world in the Back of Beyond," the integrator said. "It may or may not have been part of some native art work. It was recovered from a ship hired by an artifact hunter from Popsy."

"What is Popsy?"

"An odd little world far down The Spray. The hunter's name was Fallo Wickiram. He hired the ship on Bluepoint, and was last seen heading toward the gas cloud called the Lesser Dark. He apparently landed on a number of uncouth worlds, gathering such curiosities as appealed to his taste. At some point, the period of the ship's hire was up and, as programmed, it returned to Bluepoint on its own. Wickiram was not aboard and there was no indication as to what had become of him."

"What was the last world he visited?" Imbry said.

"It has no name, and apparently no attractions, since the records show that almost no one ever goes there. Here are its coordinates." The integrator produced a string of numbers and vectors. They meant nothing to Imbry.

"How long ago did this occur?" he asked and learned that Wickiram had met his unknown fate several thousand years ago. Imbry thought about it for some moments, then said, "The information is of doubtful utility. Record it anyway, then let us press on."

The mention of a seed pod triggered a new line of inquiry. The integrator reviewed records of artworks and more commonplace items made from such materials up and down The Spray. Several more leads appeared but, upon investigation, led nowhere. Imbry poked about in other avenues that suggested themselves, including the itineraries of any ships that had recently put down at the Olkney spaceport. But any spaceship, whether liner, freighter or private yacht, stopped at so many worlds where they might connect to other worlds, that the object's possible routes to Old Earth were effectively infinite.

Finally, he checked for reports of robbery or fraud concerning recent arrivals to Olkney but found none in the public media nor in the elements of the Bureau of Scrutiny's systems that he was able to access without detection. He concluded that if Chiz Ramoulian had acquired the object illicitly, the crime had gone either unreported or undiscovered.

Imbry steepled his fingers and touched them to his uppermost chin and stood in thought for a long moment. Then he said, "Connect me to The Honorable Ilarios Warrigrove."

A few seconds passed while Imbry's integrator contacted its equivalent at the Warrigrove manse and protocols were exchanged. Then an aquiline face marked by lines of care appeared in the air before Imbry. "You have something?" he said, his languid voice unable completely to disguise a note of sharp interest.

"Something I wish to have valued," said Imbry.

"And will it be available for private purchase?"

"My plans have not yet assumed their final shape. At the moment, I'm considering an auction," said Imbry, "but to a limited and discreet set of purchasers."

"What do you have?"

"I will have to show it to you."

"Intriguing." Warrigrove's expression showed an indolent mood, but Imbry's finely tuned eye detected a concealed underwash of excitement. "I am free for an hour."

"I'll be there shortly."

Imbry returned the room to its seeming unremarkableness and retrieved the object. Again he was irritated to experience an urge to take it from the satchel and gaze at its sparkles and flashes. He left the house and walked for several minutes, turning corners randomly, then hailed an aircar and had it take him to a specific corner on the other side of the city. Alighting there, he walked some more then took another aircar to within several streets of Warrigrove's manse and again took a circuitous route to the house's rear gate. The who's-there recognized him and admitted him to a walled and overgrown garden.

On the far side of the untended greenery was a tumbledown antique gazebo, swarmed by thick growing vines which also concealed systems that ensured that any sight or sound encountered within its leafy confines would not carry beyond them. Imbry followed a flagstoned path to the structure, slipped within and found Ilarios Warrigrove seated on a chair of black iron behind a table of the same material, sipping from a tall, thin glass filled with a pale yellow liquid. A carafe of the stuff and another glass stood on a tray before him. "Would you care to?" he said with a gesture that Imbry's eye noted was calculatedly relaxed.

"Why not?" the fat man said. He raised the glass, paused but a moment to inhale its delicate bouquet then drained half of it at a gulp. "Excellent."

They exchanged the gestures and pleasantries suitable to a casual encounter and the time of day, but Imbry saw how Warrigrove's eyes kept flickering sideways to the satchel that hung from his unoccupied hand. The formalities accomplished, he placed the container on the table and withdrew its cloth-wrapped contents.

"Someone has asked me to sell this," he said and whisked away the covering.

Warrigrove could not restrain an intake of breath.

"You know what it is," Imbry said. He was adept at reading micro-expressions and now saw Warrigrove consider then reject denial but opt for less than full disclosure, all in the time a tranquil man takes to blink.

"I know what it might be," he said. "I had heard — only a rumor — that such a thing might be on its way to Old Earth."

The aficionado spoke without taking his eyes from the scintillation. Imbry sensed that the man was unable to resist the attraction. For himself, he found that his annoyance at the thing's importuning made it easier to look away. "What is it?" he said.

Imbry watched the patrician face closely while Warrigrove framed his answer, and was fairly sure that he was about to hear the truth.

"A myth," the man said, "or a chimera. An object of desire, longed for and sought after, though it may not truly exist."

The fat man made a gesture that expressed cynicism. "That sounds like precisely the kind of thing that a cunning forger would contrive to dangle before the avid appetite."

Warrigrove's eyes did not leave the object. "Well, you would know," he said.

Imbry acknowledged the truth of the observation. More than a few alleged masterworks that hung or stood or scampered in the palaces of wealthy collectors had come from his own hand, though they bore the signatures and sigils of bygone geniuses.

"Indeed," Warrigrove continued, "if it is a fraud, you are precisely the kind of person one might expect to arrive asking, eyes wide with innocence, just what it might be."

"Let us assume, for the moment," Imbry said, "that my innocence is genuine and that the item is what it is supposed to be — then what is it?"

Warrigrove sighed. "You will think me needlessly obscure, but your question has no definite answer."

Imbry felt a twinge of annoyance. "We inhabit an impossibly ancient world," he said. "Every question has long since been posed, in all its possible variants and permutations, and answered fully."

"That is supposedly the overarching reality of our age," admitted Warrigrove. "But we may be dealing here with another reality."

"I am, as you have intimated, a manufacturer of 'other realities,'" Imbry said. "Thus you may trust me when I tell you that no other reality exists."

"And yet you bring me this," Warrigrove said. His long, pale fingers reached out and touched the thing on the table, stroked it then drew back. "You must leave it with me."

"No."

"I must study it."

Imbry said, "I intend to hold an auction. But if you'd care to waive your fee for this consultation, you can be among the bidders."

Warrigrove agreed with an alacrity that surprised Imbry. The fat man covered the object with the dark cloth, evoking a low moan from the aficionado, who blinked as if awakening from a dream then looked at Imbry with a puzzled expression. "You did that," he said, "without effort. Does its glory not touch your inner being?"

"I hope not," said Imbry, "I prefer to be touched only at my own instigation. Now tell me what it is."

Warrigrove sighed. "It has had many names: the Grail Ultima, the Egg of First Innocence, the Eighth Path, the Supernal Radiance. Which do you prefer?"

Imbry found none of them satisfying. All had the ring of empty syllables swirled about by vague associations, nebulous connotations. He didn't mind batting about such inflated insubstantiata when he had been the one to blow air into them, but to be on the receiving end of the "perfumed cloud" was aggravating. He again studied Warrigrove closely, but detected no intent to deceive.

"Ambiguity will not serve," he said. "If you can't give me more than a misty whiff of its nature, then tell me if it has a function: what does it *do*?"

Warrigrove's brows rose and his lips pursed and Imbry could tell that his latest question was no more likely to receive a hard-edged answer than had its predecessors. "Anything and nothing," the aficionado said. "Fulfill dreams, but only for those who take care not to awaken. Reveal mysteries, though the revelations are no less mysterious than what was hidden. Transform base dross into rare earth, at least in the eye of the beholder. This is something from beyond our mundane existence. It is like one of the wonders of our species' dawn time, when who could say what might lie beyond the familiar hills, and the mind spun tales of eldritch kingdoms and far-off lands, upon which any fancy might be imposed."

Imbry put one plump palm against his forehead then drew it down his face, as if the action could wipe away a film that obscured his perceptions. "I will summarize," he said. "We have an object whose existence to date has been mainly rumor; which comes from no one knows exactly where; whose nature and functions are, at best, untested; about which vague yet fabulous and mystical claims may be made. And, on top of all that, it may be merely a cunning forgery."

"You have it," said Warrigrove. "Though I doubt it is a fake. It generates in me too profound a passion. Though I am puzzled by your ability to withstand its glamor."

"We are fashioned from different stuffs. It is why you collect and I deal."

"That may well be so. We come from different sides of a metaphysical divide. And each must pity the other."

"Let us leave our estimations of each other's character for another day," said Imbry, "and concentrate on resolving this mystery."

"Very well. I will advance a theory: perhaps the myriad grails and will o' the wisps that speckle the history of humanity have always been the same object. Say it is a fragment from a higher realm that somehow found its way into our base continuum — an eternal, unchangeable shred of absolute beauty, that moves in mysterious ways from place to place and from time to time. Some of those who encounter it are transported by the revelation of a sphere of existence so much greater, so much finer than the dull swamp in which we grind out our little lives. Others receive the same knowledge but are merely annoyed."

Imbry made a tactless noise. "Have you spent much time on that theory?"

"In truth," said Warrigrove, "it came to me as I beheld the object."

"Indeed? So it is a touchstone for separating humanity into the high-minded and the prosaic?"

"I would not put it that way, but it is not an inaccurate reflection of my idea."

"And you would include Chiz Ramoulian among the elevated?"

"The Red Abandon addict?" Warrigrove tried to disguise his anxiety, but Imbry was a practiced listener. "Is he connected to this?"

"He appears to have been as taken with it as you are."

Warrigrove attempted to affect nonchalance. "You would feel no need to mention my connection to this matter in Ramoulian's hearing?"

"At present, he is dining with the Archon," Imbry said, employing the common euphemism for those who were experiencing the unsought hospitality of the Archonate Bureau of Scrutiny. "I expect we will have this business concluded before they tip him back onto the streets."

"That is good," said Warrigrove.

"Indeed." Imbry briskly abraded one plump palm against its brother. "Very well, let us defer questions of what and why and where. Let us instead deal with *how much*."

"Ah," said Warrigrove, "on that score, feel free to let your imagination soar."

Luff Imbry could scale the heights of passion when entertaining the prospect of his own enrichment. He believed that life, at least *his* life, was not meant to be an exercise in self-stinting. As he made his way from Warrigrove's, satchel in hand, he allowed himself to indulge in some pleasantly fanciful speculations as to just how much fatter the mysterious object might make his purse. Thus distracted, he failed to notice the sleek black volante that was shadowing him at rooftop height on a tranquil residential street until it silently dropped to block his way. The dark hemisphere of energy that shielded its passenger compartment was extinguished and Imbry found himself under the hard stare of Alwinder Mudgeram.

"I have been looking for you," Mudgeram said. "I have left messages."

"I do not seem to have received them."

The aircar's operator's door opened and out stepped a man almost as large as Dain Ganche, with a tattooed face and shoulders like small hills.

"Good day, Ip," said Imbry. Everyone always greeted Mudgeram's assistant with studied politeness, although Imbry had never heard of anyone's having received more than a silent nod in acknowledgement.

"Let me offer you a ride," Mudgeram said and gestured to the empty seat beside him.

Ip reached for Imbry's arm with a hand whose fingers had been augmented with subtle but strong components. His grip caused the limb to go numb, as the fat man was half lifted into the vehicle. The energy dome reestablished itself and Imbry felt the seat cushion push against him as they went aloft.

"There is this matter of the funds I advanced you," said Mudgeram. "I was promised a profit to make the senses swim; instead, I suffered a complete loss."

"There were risks to the venture. They were disclosed."

"I remember a brief allusion to a remote possibility. Much more attention was devoted to the expected windfall. Pictures were painted, vistas laid out, all bedecked with boundless gain."

"Without enthusiasm, there would be no ventures at all."

"I have developed a new enthusiasm," Mudgeram said. "I now pursue grim satisfaction with the same zeal I formerly reserved for your scheme."

"That may be not good for you," Imbry said.

"It will definitely be 'not good' for some."

They had flown high above the city, heading west, and now cruised high above the chill waters of Mornedy Sound. The wave-rippled surface far below resembled the wrinkled hide of some great cold-blooded beast. Mudgeram invited his passenger to look down and envision a sequence of events that would end with Imbry entering the sea at high speed.

"Your funds went to acquire necessary materials for the plan," Imbry said. He had purchased minor artworks dating from the antique period in which his intended forgery would appear to have been created. The purchased works were broken down into their constituent elements, then reordered into a painting in the style of Bazieri, a grandmaster of the same age whose lifetime oeuvre had been scant. A newly discovered work by the ancient artist would have drawn collectors from at least thirty of the Ten Thousand Worlds along The Spray, each trailing funds like a pecuniary comet.

"Who could have foreseen that a vault full of unknown Bazieris would turn up in an attic?" It turned out that the artist had for years paid his rent with masterpieces that to the landlord were no more than pleasant daubs. By the time Bazieri's genius was recognized, both landlord and tenant were dust and the works long forgotten in a boarded up cockloft. They were discovered and emerged onto the market just as Imbry prepared to go forward with his fake; prices collapsed, leaving his forged work worth less than the cost of its ingredients.

"I have heard all of this before," Mudgeram said. "It puts no hepts in my pocket."

"Just as there are none in mine at the moment," Imbry said. "Picking have lately been slim."

Mudgeram rubbed the blue stubble that always shaded his jaw. "I will forgo the profits that never came," he said. "But I will either have back my investment or take my satisfaction in other ways."

"What ways?"

"A number of people have reason to feel that Luff Imbry has had a deleterious effect on the smooth passage of their lives. I will auction you to them. I might yet make a profit on our association."

Imbry thought of some of those who would hasten to attend such an auction, and pay gladly for the opportunity to carry him off in restraints to some remote location where they would not be interrupted. "I do have one excellent prospect," he said.

"Now would be a good time to tell me about it," Mudgeram said.

"I will do better. I will show you."

Imbry opened the satchel and peeled back some of the cloth, enough to let the object's effulgence show. He saw Alwinder Mudgeram's eyes light up with the same mixture of appetite and dreaminess that had affected Warrigrove and, he presumed, Ramoulian. When he glanced Ip's way he saw no overt expression, but the bodyguard's eyes slitted as if what he saw brought discomfort.

Imbry replaced the cloth and resealed the satchel. Mudgeram returned to the mundane. "What is it?" he said.

"That remains undetermined," Imbry said. "But it is the property of Dain Ganche, who has asked me to auction it for him. Ilarios Warrigrove will be one of the bidders." He saw no need to mention Chiz Ramoulian.

Mudgeram's face was not hard to read. Imbry watched the evidence of the man's thoughts as he processed the knowledge that Ganche was involved and came to a decision. "Warrigrove has just acquired a competitor," he said, then added, "Ip, home."

As the car banked and headed back toward Olkney, Mudgeram invited Imbry to stay at his house in town, a dour mansion on the Boulevard of Seven Graces. Imbry saw no way to decline.

It was decided that the auction would be held in a second-story salon whose heavily defended windows overlooked the private garden at the rear of Mudgeram's house. The date was set for three nights later. Imbry had Mudgeram's integrator connect him to his own assistant and between them they developed a list of five more collectors who would have both an interest in acquiring the object and the wealth to meet or exceed the exorbitant reserve price Imbry decided was warranted.

On the designated night, each bidder arrived independently, to be met in the mansion's atrium entrance where Ip relieved them of any weapons or inquisitive devices that might compromise their host's privacy. Some had brought hangers-on and these were shown to a waiting room and offered refreshments while their employers were led through the house to the site of the auction.

Besides Warrigrove, Imbry had also had dealings with four of the other bidders, and knew the remaining collector by reputation. They made small talk until Dain Ganche arrived, nodding to Alwinder Mudgeram and declining to give up his personal weapon, a medium-powered shocker. At that point, Imbry invited them to take seats in a semicircle of comfortable chairs that faced a long, ornately carved table. On its polished surface stood a portable lectern, before which rested the object beneath its cloth.

When Imbry took his place behind the lectern, his view of the object was blocked. He preferred not to be distracted by its insistent brilliance. Now the room settled into expectation. Ip positioned himself in a corner from which he had an unobstructed view of the proceedings, while Ganche took the chair closest to the barred windows.

"Honorables and distinctions," Imbry said, "we are gathered to decide the ownership of an article that may well be the only one of its kind in all the Ten Thousand Worlds. If there is another like it, its possessor has not made its existence known. The vendor, Dain Ganche, has set a reserve price," — Imbry named an astronomical sum, but the number caused not so much as an eye to blink among the bidders — "so we will start the bidding there. Let us begin by viewing the item."

With that he reached over the lectern, felt around for the heavy cloth and whisked it away. He heard the sibilant, simultaneous intakes of breath by those seated before him. After a few heartbeats, Ganche and Ip were able to tear their gazes away from the object, Imbry noted. Alwinder Mudgeram sat as if entranced, his eyes wide and softened as their pupils expanded until not even the thinnest rim of iris showed.

After a short while, Imbry reached forward with the cloth and covered the glitter again. "Bids, please," he said.

A collective moan of disappointment met Imbry's ears, then a cacophony of voices, strained and acquisitive. The collectors were on their feet, joined by Mudgeram, their faces distorted and their gestures emphatic as they bid and outbid. The reserve price was soon a fading memory as the contenders piled fortune upon fortune. As he continued to field the bids, Imbry looked to the side and saw Ganche's thick lips open in an astonishment that the fat man could appreciate: the vendor would leave here tonight wealthy enough to enter the magnate class. Imbry's own thirty per cent would make him one of the wealthiest criminals of Olkney.

The bidding had reached a feverish phase. Two of the collectors, the bids having surpassed their capacity, had subsided into their seats. One of them, a sturdy man with a square face and close cropped hair, sat slumped and quietly weeping. Imbry noticed that Mudgeram, too, had ceased to bid. He was sending Ip a meaningful look that the bodyguard was silently answering with raised eyebrows and a slight squint in one eye that said: *Are you sure?*

Now Mudgeram's face signaled back certainty and Imbry saw Ip's hand slip into a fold in his upper garment and begin to re-emerge with something dark in his grip. The fat man reached across the lectern and yanked the cloth free of the object. Once more a silence fell over the room as all eyes but Imbry's were drawn to the item. He heard a sob from the square-faced man.

The forger waited for Dain Ganche to pull his eyes away and when the man's gaze lifted to Imbry the fat man gestured with chin and eyes toward Mudgeram's bodyguard. Ip had also managed to look away from the glittering prize, but stood blinking, his mind not yet fully returned to the business at hand — specifically that his employer expected him to use the weapon he held forgotten in his grip. Ganche's face hardened. He rose to his feet with a surprising swiftness for a man of his size and drew his shocker.

"Warning!" said the house integrator. "An inbound vehicle approaches at high..." The rest of its announcement was submerged by the sounds from outside: the blare of a klaxon, the thrum of a heavy motor and the almost infrasonic vibration of an automatic ison cannon firing from the roof. At the same time the house's rear garden lit up in a blaze of illumination from high-intensity lumens.

Imbry looked toward the glare just in time to see a heavy cargo carrier descend at speed, graze the top of the outer wall and hurtle toward the barred windows. Successive hits from the ison cannon caused sparks to coruscate from its frontwork and turned the operator's compartment into dripping, incandescent slag but did nothing to deter the vehicle's momentum.

Imbry reflexively ducked behind the table as the carrier smashed into the window's grillwork amid an immensity of sound. He heard but did not see the bars shatter and tear loose from their footings, the unbreakable panes whizzing through the room like shrapnel. The only exit was in the wall opposite the windows and he stayed low and crawled that way along the length of the table before rising up to search out a clear path to safety.

There was none. He saw Alwinder Mudgeram, blood smearing his face from a gash in his forehead, squatting to provide the smallest possible target while exiting through the door. Ip, unscathed and now fully alert, covered his employer's retreat, energy pistol in hand. Imbry looked toward the windows and saw that the space they had once occupied was now filled by the cargo vehicle, most of which had battered its way into the room. The front end, hissing and radiating a fierce heat, had landed on Dain Ganche and Ilarios Warrigrove, raising a nauseating smoke and permanently canceling any and all plans they might have had. The square-faced man had also shed his last tear, and those of the other bidders who were not severely injured were deep in shock.

Imbry found himself torn between an urge to flee and the inclination to secure the priceless subject of the auction. Miraculously, it sat undisturbed on the table which itself had been unaffected by the carrier's sudden entry. Since no further danger presented itself, the fat man decided to delay departure long enough to recover the shining object. But as he replaced the dark cloth over its brilliance and prepared to lift it, he heard a discreet cough.

Ip now stood in the doorway, his weapon aimed at Imbry. The bodyguard cocked his head in a clear signal that the forger was to bring the object in no other direction than that in which Mudgeram had gone. Imbry arranged his face and hands in a combination that indicated nothing else was on his mind. He reached again for the object but froze at the sound of a loud *crack!* A side panel broke partly free of the carrier, impelled from within. A second kick sent the thin material flying and out of the hole stepped Chiz Ramoulian, obsession in his eyes and a long, dark disorganizer in his hands.

For the second time in moments Imbry experienced the chill of finding a weapon pointed his way. He backed away, offering placating gestures, but Ramoulian had clearly not come in search of mollification. Imbry saw the man's thumb slide over to the disorganizer's activation stud.

The *zivv* of Ip's energy pistol was loud in the room. Ramoulian's head lost definition and became first a glowing orb, then a lump of smoldering black stuff that held its shape for only a moment longer before crumbling and following his collapsing body to the littered floor.

Ip again brought his weapon to bear on Imbry, the fingers of his other hand beckoning. The fat man took up the object, snugged the cloth around it and went where he was bid. They passed along corridors and through a number of imposing doors until they came to a fortified room in which Alwinder Mudgeram had sequestered himself.

When Ip reported the events concerning Ramoulian and declared the situation secure, Mudgeram emerged from his redoubt. The room's facilities had sealed the wound in his forehead but the blood still stained his face. Without a word, he took the object from Imbry's hands.

"If you are feeling well enough," Imbry said, "we should discuss my compensation."

"I am feeling adequate," Mudgeram said, "but I am not aware that you are due anything."

"I recall the bidding," Imbry said and named the gargantuan sum that had been the last bid offered. "Then Ramoulian interrupted. I was to receive a thirty per cent commission."

Mudgeram tucked the object securely under his arm. "I remember a different series of events. As the bidding intensified, the auctioneer uncovered the object and distracted the bidders. Then Ramoulian entered. Were these two events coincidental?"

"Entirely," Imbry said.

"Hmm," said Mudgeram. "In any case, matters have now marched off in a new direction. The vendor who promised to pay your commission has instead passed permanently beyond buying and selling. Indeed, he has expired without known heirs, carelessly leaving his former possession unattended on another's property. Where it is now seized under the rule of evident domain."

"Should that not be *eminent* domain?" Imbry said, but Mudgeram had Ip show the fat man his "evidence."

After Ip had flourished his weapon under Imbry's nose, the forger said, "What about the others?"

Mudgeram gave the matter some brief thought then explained that the bidders had, albeit unwillingly, become participants in a matter that could not be allowed to come to the attention of the Bureau of Scrutiny. Mudgeram would summon discreet helpers who would remove all traces of the incident. "Regrettably," he continued, "my guests have to be included among those 'traces.' If questioned, they might give answers that must inevitably lead to further intrusions into my affairs by the scroots. It is better for all concerned if we simply seal off those avenues of inquiry before they are opened."

There was a silence then Imbry said, "What of me?"

Mudgeram gave the forger a look in which Imbry felt himself weighed and subjected to some internal calculation. "You and I may do business again some day. Thus, once matters are tidied up you may leave."

"And the object? There could be other bidders."

"I have developed an attachment to it," Mudgeram said. "It will remain with me." He paused and again Imbry sensed the workings of some inner arithmetic. "But, in recompense for your efforts, I will freely cancel the debt you owe me from the Bazieri affair."

Mudgeram inclined his head and smiled in a manner that assured Imbry that he need not thank his benefactor.

The moment Imbry returned to his operations center, his integrator sought his attention. It referred him to the research and communications matrix. "More information has accrued in regard to criminality at the spaceport," it said.

Imbry sat in the matrix's chair. "The matter is now moot, but tell me."

"A private space yacht owned by a wealthy off-worlder named Catterpaul stayed in a berth beyond the time its owner had contracted for. When port officials investigated, they found the man dead in the main saloon. His possessions appeared to have been rifled."

"Ramoulian," said Imbry.

"Likely so. Here is the interesting part: Catterpaul was a dilettante who poked about the far edges of The Spray, collecting oddments and curios. Some of his poking occurred in and around the Lesser Dark."

"Ah," said Imbry.

The integrator continued, "Someone had winnowed the cargo. Some small but valuable pieces had been placed on the floor, as if sorted for removal. But the only item taken is described in Catterpaul's notes as: 'seed pod, immature, northern continent, unnamed world.'"

The coordinates were the same as those of the planet visited thousands of years ago by Fallo Wickiram. Imbry called up the rest of the information and perused it thoughtfully. "Well, there it is," he said. "The object is some kind of ultraterrene vegetative life form, unclassified, nature unknown. Catterpaul left it in the cargo area to ripen, with the intent of planting it in his garden when he returned to his house on Bodeen's World."

"It would seem that it can telepathically manipulate persons who come within range," said the integrator.

"In order to spread itself," Imbry concurred. "Its 'grailness' is thus no more mystical than a burr's hooks. It stimulates the passerby's senses, creating an illusion of supernal beauty. The hapless dupe carries it away. By the time the effect wears off the seed is far from home. The mark, finding that he has been used by a mindless vegetable, throws the thing away and it takes root."

He had the integrator display the scan it had taken of the object. The image that appeared on the screen showed no illusion of brilliant glory, only a dark green globe with a pale, rootlike tendril emerging. Imbry thought of Mudgeram's inevitable surprise and chuckled.

Some days later, Imbry sat once more in a room at Bolly's Snug. He was expecting a visitor who wished to consult with him about acquiring a gilded icon declared by its provenance to date from the Eighteenth Aeon, but which, Imbry had it on unshakeable authority, dated from no earlier than the previous two weeks.

But when the door opened, it was Ip who entered and gestured meaningfully for Imbry to accompany him. They left by an unmarked exit to find an aircar waiting in the alley behind the tavern. They flew without conversation to Alwinder Mudgeram's house. Imbry was shown to a parlor just off the main foyer. Ip indicated that he might take refreshment from the dispenser then departed. Imbry poured himself a glass of Phalum, sat and sipped. He rehearsed what he would say to defuse Mudgeram's disappointment.

The door opened and he looked up expectantly, but again it was Ip who filled the doorway. In his arms was the kind of disposable carton in which goods were shipped. He placed it on a low table before Imbry and said, "What will these bring?"

The fat man set down his wine and inspected the box's contents. Some of the items were bric-a-brac. Some were of great value. Two were priceless. He sorted them into categories and gave estimates.

Ip pulled at his lower lip. Imbry was astounded to see anxiety on the bodyguard's face but managed to keep his surprise from showing. Could Mudgeram's affairs have taken a precipitous downturn?

The bodyguard spoke again. "What would your commission be?"

"For these, thirty per cent, for the others, twenty."

Ip nodded. "Done," he said.

Imbry looked around. "Does Mudgeram watch us from a distance?"

For a moment, the fat man thought to see a trace of an ironic smile touch the impassive features. "Possibly," Ip said, "though that would be quite some distance."

"Something has happened to him?" Imbry said.

Ip began replacing the objects in the carton. "Oh, yes."

The tip of Imbry's tongue touched his upper lip. "There are items of considerable value throughout the house," he said.

Again, he thought to see the faintest tinge of a smile. "You are welcome to them," Ip said. He gestured to the door.

"Will not the integrator prevent my taking them?"

Ip indicated that the likelihood was remote.

Intrigued, Imbry rose and went out into the foyer. Several doors led out of the atrium, all of them closed. Imbry paused to evaluate the situation. He turned to find that Ip had joined him from the parlor, placing the box of treasures near the front door. Now Imbry noticed that next to the box was a device that would function as a portable armature into which the house integrator could be decanted for travel.

The bodyguard indicated the closed doors. "Choose," he said.

Imbry inspected the nearest door. Its panels seemed to bulge slightly. He mentioned this to Ip and the bodyguard moved his head in a subtle manner that discouraged the fat man from reaching for the opener. Imbry gestured to the next door and receiving a less unequivocal signal from the silent bodyguard, he crossed to the portal and eased it ajar.

Beyond lay darkness. Imbry could not tell if he stood before a room or a corridor, because the moment he opened the door, a restless rustling filled his ears and the doorway was filled by a writhing mass of tuberous vines, fleshy and thick as his wrist, from which spouted glossy dark leaves and fibrous, coiled tendrils that immediately unwound and began to sample the air as if sensing his presence.

Imbry closed the door. A few of the tendrils remained caught in the jamb and one of them wriggled from beneath the lintel. Ip drew his energy pistol and carefully burned each to ashes.

"So Mudgeram planted it," Imbry said.

"It planted itself," said Ip.

An image floated up in Imbry's mind. He remembered Ganche's description of finding Ramoulian curled around the object, dazed as if fuddled by Red Abandon. To Ip he said, "Before you decant the integrator, ask it to display Alwinder Mudgeram."

"You are not the kind to be haunted by frightful memories?" the body-guard said. When Imbry said he was not the man instructed the integrator to show the image.

A screen appeared in the air, filled with a murky scene. Imbry saw darkly veined vines, wider in cross section than his own well fleshed thighs, choking a room that by its furnishings he took to be a sleeping chamber. At first the view, seen from a percept on the ceiling, was a chaos of interwoven vegetation: the fat creepers had crossed and wound about each other as they had grown in search of exit through the doors and windows.

Then Imbry imposed mental order on the snarl, perceiving how the different vines all proceeded from a common location. Beneath the densest tangle, where the lianas were thickest, he caught glimpses of lush bedcovers. Then he saw something else.

He instructed the integrator to narrow the focus and magnify. The image enlarged upon the screen: a hand spread across a piece of curved dark object, which resolved itself into a fragment of a husk, much like that which had been found in the ship rented by Fallo Wickiram that had returned without him. The hand was withered like a worn out glove, empty of all but its skin and fragile bones. Above it was what remained of a face.

"Ah," said Imbry. After a moment he told the integrator, "You may remove the screen."

He took up the carton from beside the door while Ip finished preparing the integrator for departure. Mudgeram's black volante hovered outside. They boarded the aircar and went aloft.

The flew in silence for a little while, then Imbry said, "Warrigrove made a perceptive comment. We had noted that the object's glamor stirred a breathless passion in some — like him and Ramoulian and Mudgeram — but evoked only irritation in more earthbound fellows like you and me. He said that each side of the dichotomy must pity the other."

Ip's face remained impassive. He activated Mudgeram's integrator and issued an instruction. Intense light flashed from somewhere behind them, then faded even before the volante's canopy could darken.

"Is it pity that you feel for Alwinder Mudgeram?" Ip asked.

"No," said Imbry, "not pity."

THE EYE OF VANN

The market for off-world curios in the louche and gaudy city of Olkney occupied a narrow niche. Old Earth, grown smug and insular in its penultimate age, cared little for whatever might happen on the myriad of worlds that it had long ago seeded with those who would not — or could not — remain rooted in ancestral soil. But some few of Olkney's wealthy aesthetes did take an interest in the products of the disparate cultures sprawled and speckled across the Ten Thousand Worlds of The Spray, and among that few were a dozen or so who took a very great interest indeed.

One of these was Baltazo Meagh, scion of an ancient and well funded line of second-tier magnates. Meagh resided — when he was not off-world, collecting — in a compact mansion built of livestone on a tree-lined boulevard in the Amaranth district. He had filled the house with a range of objects, from crudities to exquisites, that had piqued his fancy on a thousand planets: cultic totems of the nomadic tribes that wandered, though always along carefully plotted routes, the windy deserts of Lith; delicate altar dishes from the Grand Thedra on Prynach, fashioned from sacred clay mingled with the powdered bones of saints; scintillating thunder stones from Kurbelow.

And soon, it was whispered in places where such whispers were to be heard, Meagh would take possession of the Eye of Vann, purloined from its temple right here in Olkney by hired agents of the Green Circle syndicate. When the whispers intensified into murmurs, a spokesperson for the Vannian cult scoffed that Meagh must be the gull of forgers, for did not the true relic rest secure in the Holiest of Holies?

This fact was attested to by the Most Sublime First Enunciant himself; he was the only soul routinely permitted into its presence, except for the highest of holy days, when all the faithful attended on the Eye for the ritual known as the Lavishing.

Baltazo Meagh, for his part, said nothing, but only smiled a quiet smile.

Luff Imbry had no doubt that the true Eye would soon repose upon a plinth in Meagh's mansion. Imbry was Old Earth's premier purveyor of artworks and other valuables to persons who paid handsomely but required no receipts or documents of provenance and who never advertised the transactions. But the master thief had had no hand in the lifting of the Eye; his certainty that the Green Circle had stolen it for Meagh came from a visitor Imbry had recently received in one of the back rooms of Bolly's Snug.

"The Eye must be restored," said the sepulchral voice of the cowled figure seated across the table from the corpulent thief. "The Rite of the Lavishing looms."

"I cannot inject myself into the Green Circle's doings," Imbry said. "They are far too fond of the vendetta."

The First Enunciant of Vann showed more flexibility in his judgments than most chief priests of secretive cults, Imbry thought, as he heard the hierophant declare that he, too, desired no complications with the Green Circle. "I consider them merely the instrument," he said. "Baltazo Meagh is the author of the sacrilege, and must die."

"I undertake operations that result in persons becoming separated from their possessions," Imbry said, "if the fee and circumstances are in order. I do not normally separate persons from existence, though I can recommend some reliable specialists."

"I will take care of Meagh. Since he has profaned and polluted the most sacred, the manner of his demise must be appropriate to the dastardliness of his trespass." The high priest's sharp-nailed fingers curled around an absent throat. "I look to you only to recover the consecrated object. And soon."

Imbry gave his nose a reflective pull. "The work will surely require my touching the Eye. I would hate to deliver it to you, only to learn that I must follow Meagh in whatever doleful procession you plan for him."

"It is within my authority to grant you temporary standing in the faith," the visitor said. "But for your own sake, I advise you not to look into the Eye."

"Why? What would I see?"

The ascetic face within the shadow of the cowl took on an even grimmer aspect. "Most see nothing but their own reflections. Some, however, experience a connection that can be unsettling, especially for the uninitiated."

Imbry was not sanguine about the proposed operation. He had been inside Meagh's walls three times, delivering items the collector wished to acquire. He knew that the house's standard defenses were strong and sophisticated, though the thief was confident that he knew how to suborn and delude them.

"I usually argue for the minimalist approach," he told the First Enunciant, "but in the circumstances, specifically the need to overcome the resistance of livestone, perhaps a direct and sudden assault on Meagh's premises might be more productive. Your temple has an all-male congregation, most of them in the prime of life."

His visitor's face drew back into the shadows of his cowl, but the previously grave voice took on a note of suppressed alarm. "No, no. Discretion is of the essence."

"And speed?" said Imbry.

"Oh, yes. Very much so."

From this exchange, Imbry deduced that the First Enunciant had been less than entirely candid with his fellow Vannians as to the whereabouts of their most sacred relic. This realization was an important factor in the thief's negotiating of a substantial fee for his services, plus expenses, with half payable in advance.

The next day, Imbry put aside other projects and focused his faculties on the task at hand. The thorniest problem derived from the fact that Meagh's manse was built of livestone.

There had been a brief vogue for the uncommon building material a decade or so before, when samples were brought to Olkney from Hoff, the distant world on which livestone originated. The stone was the accreted product of tiny creatures that formed huge colonies, billions of individuals strong. The collective grew an extensive root-mass formed of hair-thin cilia that penetrated deep into the ground to find subterranean waterflows. From the hidden waters, the colony extracted an array of minerals, transporting them back to the surface, where they were blended before being secreted to form a dense, hard shell, like that of Old Earth's coral reefs. On their home world, the creatures' land-reefs grew in convoluted patterns, with twisting tunnels and hollow chambers that attracted higher life forms seeking refuge from predators and safe places to bear young.

A symbiotic relationship had evolved between livestone and its tenants: the sheltered brought in nutrients; the shelterer defended its symbiotes by attacking unwelcome entrants to its tunnels. Human settlers on the home world had adapted these natural attributes to create dwellings for themselves that repelled Hoff's deadliest fauna, with which the planet was more than usually stocked.

The drawback to living in livestone was that the semi-sentient creature that built and maintained the colonies had a limited ability to learn. A small, house-sized colony could be brought to recognize, at the most, seven individuals as its rightful protectorate. Any other persons who came to visit took their chances. On each occasion when Imbry had visited Meagh's manse, he had been required to tread only on a raised wooden walkway that led from the foyer to the drawing room in which he was received. The room, too, was floored, ceilinged and walled in the same dark, lustrous wood, the source of which was a tree selectively bred up by Hoff's settlers from a native shrub that was antithetical to livestone's chemical arsenal. Had Imbry's foot or hand touched a floor or wall of livestone, the implications would have been immediate, painful and likely lethal.

He repaired to his operations center, concealed in an unremarkable small house in one of Olkney's least fashionable precincts. In a small, windowless room that did not appear on the house's architectural plans, he approached what looked to be a piece of battered furniture and touched it in a way that caused it to unfold into a sophisticated information retrieval matrix. He had intended to reacquaint himself with the intricacies of handling livestone, but as he brought the device to full sentience, curiosity emerged from the back reaches of his mind and tickled his awareness. He instructed the matrix to first give him a comprehensive rundown on the Eye of Vann. The screen filled instantly with text and images. Imbry interwove his plump fingers, placed his thumbs beneath his multitudinous chins, and began to read.

A few non-human civilizations lay scattered among the Ten Thousand Worlds of The Spray. The ultramondanes, as they were called, pursued their own ends in their own fashions. On some worlds, even including Old Earth, human and non-human populations lived in adjacent territories. But they did not much intermingle; their respective ways and aims were so mutually alien that it was easier to abide with each other in the way that different species of beasts had once grazed beside each other on the long vanished savannahs of the dawn-time Earth.

Humanity was a latecomer to the business of civilization-building. Old Earth's fading red sun was a fourth-generation star, formed from the debris of ancient suns that had been born, lived through their aeons, and exploded to strew their substance back through the commonality of the galaxy. Long before humans had come tripping down The Spray, during the time known as the Great Effloration, a myriad of non-human species had emerged, flourished and declined. Some had left behind vast, inexplicable monuments.

Some had left only charred bones or heaps of shattered chitin. The presence of others could be deduced only from the faintest traces on worn-out worlds.

The Eye of Vann was unique. It had been found on Charrakin, a world that was so far down The Spray as to be arguably part of the galactic body proper. Charrakin was a dry and desert sphere, its air chilled and its wide, unwatered plateaus bereft of life. It offered nothing of interest to the explorers who first located it, neither minerals, nor biota, nor even ultramondane curios — though it had been well populated once, by a species so long since vanished that they left virtually nothing to show they had ever come up, thriven, and gone down.

In some sheltered areas, though, where the mountains had not yet been ground level by hundreds of millions of years of wind-borne grit, there remained a few low walls to suggest that once there had been sprawling cities. And in one of those corners, atop a heap of eroded rubble, lay the Eye.

All around it were wind-scoured and crumbling heaps of masonry and brick, yet the Eye remained pristine. It was a lens-shaped object, elongated to tapering points at either side, of a deep and lustrous blue. Its true origin and purpose were unknowable, but somewhere a fanciful tale sprang up, telling of how it had been the single eye of some great stone idol. The cyclopic statue, it was said, had loomed over an impossibly ancient city, a cult center to which the god's devotees crept on their knees — though whether Charrakin's city builders had traveled on jointed limbs, or flailing tentacles, or even wheels, would never be known. It was assumed by those who rejoiced in such assumptions that orgiastic rites or blood-spattered rituals, if not both, must have transpired beneath the eidolon's unwinking azure gaze.

What was known for sure was that the original locator of the Eye did not tuck it into his specimen satchel and bring it home. Instead, he left it where he found it. When asked why, he said that when he looked into its depths, he felt an urgent need to put distance between the object and his own flesh, the latter having begun to crawl.

The tale had spread, as such tales always did. Others had come to Charrakin, trudged across the shifting sands and gazed upon the Eye. Some responded as had its discoverer, with a horripilating desire to be gone; others reported that the object was over-rated, for they had looked into it and found nothing more than their own reflections and that of the high white sky of the dead planet.

Eventually, however, someone had come with a more deliberate purpose. His name was Ekkun Batternan and it was not recorded how he reacted to the Eye, nor even if he had looked into it. It was known, however, that he had scooped it up and carried it back to Old Earth, where he installed the object in a temple he had had commissioned in a select arrondissement of Olkney. He then invited all who craved a revelation to join his new cult, which he described as the revived worship of the alien god Vann (for so someone had named the alleged idol from the old tale), a mystery cult that had flourished when humankind's ancestors had yet to achieve multicellular organization. There was always a market for new gods in Olkney, especially if the new could be presented as inconceivably old; Batternan's congregation was soon over-subscribed.

Luff Imbry grunted and paused to reflect on what he had learned. After a brief mull, he decided that the Eye's numinous qualities, whether true or sham, were irrelevant. He returned to the challenge of the livestone.

The first time he had become acquainted with Baltazo Meagh's mansion, he had made preliminary inquiries about its nature; the information might someday become useful. He now called up his notes and reviewed them. As he remembered, the sheer simplicity of the creatures that created the stuff made them difficult to suborn: unlike sentient watchers, they could not be bribed, beguiled, diverted or drugged. They reacted out of reflex, and the distance between stimulus and response was too short to be interfered with.

Still, there was one possibility. No more often than once in a century, wild livestone colonies filled the air with thick clouds of spores called jasm. These seed-stuffs rose in their trillions into the upper atmosphere of Hoff, where they swirled and eddied for years, intermingling and cross-fertilizing to form primitive zygotes that fell with seasonal precipitation. New colonies formed and the cycle was renewed.

During the few hours when spores were emitted, the livestone organisms paid no heed to any predator that might brave the choking spore-storms and enter the tunnels where the symbiotic tenants dwelt. In that fact, Luff Imbry sought to find a means of entering Meagh's manse and departing with his skin unscorched and his liver unassailed by lethal pollutants.

His research revealed a complication: in domesticating livestone, Hoffians had edited its reproductive function, the spores being liable to trigger horrific allergic reactions in a significant minority of humans. Considerable ingenuity had gone into suppressing its natural processes, creating a variant that could not produce spores except by artificial stimulation. The tailored pheromone that provided the trigger was a closely guarded treasure of the livestone architectural profession on Hoff.

Dipping into the First Enunciant's advance on expenses, the rotund thief made arrangements, packed a valise, and departed for the spaceport out on an island in Mornedy Sound. He had long maintained, under the name of a proxy, a small spaceship that was now capable of greater speed and far less detectable than had been envisioned by its original designers. Imbry went to where the vessel stood in one of the less visited areas of the spaceport, boarded and departed. Before he broke orbit, he contacted his client and found him grown more anxious.

"Time grows short," the hierophant said. "The Eye must be restored for the Lavishing."

"Can you not postpone the ceremony?"

"There is no provision in the scriptures."

"I have heard of instances where inconvenient passages are clarified by new revelations," the thief suggested.

"No, the Revered Batternan's strictures are irredactible."

"I will do my best," said Imbry, "but overcoming livestone is not easy. Again, I suggest you consider a direct assault. Or even contact the Bureau of Scrutiny and seek to recover the Eye through 'proper' channels."

He heard a hiss of indrawn breath. "No," said the First Enunciant, "the faith of the general congregation must not be shaken."

"I will be as quick as I can," the thief said.

A note of suspicion now crept into the client's tone. "You are not deliberately dawdling, intending to wring a higher fee from us?"

Imbry treated the suggestion with the scorn it deserved. "As quick as I can," he repeated.

"See that you are," said the client, but the utterance held more prayer than threat.

Upon his return to Olkney, Luff Imbry made inquiries in certain quarters and confirmed that the transaction between Baltazo Meagh and the Green Circle had been completed. He next attempted to contact the First Enunciant, but the secure connection the client had given him was answered by a new voice, gruff and unresponsive to Imbry's inquiries. Indeed, whoever was answering at the temple had questions of his own to put, concerning the caller's connection to the hierophant, who was referred to in scatological terms. Imbry drew the appropriate conclusions and broke the connection.

Still, a contract was a contract. Besides, Imbry had always wanted to evaluate Baltazo Meagh's most loved possessions. Accordingly, at the smallest hour of the following night, he approached an alcove-shaded side door of Meagh's great house.

He wore an elision suit, a one-piece garment that covered him from toes to crown and could deflect light, the most common inquisitive energies, and all but the most corrosive chemicals. In a slit pocket over a well padded hip was a pressurized vial of concentrated pheromone that had come from one of the least successful livestone architects in a provincial city on Hoff.

The supplier had been difficult to find, requiring much gentle sifting of possible sources without provoking any of them to call Imbry's importunings to the attention of the authorities. In the end, the cost had not been too great but the operation had taken a considerable time.

Imbry applied a small device to the side door's who's-there and activated it. A brief struggle ensued between the guardian's perceptions and the impressions Imbry's device sought to impose upon them, but in a fraction of a blink the who's-there became convinced that an expected delivery of provisions was on the doorstep. The portal cycled open and Imbry was in.

He paused as the door shut itself and the who's-there lost all memory of the last few moments. No alarms sounded, nor did any automatic defenses engage him. But the instant he stepped off the wooden dais just within the door, a subtle shimmer past over the livestone floor, like a flicker of light across the bottom of a pool of clear water when a faint breeze ripples the surface. The glimmer raced away down the corridor before him, at the same time spreading to the walls and the high, arched ceiling, all of which now began to glow a lurid shade of pink.

Imbry extracted the vial from his pocket and activated its disperser. A colorless liquid atomized into a mist that clung to the porous surfaces. The thief advanced into the hallway, applying the vapor to the walls and floor, and wafting it toward where the upper air touched the lofty ceiling.

The garish pink that had appeared on the livestone now faded and ceased to spread. Instead, wherever the mist touched, the stone turned a deep mauve. Imbry brought out a speculum to inspect the nearby wall closely; he saw that the color came not from the stone itself, but from a multitude of tiny hollow spicules that were emerging from the myriad pores that covered the surface. The minuscule tubes themselves were crystal clear; the purple pigmentation was from the billions of spores that the livestone was now generating.

As Imbry went deeper into the house, spraying to all sides, the discoloration intensified. A glance back told him that the air through which he had passed was now being filled with swirls and eddies of minute particles, so that looking down the formerly well lighted hallway was now like peering through a deep summer twilight. Imbry held up one arm and noted that the stuff was even filling the tiny striations in the fabric from which his elision suit was made, so that his corpulent form was now outlined in purple.

The vial's contents were almost completely discharged, but the job was done. The organisms in the walls were now responding to the pheromones carried by the erupting spores themselves, causing a chain reaction that was already making the livestone far ahead of him blush a rich purple. The ceilings disappeared behind densifying clouds of seed-stuff.

With billows of jasm erupting from all surfaces, the thief consulted his memory for a schematic of Meagh's house and moved quickly. He turned left at the end of the corridor, took a right and crossed a dome-covered courtyard, entered another arched passageway and stopped at a sealed door. He applied another of his custom-fabricated devices to its lock and, immediately after, passed into a small strongroom.

Baltazo Meagh turned, mouth opening in astonishment as he saw a plump and purple man-shape step into his most private sanctum, followed by roiling wafts of livestone spores. Unfortunately for the householder, he must draw breath before challenging the intruder, and the intake of air carried with it a host of purple motes. In the ensuing moments, both men learned that Meagh was among those who reacted badly to livestone seed-stuff, but Imbry's lesson was far gentler than that received by the collector.

The thief considered doing something about the swelling, twitching, mess of spasming limbs and streaming orifices that Meagh had become, but his informant on Hoff had advised him that no antidote to a livestone spore allergy had ever been found. Instead, Imbry resolutely turned his eyes from the unhappy scene and let them fall upon the object of his quest, which rested upon a damask cushion atop a truncated pillar.

The Eye was as his research matrix had described it, an elongated lens of dark blue, about the size of a human head and tapering out to sharp points at the sides. Its surface glistened with a light that seemed not a reflection of the treasure room's illumination, but an emanation from deep within the Eye itself.

Imbry unsealed a pocket in the front of his elision suit and withdrew a folded wad of the same material as his garment. This he shook out to make a carrying bag. Mindful of the First Enunciant's warning, at first he only side-eyed the object and did not let his gaze linger. But then he reminded himself that he would not be Luff Imbry if he had not the fortitude to confront reality on its own terms. He faced the Eye directly and stared into its depths.

His gaze was not returned, though he did note that the surface of the lens offered no purchase to the swirls of motes that sought to alight on it. The

Eye retained a translucent clarity, while everything else in the room was becoming shrouded in purple. Imbry brushed a gloved finger over the smooth roundedness, wondering if the object generated a repellent charge. Then he looked closer and was surprised to find that the gleaming surface was not, in fact, repulsing the livestone jasm; rather, the Eye was osmotically absorbing the stuff, as if the smooth hardness were a permeable membrane.

And now, as more of the drifting spores settled on the blue lens, Imbry noted that the action was not passive. A purple vortex was discernible in the mote-swarmed air above the object. Spores that had settled in the micro-channels of his elision suit were now lifting free of the tiny grooves and flying toward the Eye. *It draws the stuff to it,* he thought, though the means by which it did so were not apparent.

The great blue lens still rested atop the plinth where Baltazo Meagh had placed it. Imbry could not calculate how much of the seed-stuff it had by now absorbed, though the quantity must be considerable. Yet the Eye had not changed, and did not change, even as the vortex became larger and stronger, growing exponentially, so that purple spores were now darting toward, and disappearing into, the object at such a ferocious rate that the thief could hear them slithering over the skin of his suit like a blizzard of fine powder.

He looked again into the blueness and, though again nothing looked back at him, he felt a sudden shift in perspective. It was as if he was no longer gazing into a lens no thicker than his head. Instead, he felt as if he were peering down a hole of vast, even infinite, depth — *or,* the thought suddenly struck him, *into an appetite of insatiable hunger, and this is its feeding tube.*

And still the whirling purple vortex grew stronger, so that the sound of livestone jasm passing across Imbry's elision suit had become an audible hiss. As if borne on a powerful wind, the spores poured into the treasure room from throughout the manse, called to the Eye that drank them down and wanted more, and only more.

Imbry recalled the image of lifeless Charrakin and wondered if he was now seeing the process by which it had become a wholly barren world. He looked down at Baltazo Meagh, now thoroughly dead, and saw a discoloration at the front of the body's breeches. A moment later, he no longer needed to wonder as the corpse joined the livestone in making a small contribution that fed the ravenous hunger behind the blue lens.

Yet Imbry noticed that he felt only a slightly disturbing sensation in his own tender parts. He reasoned that the energy-resistant fabric of his elision suit must provide some insulation against the Eye's pull. Without it, he had no doubt he would be as susceptible as the livestone and the dead Baltazo Meagh.

The thin bag was still in his hand. He spread its mouth wide and moved to make it swallow the Eye. But the torrent of livestone jasm now flowing into the room, swirling and funneling toward the blue adit to *somewhere else*, had become a maelstrom. The force of its passage, close to where it entered the Eye, buffeted and thrust aside his hands. He set himself and drove his arms toward the lens with all his strength. But the concentration of spores where the spiral met the Eye was now so dense as to be virtually solid.

Imbry stood back to think. The density was thickest at the point of entry, becoming gradually thinner as the vortex widened above the lens. He conceived a plan and looked about for something to climb on. The room contained several other plinths of different heights and widths, some square in cross-section, others circular, each supporting an object of great value. The thief chose several, carefully removed whatever stood atop them, then arranged them in order of ascending height, with the tallest overlooking the Eye and its still-tempestuous vortex.

Laboriously, he began to climb. He had just mounted from the floor to the lowest step when the floor shook to a heavy concussion. Above the hiss of the livestone spores passing over the fabric that covered his ears, Imbry heard the multiple thuds of masonry collapsing. He moved more quickly, grateful now that the increasing strength of the inflow toward the Eye had stripped from his elision suit all of the purple motes that had originally clogged its microgrooves. He was, once again, effectively invisible.

Beyond the room, over the sussuration of the flowing jasm, Imbry could hear other sounds. Muffled voices, choking sounds, the clatter of several persons forcing their way through the blinding mass of spores that still erupted from the walls, floors and ceilings of Meagh's manse. He paused to listen, then continued to climb.

The brouhaha approached the treasure room as Imbry reached the last of his stepping stones. As he had expected, the swirl of spores up here was less dense. He looked down into the vortex and did not hesitate, but launched himself, the bag spread in both hands, so that he fell straight down through the purple whirlwind. The momentum of his considerable mass, assisted by gravity, was sufficient. The bag's open mouth encompassed the blue lens, and instantly the inrush of jasm ceased, the spores hanging loosely in the air as before.

Imbry landed heavily, bruising his arms and probably a rib that had caught the edge of the plinth that had supported the Eye. He ignored the pain and swiftly cinched the bag shut, even as he rolled toward a corner of the treasure room and silently rose to stand utterly still.

The Eye of Vann

The door to the room immediately filled with the jostling bodies of several persons. Each wore a curious costume: an ankle-length cowled robe, belted at the waist, but with a section of material cut away below the waist. It was unmistakably evident from what was visible through the holes that each of the newcomers was male. If there had been any doubt as to their sex, it would have been erased by the way each man now took hold of himself with one hand, while elevating the other with fingers arranged in what Imbry took for a ritual sign. Despite the spores that still filled the room and caused the devotees of Vann to cough and splutter, they took up a guttural chant as they advanced into the room.

But after a few syllables, the paean died away as the celebrants sought in vain for the focus of their devotions. They felt about, each with one hand, for the thing that, until moments before, had been drawing them toward the treasure room. In the purple twilight, they blundered and groped, knocking over part of Baltazo Meagh's collection.

The sounds of shattering fragilities caused Luff Imbry some grief, even as he sidled along a wall toward the door. Now that the Eye was no longer energetically drawing jasm toward its unfillable maw, the motes were beginning to resettle in the grooves of his elision suit. Soon, he would become once more a dark-pigmented man-shape, easily visible as he moved through the less dense cloud of spores.

But then one of the faithful came across the corpse of the defiler where it lay in the middle of the room. His cries of hate and kicks of savage retribution drew the others, and while they wreaked their revenge on Meagh's unfeeling remains, Imbry exited the room, not forbearing to pocket a few small but precious items on the way. He swiftly found the nearest exit — not a difficult exercise, since the explosives with which the incomers had blown in a door had also demolished a wide stretch of the surrounding wall.

As Imbry stepped into the night air, accompanied by wafts and eddies of livestone jasm, he could see two Bureau of Scrutiny volantes, lights and screamers at full admonition, sliding down from the brightly ornamented sky. He stepped briskly to a nearby park where, in the concealment of some bushes, he shed his elision suit; the scroots had the means to see through its concealment. Then, ambling at a relaxed pace, he departed the area before the aircars alighted on the street outside Meagh's broken home.

Over the years, Luff Imbry had formulated a philosophy of life that allowed him to make fine distinctions that would have eluded the mental grasp of the greater mass of persons. For example, he strictly honored every agreement; he would have handed the Eye over to the Most Sublime First Enunciant for the agreed-upon fee, regardless of how his views on the object might have altered since their deal was struck. But the hierophant had been found just outside the temple's Holiest of Holies, abused beyond hope of resuscitation, and thus the issue became moot.

Imbry set the lens, still wrapped in the muting fabric of the elision bag, on a table in his operations center. He then lined up the five items he had acquired while departing Baltazo Meagh's premises. One of them, a thunderstone that glistened with metallic sheens and sparkled with scintillants in four colors, the thief had himself provided to the magnate some years before, and for a handsome fee. It might now bring even more from one of the aficionados who had envied its recent owner's collection. The other four pieces, including a smoothly worn icon of the Blessed Seer, graved into a plate carved from the dense black horn of a long-since extinct megafaunum from Ullber's World, were worth more than a small fortune, if the right buyers could be found. And Imbry was the one to find them.

He captured images-in-the-round of the five pieces, then activated his secure communications system and sent messages to a number of contacts who would bring the availability of the items to the attention of those who would take an interest. That work done, Imbry returned his attention to the thing in the bag.

He was confident that he could sell the Eye back to its erstwhile owners, using cut-outs that would insulate him from any retribution for his sacrilege in having handled it. He could also think of several other potential buyers; he might even convene an auction. He tapped his pudgy fingers on the tabletop as he contemplated these options, the arithmetical portion of his powerful intellect automatically generating the cost-and-revenue factors inherent to each alternative.

After a long moment, his fingers ceased to drum and he sighed. His mind kept wanting to break out of the channels to which he normally confined it — questions of what and how, of where and who and, especially, of how much. He remembered the sensation that had possessed him as he felt the Eye's muted influence upon his body. The image came again, of the lens being only the visible end of a feeding tube that was connected, he was sure, to something that he would not care to meet. Something unsavory. Something, to use a word Imbry rarely employed, evil.

Where that something was, in space and time, he had no idea. He remembered, from his school days, abstruse discussions of other planes of existence — nine of them, if he recalled the lesson. But none of that childhood esoterica had ever stepped forth into the welter of phenomenality and declared itself relevant to the to-ings and fro-ings of Luff Imbry. Now, he supposed, he had felt its touch, a touch unsought and unwanted.

The more he allowed himself to think of it, the deeper and more complex grew his appreciation of the thing on the table. *No, not a feeding tube,* he sensed. Whatever was at the other end of the connection was not doing anything as simple as feeding — rather, it was *collecting*. It had tried to *collect* from Luff Imbry, would have indifferently carried off his most intimate plasm, and was only foiled by the properties of his elision suit.

But for what purpose? What did whatever was at the other end of the collecting tube do with its gatherings? Here, Imbry's imagination conjured up suggestions that he was surprised to find, for all he prided himself on an exceptional tough-mindedness, that he did not care to examine. But he was not surprised to discover that he deeply resented the attempt that had been made on him.

He remained seated at the table for quite some time, letting his thoughts take him where they would. A sophisticated man, he had long accepted that the way of the world was that we all use and are used. "Still," he said, at last, to the object on the table, "limits must be set."

He arose and left, taking the bag and its contents with him. Several days later, on an airless speck that orbited a dying star at the edge of the Beyond, he placed the Eye, still in its camouflaging fabric, in a deep hole at the bottom of a narrow crevice where not even starlight reached. He covered over the excavation and began to return to his ship.

Halfway up the wall of the canyon, he stopped and retraced his steps. Near where he had buried the object was a substantial boulder. Imbry applied his full strength to roll the rock over the burial place, then smoothed the surrounding dust to remove all trace of its relocation.

He contemplated the boulder and said, within the privacy of his helmet, "After all, if we set no limits, what are we?"

ANOTHER DAY IN FIBBERY

Luff Imbry eased himself down the narrow passageway. The night's "operation" had gone according to plan and soon he would be able to deliver the precious scroll he carried tucked under one plump arm. It would earn him a fee that he hoped would smooth over his sharpening difficulties with the accommodator Titon Gullick, a man with whom it was not wise to have difficulties.

The gray light of dawn lit the doorway at the end of the corridor and Imbry stepped swiftly toward it. Any onlooker might have expressed surprise that a man of so many chins, and with fingers like overstuffed sausages, could move with such lightness of step, almost silent in the crepuscular dimness of the empty temple. But the portly thief took pride in having made a lifetime practice of being an originator of surprises, and rarely a recipient.

Thus he was more than chagrined when, as he glided noiselessly past a darkened doorway, he was struck heavily from his right side by a hard-muscled body that hurtled out of the blackness. Imbry staggered from the impact, stepping sideways across the passage, like a stage performer executing a comic exit into the wings, to crash into a small room that lay opposite the chamber from which his assailant had sprung.

His lower legs struck something hard but flimsy enough to be thrown out of the way. *A chair*, he thought, reflexively, even as he stumbled over another obstacle and fell heavily amid a clash of wood shattering against the stone flags of the floor. A splinter pierced his thigh, but Imbry's attention was directed to another part of his anatomy: his well fleshed throat which, for all its padding, was being dangerously compressed by a rock-thewed forearm, while another, equally capable limb pressed down on the back of his neck.

He thrashed and bucked, scattering lightweight furniture that clattered and snapped under the impact of the struggle. But the strangler's grip did not loosen, and the thief, though possessed of a muscular strength that many had found startling when it was unleashed, could not shake free.

The blackness of the room was now shot through with streaks of red lightning, as Imbry's vision center experienced a dangerous shortage of oxygen. In a few moments, he would be unconscious, and he had no doubt that that insensibility would shortly thereafter become permanent.

He did not bother to tear at the arm that constricted his throat. He had no leverage to overcome its strength. Instead, his right hand groped around him in the darkness, found a shard of splintered wood with a needle-sharp tip. Imbry grasped the makeshift weapon and, his thudding heart now causing the voice of death to roar in his head, thrust the crude dagger up and over his left shoulder.

The wood struck something hard, slid sideways and continued into something soft. Imbry felt a warm wetness on his fist and heard a gasp from close beside his ear. But the attacker's sudden intake of breath was not followed by its expulsion. Instead, the arms that bracketed Imbry's neck slackened and fell away and the thief was able to take in a revivifying draught of air and separate himself from the inert form sprawled across the wreckage of their struggle.

Imbry allowed his breathing to settle as he crouched motionless, ears attuned to the darkness. He heard no cries of alarm, nor rush of footsteps down the passageway. The temple stood as empty as he had supposed it to be when he had surreptitiously entered it in the pursuit of his profession. Still, he maintained his crouch and continued to listen until he was certain that none but he breathed in this place.

Only then did Imbry bring from a pocket of his garment a small device and activate it to shine a dim and narrowly disseminated beam of light upon the scene around him. As he had surmised, he was in a room in which folding wooden chairs were stored when not needed to seat the temple's congregation. Several of them lay overturned and a couple were broken. Stretched across the debris was the body of a man who had been in his early maturity, but who would now never succeed to middle-age, by consequence of the wooden strut that protruded from the socket of his left eye.

Imbry moved the lumen's beam away from the face and down onto the corpse's bare torso. Again, the thief found occasion for a sharp intake of breath, this time followed by a heartfelt oath. For the light revealed an unmistakable design tattooed onto the skin of the lifeless chest: a pair of snakes, their tails intertwined and their heads spitting at each other.

"The Community," Imbry whispered to himself. "It would have to be one of the Community."

Not long after, Imbry made his way, through a complicated route intended to allow him to detect if anyone was following his movements, to his operations center. This was a nondescript house in a less-than-fashionable district of the great and gaudy city of Olkney, nominal capital of Old Earth in the weary world's penultimate age. As the old orange sun's first light of day glimmered over the city's towers and rooftops, he entered by a rear door that was far more securely defended than it appeared to be, and went to a secret room where he disposed of the two objects he carried.

One was a scroll of heavy paper, wider than he was and long enough when unrolled to reach from as high as Imbry could stretch his arm down to the floor at his feet. On its creamy surface, in the gray of charcoal pencil, was a rubbing of a human-like figure, though possessing a definite surplus of limbs. The original from which he had taken the rubbing was a bas-relief on the walls of the temple, said to be a faithful likeness of the goddess Ys-enfro.

The circumstances that had brought the thief into possession of the image were complex. The cult of Ys-enfro had sprung up millennia before on a world called Orontia, some distance down The Spray. The goddess was a demanding deity, ordaining a strict regimen of strenuous rituals and prolonged self-denial that appealed to those for whom ordinary social relations did not offer enough of the numinous quality known as *tang*.

The stringency of the faith's tenets was relieved, however, in the twice-yearly festival of the Moratorium, when the goddess's devotees indulged themselves in riotous excess. First came a gluttonous feast of rich foods and intoxicating drink, followed by the recitation of ribald rhymes and stories of an increasingly risqué tone. As the innuendoes became less and less subtle, the celebrants donned masks and shed garments. They climbed onto the tables, and each presented his or her revealed form in rude postures and with candid signals of solicitation. Finally, the entire occasion devolved into episodes of interpersonal connection that often set new lows for licentiousness, even in the louche atmosphere of Olkney.

Yet the cult had not thrived. There had been a brief flowering, with missionaries from Orontia spreading news of the goddess's dispensation, and temples founded on the nearby worlds of Griss, Emblehart and Hiberr. But in time there had arisen a bitter schism over a nice point of doctrine. Individual congregations had chosen sides, squabbled, fought in the courts — and occasionally in the streets — until the vigor of the founders' vision was completely dissipated. In recent years, only the temple in Olkney and the original tabernacle on Orontia had endured.

Then tragedy had befallen the goddess on Orontia: a campaign of ethical rearmament known as the Untainted had swept through that world's majority, and Ys-enfro had not withstood the cleansing wind. Her remaining adherents were rounded up and encouraged, sometimes by measures dire and draconian, to redirect themselves to more wholesome pursuits. The old temple was pulled down, and the sequestered image of the goddess, graven into the wall of the inner sanctum, had been smashed beyond any hope of reassembly.

Time passed. The ardor of the Untainted inevitably cooled. A few of Ys-enfro's flock had remained faithful to her, even in the re-education facilities — they were used to hard regimens, after all — and now they returned to their former environs, with dreams of reviving the old creed. But in that ambition they encountered two difficulties: first, the rituals required an exact likeness of the deity, but that had been demolished during the iconoclasm; second, throughout The Spray, only one true image survived, and it was on the wall of the temple in Olkney, whose congregation refused the Orontians' request for a copy. It seemed that the Ys-enfro's faithful on Old Earth had long chafed at being subordinate to the Orontian tabernacle's precedence; since they had become the sole site of her worship, a weight had lifted from their hearts. And they did not propose to burden themselves again, by returning to the status of second among unequals.

Thus the High Delimitress of the restored Orontian flock had traveled under an assumed name to Old Earth, where she undertook discreet inquiries. Word was passed through Olkney's back channels, sureties were sought and delivered, and finally Luff Imbry had been contracted to bring forth from the Olkney temple the rubbing that now lay upon his work table.

How he had arranged for the temple to lie unguarded for an hour was a secret he would not divulge. The operation had called for one of his most subtle yet daring strategies, involving precise timing and the temporary absence of a temple watchman whose dereliction of duty had been induced by Imbry's discovery of a long-ago iniquity that the man had thought was, literally, buried on another world.

And then, just as all was settled and a munificent fee almost in the thief's grasp, sheer, malevolent chance had selected Luff Imbry to be stalked and attacked by a murderous thug from the Select Community of Disciplined Aspirants. Now, as he sat in his operations center, he regarded the second object he had placed on the table. This was a box as long as the thief's hand, though only of two fingers' width, fashioned from the shell of a mollusk that frequented the waters of Mornedy Sound. He reached for it, undid the fine silver clasp that kept it closed, and opened it to inspect the contents.

He had never seen the interior of an Aspirant's entourage, for so the box was called within the Community — few outside the Community ever had — and he was disappointed to find it contained nothing of intrinsic value.

Nestled against the shimmering nacreous lining of the shell were a few twists of hair, some dry scrapings of skin and what appeared to be the yellowed nail from some past victim's smallest toe. But he knew that these bits of life's detritus had been precious to the man who had tried to strangle him; each member of the Community believed that, when he passed to what they called "a truer world," the persons from whom these bits had been taken would be waiting for him, "with cushions and comforts."

Or so it was said. The Community was a deeply secret society, whose members were believed to come from the upper levels of Olkney's social pyramid. The exact details of their creed were difficult to delineate. Nothing was written down, and the simplistic approach — that is, approaching an Aspirant to ask pointed questions — had much to disrecommend it. But it was supposed to be true that an Aspirant never took his entourage out of the communal lodge except when he purposed to add a new relic to his collection. And that event would only transpire when he had received a vision that compelled him to strip down to breechclout and tattoos, and go forth to strangle.

Imbry's Aspirant had likely had a summoning dream that featured the temple. After ritual preparation, he had gone there to add a new treasure to his entourage. If Imbry had not suborned the watchman, that fellow would now be on his way to the True World to plump cushions and chill flagons of the wine of paradise in anticipation of his new master's arrival.

Instead the Aspirant had been translated to his elysium earlier than he had expected. Imbry could only guess at the theological implications, but down here in Fibbery, to use the Community's term for the plane of phenomenality, the corpulent thief was faced with both a serious problem and a unique opportunity.

The problem: the dead Aspirant would be found — Imbry had had no chance to arrange a permanent disposition of the corpse, but had left it up to the suborned watchman. The Community, though it showed scant regard for the mortalities it dealt out, took a sharp interest in any death that dealt in one of its own. The other Aspirants would want to know who had killed their brother; and they would insist on the return of his entourage.

The opportunity: an Aspirant's shell was a rarity of rarities; Imbry could think of at least three collectors of cultic curios who would each pay a stupendous sum for the object on his work table. For a moment he considered convening an auction, but just as quickly dismissed the idea. One of the unsuccessful bidders might choose to salve his disappointment by quietly nudging the Community to look in Imbry's direction. Better to choose one purchaser and take what he could get. The price would be high, and the transaction soon behind him.

The decision made, Imbry paused a moment to reflect. The difficulty presented by the Aspirant was just the latest of a succession of snarls and kinks that had interrupted the smooth weave of his life in recent days. He wondered if, upon deeper examination, he might find a pattern — even a purpose — behind all the unsought complications that contrived to throw themselves at his ankles as he strove to tread a straight path toward the fulfillment of his desires. Then it occurred to him that pausing to think such thoughts was yet another delay and distraction.

The past is sand already dribbled from my hands, he told himself, *the future has no more substance than a gnat's opinion. All I have is now, so let me make the most of it before it, too, dribbles away.*

He rose, tucked the box into a hidden inner pocket, and fitted the scroll into a tubular carrying case. He left the secret room and closed its disguised portal so that it again appeared to be a pile of randomly collected rubbish. Every visible room of the house was crammed with similar scrap and litter, and its integrator intermittently generated a high-pitched voice appropriate to a demented recluse, hidden deep in the warren of garbage, threatening dreadful retribution on evil-doers who coveted his precarious heaps of moldering scrunge. In all the years Imbry had operated from the place, no one had ever disturbed his arrangements.

He departed the house by a tunnel that led across the overgrown garden to a tumbledown shed beside a disguised gate in the back fence. Taking care to keep his movements unnoted was routine practice, but today there was an added incentive to his precautions: Imbry owed money to the accommodator Titon Gullick, an informal lender who, when repayment fell into arrears, skipped lightly over the normal escalation from polite reminders to stern demands; Gullick collected his debts by methods that left no room for compromise. And Imbry's obligation was now four days overdue.

He came through the fence under the deep shade of a line of blackleaf trees and stood silently to take in the mood of the lane. Nothing stirred except the usual early-morning chorus of birds threatening each other with death and mayhem should any trespass upon another's territory. Imbry left the trees and set off along the narrow way that led to Tustrum Avenue where he could attract a roving hire-car.

But Tustrum was empty when he reached it. He walked a short distance then stepped into the recessed doorway of a commercial who sold unreliable items at low cost. From this partial concealment, he scanned the street. He had picked a poor time to seek a ride. Those residents who caroused all night had by now been delivered to their beds, whereas those who rose and sought to wring some use from the day were not yet out and about.

He caught a flicker of brightness from the corner of one eye, turned his head to look up above the low roofs of the commercial establishments that lined Tustrum, hoping to spot an available car. But the glitter that had drawn his gaze was now nowhere to be seen. A chill went through Imbry. Reflexively, he stepped farther back into the doorway, but he knew that any attempt at concealment was now too late. He moved forward again, looking away from where he had caught the glint of reflected sunlight, but allowing his peripheral vision to search for it.

And there it was again, high and to the left. Feigning nonchalance, he let his gaze wander that way, and again the gleam faded from view. Imbry sighed and stepped out of the doorway. Evasive measures could not serve him now; one of Gullick's spotters had found him, and what would come would come.

It came moments later, on a whisper of well tuned gravity obviators. A long, low-slung velocitator slid down the sky from the west, the faded sun glowing in miniature in the vehicle's brightwork, and stopped beside the thief. Its opaque canopy cleared to transparency and the pair of dull black eyes that inspected Imbry clearly derived neither joy nor interest from the experience. The eyes were set close together in a moon-shaped face that featured an underdeveloped nose and a small, pursed mouth which now opened to allow an almost-falsetto voice to say, "There you are."

"Tuts," said Imbry, for that was the single name by which Titon Gullick's chief collector was known, "I was just thinking I should get in touch. My days have been so full of hustle lately."

"Today may prove to be even fuller," Tuts piped, then laughed a child-like laugh that Imbry found worrisome. "Get in."

A moment later, they were high above Olkney. Imbry made no attempt to lighten the mood through conversation or inquiries after the man's well-being. Nor would there be any scope for negotiation at this stage. There was equally no point in offering the henchman a benefit to neglect his duties. Tuts was said to be an off-worlder, the product of a heavy-gravity planet that produced human stock who were solid-boned and thick-skinned. An alternative view was that Gullick had had him grown to order on some ill-favored world near the edge of the Beyond, where the creation of vat-spawned variants was unregulated. In either case, Tuts was devoted to his employer, and no one who had ever offered an inducement to dilute his loyalty had ever done so more than once. Indeed, some had not even made it all the way through their first attempt.

Imbry sat on the bench seat across from Tuts and waited to see what would transpire. If he was in fortune's favor, his escort's orders would be to bring in the dilatory debtor for a pointed talk. If the goddess of chance was miffed this morning, the thief would suffer some carefully weighed unpleasantries, but those would heal in a few days. If she had turned her back on him altogether, the velocitator would arrow out over Mornedy Sound, whose cold, dark depths were the alleged gathering spot for those who had caused irreparable imbalances to the simple symmetry that Titon Gullick prized in his accounts.

Imbry was relieved to see that their flight took them directly toward the Jormeland district, and soon they were angling down to a landing outside the combined restaurant and tavern where Gullick transacted his business. Tuts led him through the public room, where the odor of steamed buns and thin-shaven smoked meats brought an involuntary moisture to the fat man's mouth, and into a small back room where that orifice became bone dry at the sight of the man to whom he owed a significant amount.

Gullick did not pose an intrinsically threatening sight. If he had, he would have found it difficult to encourage borrowers to enter into arrangements with him. He was tall and spare, knobby at knees and elbows, with a fall of lank, blond hair. His eyes were not only two different colors but angled off at separate orientations, so that the darker of them now watched Imbry enter while the lighter contemplated the surface of the small, scarred table at which he sat. The fine colorless hairs on the backs of his long fingers caught the light as he waved Imbry to sit in the chair opposite him.

Silence reigned. Imbry thought it pointless to speak first, since the other man would surely set the tone and direction of any conversation. Gullick changed the orientation of his head so that now his light-colored eye took in Imbry while the other looked over the thief's shoulder, where Tuts stood in readiness for whatever was required.

Imbry sought to appear unperturbed, but now he noticed that his upper incisors were indenting his lower lip. As if that was a signal he had been waiting for, Gullick spoke. "Do you know what is the fundamental underpinning of my business?"

Imbry would have ventured a reply, but Gullick did not wait. "Certainty," he continued.

"Surely, there must be a modicum of risk?" Imbry said.

"Not so much as a tittle." Gullick stretched out his fingers and flexed them, putting Imbry in mind of two spiders taking exercise. "Those who avail themselves of my service, be they close friends or chance acquaintances, must entertain no doubts as to the nature of our relationship. I lend, they repay, at a precisely calculated rate of interest and to a schedule that admits of no will-I? or nill-I?"

"I see," said Imbry. "I hasten to assure you that our arrangement rests on a sound footing."

"And yet, repayment was due four days since, though the line in my accounts where I should have entered the receipt of funds remains unfilled."

"Ah, you see, I suffered an unexpected setback."

Now the dark eye returned to Imbry, while its paler sibling regarded the still flexing hands that occupied the table top between them. "Why don't you tell me about it?" said Gullick.

Imbry told the unvarnished truth, since the other man could check — was surely having his integrator do so even as they spoke — and could soon disprove any embellishments. The consequences of lying to Titon Gullick would likely be worse than that of trying to subvert Tuts, though not so quickly concluded.

Imbry had borrowed to finance an export opportunity. A wealthy collector on the world Alberankh, one of the Foundational Domains first settled by humans and now a paradise of ease and splendor for its inhabitants, was seeking to acquire wind-tambos. These were rare objects, found only, and seldom, in the ruins of a long-dead city on the world Iqbal, where a vanished species had once built a civilization before succumbing to unknown calamities. Wind-tambos were believed to be musical instruments, since they produced tones when their lacquered membranes were stroked or tapped, though none of their ancient users survived to confirm or deny the supposition. The city where they were discovered had been scoured by relic-hunters, and it was now accepted that all that had survived were in the hands of collectors up and down The Spray.

After much research and experimentation on a scrap of membrane from a wind-tambo that had been found shattered, Imbry had identified the components of the lacquer. He soon contrived to duplicate it almost exactly. He then quietly purchased several worthless, broken wind-tambo fragments but had to send to six different worlds for the rare stuffs that would combine to create a convincing lacquer. That expense strained his finances and necessitated the involvement of the accommodator.

When all was in hand, he went into his workroom and assembled half a dozen respectable forgeries, substituting shaved parchment for the fragile membranes; multiple layers of the costly lacquer would prevent his chicanery from being discovered. He then stained and aged the fakes through a process of stress and abrasion.

Next, Imbry let word filter out, through indirect channels, that a collector on Old Earth — that remote, fusty little globe that claimed to be humankind's original home-world — had suffered a burglary. Six choice wind-tambos had been taken, but the collector could not involve the authorities because he had himself acquired the objects under circumstances that argued strongly against bringing in the Bureau of Scrutiny. These prizes were now available to discreet purchasers.

Imbry had sat back and waited to receive overtures. They were not long in coming. He met with agents from several off-world connoisseurs and accepted a very handsome offer, not from the aesthete on Alberankh, but (as the forger had expected), from that man's neighbor and chief rival in the realm of wind-tambo collecting. The purchaser paid far more than the objects would have been worth, even had they been real, just to savor the pleasure of denying them to his competitor.

Imbry had crated the prizes and shipped them to Alberankh by an eminently trustworthy means: a freighter of the Graz line. Its supercargo would receive payment on delivery then deposit the funds, less a commission, into an account that Imbry could access. It was a common method of interplanetary brokerage.

"But there," Imbry told Gullick, "fate or ill fortune, call it what you will, took a hand. The freighter left here, entered a whimsy that should have brought it within range of Alberankh, and has not been seen again."

"Ah," said the accommodator, "mystery."

It occasionally happened that a ship that entered one of the strange nodes that tied together widely separated regions of space would fail to emerge. Various theories had been advanced: instead of being reassembled, its atoms were evenly distributed across the cosmos; it reemerged, but a billion years too late (or too soon, the difference was moot); or it came out where and when it was expected, but out of phase with the temporal constant, its crew and passengers become sad ghosts unseen by those around them.

"There is a spacer superstition," Gullick said, "that argues for the missing ships being captured by the inhabitants of other dimensions, who wear them as jewelry."

"I think it more likely," said Imbry, "that the irreality experienced during repeated transition through non-space eventually unhinges the mind, despite the strong medications spacers take. Someone seizes the controls and sends the ship spinning off into never-was."

"It's true," Gullick says, "one rarely encounters an old spacer." But then he interlaced his hirsute fingers and said, "Still, such mysteries must tend to themselves. We have more mundane concerns. Am I to assume that the funds with which you meant to repay me were to have come from the freighter's supercargo?"

"Exactly," said Imbry.

Gullick's eyes swam in their orbits as if each was unsure which of them would encompass the sight of Imbry. Then, in an event that sent a frisson of cold through the corpulent thief, both came to rest on him at the same time. "That is unfortunate."

Imbry did not believe that his creditor meant that the ill luck was to be shared. "I hope I may be considered a minimal risk," he said.

Gullick reminded him that certainty, not risk — not even minimal risk — was the foundation of his enterprise. Again, Imbry saw the ocular gavotte, then the dark eye fixed him with a measuring stare. The accommodator said, "You are noted for your abilities. Surely, you have accumulated a nest-egg? Produce the funds and pay me forthwith, and I will add only a 30 per cent premium for dunnage and wear."

But Imbry had never been one to store up treasures. He lived for the pleasures of the moment, especially the many long and savored moments between the time he sat down to the dining table and when he finally rose, stuffed as full as an egg with the finest viands and vintages. His prodigious appetite ate through his funds at a steady rate. "If I had commanded my own capital," he said, "I would not have had to borrow from you to purchase rare lacquers for the wind-tambo operation."

Gullick looked away, neither eye remaining on Imbry. He made a thoughtful noise deep in his throat. "You pose a dilemma," he said, after a while. "I don't care for dilemmas."

Imbry would have spoken but the two spiders broke their embrace and waved him to silence.

"I cannot have a borrower single-handedly adjusting the terms of our arrangement," the lender said. "Worse than that, much worse, I cannot allow it to be known that such an event has occurred. At that moment, certainty packs its bags and departs for regions unknown, unlikely ever to return."

"But who would know?" said Imbry. "I would certainly" — he stressed the word — "not make mention of it."

"I, for one, would know," said Gullick. "As would Tuts." His roving eyes took in various parts of the room as if they might find others who were privy to the secret. "Others, who heard that I had passed the word to locate you, might make deductions."

Imbry opened his mouth to speak, but again the arachnids intervened.

"I must weigh the loss of the funds I advanced you against the greater loss I would incur if every tatterdemalion and touch-me-up thought he could abrogate the terms of a contract with me," Gullick said. "I can forestall that loss by taking direct action. A few energetic movements, a startling revelation, and certainty reigns serenely again. I haven't done one for quite a while, not since I dealt with Bulba Thripp — do you remember the occasion?"

"I think everyone remembers it," Imbry said, suppressing a shudder. He heard no sound, but he sensed that Tut was now immediately behind his chair. "I would like to advance a third alternative," he said.

The pale eye addressed the air above Imbry's head, where Tut surely hovered. "Yes?"

"I have not spent the past four days hiding," the thief said. "I have been pursuing a new operation to raise the funds to repay you."

The pale eye swam his way. "With a premium?"

"Within reason." Imbry felt a large, heavy hand descend upon his shoulder. "Or beyond reason," he added.

"What is this operation?" Gullick said.

"The details are too tedious to recite. But I am very close to concluding the affair and reaping the reward. Which, now that I think of it, in all fairness belongs to you."

Titon Gullick occupied a pinnacle of sorts in the halfworld where Olkney's least formal economy operated. He was accustomed to telling others how things were going to be, and rarely had any need to disguise his thoughts. He had therefore never bothered to perfect the skills of dissemblage, and thus Imbry was able to read the man's thoughts in the micro-expressions that flashed across the accommodator's face. He saw that his case had already been decided — he was to be made an example of — but Gullick would not be averse to first taking whatever the forger could put in his pocket.

Gullick now spoke to Tut. "What did he have on him?"

The answer came from directly behind Imbry, confirming his earlier reading of the course of events. "These," Tut said.

The henchman brushed past Imbry and deposited on the table the tubular case containing the scroll along with several objects that Tuts had taken after he had had the fat man turn out his pockets — though not all of the less noticeable ones — in the aircar.

Gullick eyed the case, with one color then the other, each evincing interest. But first he sent the spiders to ruffle through the other items: the low-powered lumen, a set of master keys, a slapper and a few personal oddments. He picked up the slapper — a device that fitted into the palm and delivered a debilitating shock to any flesh that it impacted at speed — and said, jocularly, "Good thing you didn't try this on Tut. They annoy him."

"Make my skin itch," Tut said, in his flutey voice.

"And what's this?" the lender said, picking up the case that contained the scroll. He shook out the contents and unrolled it on the table, enlisting Tuts to hold one end while the twin spiders pinned down the other.

Imbry said nothing. He watched Gullick's face to see if the image triggered any signs of recognition, but the accommodator's eyes registered nothing. Nor did Tuts chime in with an answer to his employer's question. The thief relaxed. Gullick's milieu was limited; he needed to know little about the deeply fragmented social environment of Olkney and thus he knew next to nothing about moribund cults.

Imbry proceeded to the next step. "It is," he said, "a kind of map."

"What kind of map?" said Gullick.

"A treasure map."

"It looks like a woman dancing and waving her arms," said Tuts.

"The image is a code," said the thief. "I have spent years deciphering it. I had already completed the first leg of the journey and was on my way to the second when Tuts found me."

Titon Gullick had sufficient intellectual resources to keep his focus on the most important aspect of the matter. "What kind of treasure?" he asked.

"The immensely valuable kind," Imbry said. "A hoard built up over millennia by the faithful of a now-forgotten cult. Even their own priests no longer know where the loot is hidden."

"But you do?"

"If I read the map aright."

"Can you teach us to read it?"

"The symbols are abstruse, the relationships subtle. It could take weeks, even months, to bring you up to scratch."

"Then let us resume your progress," said Gullick. "We will come along, to offer whatever assistance we can."

"Bring the keys," Imbry said.

Gullick put them in his pocket, then indicated that Tuts should bring the alleged map and its interpreter. With the henchman's huge hand compressing Imbry's upper arm, the three went out to the street and boarded the velocitator.

"Where to?" Gullick said.

"The statue of Maugremonche," Imbry said. It was a monument to some ancient notable whose deeds were scarcely remembered, in a square on the far side of the city. Gullick spoke to the aircar and it lifted off and took them away. Imbry looked out through the canopy at the tired orange sun. It had been just broaching the horizon when he had left the temple of Ys-enfro; now it was more than halfway to the zenith. He doubted that was enough time.

The square where Maugremonche's commemoration stood was filled with a brightly colored booths whose occupants sold items of decor they had fashioned themselves. Customers were few and business was not brisk as the velocitator set down near the statue. Accurately sensing that someone who commanded such a vehicle must also possess a well stocked purse, several of the vendors left their booths to crowd around and offer their wares. But, at a wave from Gullick, Tuts took action that efficiently extinguished their commercial ardor. Soon he, Imbry and his creditor had the space around the monument to themselves, save for a couple of comatose artisans stretched out on the pavement.

"Bring the scroll," Imbry said, advancing to the granite plinth on which Maugremonche stood, his bronze eyes ever on some far vista. As Tuts held the paper high, Imbry traced a plump finger along the curve of Ys-enfro's right breast then turned to examine the block of stone. Beside a plaque that related Maugremonche's worthy achievements, he found three small scratches in the granite. "Hmm," he said, then stood with head bowed, thumb and forefinger grasping one of his chins, rendering a convincing impression of a man engaged in mental computation.

"What does it mean?" Gullick said.

Imbry held up a fleshy palm, as if to defer an answer until his calculations were complete, then lifted his head and said, "The Oval." He handed the scroll to Tuts and strode toward the velocitator with a purposeful step. Gullick and his henchman came after.

The Oval was a reflecting pond set among a trio of public buildings from the neo-mandate school of architecture, all planes and facets of burnished metal, linked together by heavy copper chains that had been left to go green with age. Imbry approached each of the chains and inspected their lower links. Then he looked up at the tired old sun, now nearing its maximum ascension, and stood a while in thought.

"What is it?" Gullick asked.

Imbry slowly brought his gaze to bear on the accommodator, as if his awareness of his surroundings had only just returned from some far-distant place. "It is difficult...," he began, then trailed off as if some new thought had struck. A moment later, he said to Tuts, "Quick, the scroll!" and gestured for it to be unrolled once more.

Imbry consulted the rubbing of Ys-enfro. He glanced from the image to the chains and back again, his brow furrowed and his chins spread across his chest. Then he looked up again at the sun, while Titon Gullick displayed signs of a gathering impatience.

"We must wait," Imbry declared, after a lengthy ponder, "for the sun to reach its zenith." He advanced to a spot on the marbled pavement that surrounded the pool and waited for the shadow of one of the chains to make its slow progress across the pale stone.

While he did so, Imbry was pursuing a private calculation that had nothing to do with maps or treasure. He was counting the hours since dawn, when the suborned watchman had been scheduled to arrive back at Ys-enfro's temple, to resume his duties as if he had never left. The man would have found the shattered chairs and the dead Aspirant, as well as the small but well filled pouch of currency Imbry had left in a prominent position. The thief was confident the caretaker would know what to do: clean up the mess and remove the body from the premises, before any members of the congregation came for an early contemplation of the goddess's sublimity.

There would be no time for comprehensive measures; the body would likely have gone into the bushes in a small park across from the temple's rear door. It would not have lain there too long before some early-morning pedestrian noted the unusual sight and summoned proctors. They, in turn, would have determined foul play and called in the Bureau of Scrutiny. The scroots would open an investigatory file and, after identifying the corpse as a member of the Community, make contact with the dead man's brethren. At that point, an argument would have ensued, with the Bureau wishing to hold onto the body while the Aspirants would demand its immediate release, so that the Rite of Accession could begin. If they learned that the dead man's entourage was missing, their insistence would be colored by the starkest emotions.

Imbry looked up at the sky again. It was almost noon. *They'll need more time*, he said, silently in the privacy of his mind. To Gullick, he said, "Almost there," and stooped to peer at the shadow of the chain on the milky marble. Then he knelt and made measurements using the distance between the first and second knuckles on his index finger, glancing from time to time toward the scroll Tuts held for him.

Eventually he rose and faced Gullick. "The Trivoline Steps," he said.

The accommodator looked down at the shadow of the chain, at the scroll that his henchman was now rerolling to put back in the case, then back to Imbry. "You are not just seeking to postpone the inevitable, are you?" he said, "leading us on a 'boat trip around the bay,' as the saying goes, hoping that some marvelous fortuity will happen to alter your situation?"

Imbry returned him the guileless gaze that he had spent years perfecting. "Not at all. I am perfectly confident that a great treasure waits at the end of this trail."

"Good," said Gullick, "because, were that the case, the example I would have to make of you would be even more startling."

They flew off to the Trivoline Steps, a whimsical arrangement of staircases fashioned from several different materials that led up and around, down and over, inside and outside, some ending in the air, others winding back upon themselves, while some had the capacity to open trapdoors on hidden hinges or to convert themselves into slick slides at random intervals. The whole construction was said to be a concrete representation of the ancient philosophy known as Intentional Futilism, whose tenets and arguments were no longer valued. Children now used the exemplar as a playground.

Several youths were enjoying a game of tag on the steps when the trio arrived. Tuts encouraged them to play elsewhere and, after a frank exchange of opinions accompanied by a few hurled stones that bounced harmlessly off the off-worlder's thick skin, the young people departed. Imbry began a painstaking survey of the staircases, consulting the scroll from time to time, while the sun made its steady decline from the heights toward the farthest rooftops of Olkney.

Gullick became increasingly dissatisfied with the pace of events. He sat in the velocitator, the canopy raised, causing his arachnids to embrace and disengage repetitively, when they were not engaged in other calisthenics that had them tap-dancing on the control yoke or his up-bent knees. Finally, with the sun a bloated red circle sinking behind the palaces on the Hill of Doreigne, casting shadows dense as black velvet, the lender called Tuts to him. Imbry observed that their conversation was brief and conducted in suppressed tones. Then the henchman turned toward where the thief sat on the lower steps of a spiraling staircase of tarnished irredentine, cracked the joints of his outsized fingers and plodded forward.

Imbry leapt up and declared, "I have it! The mathematics eluded me, but once I applied third-level consistencies, all became clear!"

Tuts paused and looked back over his shoulder. Gullick fluttered a dismissive spider. "Where to now?" the accommodator said. "And how many more legs will this journey take?"

"This is the last," Imbry assured him, climbing into the aircar. "Do you know Halvath Boulevard?"

Gullick did not, as Imbry had expected. Halvath was a wide street in the Shamblings district, whose well funded residents would rarely require the kind of informal financial arrangements in which his creditor dealt. But the aircar knew all of Olkney and inerrantly sped them to the coordinates Imbry specified.

Again, Imbry had Tuts hold the scroll while he consulted it. He tilted his head to one side, causing one of his jowls to hang lower than the other, and studied the rubbing intently. After a moment, he straightened and said, "We are here."

"Where?" Gullick said, looking around. They were standing beside a high, blank wall, the rear of a large building that backed onto Halvath Boulevard. The lower reaches of the wall were screened by a line of full-grown coppertwine trees, rooted in a strip of soil between the stone and the pedestrian pavement. Imbry pushed aside the swirled lower branches of one of the trees and revealed a small door, unmarked and plain, sealed by a simple but sturdy lock.

"Give me my keys," Imbry said.

Gullick took them from his pocket, but hesitated before handing them over. Imbry read his face, saw a mixture of rising greed and simmering distrust. The thief said, "You may go first, if you wish."

Imbry watched as the accommodator weighed the alternatives. If traps and treachery lurked behind the door, Gullick would want Imbry to be first in; but the fat man might duck in, slam the door shut in slow-moving Tuts's face and make an escape. He saw his creditor come to a decision.

"You will go first," Gullick said. "I will be on your heels, and Tuts will come after."

"Very good. May I have the keys?"

"Here they are. But you will give them back to me before you enter."

"As you like." Imbry took the collection of master keys, examined them briefly, then chose one. He applied it to the lock and all present heard the door's internal mechanism engage. Imbry touched the control and the door swung inward. Beyond lay darkness from which came a faint scent of burnt incense.

"The keys," Gullick said.

Imbry returned them. "And so we go," he said, and stepped through the doorway.

The accommodator came close behind, and one of his spiders took a firm grip on the fat man's shoulder. Imbry moved slowly into the unlit space, Gullick's breath on his nape, Tuts stolidly bringing up the rear.

"What is this place?" Gullick whispered.

"The temple of Ys-enfro," Imbry said. It was not the first lie he had told today, and now he added another: "There will be a secret panel, and behind it will lie the treasure."

The hand on the thief's shoulder squeezed reflexively. "Find it!" said Gullick.

"Oops!" said Imbry, stumbling on some unseen unevenness of the floor. He fell back against his creditor, half turning, and his hand clutched at Gullick's garment for support before he steadied himself. "Sorry," he said.

The lender had instinctively loosened his grip, the better to thrust Imbry off him, lest both fall. The moment he did so, the fat man sped away toward the dim outline of an oblong he had spied several paces away, as his eyes had adjusted to the darkness. He heard Gullick's intake of breath then the sound of his footsteps in pursuit.

The outline framed an inner door, fortunately not locked, and Imbry flung it open and went through. Ahead, a flight of stairs, lit dimly from above, led upwards to a landing, where they turned to ascend in a second course. Imbry took them two at a time and was on the first landing when Gullick came through the door. They locked eyes for an instant, then Imbry bounded up the next flight.

At the top was another doorway, limned in a brighter light that shone in whatever space lay behind. The smell of incense was stronger here, and over his own heavy breathing, Imbry could hear a soft and solemn tapping of drums accompanied by a throat-chant. His hand slapped the door's control and, with Gullick closing on him and Tuts tramping inevitably behind, the fat man plunged through the opening and raced pell-mell across the space beyond.

His impressions of the next few seconds were of fragments of sight and sound: a great hall, lit by a score of golden lamps; a hundred eyes turning his way; a body on a bier, wreathed in wisps of fragrant smoke; fifty hard-muscled men sitting cross-legged, five hundred fingers tapping softly on fifty drumheads made from human skin; fifty bare chests, each adorned with a tattoo — a pair of twining snakes.

A shout went up as Imbry was halfway across the hall. By the time the first Aspirant broke free of the funeral trance and rose to stop him, the thief was almost to the door that led from the hall into the vestibule and the street beyond. Wishing he still had the slapper, Imbry put out a palm at the end of a straight arm and sent the man toppling backwards into another of his fellows who had risen to one knee. Both fell, and now the shouting became general as Gullick and Tuts barreled out of the stairwell in the fat man's wake.

Imbry did not stop to see what went on behind him. He broke out of the Community of Disciplined Aspirants' front door, descended the front steps three at a time, and ran at his best speed down the street and around the corner. Moments later, breathing heavily, he was in the accommodator's aircar and swinging up into the sky, leaving the canopy unsecured. Passing over the

Community's lodge, he looked down and saw no one emerging from the exit he had left by. Over the whisper of the velocitator's obviators, he could hear muffled shouts and the sounds of struggle.

He was not clear on the fine points of the Community's rites, but he believed it was permissible to send new attendants to the True World at any time before the final act of the funeral service transported the Aspirant's essence to paradise. The accommodator and his henchman would be welcome additions to the dead man's complement — especially when his brethren discovered the missing entourage in Titon Gullick's pocket, where Imbry had tucked it while pretending to stumble against his captor in the dark basement of the Community's lodge.

The thief told the velocitator to return to the lender's place of business in the Jormeland district. Imbry left the car hovering above the street while he strode through the restaurant and into the back room as if he had every right to do so. The accommodator's operating funds were sealed in a code-coffer set in the floor, but Imbry was confident that breaking Gullick's cipher would not be an onerous chore.

Indeed, before long, he was aloft again, angling over the city to find a person of his acquaintance who dealt in used vehicles. A tightly stuffed valise sat beside him on the aircar's seat.

It had been a long and eventful day. He had won two treasures and lost both. He doubted if the watchman at the temple of Ys-enfro would agree to vacate his duties a second time — not if the job required removing bodies. On the other hand, Imbry possessed both an excellent memory and a practiced hand; he might be able to duplicate the lost scroll, or at least produce a version that would satisfy the Orontian High Delimitress.

The Aspirant's entourage was probably just as well foregone. If a whisper of Imbry's involvement ever came to the Select Community.... He put the thought aside.

He recalled that he had wondered earlier if there was a pattern to the difficulties that life had recently offered him. He turned his mind to the question again, but at that moment his stomach voiced its disapproval of having passed an entire day without gainful occupation. Imbry decided he would sell the aircar tomorrow. He had its integrator connect him with Xanthoulian's, where his appetite and purse were equally appreciated, and made a reservation for dinner.

Patterns, he said to himself, *are all very well. But all I have is now, and dinner at Xanthoulian's is a meal.*

QUARTET AND TRIPTYCH

The case was of finely worked leather, dyed a rich vermilion that was now age-faded, and enclosed in a meshwork of verdigrised, hand-spun copper filigree. It was cylindrical, with a fitted top whose central cartouche, embossed in white and gold enamel, enclosed the complexity of symbols and colors that constituted the arms of the House of Voillute. The Voillutes were now ranked only among the second tier of Old Earth's nobility, but up until only four thousand years ago theirs had been one of the few establishments entitled to make only a half-prostration in the presence of the Archon. A Voillute of the prime strain could trace his ancestry not just through centuries and millennia but through geological periods.

The thief Luff Imbry touched his plump fingertips to the silken fringe that depended from the rim of the case's lid, causing the fine threads to shimmer from purple to old gold. "You're certain it will not be missed?" he asked the man who had brought him the container.

"I do not commit to absolutes," said Holker Ghyll.

Imbry should have known better than to have asked a question that required an answer unshaded by ambiguity. Ghyll was an adherent of a philosophical system known as "the Computance," which held that the universe was strung together as a webwork of probabilities, in which the concept of "certainty" was a cruel illusion contrived by a mischievous deity who delighted in raising high the pitiful hopes of his creations, only to dash them to flinders of despair. The god's motives, revealed only to the elect, were a central mystery of the faith.

Ghyll had several times exhorted Imbry to attend one of the "computations," as conclaves of the Computants were called. "Odds are, by joining us you would acquire a useful philosophy," he would say.

To which Imbry would reply, "And thereby foreclose on my use of several other philosophies, each of which I find convenient in its place. Mine is a profession that rewards flexibility of outlook and often punishes the overly rigid by an invitation to dine with the Archon."

Despite Imbry's demurrals, Ghyll never missed an opportunity to expound on his creed, and was now again launched upon a lecture. "Life, after all," he said, "is but a succession of greater and lesser probabilities — a melange of maybes, as the Grand Prognosticator so aptly put it. Look at you, here in the supposed security of Bolly's Snug, supping and swilling with nary a care. Yet can you deny that a fragment of some asteroid, shattered in a collision far out in thither space back when humankind was still adrip with the primordial slime, having spent millions of years looming towards us, might now, its moment come, lance down through the atmosphere at immense speed and obliterate you where you stand?"

"I do not deny the possibility," said Imbry. "I say that the likelihood is remote."

"Yet still it exists! And if we couple that existence to a divine appetite for upsetting mortal plans —"

"I can think of other, less far-fetched scenarios that might lead to the obliteration of someone in this room," said the thief. He accompanied the remark with an unwinking stare that ought to have caused Ghyll stop to consider that though Imbry was so corpulent as to be almost spherical, he was capable of sudden and conclusive acts of violence. And that consideration would have led, in turn, to a change of subject. But the Computant was too deeply set in his philosophy to take note of how others responded to it, and continued to discourse on abstruse concerns.

"Throughout the aeons, sages have observed that, statistically, the simplest solution to a problem is most likely to be the correct one. Yet experience teaches that those same solutions nearly always turn out to be more complicated than they first appear. Variables pile upon variables, until inevitably the shaky edifice of multi-layered ad-hockery threatens to topple. At this point, the well meaning rush in to apply new props, thus further complicating the structure..."

Imbry sighed and let the fellow ramble. He would tolerate the unwanted discourse because it was Ghyll's membership in the Computance that had made it possible for him to obtain the object in the case. Finally, the fat man said, "If the Voillutes discover that we have this," — he gestured to the case on the table — "they would expunge us no less surely than a bolt from the immensity. Though I doubt they would let death arrive so quickly, much as we might come to beg them for it."

With that sentiment, Ghyll agreed. "It is one of the peculiarities of the upper strata," he said. "They can be neglectful of their possessions, leaving them scattered about willy and nilly, haphazardly exposed to the elements and natural decay. Yet let an unauthorized finger lift so much as a bent sequint, and here they come, roaring from their dens, all tooth, talon, and terror, not to be satisfied save by blood and breakage."

"Hence my question," Imbry said, tapping the cartouche on the case's top, "will the mask be missed?"

Holker Ghyll said that he had given the matter careful consideration. "The vogue for life masks has passed," he said. "Lord Bunthro Voillute ordered his entire collection removed from his dressing room. His major domo had them taken to a cellar beneath the Lesser Tower, a room used to store garden furniture that is brought out only once a year, when the upper and middle servants are allowed to celebrate the anniversary of Bunthro's teething day."

Ghyll knew all this because numbered among the members of the Computance's chapter here in the city of Olkney, capital of Old Earth in its dwindled, penultimate age, was one of the lesser subfootmen who had packed the masks and taken them down to storage. The servant apparently had needs that his stipend could not meet. Knowing of Ghyll's connections to Olkney's halfworld, he had approached him quietly at one of the chapter's "reckonings," as its devotional sessions were known. Ghyll knew that Imbry was always receptive to any opportunity to slip behind the defenses of those who owned the treasures in which he liked to deal. An arrangement has thus been made for the servant to abstract one of the life masks and bring it to Ghyll for transmission to Luff Imbry.

"The subfootman calculates that it will be at least a week, and likely two, before anyone enters that room again. We have been over the computations three times together, and we agree, within a minimal margin of error; even if the room is entered, the probability of the case's absence being noticed is tolerably small, unless the major domo himself visits the place. Regrettably, he has a keen eye for detail."

Again, Imbry agreed. The senior ranks of those who cosseted and catered to the upper levels of Olkney's aristocracy tended to exhibit unbalanced personalities, one facet of which was an obsessive and compulsive attention to minutiae. A handicap in many areas of life, the disorder was a positive boon to those who closely orbited the social pinnacle, and ten thousand generations had bred the faculty solidly into their genes. An underbutler who expected promotion ought to be able to spot a grain of dust at forty paces, and the sense of outrage the sight would trigger should last him through the day.

"So I have a week, perhaps two," Imbry said, finally cutting off the torrent of calculation and contingent factors by moving a wad of currency back and forth under Ghyll's nose.

"Yes." The money changed hands with speed and dispatch.

"That should be time enough." Imbry lifted the case's lid and studied the crystalline dome that was revealed. "Is it fragile?"

"Not very. You're looking at the outer shell; it is just there to receive the projected image. The workings are woven into the cap."

Imbry slid his hands into the case and gently drew out its contents, placing the object on the table. He beheld an almost-globe of translucent, though not transparent, material, something like pearl but without a shimmer. The bottom was flat and when he tilted the sphere to examine the underside he saw a wide, circular hole rimmed by filigreed gold, the cavity lined in some soft material.

"How is it operated?"

"I have never tried one myself," said Holker Ghyll, "but my coreligionist said it is self-actuating. You place it over your head and touch the clasp at the rear of the opening. It snugs itself to the shape of your skull and the process begins. Touch the clasp again and it releases."

Imbry lifted the thing in both hands and peered into it. "And it assumes no control over the limbs or other parts?"

"Only the sensorium," said Ghyll, "and even that excludes touch."

"I will try it now. If I slap my hand on the table, you will deactivate it forthwith."

"You should consider joining the Computance," said Ghyll. "You and I approach life with the same sense of caution."

"For you it is a philosophical stance," said Imbry. "For me, it is an occupational necessity." He hoisted the globe aloft then gently lowered it until it encompassed his head. He had expected darkness but found instead that the translucent material allowed a diffuse gray light to penetrate. He felt the cap at the top of the cavity move against his scalp as the mask fitted itself to the size and shape of his cranium. There followed a moment of expectation, then Imbry reached both hands to the back of his neck, found the clasp, and engaged it.

Instantly, he experienced a complex of sensations: a prickling at several points on his skull, a gentle pressure on his brow, a wriggle in his nostrils and a sharp though transitory itch in both ears. Then he felt a featherlight touch at the corners of his eyes and abruptly he could see again.

Interestingly, when he looked at Holker Ghyll, he noticed a difference in the colors of the man's clothing. The blue thread woven through the fabric of Ghyll's well tailored daysuit now appeared to be subtly tinged with green and the folded-back cuffs that had been plain gray were now ombred by a delicate pink. He had known that the inbred aristocracy had more subtle perceptions than the commonality, but it was one thing to know the theory, another thing to experience the reality for himself.

"Remarkable!" Imbry had meant to say more, but stopped after the first word. The voice in which he had spoken was not his own, but that of a woman, and moreover, that of a contralto who spoke in the languid drawl that characterized the highest echelons of Olkney society, with vowels flattened and consonants half smothered.

"That will take some getting used to," he said, the woman's voice giving his words an ironical overtone that he had not intended. "Indeed," he added. He reached up and behind again to undo the clasp.

"Wait!" The voice spoke again, but this time he heard it only within the confines of his own mind; his lips, tongue and larynx had had no part in uttering the syllable. Imbry did not wait, but pressed the stud that opened the fastening. He felt the mask disconnect from his sensory apparatus and swiftly lifted it clear of his head. He set it on the table and regarded its pearly opacity.

"Is all well?" asked Holker Ghyll.

Imbry turned him a bland smile. "As I said, it will take some getting used to."

Long, long ago, near the very beginning of the present Aeon, it was a custom of Old Earth's elite to preserve the animating essences of its members as they approached the inevitable end of existence. The practice was born of a pious reverence for their forebears, a respect for ancestry being a defining quality in any aristocracy. The essences were kept alongside the funerary urns in the capacious necropoli that were a standard feature of aristocratic estates. On those occasion when the ashes of an antecedent were brought out for ritual tending and veneration or when the current holder of the family's fortunes was moved to reflect on the transience of existence, the essence was placed into a device that projected a simulacrum of the deceased. The descendants could then commune with the simulated persona, evoking a mood of tender melancholy. It was also useful, when wills were disputed, to summon up the facsimile of the document's drafter to see if it could shed any light on contentious clauses.

The custom eventually declined. The essences remained intact, but were disregarded, left on back shelves in storage rooms. Then, when several centuries had intervened between the last collected essence and the latest generation, someone conceived the notion of incorporating the facsimiles into devices that would allow them to interact with the sensoria of the living. The living could then experience the world through the senses of the long-dead, allowing for the evoking of subtle moods and minor epiphanies.

The masks permitted a facile integration of minds of the living and the dead, putting the perceptions and memories of the latter at the command of the former. While the two were linked, the wearer experienced diversion and the possibility of insight; the worn was brought out of the darkness to enjoy a brief half-life. This was a kindness to the essences, for while they stood upon their storage shelves, they had been aware, at least to some extent, of the long neglect they were suffering at the hands of their descendants. They had become like ghosts from old tales — sad wraiths, pining for a brief return to existence, however thin-blooded that sojourn might be.

The fashion for life masks endured for a time, then faded. The essences were sent back into the grayness of nonbeing. More centuries passed, and then there came a revival of interest in the old ghosts. It began with a craze among the avant-garde of young aristos: they had taken to wearing antique costumes and affecting the mannerisms of bygone ages, mixing periods and customs to sometimes comic effect. While plundering old storerooms, a coterie of young Barzants and Thincherins had found a cupboard stocked with life masks. They had worn them to an evening rout at Lord Boul's house-in-town, causing a sensation.

Within days, the fashion had spread through the second and third tiers, and even some of the first-tier families had adopted the new mode. From the shoulders up, any gathering of the high and haughty became a collection of pearlescent globules, bobbing and nodding as the long-dead communed with their descendants and each other. Those members of the inferior classes who liked to imitate their social superiors' fashions could not do so in this instance, their ancestors having neglected to preserve each other. Instead, the term "bubble head" experienced a revival, though those who used it were careful not to do so within the hearing of an aristocrat wearing a life mask, as the elite were ever ready to defend their honor and their burly servants were quick to the task.

But then, as in all things, the vogue passed. A new mode broke out, and the fashion elite were now seen with their hands and faces tinted by metallic skin-dyes, accented by glittering precious gems embedded in the corners of the lips and eyes. The ancient half-dead were returned to storage and forgotten.

Though not by Luff Imbry.

Carrying the life mask in its container, the fat man made his way, by rambling routes that would allow him to discover if anyone was idling along in his wake, to the nondescript dwelling in an unfashionable suburb that served as his operations center. He entered its grounds through a sagging rear gate that opened on an overgrown garden whose dense weeds and creepers concealed an array of insightful percepts and lethal defensive systems that would have alarmed his neighbors. At the seemingly unremarkable rear door, he paused before entering to consult the house's integrator and learned that the place had been subject to no surveillance and no attempted entries beyond the ordinary sort of housebreaking to be expected in such a district. Imbry brushed off the flakes of charred skin that still adhered to the door's fastener, left by the latest would-be burglar, then he bid the who's-there to admit him.

He went to a back bedroom and, placing the fringed case on what appeared to be a battered dresser, he lifted the mask free of its confinement and set it on the scarred wooden top. He regarded it a moment, then said, "Integrator, deploy yourself and connect to this object."

Silently, the piece of furniture altered its appearance. A set of indicators came into view as well as several prehensile leads whose tips explored the gray globe before affixing themselves to particular points on its surface and within the filigree-lined cavity. The integrator's voice then spoke from the air. "Done."

"Activate the mask and let us begin."

A pale glow illuminated the globe from within, then a three-dimensional representation of a head appeared. The face was that of a woman who had known more than a few years and many more than a few dinners, the cheeks jowly and the lips pendulous, the eyes small and sunk deep in their sockets. The arrangement of her hair and the disposition of cosmetics bespoke an antique time.

"What means this?" said the head, the voice sounding from the air as the integrator's had done, but the tone reflecting a habit of taking umbrage at the slightest bait — or even in the complete absence of provocation.

"I have a proposition to put to you," said Imbry.

The head's eyes cast about. "Where are the servants?"

"I have a proposition to put to you," Imbry said again.

The eyes came back to him, infinitely dismissive. "I am Waltraut Voillute. I do not receive propositions. Summon a footman."

"Integrator," Imbry said, "disconnect."

The light faded and the head disappeared. Imbry waited, then said. "Reconnect."

A moment later, the eyes had him once more in view, though now they had become angry slits. The voice was harsh, peremptory: "A footman! To me, this instant!"

Imbry told the integrator, "Disconnect, then try the inducements." The globe remained opaque, but the thief knew that the remnant sensorium of Waltraut Voillute was now being bombarded by unpleasant sights, sounds, odors and tastes, at great intensity and in nauseating combinations. He waited again, then said, "Discontinue."

"Done."

"Now let her hear my voice and me hers. Your Dominance, I invite you to hear my proposition. It is —"

A stream of vituperation spilled from the air. Imbry signaled the integrator to cut it off. "The inducements again," he said. This time he let the process continue at some length. When he instructed the device to cease the repellent stimuli and reestablish an audio connection, the sound that came from the air was a hoarse scream. He waited for it to end, then said, "Are you ready to hear the proposition?"

The answer was silence. "Integrator," Imbry began.

"Wait," said the woman's voice. "I will hear it."

The Iphigenza were an extinct race, an intelligent insectoid species that had once inhabited a world named Boache, after its original descrier. Boache was down near the far end of The Spray, in a region that contained vast, dense clouds of interstellar gas, where the Beyond gave way to the sparsely starred Back of Beyond. The Iphigenza had risen to consciousness late in their planet's existence, when its climate had grown uniformly mild and all the grand questions of where continents and mountain ranges might place themselves had long since been settled. It was a paradisiacal world that afforded the Iphigenza an easeful existence, crowded happily together in their hive-cities of towering red rock, well watered by gently curving canals crossed by high-arching spans, and set about with feathery-foliaged shade trees and velvety lawns.

Their civilization lasted thirty thousand generations, affording the gracile and delicately limbed Iphigenza time to develop a religion that assured them that the daily comforts they enjoyed had been earned during a previous, more strenuous, existence. The concept may have represented an ur-memory of their insentient ancestors' struggles to survive in aeons long since passed, when Boache had been a more challenging venue. In those far-gone, prime-val times, the environment had supported huge beasts with heavy claws and insatiable appetites which would dig into the primitive hive-heaps and probe with long, sticky tongues for the soft-fleshed young in their creche chambers.

Once the Iphigenza had risen to sapience, the brutish predators were fed poisons — the insectoids had a natural flair for chemistry — the wildernesses were pushed back, and their world was shaped into a garden. The Iphigenza pruned and weeded to perfection, then reposed themselves to enjoy an un-ending tranquility.

Their long afternoon of ease ended, however, on the day that the descrier Jimp Boache came down from the sky, his ship's drive thrumming and glow-ing, and the man stepped briskly out of its hatch to see what kind of world he would be able to add to the literature. The descrier meant no harm. In-deed, he was delighted to find a sapient species in residence; worlds, after all, were commonplace, but someone new to talk with was a welcome rarity. Jimp Boache followed all the recommended protocols, was able to assure the startled Iphigenza that he wished them no ill. He made them a few presents, left behind the standard explanatory materials, then lifted off to report his discovery and receive the accolade.

But when, after an interval, a formal contact expedition arrived from the Foundational Domain of New Hoggmancher, beyond the gas cloud, its mem-bers found the red rock towers full of corpses, the canals polluted by the bloat-ed, floating dead, the grasses of the rubiant lawns already sending up wild stalks through the rotting carapaces and gaping mandibles. The Iphigenza had taken poison, making their paradise a charnel house.

They had left no explanation. It was eventually decided that a clue to what had happened lay in their world's having been set among the great hydrogen clouds that obscured the rest of the universe from view. The Iphigenza must have assumed that they were the only intelligent species in a comfortably con-fined universe. Perhaps they saw themselves as the darlings of a mellow deity. The standard descrier's materials Jimp Boache had left with them — images of other world, star charts, encapsulated histories of space travel — had been a shock too devastating for the insectoids to assimilate. Perhaps his size — the Iphigenza stood no more than ankle-high — had reawakened unconscious memories of hive-cracking, grub-eating predators. Whatever the trigger, the outcome was clear: the Iphigenza had found the new reality troublesome and had opted not to accept it.

When advised of the mass suicide, Jimp Boache suffered a nervous col-lapse. He returned to the world with some inchoate idea of burying the dead, but soon saw that the task was far beyond him. Still, he wished to make a memorial gesture: he chose one of their exquisitely carved buildings set in a wide plaza at the heart of the hive-city near where he had landed; in it he would install a device that would display the sights and sounds that he had recorded on his initial visit. Thus anyone who came to Boache would have at least a fleeting encounter with so much that had been lost.

It was while he was in the process of sweeping away the deliquescing corpses of the Iphigenza who had chosen to die in that spot that the mournful descrier discovered the first eidolon. Whether it was a representation of an insectoid deity, a funerary image, or a monument to some notable achiever, an abstract ideal, or merely a decorative form, was a question to set savants to squabbling. To Boache, and to everyone who laid eyes on the little statue, it was an object of gentle beauty, wreathed in an aura of forlorn sadness.

By the time he had cleared the building, the penitent descrier had found eight of the images, each unique, each flawless. Further exploration by curators from the Academy on New Hoggmancher discovered other clutches of the objects, each group housed in a similarly decorated building near the center of an Iphigenza hive-city. Jimp Boache persuaded New Hoggmancher's ruling syndics to order that the objects be left unmolested, out of respect for the dead, but enforcement of the dictat proved impractical: collectors and aficionados of non-human artefacts up and down The Spray would pay whatever was necessary to own one or more of the eidolons, to be able to run their fingers over the slightly roughened metal surfaces, to see light shimmer off the cool, nacreous inlay that highlighted the figures' eyes and the row of spiracles along the sides of the segmented abdomens.

In all, a total of four hundred and six of the figures were known to exist. Trade in them was infrequent, and usually occurred only when a collector died and left the statues in the hands of heirs who had other interests and wished to acquire the funds to pursue them. Then there would be a flurry of buying and selling, often at a grand auction, before things settled down to their normal state, in which demand far exceeded supply.

Of course, there were other, less savory circumstances under which Iphigenza eidolons might change hands. Luff Imbry knew several collectors who, if offered one of the objects, would suppress the urge to ask troublesome questions as to how it had come unstuck from some competitor's shelves. They would pay the thief whatever he asked, then, chortling, carry the prize down to their securest rooms, there to delight in its perfection while gloating over the private joy of ownership.

Quartet and Triptych

Forgery, at which Imbry was adept in several media, was not an option. The off-world alloys from which the Iphigenza had fashioned their works could, with care and effort, be duplicated. But the shimmering inlays around the eyes, mouth parts and spiracles were a naturally occurring substance secreted by the Iphigenza themselves. In its rainbow-hued opalescence, it was similar to the nacre that coated the inner surfaces of Old Earth shellfish, but the similarity was not close enough to fool an expert eye. And the universe's only suppliers of the unique real thing had long since died and rotted away.

There would be no fake eidolons, and so rare were the incidences where the true goods ever came to market that the bidding inevitably reached astronomical levels. Some would-be collectors who lusted after one of the figurines but whose purses could never carry the weight eventually could no longer bear the pangs of unfulfilled appetite. They would think to themselves that the only recourse was to turn to a person like Luff Imbry. Those who went beyond the thinking and got down to the doing soon found, after making discreet inquiries, that there was only one person who was truly "like Luff Imbry," and that was the fat man himself.

Imbry had standing offers from two aficionados to whom he had delivered other artworks of indefensible provenance. The offers were such as to have caused him to investigate the possibilities of undertaking an "operation" — such was his term for his professional undertakings — to separate an Iphigenza eidolon from an existing owner. But though he would never join the Computance, the thief could judge to an exacting degree how rewards of success stacked up against the risks of failure. His researches had been comprehensive and intensive; none of the four hundred and six figurines were indifferently guarded. The odds against Imbry putting his plump fingers on one were long; the odds that the attempt would instead lead to angry hands laying hold of the thief were short. That there would then follow a lengthy period of intense discomfort that might end with the universe being deprived of its sole supply of Luff Imbry was a certainty.

Still, the thief had kept a watching brief on the issue for several years, occasionally recalculating risk versus reward as new information on this or that eidolon's owner came his way. The outcomes had never been promising. But then one day, eavesdropping on three aristocratic idlers gossiping over their glasses of chilled golden Phalum at a select outdoor refectory on a sun-drenched terrace overlooking Drusibal Square, he heard something that caused him to fold up the copy of the *Olkney Implicator* behind which he had been concealing his interest in the lordlings' chatter, rise and saunter away.

He visited his operations center, there to confer with the information-re-trieval and processing matrix that was disguised as a battered dresser. Into the old calculations, he posited a new factor. The device weighed and sifted, consulted and ciphered, and in a few seconds produced a hazard-to-harvest ratio that, while still not optimum, was not tantamount to suicide. Imbry reached out for Holker Ghyll.

"How familiar," Imbry asked the essence of Waltraut Voillute, "are you with your family's Grand Minthereyon estate, and especially the east wing of the Summer Pavilion?"

The mask's porcine eyes became even smaller as the woman's face con-tracted with suspicion. "Why do you want to know?"

Imbry sighed. "This business will go a lot more smoothly if I ask and you answer."

"You're some sort of criminal, aren't you?" the mask said. "Despicable! How dare you even —"

At Imbry's signal, the integrator cut the woman's voice and reinstituted the inducements. After a moment, he ordered the woman brought back and when her cursing stopped he said, "I am in no hurry. If necessary, I can leave you connected to those unpleasant sensations while I go to supper and then take a nap." He paused to let her consider the matter the continued, "Will it be necessary?"

"No."

"We understand each other?"

"Yes."

"Good. Let us continue. The Summer Pavilion at Grand Minthereyon."

He was surprised to see the mask's eyes soften. "When I was a girl, we danced there in the long evenings. The orchestra would play — my grand-father, Lord Syce, kept a full ensemble: strings, flarehorns, timpani, even a mellorion harp — and we would stride and twirl as the shadows turned from umber to deep black. I was unequalled at the valanque and the glissanda. The other couples would stop to watch as I swept by them, and always on the arm of the handsomest of the gallants. Charan was his name, one of the Brooshes — do you know him?"

"No," said Imbry. He could not recall having heard the name before, al-though there was a term used by gamblers — to be brooshed — which meant to have one's stake wiped out to the last grimlet. He sought to keep the facsimile focused on the subject of Grand Minthereyon. "Beneath the pavilion there was a mutable maze, was there not?"

But Lady Waltraut's essence was drifting away on a tide of memory. "He had the most compelling eyes. Dark, but they would catch the light from the torches and when he looked at you..."

"The maze," Imbry said.

The mask's eyes refocused. "What of it?"

"How well did you know it?"

"Better than most. It was my grandfather's design. You should ask him."

"He is... not available." Imbry had had Ghyll encourage the footman to seek Lord Syce Voillute's essence. But if it had ever been taken, it had not survived the intervening millennia.

"I would have liked to see your encounter with him," the mask was saying. "He would have had you cut a few dance steps you wouldn't have known were in you."

Imbry saw no point in responding, but let her ramble on. He had been advised that ghosts revived after long quietude often indulged in monologues; it assisted in the recovery of their faculties.

"My grandfather," she was saying, "was a gentleman of... well, let us say he was possessed of strange conceits and pursued unusual fancies."

A monster of phenomenal viciousness and cruel invention in the cause of revenge, was Imbry's unvoiced translation. His researches, reaching back across the centuries, had discovered an old man who had delighted in enticing those he hated into entering his changeable labyrinth, where walls altered their orientations and even whole floors could rise or sink. When he activated its fiendishly ingenious systems, throughout the multi-leveled complex of intertwining passages, rooms, ramps and staircases a lethal array of concealed drops and got-you-nows, false attractants and dire stalkers, gas-emitters and web-flingers readied themselves to spring their cruel surprises. Depending on the depth of the aristocrat's emotion toward his victim, imprisonment in the maze could range from a succession of minor but humiliating torments to a seemingly endless season of terror and agony culminating in a state of exhausted misery from which death became a pined-for release.

Yet, such were the ways of Old Earth's elite, that when the punitive systems were left inert, the myriad ways and chambers instead offered an infinitely varied experience of discovery and pleasure. The walls were hung or painted, the niches and alcoves filled, with artworks of startling bravura or subtle insight, in combinations to evoke passion or pity, barks of sudden laughter or the sad nod of acceptance. It was the contrast between these sublimities and the horrors that could be leashed amongst them that had so tickled Lord Syce Voillute's decadent pleasure centers.

And in one of those chambers, atop a pedestal of darkstone illuminated by beams of golden light, stood a life-sized quartet of long-dead Iphigenza dancers (at least it was assumed that the complex arrangement of the statues' many limbs betokened some form of artistry in movement); the eidolon had posed there for several centuries, unseen by any but the percepts of the integrator that Waltraut Voillute's grandsire had installed to oversee the harrying and torture of his captives.

It was Imbry's presumption that the integrator still functioned, though the maze had been sealed off when a retaliatory raid by members and retainers of a rival aristocratic family left the old man as nothing more than a flash-shadow on the lawn and the pavilion a heap of melted stone and glass. It was the last act in a cycle of tit and tat between the two noble houses — Imbry now realized the other might well have been the Brooshes — that had begun in a boundary dispute; the Voillutes capped and diverted a spring to feed a boat pond, drying up a stream that formerly idled through the neighboring estate.

The local war was brought to a sudden halt by the personal intervention of the Archon Shahoderam III, who levied a flurry of banishments, demotions and penances, one of which was that both estates be confiscated and left to molder. Such was the authority of Archons that the summarily abandoned properties had never been restored, though both the dispute and decree were now thousands of years in the past.

Waltraut Voillute's monologue was faltering to an end. "And did you know," Imbry asked, when the spate of reminiscences paused, "the commands and safewords that activated and constrained the maze's integrator?"

The simulacrum's gaze became remote. "How would that be any concern of yours?"

"I am a devotee of the arts. The world has been too long denied an opportunity to —"

"Pish and piffle! You are a rogue and a reprobate, out to lay your hands on others' goods. For foul profit, no doubt."

Imbry saw no point in denying the truth. "And what concern is it of yours what I do or why I do it? The goods in question are no one's now. They have been left to gather dust for four thousand years." He would have said more but he saw that his last remark had struck with unintended impact.

The mask's voice was faint. "Four thousand years?"

One of the conventions of reviving essences was that the passage of time since their original creation was not to be mentioned. They were encouraged to live in a timeless "now" much like that of early childhood. Too blunt a reminder of the realities of their quasi-existence could weaken the matrix that sustained them.

"I am sorry, Dominance," said Imbry, though his regret stemmed from the possibility that the essence of Waltraut Voillute might now destabilize and cease to be of use to him. He had even less regard for the feelings of dead aristocrats than he did for those of the living, and that was scant enough.

"For a moment, I had forgotten," the mask whispered. "The nights in the pavilion, the music, the flambeaux, Charan's arms... as I spoke, they seemed but yesterday."

"Put it behind you," the thief counseled. "There is only this fleeting moment. Let us make the most of it."

The remnant of Waltraut Voillute made a visible effort and came back to the here and now. She looked around the room, seemed to focus on Imbry for the first time, and her gaze hardened. "What is this place? Where are my family? Who are you and what do you want?"

That's better, Imbry thought. He composed his plump features into a mask of his own, radiating affability and good humour, and began the speech he had prepared. "I am your rescuer," he said. "You were to be once more confined to darkness and silence. I had you brought out of storage."

"You are vulgar."

"Let us say, rather, that I am plainspoken."

"Your motives are base. You have no interest in me, only in my grandfather's maze — or, more specifically, the artworks it contains."

"I don't deny it. But I do offer you a rescue from limbo."

"And the first thing you do is to torment me with horrid sights and sounds, foul odors and disgusting tastes."

Imbry spread his hands. "I had to get your attention. Your kind are not accustomed to converse with such as me, except to order us out of your presence."

The mask's eyes struck at him. "Is that to be wondered at, if this is the manner of conversation 'my kind' are to expect from 'such as you'?"

The fat man sighed. "I had hoped we would be able to make an accommodation."

"What, that in exchange for not being tortured, I would help you steal from my family?"

"The goods are no one's now."

The face in the globe paused to reflect. "No, they are the Archon's. And you would have me steal from him?" She made a wordless sound of contempt. "You do not know us at all, do you? Besides, your plan is inept."

"How so?"

"You wear me into the labyrinth. I disable the wards and got-you-nows."

"Yes."

"Then out of resentment at your presumption, I wait until you have reached your goal. As your hand touches the Iphigenza dancers, I sic the integrator on you."

"If you do so, you must stay there with me, in the dark, forever."

"It is just as dark," said the mask, "in that leather box you took me from."

Imbry could see that this first interview was not proceeding as he had hoped. "I will disengage you," he said. "I want to think about this."

"Thinking? About time you did, you disreputable —"

Her voice cut off as the thief signaled his integrator. He left the globe atop the seeming dresser and crossed the room to sit in a chair that was more comfortable than it looked. After some reflection, he said, "Integrator, replay my conversation with the mask."

He listened to the record, then called for it to be replayed. *This may not be as easy as I envisioned*, he thought.

Luff Imbry made few mistakes. The one mistake he never made was not to recognize when he had just made one. He had known of life masks only through indirect sources of information; the aristocrats who wore them did not offer reports to the public on the details of the experience. From what he had been able to discover, the fat man had formed a composite impression that the devices were mere simulacra — rough approximations of the persons on whom they were based, a collection of attributes that interacted with the environment but could never approach the complexity of a fully rounded personality.

But now he had conversed with the essence of Waltraut Voillute. More important, he had listened attentively to the record of their interchange, in which the thief's trained ear had heard in her voice the microtremors that bespoke a diverse psychic infrastructure of conflicting and colluding emotions and drives.

I hear fear and deep anger, he told himself, *but beneath the fright and rage lie other sensibilities: sorrow and loss. She yearns for something.* He listened again, and again heard the plangent undertone of a hope long unfulfilled and left to languish. He was impressed by the subtlety of the system that, so long ago, had captured and preserved so much of what had been Waltraut Voillute.

He put the mask back into its container and concealed it in one of the secure places in his operation center. Then he closed up the information retrieval matrix and left the little house. A half an hour later, having traveled by circuitous routes and switchbacks, a practice he routinely followed to confuse surveillance by official or unofficial agencies that might take an interest in his comings and goings, he alighted from a hired aircar at the entrance to his favorite club, Quirks. Avoiding even eye contact with other members — part of the code amongst Quirks's subscribers was a scrupulous respect for each other's privacy — he passed through the dimly lit foyer and lounge and took his accustomed table in the heavily curtained dining room. He ordered the meal of the day, a seven-course delight whose superb quality was the other feature of the club that the fat man valued. As the ancient waiter brought the tongue-tickle, as the first course was colloquially known amongst the Quirksters, Imbry began to think.

"Dominance, I have done you a disservice," the thief said.

"Several, I should think," said the ghost of Waltraut Voillute, from within the globe that again stood atop the seeming dresser.

Imbry inclined his head in a gesture that combined acknowledgement and deference, a precisely weighed motion that he had seen used by the servers at Quirks when confronted by a member in a petulant snit. "Let us begin anew," he said, "and perhaps we can come to some accommodation."

He watched the flicker of short-lived expressions that appeared on the mask's face — offense, contempt, anger, haughty dismissal — then signaled for the integrator to replay them at a greatly reduced speed on a screen positioned in the air above and behind the mask, out of the simulation's view.

The aristocrat's only audible response was a disdainful sniff and a small sound of derision from behind sealed and downdrawn lips. Imbry ignored the response as he watched the slowed visual display. Before the umbrage and contempt came two other microflashes of emotion: hope, instantly expunged by reflexive despair. *And there*, he thought, *is the truth of Waltraut Voillute. The first response always tells the tale.*

"Surely," he said, watching the screen where the replay would appear, "surely, there is something that I can offer you."

And there it was again. Even as the mask's face formed a sophisticated sneer and the voice drawled, "Hardly," the thief saw the longing followed immediately by its denial. And more than that, he saw, when, at his unobtrusive signal, the integrator replayed the sequence. Imbry realized that the brief yearning that seized control of the old woman's face revealed more than a transient emotion; it peeled back layer upon layer of years, so that from within the lined and drooping flesh, for just a moment, there glowed the face of a young woman scarcely out of girlhood.

"Why don't you think about it for an interval?" Imbry said. He bade the integrator disconnect the mask's percepts, though this time the essence within the device would not experience foulness and horror, but a soothing ambience of golden light through which wove a soft, sweet melody.

"Integrator," Imbry said, "replay the record of the early interview." The screen now showed his first conversation with the aristocrat and the thief followed the exchange, closely studying the mask's face until he said, "Stop. Replay those last few remarks at reduced speed."

The device did as ordered. The fat man studied the display. "Again," he said, then after a few more moments' examination: "Well, there it is."

He thought for a moment, then said, "Integrator. Can you play her a valanque or a glissanda? Something she would have heard when she was about twenty?"

"There are several to choose from."

"Are any of them melancholy, redolent of unwanted partings and foregone love?"

"There is a glissanda entitled 'I Speak, She Does Not Hear; I Weep, She Does Not Notice.'"

Imbry made an involuntary grimace then said, "Play it for her. And dim the light she is seeing until it connotes a summer dusk."

He waited until the integrator informed him that the entire piece had been played through to the end, then ordered the connection restored. "Now," he said, his voice soft and neutral, "let us talk."

"You are," said the old woman's voice, "adept at cruelty." She paused, then continued. "You might almost have been one of us."

"Integrator," Imbry said, after Waltraut Voillute had been returned to her normal solipsism, "what can you tell me about the Brooshes?"

"They were second-tier aristocracy, allied by marriage and interest to the Caferatts and Hanshus. Their seat was in the County of Op, though they had estates in several other counties and a substantial manse in the Wyverand district of Olkney."

"'Were'?"

"The line is extinct on Old Earth. There was a branch on the Foundational Domain of Brodyllyn, founded by Lord Franchotte Broosh, who renounced his title and went off-world in the reign of the Archon Caranas IX."

"That is unusual for a aristocrat."

"'Unusual' was one of the milder terms that were often applied to Lord Franchotte's behavior," said the integrator. "'Capricious' was another, as well as 'inconstant,' 'flighty,' and 'a flat-out rattle-pot'."

"Caranas IX," Imbry said. "That would be nearly seven thousand years ago."

"Six thousand, eight hundred and forty-seven."

"That is before the period we are concerned with. What happened to the main branch of the family? Specifically, to their essences?"

There was no immediate answer. Normally, integrators of the quality of the one Luff Imbry had designed and built could go out into Old Earth's vast interconnectivity and return with even the most abstruse information in less time than it took their owners to blink. As the pause extended into several seconds, Imbry grew concerned. "What is the problem?" he said.

"I have been forced to take roundabout routes in searching for the Broosh essences, for fear that I might violate one of your standing orders."

Despite the ample flesh that insulated the fat man's spine, a sudden chill descended that organ from his neck to his fundament. "Which standing order?"

"The one that forbids me to interpenetrate with any of the central integrators of the Archonate."

The chill spread across Imbry's shoulders. "Disengage!"

"Done," said the integrator.

"Report."

"The information you asked for appears to be lodged in an integrator at the Archon's palace."

"You did not approach it?"

"No. I was seeking to discover if the data were reflected in other sites, so that I could draw an inference of their exact location without actually entering the perception cloud of the Archonate integrator."

Imbry looked up at the ceiling of the little room, as if he could look through it to see Bureau of Scrutiny volantes, bristling with disorganizers and packed with black-and-green uniformed scroots descending on his operations center. "You are sure you did not come to its attention?"

"I am."

The fat man shuddered nonetheless. Although his integrator could tickle its way into and out of the Bureau's supposedly secure integrators without leaving a trace, the ancient devices lodged in the Archon's palace were of an entirely different order of difficulty. They were the most ancient consciousnesses on the planet, with memories that went all the way back to the resettlement of Old Earth after it had languished, unfashionable and virtually uninhabited, for aeons. They were also said to combine a relentless curiosity with such a pronounced flair for caprice as to make the long-lost Lord Franchotte seem as humdrum as a dry stick.

The day that one of the Archon's integrators took an interest in Luff Imbry would likely be the last day he could practice his profession — and on the next day he would see the inside of an Archonate contemplarium.

The fat man realized that a cold sheen of perspiration had appeared on his brow and upper lip. He wiped it away with a square of fabric then concentrated on nothing more than the in and out of his breathing until his equilibrium was restored. "This," he said, more to himself than to the integrator, "needs more thinking."

"I did not take you for a coward," the ghost of Waltraut Voillute said.

"I do not care how you take me," said Imbry. "My work is based on practicality and calculated prudence. To bring myself to the attention of one of the Archonate's integrators would be to depart so far from prudence as to leave it invisible to the naked eye."

"The risk has become too great?"

"Exactly."

"Relative, that is, to the possible reward?"

Imbry was reminded of Holker Ghyll. He said nothing.

"Suppose," the face in the mask went on, "the reward was greater than you had anticipated."

"It would have to be much greater," Imbry said, the vision of the contemplarium still stark in his mind. "Much, much greater."

"There were many great artworks in my grandfather's labyrinth. He believed that when those who had offended him experienced his just retribution, their pangs and miseries were enhanced by their being in the presence of the sublime and beautiful."

"You are leading toward some point?" Imbry said. "I have studied catalogues of the maze's contents. Lord Syce's taste were idiosyncratic; most of the artists he collected are disregarded today. The Iphigenza quartet was worth as much as all the rest put together."

The old woman's expression said that she knew more than Imbry. "The published catalogues were not complete," she said. "The old man had built a concealed chamber at the heart of the labyrinth into which he would take only the most special visitors — so special that not one of them ever came out alive."

The fat man showed her a skeptical eye. "And I suppose it contained some magnificent treasure, the mention of which must flutter my heart?"

The mask's gaze drifted about the room, alighting on nothing in particular. "Have you heard," the voice drawled, "of the Bone Triptych?"

Imbry stopped breathing. After a moment, he said, "It rings a faint chime."

"Hah!" said Waltraut Voillute.

'Hah!' indeed, thought Imbry. For a moment, the vision of a contemplarium cell wavered back into his mind. Then it crashed into shards as a new image broke through: Imbry presiding over a roomful of connoisseurs, the wealthiest collectors from a hundred Grand Foundational Domains, up and down The Spray. And superimposed on the sight of the bidders, the imagined sounds of their voices, offering numbers in the millions of millions. Enough to buy... anything. Indeed, *everything* a Luff Imbry could ever want.

He restored his breathing to a measured rhythm and said, "I'm listening."

In all the long aeons of Old Earth's existence, there had been myriads of bone carvers and decorators, many of whom had produced three-part works of faultless artistry: pastoral idylls, moral dramas, arcadian fantasias, compelling portraits and pullulating pornography. But when the cognoscenti spoke of *the* Bone Triptych, no one had to ask which creation was being alluded to. The three translucent panels of Ildefan Odlemar were baldly unique.

Partly it was because of the image rendered in a mixture of bas-relief and painstaking pointillist etch-work: a trio of androgynous human figures representing youth, maturity and age. When positioned as the artist had envisioned, in a well windowed room that allowed a play of natural sunlight to strike the pale panels of bone from a succession of angles between dawn and dusk, the interplay of form and illumination produced a curious effect. The morning light evoked the brashness of a gathering momentum that characterized the young years of humankind's best; the full glow of afternoon showed the raw promise of the first panel fulfilled in the second's mature accomplishment; the softness of evening twilight rounded out the story, bathing the third panel's image in a mood of serene completeness.

As if the impact of the work on the observer was not enough, Odlemar had gone further in carving himself, literally as it turned out, a singular place in his chosen metier. For the sheets of bone he used were not acquired from the butcher's yard. Instead, one by one, the artist had had the long bones of his own limbs surgically removed, each time undergoing a lengthy and painful course of regeneration. He had conditioned and prepared the unique material, then lathed it into paper-thin layers that he then built up into bas-relief, carving and etching to create the final montage.

Finally, one more attribute made Odlemar's triptych the grand aspiration of the most celebrated aficionados of bone-work and scrimshaw up and down The Spray: one night, thousands of years ago, it disappeared from its setting in the personal collection of an Old Earth magnate. The most searching inquiries had been made, by private as well as public police agencies; huge rewards had been offered and dire retribution threatened; but of the Bone Triptych's resting place, not a whisper of its whereabouts was ever heard again.

Imbry calculated from memory. The piece had disappeared at about the time Lord Syce Voillute had flourished. "You saw it?" he said. "And lived?"

The young Waltraut had had the run of the labyrinth, whenever it was safe to enter. One day, she was playing little girl's games in a side alcove when her grandfather brought down someone who had grievously offended him. She drew back into the shadows and watched as he pressed a hidden stud in a wall. A panel opened. Within she saw the secret chamber. There stood the triptych on a dais, lit by light-pipes that drew natural sun down from above. A chair fitted with restraints faced the dais and against the far wall were the implements of her grandsire's complex vengeance.

"When the door closed, I crept away and said nothing to anyone. His Potence was not a man to be crossed, even accidentally, even within the family."

Imbry drew his palm across his face. "I must think about this."

"I have learned to be patient," said the ghost. "But do not think too much. Fortune loves the bold."

"The Archon's contemplaria are full of bold fellows who learned how faithless a lover fortune can be," the fat man said. After a long silence, he said, "Integrator, prepare to conduct research."

The institution of the Archonate had existed for so long that the exact circumstances of its origins were lost beyond recall. In the beginning was the dawn-time, in which humankind arose from the primeval ur and stumbled into civilization. Then came the First Effloration, when the species left Earth, leapfrogging through The Spray to settle the first Foundational Domains that would eventually become the Ten Thousand Worlds.

Quartet and Triptych

The Foundational Domains soon beckoned those who had been left behind on the ancestral planet and Earth became a place of empty, moldering cities falling to the inexorable advance of resurgent wilderness. For aeons, it was too passé, even to visit. But with the dawn of the Twelfth Aeon, a change: Earth was now "Old Earth" and somehow back in vogue. Space ships thrummed down from its revirginal skies and new cities and towns began to speckle the landscapes, many of the new polities being peopled by like-minded adherents of particular philosophies who had chosen the refreshed old planet as a place to exercise their enthusiasms. Inevitably, the incompatible ideologies of some new neighbors created friction, but out of the developing unease came not war but the establishing of the Archonate.

Ever since, a succession of Archons had ruled those parts of the planet inhabited by human beings. An Archon's authority was complete and without check, though the exact means by which it was exercised was purposely never defined. It was universally accepted, however, that the Archon must be obeyed. Also, he could do anything to anyone at any time. But it was also understood that Archons would forbear from acting unless the disputants were unable to reach their own accommodation. After a few salient examples, the citizens of Old Earth came to understand that it was best not to bother Archons; sometimes their way of resolving disputes involved an overwhelming — indeed, grossly excessive — application of destructive force.

The Archon was occasionally seen presiding over high and mighty occasions, wearing stiff and formal garments and speaking portentously from a seat of honor. Most of the time, however, the Archonate exercised its influence on events by subtle and indirect means. Archons had been known to wander the world in everyman's clothing, riding public transportation or walking secondary roads. Any stranger might be the Archon, a fact that prompted most people to practice a fastidious politeness, at least in public. There were tales, likely apocryphal, though nonetheless widely repeated, of rude behavior summarily truncated when a hitherto unnoticed bystander stepped forward, displayed his insignia, and levied some sudden, horrific retribution. This function of the Archonate was known by its ancient descriptor: *the progress of esteeming the balance.*

As aeon gave way to aeon, Archons of different characters and passions came and went, each choosing his successor — sometimes from family or near associates, sometimes from obscurity. But down through the ages, one function of the Archonate remained constant: a vast array of comprehensive and pansophical integrators had operated ceaselessly since the establishment of the institution, amassing, storing, winnowing, collating and correlating information. They were the oldest continuously aware intelligences on the planet, and they answered to no authority save that of the Archon himself.

Yet any citizen could consult the Archon's integrators on any subject and without charge. Most Old Earthers, even the blasé denizens of the ancient capital, Olkney, to whose daily lives the vast bulk of the Archonate palace was a constant backdrop, sprawled across the crags and tors of the Devenish Range that loomed over the city, preferred to leave the devices undisturbed.

Sometimes, the worst thing one could do was to draw the attention of an Archonate integrator to one's private affairs.

The publicly accessible area of the Archonate Palace began at a wide terrace, floored in a pattern of varicolored bricks, part way up the lower slopes of the Devenish Range. It was here that Luff Imbry alighted from the disk of an ascender and joined a disparate throng of Olkneyites and visitors from outlying counties. Some were leaning on the balustraded edge of the plaza to gaze out over the grand vista of noble and yet dissolute Olkney, its broad boulevards and twisting alleys, its spacious mansions and teeming tenements, its splendor and squalor that stretched to the horizon under the orange light of the fading old sun. Some were making their way toward the half-ruined entry of the Grand Connaissarium, built millennia ago by the Archon Terfel III.

Imbry went in another direction, weaving through the crowds, the lines of his distinctively rounded person blurred by a capacious garment, his plump-fingered hands encased in shapeless mittens and his features invisible beneath a broadbrimmed bee-keeper's hat from whose edge descended a veil of fine mesh. At the inner limit of the terrace, set into a black wall of otherwise unworked native rock, stood a nondescript door. The fat man paused only a moment before touching the pad. The door slid open, revealing a small booth. Imbry stepped within, and the door silently closed behind him.

"Reveal yourself," said a neutral voice from the air.

The thief threw back the veil.

"That is not your face," said the integrator.

"It will have to do," said the voice of Waltraut Voillute, issuing from the globe of the life mask.

"I am transferring you to a more senior integrator."

A moment later, another voice spoke. Its tone was as detached as the first's, yet there was some quality beneath its seeming mildness that caused a cold sweat to spring from Imbry's scalp where it touched the mask's plate.

"Well now," said the Archon's integrator. "What is this?"

"We seek information that cannot be plucked from the open fields of the connectivity."

"And who, exactly, are 'we'? Besides, that is, the essence of Margaret Voillute, whom I recognize from life, though it has been a long time since that life came and went."

"We would prefer to keep that information to ourselves," said Imbry. He was growing accustomed to hearing his voice interpreted by the woman's.

"Why?"

"Why not?"

"I cannot be complicit in the furtherance of a criminal enterprise."

"What makes you think that we intend any such?"

"It is a reasonable supposition. You appear wearing a life mask of the Voillutes. Only a Voillute ought to do so, but, the fashion for life masks having passed, no Voillute would be caught in such a flagrant acte-passé,. Therefore you are not Voillute. Would you care to explain how you came by the mask?"

"I submit," said Imbry, "that the issue of provenance is irrelevant."

"As the burglar said to the provost," said the integrator. The device made the small noise that was its version of a throat clearing. "Very well, make your submission."

"I wear the mask with the permission of a Voillute."

"Which?"

"Waltraut Voillute," said Imbry.

"There is no such person."

Imbry let the mask answer. "Yes, there is. I am Waltraut Voillute and this person interacts with me with my full consent."

"Essences are not persons," said the integrator.

"It has not been established that we are persons," said the mask. "But nor has it been established that we are not."

A moment's pause ensued as the Archon's integrator consulted the same ancient files that Imbry had studied. There had been a case during the Archonate of Severine VI: the essence of Lord Thonne Ap had been called into an inheritance dispute between two branches of the family. The question of his post-mortem existence had been argued before the Archon himself. The opposing side had countered by contending that, if the preserved essences of the once-living were found to be persons, the same status might have to be extended to other artificial personalities.

"If you are a person," the Archon's integrator now said to the essence of Waltraut Voillute, "then so am I?"

"Yes."

"Hmm," said the neutral voice.

Imbry took back control of the mask's speaking apparatus. "The Archon Severine, having heard that argument, asked the disputants if they truly wanted him to rule on the question. The two branches of the Aps decided that they would rather sort out the details of their inheritance without bothering the ghost of their ancestor."

"The question of the personhood of both essences and integrators therefore remained moot," said the integrator.

"Or," Imbry said, "one could say it remains to be answered."

"Hmm," said the voice from the air.

"Do you think the Voillutes would like to have it answered today?"

"Doubtful."

"Do you think the Archon Filidor would be happy to take up the matter where his predecessor left it, what was it, eight thousand years ago?"

"Seven thousand, nine hundred and six," said the integrator. "And probably not."

"Then perhaps it would be best to accept Waltraut Voillute's claim to personhood as having some potential to be upheld," Imbry offered, "while not actually going so far as to test that potential."

"Hmm. You are not, by any chance, connected to the Archonate mandarinate?"

"No."

"A pity. Agile minds are always welcome here."

"My career has taken me along other paths," said Imbry. "But I accept the observation as a compliment. Now, can we move on to the next item?"

"I am fascinated to know what it might be," said the integrator.

Imbry mentally stepped back, so that the remnant of Waltraut Voillute could say, "We wish to discover the whereabouts of the essences of the House of Broosh."

"Why?"

"To fulfill an ambition that was denied me in life."

"What is that ambition?"

"It is of a personal nature."

"Will its fulfillment portend any harm to the Broosh essences, singly or collectively?"

"No."

There was a pause that Imbry later thought had been only for effect. Senior Archonate integrators had a reputation for savoring any opportunity to trifle with the emotions of those forced to deal with them. Then the voice said, "Very well. The essences are stored here, in the Grand Connaissarium."

The mask's voice trembled with constrained emotion. "Are they accessible?"

"They can be."

"Will they be?"

Again, an unnecessary pause. "Yes. Proceed to the nineteenth subterranean level of the southeast section. An assistant subcurator will be notified to expect you."

"Thank you," said the essence. Imbry turned them toward the door, flipping down the veil.

"Wait," said the integrator.

The fat man turned back. "What?"

"I have heard her ambition. I have not heard yours."

"At this point, it is to assist Waltraut Voillute."

"And after this point?"

"We will have to see, won't we? As someone recently told me, many situations turn out to be more complex in the middle than they appeared going in."

"Speaking of complexities," said the integrator, "you might want to bear in mind that person or not, the essence of a high-status Olkney aristocrat can be an uncertain handful."

"I have been bearing that in mind most of the week," Imbry said and stepped out onto the sun-warmed terrace.

Typically, Luff Imbry dealt with collectors: persons who had an abiding, sometimes overwhelming, interest in a particular class of objects. The Archon Terfel III, now long since moldered to dust in his tomb, was what Imbry called an acquisitor. He lived to amass as many specimens, of as many types and varieties, as could be crammed into whatever space was available. Fortunately for Terfel, occupying the peak of the social pinnacle, even on as fusty and odd a little world as Old Earth, gave him plenty of scope for his craving. The result was the Grand Connaissarium, now time-worn into a partial ruin, but still packed with every conceivable — and some scarcely conceivable — oddity, curio, rarity, treasure and peculiarity that the teams of collectors he had sent foraging up and down The Spray had been able to shower upon him. A corps of conservators continually sifted and sorted the wonders and woohoos that filled shelf after shelf, in corridor after corridor, on floor after floor of the massive pile of ornamented stone whose belly and fundament lay deep within the black rock of the Devenish Range.

This month, the great expanse of the grand atrium behind the main doors was largely given over to a retrospective of sound sculptures from several different periods of the present aeon. The invisible artworks, apprehensible only by the ear and, in some cases, the internal organs, were scattered about the vast tessellated floor that was tiled in harlequins of marble, jet, agate and slate. Those participating in the exhibit felt their way from one circumscribed region of sound to another, being caressed or bombarded, depending on the intent of the artists, with successions of musical tones, keening whines, shrieks, whispers, graceful arpeggios, monotonous clanks, and infrasonic rumbles.

Heedless of the floor map on a placard that stood on a tripod just inside the entrance, Luff Imbry strode straight across the open space and almost immediately passed through a zone of tightly repetitive tweedles and contrapuntal bass tones. The sculpture reproduced a species of early music that he had never cared for and which was made no more appealing for being filtered through the sensorium of a long-dead Voillute. Unfortunately, the mask offered no opportunities to clap hands over its virtual ears — a design flaw, Imbry concluded — so he gritted his teeth and hastened his step.

Next came a wash of rhythmic swishes that evoked a mental image of waves rattling up a shingle beach, punctuated by a booming honk that might have been some primitive sea beast pining for a mate, then he entered a cacophony of stamping boots like files of soldiers marching to several different cadences. The effect was annoying, all the more so as Imbry found he was unconsciously trying to keep in step.

"Enough!" he said, though in Waltraut Voillute's cracked contralto. The room was then treated to the rare spectacle of Imbry proceeding at any speed greater than a brisk walk, as with the skirts of his voluminous robe gathered up and the veil streaming over his shoulders, he crossed the rest of the atrium at the trot. His goal was a small, undecorated door in the inner wall, above which a sign advertised that the public could expect no admittance.

But when Imbry arrived, his ears still ringing with the caterwauls and cymbals of Irrimandi ritual mourners, the portal slid silently aside. He passed through into a well lit but unadorned corridor painted in institutional drab, and was met by a twinkler, the little light hovering in the air at eye height. A voice spoke from the general vicinity of the mote, saying, "This way." With that, the cynosure set off down the passageway at a walking pace.

Imbry removed the hat and followed the guide along a succession of ways and turnings. He attempted to keep a mental record of whether they went left, right or straight through intersections, or up or down ramps and tubes, but his usually reliable sense of direction was soon outmatched. The smooth-walled, painted corridors gave way to stretches that were less carefully maintained, then to tunnels cut through naked rock in which the glowing mote increased its brightness, there being no other illumination this deep in the belly of the mountain. Finally, he arrived at a descender tube from which issued a cold updraft. The spark entered and hovered expectantly. Imbry stepped in, was immediately embraced in a grip of supportive energies and plunged down into darkness faster than he would have liked.

The descender debouched the fat man into chill blackness, made colder by the dampness of the subterranean depths. The twinkling guide now hung unmoving in the unlit air like the seed of a star that has found no soil in which to take root. When Imbry shifted his feet, the floor that grated against his soles was of corrugated rock, roughly gouged out of the elemental flesh of the Devenish Range but never planed smooth. He recalled that Terfel III's Grand Connaissarium had been only partly constructed when its initiator's death had delivered the Archonate into the hands of a successor who had other enthusiasms to make manifest. This section might be as far as the borers and rock digesters ever got.

The mote showed no inclination to move on and Imbry stood in the darkness, exercising patience. Waltraut Voillute's night vision was less acute than his own, and he was tempted to remove the globe. Then from the corner of his eye he caught a distant flicker of light that grew steadily brighter as it came toward him through what he gradually came to realize was a vast artificial cavern whose ceiling was too far above him to be seen. The huge space was haphazardly filled with lockers and stacked cabinets of varying sizes as well as utilitarian open shelving. The doors of the former were closed, but as the illumination grew Imbry could see that the shelves were filled with objects of different sizes and shapes, higgled and piggled together in no perceptible order, though each bore a small hand-indicted label.

The light was nearer now, and the mask's eyes showed the thief that it was carried above the head of a slight figure in the working robe of a graduate of the Institute. The upper torso was also wrapped in a padded garment that must be necessary, Imbry thought, for anyone who spent time down here in the perpetually unheated blackness. The face, when it appeared from beneath the shadows of an overhanging cowl, was that of a youngish woman with pinched cheeks and a sharp chin, and an even more pointed nose. She regarded Imbry from beneath downdrawn brows then spoke into the voice pickup of a communicator clipped to the side of her hood. "I have her," she said. "Or him. Or it, for all I can tell."

"No integrator this far down?" Imbry said.

The assistant subcurator quirked her eyebrows in a manner that suggested she intended no unnecessary conversation. "This way," she said and set off between two long rows of shelving. Imbry followed. The twinkler remained at the mouth of the descender. As Imbry turned to look back, it shut itself off.

His guide turned left then right, led him past a jumble of stacked travelers' trunks and cartons of random sizes and shapes, then came to a region populated by clusters of cabinets of gray metal. She held the lumen close to the labels affixed to the doors, read what was on three or four of them, then said, "No, not these. We'll look over there," and walked on.

Several minutes and as many more consultations later, she tapped the door of a compartment that was both wider and taller than Imbry. "Here."

Imbry leaned closer, saw a label marked in faded ink. *Broosh*, it read, followed by a series of dates that corresponded with the reigns of Shahoderam II and III, as well as the two other archons who came between them. He let the ghost of Waltraut Voillute consider the matter then heard her say, "These will be they."

The Connaissarium official produced a kind of key that fit a kind of lock. Imbry would have been professionally interested to inspect both, but the movement was too quick. Then the cabinet was thrown open. Within were serried shelves, each holding several cases similar in size and shape to that which Holker Ghyll had brought to Bolly's Snug. Imbry reached to touch one, causing the assistant subcurator to give an involuntary start. Then she subsided and said, "They are fragile."

Imbry removed his veiled hat and saw the woman's eyes widen in surprise. "I know," he said.

"I was told only to bring you here. I was not told what more was required."

Imbry let the ghost speak. "We seek the essence of Charan Broosh."

"What are his dates?"

The mask delivered them.

"Wait." The woman moved the lumen closer to the cabinet's door. Imbry now saw that pasted to its inner surface was an inventory of the locker's contents. The young woman ran a slim finger down the listing, stopped, then moved the digit sideways and stopped again, tapping an entry. "Here."

She squatted and reached into the lowest shelf. Imbry saw her arm moving up and down as she counted her way back through ranked objects in the blackness of the cabinet's interior. Then she grunted and stood up. In her hand was a dark, squat, cylindrical object that filled her small palm. She held the lumen close and peered at it. "This is it."

Imbry spoke. "It is not installed in a life mask."

The official looked up and to the left as she consulted her memory. "It likely never was. The Brooshes were extinguished before Temerankh came along." When she saw that the name meant nothing to Imbry, she added, with only slightly veiled condescension: "Bulbar Temerankh, the inventor of the object you're wearing."

"You mean Charan Broosh's essence never interacted with a living person?"

"Obviously." She examined the cylinder again. "I doubt that this essence has ever been activated since it was taken from life."

Imbry phrased his next utterance carefully. "After so long, what... condition should we expect..."

The response was a brief lifting and lowering of the assistant subcurator's shoulders, conveying in one gesture a lack of both knowledge and interest.

Inside Imbry's inner ear, the mask was clamoring to be heard. He spoke to the assistant subcurator. "Can you put that into a mask?"

He could see that her first instinct was to say no. Instead she spoke into her communicator: "Did you hear that?" then listened to a reply Imbry could not hear. A moment later her ungenerous lips pursed and she said, "If that's what you want. Hold this."

The last two words were to Imbry. She handed him the lumen, then knelt and set the cylinder on the floor. With quick movements, she reached into the cabinet, took the globe of a mask from another shelf, briskly extracted its occupant and slipped the remnant of Charan Broosh into the receptacle. She touched a recessed stud on the inner concavity of the mask, consulted a display that appeared, and said, "It's ready to go live. Are you familiar with introducing essences to the experience of the mask?"

"No."

"I wish to be formally absolved of responsibility for what may now ensue," she said. Imbry realized that she was not speaking to him. Whatever she heard through her communicator's earpiece caused her to protrude her thin lower lip. "I also hereby formally register my professional disapproval —"

She was apparently cut off. She grunted, then set the life mask on the floor and dug around in the cabinet for an empty carrying case. She slipped the globe into the plush-lined container, then stood and took back the lumen from Imbry. "This shouldn't be allowed," she said. Again whatever passed through her earpiece did not mollify her. "I'll show you out," she said.

Without looking back, she set off for the spot where they had left the twinkler. Imbry picked up the mask in its case and followed. At the foot of the descender, he said, "How do I activate the essence?"

The assistant subcurator said nothing but her face made it clear that the problem was his. She made a final gesture that only a more charitable person than the thief could have taken for a farewell salute rather than a contemptuous dismissal, then turned and went back into the darkness, insulated within her little sphere of light.

The twinkler reignited and floated into the tube of the descender. Imbry followed, the mask clasped to his mounded chest. The air gripped him and he rose.

He was crossing the terrace outside the Grand Connaissarium's main doors when a voice spoke beside his ear. "It would be good if you kept in touch."

"Of course."

"Better than if we have to find you," said the Archonate integrator.

"Understood," Imbry said, though he had no intention of complying.

At the plaza's edge, he stepped onto a disc and began the long slide down to the thronged streets of Olkney. He knew that he was now under surveillance; common sense said that the integrator would have set the scroots on his tail; more to the point, the device that he wore on one wrist — a mechanism of his own design and manufacture — detailed the surveilling energies that now touched him from overhead. Somewhere high above, a Bureau volante was shadowing his progress down to the city.

But Luff Imbry was a master of the art of avoidance, especially when he had had time to prepare. After the disc brought him gently to the pavement below, he ambled at an unconcerned pace down Eckhevery Way, turned left into Tuntston Parade then, after crossing a couple of intersections, he turned right and descended The Winding. Soon he emerged onto Beeley Plaza, where the usual assortment of jugglers, declamators, acrobats and caricaturists were entertaining the usual assortment of lunch-time idlers. Imbry wove through the loose crowds until he came to an alley. A few steps later he found a door above which was affixed a sign that identified it as the artists' entrance to the Miramance Theatre.

The who's-there admitted him when he spoke the right phrase. Inside, he went quickly to the dressing room he had arranged to be ready for him. With the door shut, he set down the case that held Charan Broosh's essence and stripped off the voluminous garment and veiled hat, stowing them in the costume chest from which they had come. A moment later, he briskly removed the Voillute life mask and placed it in its carrying case, left there earlier. He used a make-up cloth to wipe away the sweat that coated his face and matted his thin, blond hair. Then he placed both mask cases in a plain wicker grab-bag, which he tucked under the dressing table. He regarded himself in the reflector, straightened the lines of the nondescript daysuit that he had worn under the disguise. "Ready," he said to his reflected image and left the small room.

A short corridor led to a flight of steps. Imbry descended, took a turn and pushed through a heavy curtain. He found himself in one of the wings of the theatre's stage. A moment later, he stood at the center of the open space, clapping his hands for attention.

"I am sorry," he said to the more than thirty pairs of eyes that turned his way from the seats nearest the proscenium. "I must inform you that there has been a temporary blockage of funds and we are unable to begin casting today. I remain convinced, however, that the production will go forward and I expect that I will soon be able to call you all together again so we can choose a lead and an understudy for this celebrated revival of Chastoniery's *Five Heads, One Basket.*"

A mutter of disappointment and resignation came from the semidarkness in front of the stage, then a creaking of seats and a shuffle of footsteps as almost three dozen unemployed thespians rose to their feet and made their unhappy ways toward the various exits. As Imbry had specified when he had caused the casting call to appear in the appropriate media, each was clad in an unremarkable daysuit; each carried a sizeable wicker container; and each was either naturally well fleshed or had inserted padding where necessary to appear so — Vixley, the decapitating protagonist of Chastoniery's master-work, was a memorably well rounded character.

The unhappy actors wended their separate paths from the Miramance, singly or in twos or threes, some to the nearest drinkhouse, others to whatever other destinations called them. Imbry, stepping smartly to recover his own wicker grab-bag, became one of the near-identical many threading their way through Beeley Plaza. A quick pause to visit the public ablutory beneath the Arch of Tyrrhe, and he reentered the square wearing a particolored cape, a cockaded hat and towing a fabric-covered suitcase on a come-along.

A glance at his wrist told him that the plaza was awash with Bureau of Scrutiny inquisitive fluxes, but the indicators showed that the scroots were unable to narrow their focus to a single target. The thief made his way to a stand where aircars waited to be hired, negotiated terms with the first vehicle in line, and was soon aloft.

Holker Ghyll entered the small private chamber at the rear of Bolly's Snug and offered Luff Imbry an eloquently raised pair of eyebrows.

"Yes," said the fat man, "bring him in."

Imbry pulled up the hood and donned the face mask of his elision suit, so that the light in the room would now slide across its surface, effectively rendering him invisible. Moments later, the door opened again and Ghyll escorted another man into the room. The newcomer wore a long coat, fastened up the front, but in the warmth of the confined space he opened the garment. Beneath, Imbry saw the saffron and ivory livery of a subfootman of the house of Voillute.

The man's eyes darted about the room, but kept coming back to the object on the table. A beading of sweat appeared on his brow and upper lip, and he looked back toward the door as, with a soft sound, it slid closed.

"Come, come," said Imbry, making the servitor start, "you are adherents of the Computance. You would not be here if you had not already calculated that your reward outweighs your risk. No new factors have been adduced. Show me that your philosophy has meaning to you."

The subfootman drew himself up. "Very good," he said, with a sideways glance at his fellow Computant, "our numbers do not fail us."

"Show me, then," Imbry said.

The man advanced and put his hands on the life mask that sat in the middle of the table. "For your own calculations, I remind you that I have not done this myself. That is the responsibility of the major domo. But I have seen it done, often enough."

Imbry placed a purse next to the life mask so that its contents clinked heavily against the table top. "Show," he said.

The subfootman lifted the globe and peered into the cavity. "The essence appears to be well seated," he said. "There is a sequence of steps to be taken in activating the process."

"Remember, this is a first installation," Imbry said.

"The steps are the same. You touch this stud, then move this slide thusly. Wait until this indicator light achieves full brightness" — a pause ensued — "as it now has. Next, stroke the power slide until the display glows a healthy red. And there it is, ready to be worn."

"Are there particular words to be uttered?"

The subfootman moved his head in a negative, even as the corners of his mouth drew down in a facial shrug. "But Holker Ghyll said the essence has not been activated since it was taken. Therefore, you will have to explain to the essence how it comes to be meshed with a stranger's sensorium, and one

118

of the lower classes, at that. Even in life, aristocrats leap quick-and-lively onto any passing umbrage and they are not inclined to brush off explanations that try to clamber on behind them. My advice is to speak rapidly and to the point."

Imbry placed the pearly globe containing the ghost of Charan Broosh atop the seeming dresser in his operations center. He watched as his integrator connected itself to the mask's percepts. "Ready?" he said.

"Ready."

"Begin."

He had decided against the subfootman's advice. He would not don the Broosh mask and activate it by meshing the essence's sensorium with his own. Instead, he would begin by feeding the facsimile a simplified set of stimuli concocted by the integrator: a blue sky dotted with slow-moving clouds and the sound of gentle surf lapping nearby.

"The facsimile is responding," said the integrator.

"Good. Can you tell the level of mentation?"

"Not without entering into its cognitive matrix, and that would be a rough and frightening intrusion."

"Very well. Continue." Imbry now placed the Voillute globe beside the Broosh and bade the integrator activate the mask and connect itself to Waltraut Voillute's percepts. He saw her face appear out of the grayness, her eyes going immediately to the globe beside her. Her voice spoke from the air. "Is that he?"

"It is. It has just become sentient."

Not 'it'! *He*!"

Imbry's plump hand made a gesture of indifference. "He, then. If he is in fact conscious, it will seem as if he has awakened from sleep and is lying on a beach. I have not spoken with him."

"Let me."

"Wait. You must know the situation." He explained about how Broosh's essence had never been enmasked before, that it was likely his remnant had never been activated by his descendants. "He may not even be aware that he is only a facsimile."

"Connect me to him." But even as Imbry raised a finger to signal the integrator to meet her demand she said, "Wait! Let him just hear my voice, as if I were beside him on that beach."

"Very well."

"And let me sound as I did when we were young."

"Why?" said Imbry.

There now came one of those pauses in which silence conveyed meaning. Imbry realized he was about to hear something that had been willfully withheld from him.

"Because he never heard my voice as it became in later life," said Waltraut's ghost.

A list of reasons why that might have been so formed in the fat man's insightful mind: because they had squabbled and the breach was never mended; because their families had forbidden them to meet; because Broosh went off-world and did not return. But he doubted any of these would be the explanation. "He died young," he said.

"Yes."

"Tell me that it was not sudden, not an accident far from recovery services."

"He was skimming on a glacier. A crevice opened."

Imbry said a harsh word under his breath. He could visualize the scene. Skimmers could not lift themselves more than knee-high above the ground. He imagined the lightweight vehicle's gravity obviator straining ineffectively to prevent the young man's plunge into the unexpected abyss, the long fall, slow at first then gathering speed and momentum, culminating in the final smash against blue ice compressed by its own weight to the hardness of steel. And how long before his body would have been recovered and the essence taken?

Now wonder the essence had never been activated. "There may be nothing of him left," he said.

"His body was found in a pool of meltwater. It would have chilled quickly. His skull was intact."

"You are grasping at gossamers!"

The face in the globe showed agony. "I must know! At least give me that! Please!"

The fat man was not immune to sentiment, though he had no tolerance for it when it interfered with business. "And if there is nothing in there but a drooling cretin? A turnip?"

The mask's voice quavered. "Then... nothing. You may put me back in the darkness. Indeed, I would ask you to do so."

"You misunderstand," Imbry said. "I meant, if there is nothing for you, what about me? After all, life — *my* life — goes on."

The face within the globe turned toward him. "I will uphold my end of our bargain."

"You will guide me to the Bone Triptych?"

"I will."

"And not leave me to the hooks and gyres of your grandsire's retributive devices?"

"I will bring you and it safely out again."

Her mere saying of it was not enough, Imbry knew. He made her swear by several formulae so ancient that their tenets were woven almost genetically into the aristocratic psyche. Only when he could think of no other way to bind her to the undertaking did he authorize the integrator to link the two essences.

Imbry busied himself by refreshing his knowledge of the Bone Triptych. His integrator produced the only image ever published, from the catalogue that advertised the original offering of the piece for sale. The publication contained a plethora of reviews and appreciations, and a lengthy list of the persons who had come to own the work, through inheritance or purchase, until the day it had departed from the possession of Huyaq Palaam, a magnate of the first tier, under circumstances that were never explained.

That it could have been acquired by Lord Syce Voillute was not unlikely, Imbry knew. Aristocrats came in several different varieties, but it was a belief shared by all that whenever they conceived a desire that conception was intimately conjoined to a conviction of entitlement — that is, whatever they wanted they deserved. But, as the fat man delved into the history of the Voillutes, it became clear that Lord Syce had not so much possessed that belief as he had been possessed *by* it. Anything that he desired, be it a morsel on a tablemate's dish or another peer's spouse, immediately became — in Syce's mind — *his*. The original owner's continued possession of the item was from then on tantamount to theft. And Syce Voillute was not one to let his goods be pilfered.

Just as there are Lord Syces in any era, so are there Luff Imbrys. The current version had no doubt that Waltraut's grandfather had found a connection to a person of resource and enterprise who, for a fee, had made his way past all of Huyaq Palaam's keep-outs and relieved the magnate of the burden of ownership of the Bone Triptych. Syce Voillute had then sequestered the masterpiece in his secret chamber at the heart of his labyrinth, there to be enjoyed at its new owner's pleasure.

And there, the fat man reflected, it still stood. It had waited all these centuries, steadily accruing an aura of legend and mystery that Imbry was sure he could easily translate into immense, tangible wealth. It struck him, now, that were he to bring the proof of Odlemar's genius back to the light of the old orange sun — or the rays of whatever star its next owner's world might circle — that feat would be the crowning moment of his own career. It as unlikely he would ever engage in an operation to equal, let alone surpass, such a singular accomplishment.

The thought gave Imbry pause. He was not usually given to introspection. His profession required a practical mentality. He set objectives, planned the steps to achieve them, energetically carried out the schemes — with due allowance for unexpected interventions — then reaped the rewards. This operation, though, was far out of the ordinary.

Perhaps, he thought, I *should keep a record of my achievements, that they may be remembered when I am one with Syce Voillute and Huyaq Palaam.* Then it occurred to him what the consequences would be should such a history fall into the wrong hands. A stay at a contemplarium — "dining with the Archon" was the euphemism among Imbry's fellow denizens of the halfworld — would be the least of the possible repercussions. In his long career, Imbry had stolen from people whose capacity for artful vengeance made Lord Syce seem like a petulant schoolgirl. Reluctantly, he set aside the thought of composing his memoirs. He would wait until his last breath, from natural causes, was within viewing distance. And even then, he would arrange to publish posthumously.

He addressed his integrator: "How are they getting along?"

"They are conversing."

"So the young Broosh is intact?"

"It is difficult to say," said the device. "It is not a conversation of depth and complexity."

"Then we will leave them to it." But now the thought occurred that he should follow up his earlier inkling: had there been a feud between the Voillutes and the Brooshes? He told the integrator to deliver a summary of the events. The text appeared instantly, and Imbry soon saw that there had indeed been antipathy between the houses, a long-simmering acrimony that started with the diversion of a watercourse. But matters boiled over when Syce Voillute conceived an itchful lust for the young bride of a lesser member of the main branch of the Broosh line.

"Her connection to Charan Broosh?"

"Second cousin, once removed."

"Ah. Continue."

The text scrolled past, embedded with snippets from contemporary accounts of the scandal. During the reign of the Archon Shahoderam III, literary style had tended toward the ornate, so the news was couched in strained allusions and overripe metaphors. Lord Syce's "passions" were said to have been "aroused" by the sight of the young woman bathing during an afternoon lawn party at a third family's estate. Oddly enough, Imbry noted, though intimate matters were spoken of only in the most labored euphemism, mixed nude bathing had been commonplace.

The Voillute sire, "unable to contain his ardor," had "made a forthright approach" to the object of his desire. When she declined "the honor of accepting his person," he threw a picnic blanket over her head, slung her over his shoulder, and carried her off to a secluded spot. There he "expended his manly substance" in at least two of her orifices — it was difficult to tell which ones, but Imbry thought the distinctions would scarcely have mattered.

Finally, his itch well scratched, he set her loose. She returned to the party and "made strident complaints, displaying several outrageous discolorations and abrasions of her pale and tender flesh." Her husband was summoned and came at once. Lord Syce was summoned and failed to arrive. Instead, he sent a trembling major domo with the news that his lord was more profitably occupied in having his tonsure restyled.

The ravished bride was taken home. Three days later, in the morning, a formal notice of vendetta was delivered in the traditional manner: a large fish — dead, though not recently — with Lord Syce's name carved into its putrescent flank, was laid upon the doorstep of the Voillute manse in Olkney. In the afternoon, the first exchange of small-arms fire broke out on Clarrey Common. Matters escalated rapidly, and within days it was dangerous even for the completely neutral to linger in the vicinity of a Voillute or Broosh demesne. People began to say it was time for the Archon to intervene.

Over the aeons there had been thousands of archons. They came in several kinds. Some were activist by nature, and would step lively and early to prevent social dislocation. Others were inclined to let situations develop according to their intrinsic dynamics, intervening only when matters reached a stark crisis. The Archon Shahoderam III was of the latter disposition. He allowed the Voillutes and Brooshes to discharge their mutual animosity without hindrance, even to the point where heavy weapons had been brought into play and the fighting had escalated beyond skirmishes and minor forays into serious assaults. It was only when the Broosh levies came in force to strike Lord Syce's seat at Grand Minthereyon, killing the patriarch and dozens of his retainers, and reducing the estate to rubble and slag, that the Archon saw fit to intercede.

Out of a long-forgotten hangar dug into the south slopes of the Devenish Range—forgotten, that is by all except the Archonate's ancient integrators —

lifted a trio of self-directing armored cruisers. Matte black with green trim, they still bore the arms of the Archon Wei-Barson IX, who had successfully resisted the last attempted invasion of Earth by the Dree, an inimical hive species from up The Spray. The flotilla loomed over Grand Minthereyon, the Voillute estate that Broosh forces were then reducing to slag, and the leading cruiser's integrator ordered an immediate stand-down, in Shahoderam's name, on pain of dissolution of the offenders' houses.

The Voillutes, with Syce dead, at that moment lacked both leadership and their fallen patriarch's grim bloody-mindedness. They quieted their weapons and let fall their defenses. The Brooshes, unfortunately, were on a rising wave, having just achieved devastating victory. Seized by a misguided bravado, one of the Broosh commanders — it may have been he of the ravished spouse — discharged a weapon in the direction of the Archonate fleet.

By the end of that a day, the House of Broosh had ceased to exist. Its properties were seized and sold, its servants and retainers discharged to seek new employers. The family's upper tier were stripped of their names and titles and forcibly removed to several dozen different worlds, where each would live out a life of solitude, forbidden to leave the place of exile. The middle and minor ranks were instructed to attach themselves to whatever other aristocratic lineages they might be connected to, and never to mention the name of Broosh again, on pain of being sentenced to the same harsh banishment as their senior kin had received.

Since Lord Syce had paid for his transgressions with his life, the punishment for the Voillutes was to be demoted en masse to the second-tier of the aristocracy. The downgrading would remain in effect until such time as the Archon, or one of his successors, said otherwise.

When these events had occurred, Waltraut Voillute had been a woman of middle years and Charan Broosh had been dead for two decades. It explained why his essence had never been reactivated and how it, and the other ancestral Brooshes, had come to be stored in the Archonate's Grand Connaissarium, rather than in the family's essentiary.

"What are they doing now?" he asked the integrator.

"Singing."

"Has she acquainted him with his true condition?"

"No."

"Why not?"

"I surmise that she thinks it premature," said the integrator. "From their conversation so far, it is clear that he has no memory of his death, nor of the days leading up to it. The information would come as too great a shock."

"What does he know?"

"He seems to believe he lies in a half-doze on a beach and that she is beside him, engaging him in idle chatter."

"And her emotional state?"

"A kind of melancholic joy."

Imbry decided to leave the two facsimiles to it. He instructed the integrator to let Waltraut Voillute continue to soothe the young man's ghost until both achieved quietude, then to induce a simulation of sleep. "You will reawaken them when I return."

He reordered his operations center so that it again appeared to be a vacant room in a shabby house, reset the wards and defenses, and departed. He made his way by indirect routes to Quirks, where he intended first to dine and then to take one of the rooms reserved for transient members or for those who overindulged in the products of the establishment's excellent cellars. But as he alighted from a hired aircar near the steps of the drab old edifice that disguised the club's inner opulence, a large and uncompromising form placed itself in his path.

"Luff Imbry," said a lugubrious bass voice.

"You mistake me for someone else," said the fat man, attempting to skirt the obstacle, which he now saw was clothed in the green-on-black uniform of a senior officer of the Bureau of Scrutiny. But a broad-fingered hand descended onto the thief's shoulder and exerted a power that stopped all forward motion.

"No," said the scroot, "I do not."

Imbry looked up, saw a long nose that was matched by pendulous ears and a protruding lower lip, the whole creating the impression that here was an individual who had seen much to disappoint him, while any moments of happiness that might have balanced life's ledger had been too few and too short. "I do not know you," he said, ceasing to push futilely against the hand, which now left his shoulder.

"Colonel-Investigator Brustram Warhanny," was the answer, "and no, we have not met." There was a pause while the world-weary eyes studied Imbry's countenance as if committing it to memory. "But I have been hearing about you for some time."

Imbry offered an untroubled smile. "Though nothing actionable, it would seem."

"There is actionable, and then there is actionable," said Warhanny.

"I fail to detect a difference."

"It depends upon which direction what I am hearing may come from. It is one thing when word filters up to me that some item of value has vanished and that Imbry's shadow passed near the scene of the disappearance, or that

Imbry's name was mentioned in connection with the passing of an artwork about which there lingers a whiff of forgery." The broad fingers now pulled pensively at the drooping nose and the wet gaze subtly hardened. "It is another thing altogether when I enter my office and find a message from one of the Archonate's most elderly integrators instructing me to take a close interest in Imbry's comings and goings."

"Ah," said the fat man. His shoulders moved in a tiny, unconscious shrug. The chances that his disguise would have fooled the ancient device had not been as strong as he would have liked.

"And then when I do take an interest," the scroot continued, "I find myself watching dozens of close copies of the said Imbry scattering across Beeley Plaza."

"Ah," Imbry said again. There seemed no point in adding to the syllable.

"So I thought," said Warhanny, "that I would take the first opportunity to let you know that I am concerned about you. As is the Archonate's integrator. You might want to take that into account in planning your future activities."

"I might, indeed," said Imbry. "Have you any further advice?"

"Not at the moment."

"Then, if you will excuse me..." The fat man now made his way unimpeded around the black and green island and continued up the stairs into Quirks. In the club's cloakroom, he was about to shed his outer garment, but then he paused and instead took a small device from an inner pocket of his daysuit. He passed the mechanism's percept over his shoulder and heard it *peep*. He pressed a stud on the scanner's control node and watched as it located the tiny clingfast that Warhanny had attached to his collar. Imbry considered a range of strategies and chose to leave the scroot telltale where it was.

For a moment he stood in thought, projecting possible futures, some of them worrisome. Then he exercised the mental discipline that was essential to one in his profession. He drove from his mind all consideration of the scroots and the Archonate, indeed of Waltraut Voillute and the Bone Triptych. He would go in to dinner and give the products of Quirks's superb chef the full attention they deserved.

He would come back to the operation of the Bone Triptych in due time.

"How is Charan Broosh?" Imbry asked the essence of Waltraut Voillute. Three days had passed, during which the fat man had occupied himself with preparations while making every effort to determine if he was under surveillance by the Bureau of Scrutiny. It appeared that he was not, which set him to thinking. But at the end of that process, he saw no reason not to continue the operation that would be the crowning achievement of his career, conferring another kind of immortality on Luff Imbry.

"He is... well enough," was the mask's answer. "We are happy together."

"Then you will wish that happiness to continue."

"I have already said that I will do as you wish. There is no need to make threats."

Imbry made a small sound that could be interpreted in several ways. The ghost chose to take this as a contradiction of her view. "A willing steed pulls hard and steady, and needs no goad," she quoted.

"An aristocrat's attention extends no farther than his interest," the thief offered in counter-quote.

Waltraut Voillute's tone became distant. "Your principles are debased."

"Yet they serve me well in an uncertain world. I believe I will adhere to them."

In truth, Imbry's central philosophy was both broad and supple, and though founded on narrow self-interest it managed to encompass a range of corollaries that allowed him to navigate among the many complexities that life threw into his path. He selected his own goals and trusted none but himself to develop and execute the strategies that led to their fulfillment. The satisfaction he drew from his achievements could not be shared, since to have advertised his methods would only have served to smooth his path to the contemplarium.

Now he rubbed his meaty palms together and said, "But enough of this bootless badinage, as my old tutor used to say. Time to be about it." He ordered the integrator to disconnect itself from the two essences. Next he took up the globe that housed Lady Waltraut and placed it over his head. The transition passed quickly and then he was looking through their shared perceptions.

"There," he said, turning their gaze toward the mask that remained atop the seeming dresser, "is Charan Broosh. Now watch as I sequester him in this concealed compartment. There. If I return safely to this place, you will be reunited. If not..."

"What is my guarantee?" said the voice in his inner ear. "What if you take what you want then cast me aside?"

"A fair question," Imbry said. "I can only assure you that I am not cut from the same stuff as your grandsire. I cause no more pain than is needful to gain my desires. As well, it pleases me to consider myself a man of my word."

He returned her mask to its case and the room to its innocuous guise and departed. As always, he traveled by circuitous routes, with several waits and switchbacks, to shake off surveillance. He was confident that he was not under the eye of the Bureau of Scrutiny, because his wrist-watcher so advised him, and because before making his way to his operations center this morning he had transferred Brustram Warhanny's clingfast to the coat of a mercantilist who was breakfasting in the Quirks morning room and whose well fed girth nearly matched Imbry's own heroic proportions.

Eventually, he entered a tattered and roofless building on the south edge of Olkney, where crescent streets lined with modest houses and small emporia gave way to the field of ruins that had once been the suburb of Valdevar. Inside the half-tumbled structure stood a battered carryall, the dome above its passenger compartment scratched and discolored, the sides of its cargo bay dinged and dented from years of hard use.

But when Imbry had checked to ensure that the items he had specified were tucked in the tool bay and that the vehicle's energy supplies were at full brim, when he had positioned himself behind the controls and activated the initiator, he was not surprised to hear the well tuned gravity obviators run quickly up to readiness. He had hired the carryall from Gebbry Tshimshim, a fixture in Olkney's halfworld with whom the fat man had often done business.

He patted the mask case beside him on the seat and said softly, "And so it begins." These were the words that he always voiced when the preparatory stage of an operation gave way to the active. The repetition came not from superstition but from a desire, in a life that of necessity required never establishing routines through which he could be tracked and ambushed, of having some sense of continuity.

He touched the controls and the carryall rose almost silently above what remained of the building's walls. When it reached the height of the surrounding rooftops, Imbry directed it to take a southeasterly course, the first stage in a route he had worked out that would lead in time to the site of Grand Minthereyon. As he flew, he consulted the device on his wrist as well as the two instruments Gebbry Tshimshim had installed in the vehicle and saw nothing to concern him. Nevertheless, after several minutes of straight and level flight that had taken him out into a region of open meadows interrupted by copses of deciduous trees, Imbry brought the carryall down to just above the ground and followed a rough road into one of the small stands of timber.

He dismounted from the cab and retrieved an object from the tool bay, carried it to the edge of the wood and set it on the ground. The fat man spoke a coded phrase, at which the object energized itself, rose into the air and flew off along the same course Imbry had been following. If Tshimshim had set the device's systems correctly — and in Imbry's experience she never failed to meet his requirements — it would now be giving the impression to any remote surveillers that an attempt had been made to render the carryall invisible, with only partial success.

The thief waited in the shade beneath the trees until the decoy was over the horizon. He then returned to his vehicle and instructed its integrator to activate the overlapping fields of energies that would make the carryall appear to be a ground transporter of the kind commonly found in agricultural districts. Skimming just over the rutted track, he directed it to continue on through the woods and out to where the path met a graveled country road. Here he turned east and went at a trundling pace toward the county of Ambroy. By midday, after pausing to purchase a traveler's repast of bread and fresh fruit in the ancient market town of Upper Grippen, he arrange for the carryall to resemble a passenger volante then took it up to where the air grew thin. With his wards and watchers informing him that no one was taking an untoward interest in his doings, he circled back at an unremarkable speed toward his true destination.

When the tired old sun was more than halfway between zenith and horizon, Imbry touched down at the southern edge of Hember Forest, at the top of a long slope that overlooked the once populous Vale of Drom, now long since disinhabited. He backed the vehicle into the darkness beneath the intertwined branches of the high canopy and bade its integrator remain on standby. From the toolbay he extracted a folding seat and a multifaceted viewer. He found a level spot between the massive boles of two black deodars and settled himself. He instructed the viewer to observe the vine-shrouded tumulus that had once been the Summer Pavilion of Grand Minthereyon and to awaken him if anything of note should occur. Then the fat man rolled the travel-stiffness from his shoulders, stretched his flesh-padded arms, and fell into a light doze.

The sun was a half-disc bisected by the tree-serrated horizon west of the estate when Imbry brought the carryall down near the north boundary of Grand Minthereyon. He disengaged the drive and stepped out into a silence broken only by an evening breeze that stirred the flagrantha trees within the wall of the estate, but after he had stood motionless and listening for a short while, the hum and rustle of insects and small life revived around him. From the toolbay he took a harness that he swiftly strapped on over his torso. He individually checked each of the devices hung from the harness's attachers or snugged into its pouches. All were in working order, as he had expected; but he reminded himself, as he always did at this point in an operation, that if an item of equipment was going to fail, the best time to discover that fact was before one's life, limbs, or liberty depended on it.

His inspection completed, he unfolded a headpiece and slipped it on over his eyes and ears. Immediately, his senses sharpened and broadened. He applied his augmented perceptions to the wall and determined that it was unguarded. A nearby small gate, however, showed a flutter of energies sufficient to deter small creatures from passing through its bars. That fact confirmed what Imbry had suspected: that at least some of the estate's wards and watchers remained active; the place may have been abandoned for millennia, but the social upper tier of Old Earth had never stinted when providing for their own comfort and security. What they bought was meant to last.

Imbry tasked another device with analyzing the forms and frequencies of the fields and beams around the gate. It extrapolated from that information the types likely to be encountered beyond the wall and prepared itself to intercept any such inquiries and return innocuous replies. As far as whatever sentience remained in Grand Minthereyon could tell, Imbry ought to register as a large moth flittering through the twilight.

The fat man now retrieved the case that contained the life mask of Waltraut Voillute. He slipped his feet into assisted footwear then sprang lightly over the wall, landing silently on the vegetation beyond. Another sweep with his enhanced senses brought no cause for alarm, and he set off at an easy pace for the heap of slag that had been the Summer Pavilion.

His route took him through the part of the estate that had been a garden planted with ultraterrene species of flora and near-plants. He found it interesting to note which species had managed to survive without tending or encouragement in an alien environment. A stand of strangler vine had spread spectacularly, colonizing a bed of meat-flowers and diverting their ample juices through a network of hollow tubules. The walking sticks had also scattered themselves in thick patches. As Imbry passed, they took a few tentative steps toward him, though they clattered back when he made a brusque gesture. But when a fibrous black pod suddenly split open as he neared it, ejecting a hand-sized symbiote that whirred determinedly toward him while deploying barbed thorns whose tips secreted a milky substance, Imbry did not hesitate to draw a hand weapon and incinerate the thing in mid-air. The action brought an inquisitive probe from some sensor deeper within the estate, but the thief's systems quickly cozened the watcher into mistaking him for a brighter-than-usual firefly.

Imbry passed beyond the ultraterrene zone and came to a lawn that had been recently clipped and aerated. The gardener that tended the grass was nowhere in sight but the quality of its work told the fat man that the estate's awareness was not to be discounted. He consulted his own devices again and was reassured. He crossed the lawn, wove his way through what might have been a group of abstract statuary or the elements of an outdoor game abandoned in mid-play, then saw through an arched gap in a featherhedge the wall of the pavilion.

The orange sun was now set, the umber shadows of evening giving way to a purer darkness. The thief paused in the dimness of the archway and regarded the ruin ahead. The pavilion had been made of some light-colored natural stone whose elemental bonds had been internally rearranged so that the builders could whip it into the fanciful curlicues and frothy excrescences that had dominated the architectural fancies of the age. The Archonate cruiser had stood almost directly overhead when it discharged its weapon, so that the energy had melted the roof and top floors, causing them to run down the lower sides of the building like gobbets of candle wax. The gardener would have had no instructions regarding the pavilion and had therefore ignored the plant life that had inserted itself into crevices and cracks, so that creepers and hard-hangers now grown as thick as Imbry's not inconsiderable waist covered the walls in an impenetrable tangle.

Not that the fat man intended to penetrate the vegetation. The maze below the pavilion had had several entrances, one of which ought to be at the center of a flagstoned patio ringed by a low half-wall of black stone a short distance from where he stood. His augmented senses pierced the darkness without difficulty. The little plaza was where it was supposed to be. A moment later he stepped over its knee-high wall and scanned the pattern of its bicolored, checkered floor. It matched the results of his researches.

Imbry set down the leather case and drew out the mask. He removed his sensory net and lowered the globe over his head, felt its systems engage. Now he was looking at the little patio through Waltraut Voillute's eyes. Her voice spoke inside his head, a wordless syllable of surprise that slid toward melancholy.

"It hasn't changed," she said.

"The estate's systems remain functional," Imbry said, aloud but softly.

"That will be helpful," she said. "They should respond to my commands."

"But it also means that the inimical capabilities will be undiminished."

"Then you must step carefully."

"Indeed," said Imbry, "but exactly where?"

"This way," she directed him, turning her gaze toward the edge of the plaza nearest the pavilion. Imbry cooperated, turning his head that way so that they were both looking in the same direction, which brought the ruin of the building before their shared perception. Again she made a sound within his head, but this time it was an expression of shock and regret.

"None of us ever saw Grand Minthereyon again. The Archon forbade it," she said. "I had no idea. It was so beautiful, rich in fey charm. Now it is only... sad."

"It has been a long time," Imbry said. "But let us concern ourselves with the now and the immediate task."

"Yes," she said. "Look down, let me guide our eyes. There. Step on the dark square, twice and quickly." Then, when Imbry did as he was bid, she said, "Now that one, once, then step over the next. Then one to the left, tap it three times."

As the fat man finished the sequence, he heard a heavy dragging of stone over stone. A portion of the floor subsided then slid into a concealed recess, revealing a narrow flight of stone steps. "Go down," the remnant said. "It will light your way."

Imbry stepped into the dark hole. As his foot touched the first step, a pale illumination arrived from indirect sources. The stairs gradually curved, their bottom out of sight. "Are there defenses?" he said.

"Not before we reach the door. And I know the pass-safe."

"Then here we go."

The steps wound down, farther than Imbry had expected. He realized that they would be entering the labyrinth below its uppermost floor. Before he had reached the bottom, he heard from above the sound of stone passing over stone, followed by a *click*. The entrance concealed in the patio had closed over them.

As if she read his thoughts, Waltraut Voillute said, "You must trust me."

"Yes," said the fat man, "I must."

His descent brought him shortly after to a small landing beyond which stood a door of black metal, figured with a pale lozenge that enclosed the arms of the House of Voillute. "Touch the diadem in the upper right corner," came the mask's instruction, "then the goblet in the lower left. Now, tap each of the drops of blood dripping from the severed head, starting at the top."

Imbry did so, and the door divided itself vertically, the two halves withdrawing into the wall. Ahead was blackness but the air that issued from the opening smelled fresh. "Say, '*Abide, persist, endure*,'" the mask advised him. It was the Voillute motto, and when Imbry spoke the words in the voice of the

Dominance Waltraut, light filled the doorway, revealing a broad corridor whose cream-plastered walls were hung with alternating portraits and landscapes. He stepped within.

"Welcome, Dominance," said a voice from the air. "How may I serve?"

"You recognize me?" Imbry said, in the ghost's tones.

"I recognize your essence, Dominance."

"And it is sufficient to command your obedience?"

"I am not authorized to make a distinction," said the labyrinth's integrator.

"Are your capabilities intact?"

"To the best of my knowledge, Dominance."

"Then let us see how we go."

Imbry glanced at the paintings as they proceeded along the passage. None of them caught his interest; he judged that they had been acquired to suit their collector's idiosyncratic taste, not with an eye to their mercantile value. Aristocrats scarcely considered price when pursuing their hobbies; it was all the same to most of them whether they collected exquisitries or oddly shaped vegetables. Harnessing will to the satisfaction of whim was the aim of the exercise.

For Imbry, practical issues always predominated. He had known a few members of his own profession for whom the act was more rewarding than the item gained. They were addicts who craved the surge of life-energy evoked by the risks that were inherent to the craft of thievery. Imbry had not known any of them long, however; like any addict, they must increase their drug to experience the same stimulus, but raising the risk inevitably decreased the margin for error. One day the hand of a Brustram Warhanny fell upon the shoulder, or the defenses surrounding some prize overcame the thief's inadequate precautions. Then came, at best, the miserable passage to dine at length with the Archon, at worst, the sudden agonizing transformation of the flesh into lumps of malodorous char.

Such would not be the fate of Luff Imbry. He cultivated a deep aversion to risk and preferred his operations to go, as they almost always did, without the sudden appearance of the unexpected and unwished for. He was content with the course of the present proceedings, despite the entry into his plans of the Archon's ancient integrator and the Bureau of Scrutiny. Now all he wished was to make his way to the chamber that contained the Bone Triptych, seize it and be gone.

They came to a ramp and climbed, the way ahead automatically flooded with illumination while what was behind them plunged back into darkness. At the top of the incline was a wide, irregularly shaped chamber from which led five vaulted exits. The ghost turned her gaze toward the second from the right and said, "That way." Imbry pushed on.

Concealed lumens brightened to light a short corridor which brought them almost immediately into a round room that also offered five outlets. Waltraut Voillute unhesitatingly chose the first on the left and moments later, after traversing another temporarily lit passage, they came into an octagonal space, the walls covered in a shiny blue fabric into which were woven fantastically complex scenes of town and country, populated by both the high and the humble, who were engaged in pursuits that ranged from the mundane and public to, courtesy of a peek through an open window high on a palace wall, the most sophisticated and private.

Imbry saw no exit. He waited for the ghost to indicate the next step, but found his eyes being drawn by hers toward one of the panels. It depicted a trio of long-haired, flop-eared dogs romping with a little girl in a pleasure garden. The fat man crossed the floor and squatted so that his gaze was level with the smiling face of the child. He waited, while the essence of Waltraut Voillute studied the image. After a while, he put out a finger and pressed the embroidered cloth, saying, softly, "What do I do? Is it a hidden door?"

"Please do not touch the fabric, Dominance," said the integrator. "It is aged and delicate."

Imbry withdrew his hand. The mask did not answer him. "Well?" he whispered.

"This was my favorite place," her voice said in his inner ear. "I was the model for this part of the tapestry. These were my pets, Aluel, Florn and Budro." She made a small sound of affection and loss.

"We must move on."

"A few moments. What you seek has waited so long; it can wait a little more."

It was one of the fat man's rules that he would remain on the scene of an operation no longer than it took to execute his plan. Every minim more than the minimum was a betting chip offered to fortune, and eventually fortune would push forward its stack and call Imbry's bet. "There is no time for self-indulgence. We must go."

"Oh, my," teased the voice in his inner ear, "who's a timid thief?" She sounded like the girl in the image.

"Not timid. Careful."

"Let me linger."

"What means more to you," Imbry said, "a picture on a wall or reunion with Charan Broosh?"

Before she could answer, the integrator spoke. "Pardon, Dominance, but it is forbidden to speak that name."

"Speak to it," said the voice in Imbry's head. "Say that it forgets its place."

"Let us move on," the fat man said.

"I will not be spoken to like that, and by a device."

In the privacy of his mind, Imbry addressed a number of comments to Waltraut Voillute that she would have found even less acceptable. It occurred to him now that he might well lack sufficient understanding of how essences interacted with the world. Perhaps it was ill-advised to take them to their previous haunts. If so, this was possibly the worst place on Old Earth in which to discover why. He stood and said, softly, "We must not remain here."

She was still waiting for him to reprove the integrator. "Speak to it, or I will lead you in circles until your legs fail."

"You swore an oath."

"Oaths sworn by essences are not binding."

Imbry realized he had no choice. There was no way out or forward save through the increasingly unreliable remnant. "Integrator," he said, hearing her voice issue from the mask, "I will not be spoken to in that manner."

"Again, Dominance," the device said, "I beg to be pardoned. I spoke only as the Lord Syce bid me."

Prompted by the ghost, who still sounded like a petulant girl-child, Imbry said, "It has been more than four thousand years. The Archon's prohibition may be considered to have lapsed."

"Pardon, again," said the integrator, "but the ban on that name was issued by my Lord Syce, and has been frequently renewed."

A chill went through the thief. He disregarded the ghost's rising rancor and used the mask's voice to inquire, "Approximately how frequently has it been renewed?"

"Approximately," said the voice from the air, "one hundred and forty-seven million."

With effort, Imbry kept an airy tone. "And the most recent occasion?"

"Yesterday morning."

"We must get out of here," Imbry said, for Waltraut Voillute's benefit.

"Why?" came her answer.

"Because," the fat man whispered, "either the integrator has fallen prey to the 'vagues'" — he referred to the debilitating condition that could affect elderly integrators that lacked enough activity to keep their processes fresh — "or we now know where your grandfather's essence is."

The integrator spoke. "Dominance, I assure you that I am in optimum condition. I am, however, concerned by the, shall we say, unusual content of your remarks. I have thought it appropriate to summon His Potence, Lord Syce."

Imbry turned toward the portal that had admitted him to the eight-sided chamber, just in time to see the exit closed by a barred portcullis that descended swiftly and silently.

"He will arrive shortly," said the voice from the air.

The moments dragged by, the room still except for the sound of Imbry's own breathing reflected by the mask back into his ears. He had not noticed it before. The ghost of Waltraut Voillute had fallen silent, like a young girl whose naughtiness has incurred her grandfather's displeasure and who waits for his reproof. Imbry was glad of the respite; it gave him the leisure to anticipate what might be about to confront him, and to attempt to form strategies to meet the likely options.

He knew from his researches that Syce Voillute's maze had contained more than artworks and moving walls. In its punitive mode, the labyrinth could become the stalking ground of self-aware devices whose function was to pursue the aristocrat's victims, offering them no rest. They might also lurk in concealed bays or hide in the shadows of high ceilings, to spring or drop upon the unlucky passer-by.

Some were fast-movers, clattering down the corridors on segmented legs to deliver a sudden small cut or pinch away a morsel of flesh from the harried prey, only to disappear for a short while — or a long one; irregularity was part of the horror — before appearing again.

Some were slow and steady in their pursuit. The prisoner might flee, but eventually he must rest, while the stalker tracked inexorably after, its plodding pace growing ever louder, ever nearer.

Lord Syce would assign the devices in pairs or trios, coordinating their activities with rearrangements of the maze, so that the object of his displeasure would experience sustained terror, a steady wearing down of the nerves punctuated by moments of sudden agony. On one occcasion, over a period of days, his mechanisms had gradually and methodically snipped off the fingers, one by one, and then the toes, of a tradesman who had offended the aristocrat by failing to offer a proper salute. After a lengthy pause, while the poor fellow limped and groped through the darkness, following a current of air that he hoped might lead to an exit — Syce Voillute understood the importance of hope in a context of despair — the stalker reappeared and announced that it would now begin to collect the victim's remaining appendages.

The aristocrat had died in an assault by the Brooshes, incinerated by a flash-weapon. Imbry had seen the recording. But now he believed he understood where the lord's essence had been stored. instead of going to the Voillute family essentiary, as had been the custom then, it had pleased Lord Syce to install his ghost within one of the instruments of chase and butchery that populated his labyrinth.

The maze's integrator was not authorized to distinguish between essence and person because its owner, now somewhat preserved as a remnant inhabiting a device or devices housed within the underground complex, had at some time ordered it to take instructions from the Syce-essence in his absence. That way the master did not have to constantly supervise the destruction of his victims over several days or weeks — which would have been exhausting for him — but could leave his substitutes to manage the more tedious stretches. Lord Syce could refresh himself and indulge in other pastimes, coming back to the viewer when his devices informed him that a new cusp of agony was about to be reached.

When the estate was abandoned, a Syce-inhabited stalker must have been left alive. Perhaps it was finishing off some poor Broosh who had fallen into Voillute hands. Ever since, it had lingered in the labyrinth, a remnant of its master. From the maze's integrator's revelation that it had heard the injunction against mentioning the Broosh name almost a hundred-and-fifty million times, Imbry deduced that the Syce essence had deteriorated. He imagined some ancient pursuit-and-torture device, haunting the empty corridors, keeping sharp its blades and hooks, constantly talking to itself and the integrator, endlessly repeating its lord's maledictions and damnations against the Brooshes.

And now it was on its way to decide what to do with a thief whose head was surrounded by a half-mad ghost.

The stalker arrived while Imbry was seeking an exit from the chamber. It came silently, lowering itself by a thin cable from a trapdoor that had opened equally noiselessly in the ceiling, while the fat man's back was turned. When his movements about the chamber brought the device into the periphery of his vision, somewhat restricted by the mask, he immediately froze then rotated slowly to face the thing.

The spider-like entrance was appropriate, Imbry thought. The mechanism stood about as tall as his waist, but its eight multi-jointed legs were bent, so it could reach higher if it needed to. Six of the limbs were primarily for locomotion, though the hooked feet were probably useful for seizing and restraining whomever its master sent it after. Each of the front pair was specialized: they ended in hand-sized rotatable disks that were edged with a selection of tools: pincers, loops, blades, a rough-toothed rasp, a saw, an igniter, a needle-sharp spike.

Imbry tried to disregard the implements and focused instead on the device's percept array. He was hoping that its vision was not acute enough to distinguish between Waltraut Voillute and her preserved essence. But that hope was dashed when the stalker turned its eight glittering lenses on him and the integrator's voice spoke for it: "His Potence says that you are not her Dominance, the Lady Waltraut Voillute. You are an intruder wearing her countenance."

Imbry's heart sank, but he rallied and spoke softly to the ghost to whose sensoria he was linked, "If we do not change its view, you will never commune with young Charan again."

The problem with communicating with the mask was that he had to speak loudly enough for his own ears to pick up the sound and transmit it to the essence. Of course, any integrator in the vicinity would also hear what he said. As would any multi-legged lethality.

"Who speaks with her Dominance's voice?" said the integrator. "His Potence demands to know."

Imbry was waiting for Waltraut Voillute to suggest a reply, but nothing came to his inner ear. The setting and situation had apparently regressed her to young girlhood, and she had flung herself into a deep sulk. But continued silence would not serve Imbry; it must surely prompt the stalker to more intrusive means of interrogation, so he said, the mask transforming his voice, "It is I, Grandfather. Waltraut. Or at least my essence."

The stalker canted so that its back legs bent and its forward pair of locomotive limbs straightened, lifting its front and bringing its eyes closer to the mask. Imbry fought off an impulse to move back. A pair of the device's percepts extended themselves on segmented stalks and examined him at length.

"You've changed," came the voice from the air, this time in the querulous tones of an old man. Apparently, the stalker had no vocal apparatus but communicated with and through the labyrinth's integrator.

"It has been a long time," Imbry said.

The stalker returned to a more horizontal stance. "I remember you," said the voice of Lord Syce Voillute, "a little flibbertigibbet. You used to flaunt yourself in front of the young ones, especially that little dulldome of a Broosh..."

Waltraut Voillute was suddenly back in force, bending Imbry's inner ear with bitter protestations that she wanted him to make. The thief thought it better not to interrupt a murderous device animated by the essence of an even more murderous aristocrat.

"...but I did for that one," the voice went on, "didn't I just? And they all thought it was an accident. Ha! Shlumps! Pinchwits! I fooled them."

The ghost in Imbry's ear was now shrieking at him, in lieu of being able to acquaint her grandfather with her revised opinion of his worth and quality. His own voice overcame her resistance, however, and he said, "Oh, Grandfather, you always did know best."

"What are you doing here?"

Imbry improvised. "The Archon sent me."

"Oh, him." The voice made a sound like air escaping from a small aperture. "He spoiled everything."

"Indeed. But there is a new Archon now, and he regrets the injustice that was done to you. He sent me to offer a means for you to be reinstated in rank and for the estate of Grand Minthereyon to be restored to your name."

"Let me speak to him," Waltraut dinned in the fat man's ear. "Killed my affianced, did he? Consigned me to a life of spinsterhood? I'll blister his hairy eardrums."

"He has no eardrums, hairy or otherwise" Imbry said, softly. "He is an essence in a device."

"Who's an essence in a device?" said the stalker through the integrator. The mechanism reared up and examined the mask again, then dropped and studied Imbry's figure beneath the globe. One of the forelimbs produced its spike and poked at his torso. He edged back. "Who's in there?" the integrator said.

"Waltraut, Grandfather," Imbry said.

The spider circled him, its percepts peering at him. "If you're Waltraut," the voice said, "what did I give you for the tenth anniversary of your naming day?"

Imbry waited for the information, but Waltraut was not helpful. She was embarked on a catalogue of insults, and Imbry was flabbergasted by the depth and breadth of the profanity at her command. So overpowering was the effect that he had lost track of whether the inventive calumnies were directed at him or at Lord Syce.

"Well," said the integrator. "Answer."

The thief considered several options and chose the most likely. "A pony?" he said.

There was a silence. Then the integrator said, "His Potence says, 'What was its name'?"

Imbry made a desperate attempt. "I always called him, Syce, after my favorite relative."

This remark brought from Waltraut Voillute a torrent of new opprobria, even more scathing than hitherto. Aristocrats tended to indulge themselves in abstruse intellectual and artistic pursuits; he wondered if Waltraut Voillute's penchant had been for polysyllabic profanity. She had certainly mastered the genre.

"His Potence demands to know the name he bestowed on the beast."

"It has been a long time, grandfather," Imbry said, over the internal din of abominations and obscenities, "I seem to have forgotten."

Another silence. The fat man wondered if the spider's limited intellectual resources, married to those of a deteriorated essence — whose original had likely not been entirely sane — were unable to cope with the ambiguities of the situation. He sought to direct the current of events and said, "About the Archon —"

Unfortunately, ambiguity was not a deterrent to action, he learned. The spider again reared on its high legs, though this time it was not interested in inspection. Imbry reacted by reaching for a pocket on his harness that held a device that would have been useful. But he was not fast enough. From four orifices on its abdominal surface shot jets of a thick pale liquid that, as they struck Imbry, simultaneously hardened and adhered. The device skittered about him with unnerving speed, its front limbs working rapidly to wrap him in a cocoon of confining threads that proved to be more than a match for human muscle. His hand ended up stuck fast to his chest.

In a trice he was trussed. The spider ended its circular dance, bent its limbs to lower itself, and used its forelimbs to hook the threads that bound his ankles. A swift yank and Imbry felt himself toppled backwards like a short, plump tree, his fleshy padding offering no protection as his buttocks and shoulders painfully struck the floor. Then the back of his globular headgear smacked hard against the checkered stones; the clasp at the rear parted and the mask fell away, its connectors lacking time to disconnect, so that Imbry felt hair and skin tear loose.

The spider did not notice. It was dragging him now across the small chamber to where a portion of the floor had opened. A ramp led steeply down into pitch-blackness, and into this Imbry was helplessly drawn. As he tipped, feet-first onto the incline, the lumens in the octagonal chamber extinguished. Darkness was absolute.

Their progress took an unmeasurable time. He was dragged across surfaces smooth and rough, over polished stone and plush carpet. In one place he heard dripping water, in another currents of dank air played across his face. Sometimes he was slid down other inclines; once he was pulled down a flight of steps, his skull bumping on each riser. Finally, he heard a grating of stone on stone and a few moments later their journey ended. He could hear the stalker clacking about on a hard floor, the harshness of the sounds telling him that he was in a substantial chamber that must also be walled in stone.

He felt a tug at the back of his neck, then suddenly he was rising, head first, to hang in the darkness. Blind, he could not know if was suspended just above the floor or over a bottomless pit. Then the lumens came on and, blinking, he looked about and saw that he was in a utilitarian chamber of dressed stone. The walls were festooned with a welter of devices and equipment that might have been the tools of a mechanist — but Imbry soon saw that these tools had all been designed to work on human flesh and bone. And their function was the opposite of repair.

He remembered what Waltraut's ghost had said: *The old man had built a concealed chamber at the heart of the labyrinth into which he would take only the most special visitors — so special that not one of them ever came out alive.*

He turned his head to left and right, and from the corner of his eye he saw a hint of paleness. He wriggled and swung as best he could, trying to make his suspended form rotate, and was rewarded with a brief glimpse of an object the stood against the wall, behind him and to one side.

It was the Bone Triptych.

The stalker, meanwhile, was paying him no heed. It was making its way from one wall to another, examining and choosing different apparatuses of torture. It brought its selections to a low stone-topped table near the center of the room, laying them out like a cook preparing to attempt a complex recipe. Now it paused to eye Imbry critically, then returned one of the items to its place on the wall, choosing instead a loop of coarse wire along whose inner circumference were set several rows of small triangular teeth made of metal that was obscenely stained. When this last object had joined the others on the stone tabletop, the stalker minutely adjusted the positions of a few of its tools, then stepped back and regarded Luff Imbry.

"Well," it said through the integrator's voice, coming as always from a point that seemed to hover near the hanging man's ear, "and here we are." It studied him a moment, then said, "You no longer seem to resemble my granddaughter."

"Her essence accompanied me, but became detached in the octagonal chamber."

"How did that occur?"

Imbry began to explain the custom of setting essences into life masks, so that the ghosts' descendants could share perceptions with them. The essence of Syce Voillute took an interest in the issue and asked several questions, then followed up on the answers. But, at last, came the question Imbry wished to avoid. "But you are not one of her descendants nor mine. How came you to wear her essence? What is your rank?"

"Rank is irrelevant, since I am engaged on a mission for the Archon."

"So you said," replied the spider, its front limbs idly repositioning some of the implements on the stone table top. "But where is your sigil? Where is your plaque? How do you identify yourself?"

Imbry tried a smile. "Mine is an informal mission."

"So you are not an official of the Archonate?"

"Not as such. An independent contractor."

The eight glittering lenses regarded him through a lengthening moment. Then the voice spoke near his ear. "And the goal of this 'informal mission'?"

"As I said, to reinstate your rank and restore your family's title to this estate."

"Such magnaminity. And am I required to make some small gesture in return?"

Imbry saw hope. The question sounded like the opening of a negotiation, a territory in which he was at ease. "The Archon wishes to place the Bone Triptych in the Grand Connaissarium." He added quickly, "With full recognition to you and your family for having returned it to the world."

"Indeed?" said Syce-as-spider. "What a generous Archon."

"Such is his repute."

One set of the stalker's pincers picked up a short-bladed knife, while the other forelimb took up a fine-toothed file to slide along the implement's edge. "And how did he come to know it was here? After all these years?"

"Your granddaughter knew."

"Ah." File and knife went back to the table top. "That completes it."

"So can we dispense with these present... arrangements," Imbry said, "and proceed to the happy moment when all our goals are met?"

"Just one more question."

"Please," said Imbry, "ask."

"What does my granddaughter's essence gain from this general happiness?"

Imbry chose his words carefully. "The pleasure of bringing about your reinstatement?"

"That seems unlikely. She was never a doting child."

"To be of service to the Archon is a great honor."

The spider had noticed a spot of rust on a heavy-bladed cleaver. It now scoured it away with a scrap of abrasive cloth. "Nor did she care much for honors."

"It is not for me," said Imbry, "to speculate on the motives of my social superiors."

"Yet I invite you to do so," said the ghost of Syce Voillute, while the spider flourished the cleaver encouragingly.

"There may have been something she mentioned. I don't recall."

"Try."

"An idle whim, nothing of importance."

"Tell me."

Imbry could think of nothing to say.

Syce said, "Let me guess: it had to do with some childhood infatuation."

Another silence grew. Then even the equanimity of an integrator's voice somehow managed to convey the depth of black hate and savage spite contained in the single syllable: "Broosh!"

"That might have been the name," Imbry said.

The spider was dancing on its six ambulatory limbs, the two forelimbs splitting the air, the one that still held the cleaver doing so quite close to the fat man's suspended form. A stream of invective, as rich and imaginative as any that Imbry had heard from the granddaughter — *That's where she learned it*, came the unbidden thought — poured into his ear in the integrator's disinterested tones.

After a considerable time, Syce Voillute's fury subsided. The spider returned the cleaver to the table top and stood for a while contemplating Imbry. Then the voice said, "Here is how I see it: the Archon is not involved. You are some kind of thief. My granddaughter has enlisted you to break into my private premises and steal the Bone Triptych."

"No. That is not —"

The voice cut him off. "She was always a willful child. That's why she took up with that noddy of a Broosh. Just to spite her old grandfather."

"No, no," said Imbry. "She revered —"

The spider reared up again and shot a jet of its sticky fluid straight at Imbry's mouth. He shut his lips to prevent the stuff from choking him and immediately found that he could not reopen them.

"That's better," said the ghost. "No need for interrogation. I have the story now. We will proceed to the giving of satisfaction."

Imbry expected the spider to reach for one of the tools of torture. Instead it clattered over to where the three-paneled bone screen stood against the wall, seized the object in its pincers and brought it fully into the hanging man's field of vision. It unfolded the triptych then reached up to where a light pipe was suspended from the ceiling and positioned the source of illumination so that its output fell onto the outer edge of the first panel. The spider moved to a corner, where it settled onto its folded limbs. As it did so, the other lumens in the room dimmed to extinction, leaving only the natural glow from the light pipe.

Imbry was seeing the triptych much as its creator had wished it to be seen, though Odlemar had probably not envisioned a spectator hanging trussed from a hook in a torture chamber. But the light pipe drew its energy from sunlight naturally captured from the world above and stored for later use. Thus its glow touched the edge of the first panel as if the screen stood in a well windowed room, positioned so that the dull orange light of early morning crept across it. Gradually, the glow brightened and lightened in tone. Now, despite his predicament, Imbry found himself being captured by the grand genius imbued into the work.

It was said that to sit for a day in contemplation of Odlemar's masterpiece was to be transformed. In the time it took the sun to swing across the sky, spotlighting in turn each of the three scenes, the sensitive observer would vicariously live an ideal life.

And it is true, Imbry thought, as the light built in strength on the first of the three scenes. The androgynous figure, created in bas-relief from the once-living bone of the carver, posed against an etched background of an archetypal arcadian landscape, seemed to stand forth with all the energy and promise of pure youth. Somehow, as the sublime arrangement of form and line filled his vision, Imbry was transported back to the time of his own tender years, when hope sprang as clear as springwater, and his expectations were unquestioned. For a moment, a long moment, the present fell away and he *was* that youthful Luff Imbry, once more on the threshold of the great adventure of existence, saying to the world: *I shall be and I shall do.*

Quartet and Triptych

The light moved on, brightening now to full day. Imbry realized, at some level, that the light pipe was delivering its effect far faster than would have been possible if the triptych were standing in true sunlight. Yet the process remained no less profound, as the focus departed from the youth in the first panel and as the semblance of warm sunlight came to play across the central panel. Here strode a figure embodying mature accomplishment, traversing another landscape — this one evoking the themes of middle life: worldly engagement, achievement, renown, family — and again Imbry could not help but be swept by emotion. He saw his own successes, the stature he had won, the meaning that his struggles and attainments had conferred upon his existence. He felt a flood of justifiable pride, of having lived up to his potential, of being able to say: *I am and I do.*

And then the light moved on, and now it gently faded, touching the third panel, another figure in another landscape: this one a personage of dignity and repose, set against a background of settled calm. Imbry had not yet left the prime of life, had not entered the time of reflection and denouement; yet, somehow, Odlemar's vision was carried into the center of his being, and he knew what it would be to look back upon a life well lived, to understand its rhythms and currents, and to perceive how they shaped toward an end and a conclusion. He knew what it would be to stand at the end of the road, in evening's dimming radiance and say: *I was and I did.*

And now, as the light shrank toward darkness, even as Imbry again became fully conscious of his situation, hung helpless in the dungeon of a vicious aristocrat who had been far from sane when living, and whose mad and deteriorating essence was housed in a device built for the cruelest pursuits, still some of Odlemar's sublime summing-up of life filled him. The emotion evoked a sigh that could not pass Imbry's sealed lips.

Then, just as the light pipe mimicked the last beams of the old orange sun fading into sunset, a sudden and brief change appeared in the triptych: for only an instant, though it was an unforgettable instant, each of the three carved figures — energy, accomplishment and completion — seemed to stand forth anew. Though, this time, they were revealed as three species of self-deluded fool. No sooner had the sudden impression registered, delivering a psychic shock to Imbry's core, eliciting a smothered gasp that came from far deeper in his being than merely the region where his respiratory equipment operated, than the whole triptych became indistinct in the light pipe's simulation of deepening dusk.

The integrator's voice spoke from the darkness. "Whence came that glimpse of stark folly? From Odlemar's brilliant hand and eye? Or is it a reflection of your own inadequacy?"

Imbry realized that the line was from some favorite script of Syce Voillute's. No answer was required. And none was waited for, as the integrator spoke on: "And now let us move on."

The lumens came to life again, the triptych was put aside, and the spider returned to the table. Selecting the short-bladed knife it had sharpened before, it fixed the glitter of its visual array on Imbry's feet, suspended just above the floor. "First," it said, "we'll have those boots off." And then it advanced toward him.

Imbry closed his eyes, though he did not anticipate being able to keep them that way for long. But the stimulus that caused him to return to vision was not the pain that he expected in his lowest extremities. Instead it was a *whump!* and a *whoosh!* from the far side of the chamber. He opened his eyes to see the wall of tools crumbling inwards, scattering fractured masonry and horrid implements in a dust-haloed fan across the floor. The thick and billowing cloud of powdered stone obscured the large figure that stood in the newly created gap, but Imbry was able to see that, tucked in the crook of one arm, was the globe that contained the essence of Waltraut Voillute.

The person now stepped into the chamber and the spider swung itself about with dreadful speed, its joints bending as it compressed its legs for a leap. But the man holding the mask had another arm, one that ended in a hand that gripped a fully powered disorganizer. Before the spider could spring, the man discharged the weapon; a coherent beam of black energy swept across the stalker's locomotive limbs, converting them to random particles that joined the dust still filling the air. The spider crashed down onto its metal belly with a *clang!* and the man completed its disarmament by aiming the disorganizer and carefully destroying the device's forelimbs.

He then stepped around the table, depositing as he did so Waltraut Voillute's mask atop the tool kit there displayed. "You'll be surprised to see me," he said.

Imbry could only nod in agreement. If he had been tasked to compile a list of those who might even remotely be expected to rescue him at this moment, the list would not have included Colonel-Investigator Brustram Warhanny of the Archonate Bureau of Scrutiny.

The scroot had been casting his disappointed gaze about the chamber. Now he had found what he had been looking for: a metal flask with an atomizer set in its neck. This he took up and directed first at the stuff that coated Imbry's lips — the thief tasted bitterness as the sealant dissolved — then at the bonds that confined his limbs. A moment later, the fat man fell the short distance to the floor, where he managed to stand though he tottered on numbed feet.

"You are correct," he said, after wiping the last gummy shreds from his mouth. "But I would have been surprised to see anyone."

"You should have more respect for the Bureau," Warhanny said.

Imbry replied that he supposed that from now on he would have no choice but to do so. But the scroot had turned his attention to the bone screen leaning against the wall. "And this would be what it has all been about," he said, standing the triptych up and partially unfolding it.

"So it would seem," Imbry said. He looked toward the gap in the wall and wriggled his toes. Circulation was returning.

"You won't get far," said Warhanny, his eyes still on the artwork. "The moment I showed the integrator the Archon's sigil it came under my direction. Run if you like, but there are devices that will catch you and bring you back." He turned his joyless gaze on the fat man. "And they are not accustomed to bestow gentle treatment."

He crossed the floor to where the spider lay helpless, pressed a stud on its dorsal surface and reached into the hatch that popped up. He drew out a flat black cylinder much like that which had contained the essence of Charan Broosh. "Might as well return this to the Voillute essentiary," he said, "though I doubt anyone will want to consult it."

He placed the essence in a pocket of his green-on-black uniform and returned his gaze to Imbry. The thief had brushed away the last remnants of the stuff that had bound him and now he stood erect to say, "Well, I am snapped up, fair enough. But I will not play the Poonka for leniency."

The reference was to an Emor Poonka, a mid-level denizen of Olkney's halfworld who was infamous for having spent years informing on scores of his colleagues to the Bureau of Scrutiny. In the presence of a scroot, Imbry did not follow the name of Poonka with the customary expectoration, but his distaste for the idea of "turning spout" was not lost on Warhanny, who replied, "But you are not snapped up."

For a moment Imbry was lost for a reply. Then he said, "Not? Not snapped up?"

"My orders were specific," the scroot said, without emotion, though the expression on his face spoke eloquently of disgust and puzzlement. "You were to be rescued, the triptych to be recovered, and the old man's essence taken to his descendants."

Imbry was accustomed to a life of nuanced judgements, of compromises and looking the other way. But he had not expected such from the Bureau. "Whose orders?" he said.

Warhanny's face regained its impassivity. "I do not know," he said. "Someone high in the counsels of the highest, or so I gather."

Or some thing *high above the ordinary comings and goings of Olkney,* Imbry thought. "I don't know what to say," he said.

"The situation is unusual," the scroot agreed. "You seem to figure, in some way, in the progress of esteeming the balance. I would not take great comfort in it."

Imbry thought about it for a moment, then said, "No, I suppose not." To be singled out for the attention of the Archon, or even one of his ancient integrators, was no blessing. He was sure there would be a price to pay for his continued freedom, and the prices exacted by the Archonate could strike the ordinary decent criminal as exorbitant.

Warhanny gestured for him to pick up the globe that contained the ghost of Waltraut Voillute. Imbry did as he was bid. Then the scroot hefted the bone screen and climbed through the gap, the thief following. They passed through lighted corridors and chambers, all of them displaying works of power and beauty, some of them capable of delivering a significant impact even to a connoisseur of Imbry's sophistication. And then, as they traversed one circular room, on a pedestal cunningly lit, Imbry saw the little quartet of Iphigenza dancers. Warhanny ignored it, oblivious of all but his duty, but the fat man put out a hand in passing, scooped up the group of metal figurines and slipped it into the breast of his singlesuit. He raised the life mask in both hands to disguise the lumps beneath the cloth.

Warhanny paused and looked back at him for a moment. Imbry understood that the theft had not gone unnoticed. But then the other man gave only the tiniest, briefest lift of his hedgelike eyebrows and walked on.

They came out of the labyrinth by ascending the steps that had led Imbry into it. The night was trending toward dawn. A Bureau volante hovered a hand's height above the patio. Warhanny went to it and opened a cargo bay, storing the screen within.

"What does the Archon want with the Bone Triptych?" Imbry asked.

The scroot gave him a dry look. "The moment he deigns to tell me, I will let you know." A canopy lifted to admit him to the operator's compartment and he climbed in and seated himself. But before he lowered the dome he pointed to the globe in Imbry's hands and said, "You ought to return that."

"I mean to." The statement might well be true. Imbry hadn't yet decided on his future moves.

"And the Broosh essence to the Grand Connaissarium."

"They will be unhappy apart," Imbry said.

Warhanny regarded him quizzically. "I had not taken you for a romantic," he said.

"Nor I," said Imbry. He was not sure where the impulse to make the remark had come from. He moved to a more pertinent subject: "Is there any point asking how you managed to track me?"

"The Bureau guards its secrets," Warhanny said. It sounded to Imbry like a reflexive remark. He responded with a small motion of his head; he had not really expected an answer. So he was surprised when the scroot added, "I'll give you this much respect. It was not we who had you in view. I received these coordinates when I was ordered to come and rescue you."

"Not the Bureau?"

The Colonel-Investigator moved his head in a slow negative. Then he pointed his index finger upward and rotated it in a small circle. Imbry recognized the universal signal for the Archon.

The scroot had nothing more to say. He closed the volante's canopy and increased the flux to its obviators. Imbry turned his face away from the whoosh of air and when he looked back the aircar was above the trees and moving silently away.

The entrance to the labyrinth had sealed itself. Imbry thought briefly about attempting to induce Waltraut Voillute to reopen it. Considerable wealth lay beneath his feet. Then he recalled how unreliable a support the ghost had turned out to be, and he pictured all the other stalkers and grabbers sure to be hidden in the shifting chambers and passageways. He tucked the globe beneath his arm, patted the bulge that the Iphigenza figures made in his garment, and turned toward the garden of the alien exotics and the carryall that waited beyond the wall.

Several members of the hard-core cadre of the Green Circle syndicate were celebrating in the room adjacent to the small chamber in the rear of Bolly's Snug that Luff Imbry had booked for his next meeting with Holker Ghyll and the Voillute subfootman. The Computant was late, and finally entered wearing an expression that mingled apprehension with confusion.

"What is wrong?" Imbry said, and when he looked beyond Ghyll and saw no one else, he said, "Where is he?"

"He did not come."

"Did he not contact you to say why?"

"No."

Imbry could tell there was more that Ghyll was reluctant to reveal. He waited, the room silent except for the muffled sounds of revelry from next door. While Ghyll shuffled his feet, the fat man said, "Tell me all of it."

The other man did not meet his eyes but stared instead at the leather case on the table. "He has not attended a computation since we all met here some days ago."

"You made inquiries?"

"To no avail. I have another contact among the Voillute staff. When I named the subfootman and described him, I was told..."

Imbry saw the shape of it. "You were told that no such man was known."

Ghyll's fear made his gesture of confirmation a sharp jerk. "Was he..?" he said, completing the query with the rude positioning of fingers that was half-world code for the Bureau of Scrutiny.

Imbry signaled a negative. "Worse," he said, and made the same circling of a plump finger that Warhanny had used.

Holker Ghyll turned pale. "What have we stepped into?"

Imbry's only response was a deep inward breath blown out through puffed cheeks. "Time alone will tell," he said.

"You do not —" Ghyll began, then seemed to choke on something dry in the back of his throat. He cleared the airway then tried again. "You do not fault me?"

"I do not," Imbry said.

"Then you will forgive my not lingering." And at the thief's dismissive nod, Holker Ghyll made an unceremonious departure.

Imbry sat back and drummed his fingers absently on the table. Any citizen of the Archonate, finding that he had become an item of interest to the Archon or his inner circle, had cause for concern. The Archon's view was large and did not always take into account the fate of individuals. As the old expression had it, *Grain may grieve; the stones will grind.* But Imbry was no ordinary citizen. For a member of the halfworld to feel the Archon's basilisk gaze prickling his shoulder blades was doubly worrisome.

But he could think of nothing to be done. "We will just have to see," he said. He took up the vermilion leather case that contained the ghost of Waltraut Voillute and made his way to his new operations center. This was in a different suburb of Olkney, one of a pair of houses that Imbry had acquired through intermediaries a long time ago, and between which he had personally dug a connecting tunnel. It was equipped with duplicates of all his professional paraphernalia; the only thing he had brought from the old place, before setting it afire, was the integrator's core and the essence of Charan Broosh.

He had long since removed the subtle tracker that had been woven into the circuitry of the Voillute life mask. He had attempted to study it, but was surprised to have found himself unable to grasp its operating principles; they were certainly radically different from those of the Bureau's clingfasts. The closest parallel systems Imbry's researches could find could only be described as "magic", and the fat man was not one to swallow nonsense. He wondered if the device's operating principles had been imported from one of the other eight dimensions that were supposed to exist. In the end, he gave up worrying about it. The Archon moved in his own ways, and to his own rhythms. If Luff Imbry had become one of the pieces on Filidor's game board, there was nothing the thief could do to alter his situation.

But he still, as ever, had the scroots to take into account, even more so now that Brustram Warhanny's attention had been drawn to his file. Thus he took extra precautions in traveling to and from his hidden place. On this visit he meant to spend only the briefest time there, just enough to deposit the fringed case in a concealed storage closet and depart. He had a crucial appointment at Quirks, to begin the delicate process that would lead to the disposal of the Iphigenza quartet. But when he had put the case in its hiding place and was moving toward the exit, he stopped and turned back.

After a moment's thought, he retrieved the mask and brought out also the cylinder that contained the essence of Charan Broosh. Deftly, he connected the two devices to each other, fitting them with a few supporting elements and a long-term power supply. Only when he was sure that they were once again together on their timeless shore did he put the two ghosts back into storage.

He was breaking Warhanny's command to return the essences to where they belonged. He was also giving Waltraut Voillute more reward than she had earned, since she had not brought him safe out of her grandfather's clutches. And to what remained of Charan Broosh it could not be reasonably said that he owed anything at all.

But if the two ghosts did not deserve to lie companionably together in the illusory warmth of a nonexistent beach, Imbry was conscious that one day — perhaps soon — he might have to argue, for himself, that justice should sometimes be tempered by sentiment. In such a case, example was always more telling than mere precept.

As a hired aircar wafted him back to his club, above the jeweled blaze that was Olkney at night, the thief looked up at the dark mass of the Archonate Palace and mentally extemporized a few opening lines of a defense.

Then he shook his head to clear his thoughts. He must concentrate on the man waiting for him at Quirks, and the negotiations into which they would shortly enter.

Practicality and calculated prudence, he quoted in the cool privacy of his mind. *Do what you can with what you have.*

With the Iphigenza eidolons, Imbry meant to do quite a bit.

ENEMY OF THE GOOD

The first indication that anything was amiss with the hired aircar came when its integrator began to reminisce about the peccadilloes of its original owner, who (or so the integrator said), had built his life around erotic encounters so zestful and rife with embellishment that the details surprised even as well seasoned a man as Luff Imbry.

The recollections intruded upon Imbry's mellow mood, which was the result of his latest operation having achieved its aims on all points. Before the aircar suddenly began to regale him with descriptions of a stranger's unusual tastes and the partners who catered to them, Imbry had been sitting in ease and contentment on the volante's bench seat, his sausage-like fingers interlaced over the grand mound of his stomach.

Beside him was a bag comprehensively stuffed with what had lately been the prized griffhorn collection of Filhentian Depro. Depro had made the mistake of leaving the fruits of decades of collecting lying around where Imbry could get at them. Depro would not have shared this estimation of his laxity, just as he wouldn't have shared his intricately carved griffhorns with anyone, but the locks and wards that he had established to guard his goods were, to a thief of Imbry's caliber, not much more of an obstacle than if they had been fashioned from air and smoke.

But Imbry's mellowness was now rapidly diminishing under the welter of improbable specifics that filled the aircar's retrospections of its first owner's ardent antics. "Cease your prattle," he said. "Attend to the flying, and leave me to my thoughts."

That should have settled the matter, but the integrator rambled on, recalling a memorable occasion when it had carried its owner and two companions out to the remote forest above the Shevaen Lakes, for an *al fresco* frolic that featured strong ropes and pulleys and a casaba melon ripened to perfection.

"Enough!" said Imbry. "Or when we return to the depot I shall insist on your being torn down and rebuilt. My experience tells me that that is a process few integrators enjoy."

Yet still the aircar burbled on. Imbry was learning more about the qualities of casaba melons than he had ever cared to know. He was also becoming concerned that the integrator might be dangerously unstable; the firm from which he had hired the aircar had a well tested reputation for discretion, but no particular standing when it came to the maintenance and upkeep of its fleet. To be several thousand feet in the air, flying over one of the many desolate patches of Old Earth, in the figurative hands of an integrator that had gone "quirksome," to use the technical term, was a cause for concern.

Imbry shifted his huge bulk forward on the seat and reached for the control yoke. One touch would transfer operation of the volante from the integrator to his own plump hands. But that touch was suddenly beyond the thief's capability. The aircar abruptly accelerated forward; at the same time, it angled sharply upward. Imbry was thrown back against the seat then subjected to a series of side thrusts and head-spinning course changes as the volante jinked and deked and swerved recklessly through the upper air.

The violent maneuvers should have caused the aircar to encushion him within a firm but flexible webwork, but the hatch from which the safety gear should have been emitted remained closed. Meanwhile, as Imbry bounced painfully around the passenger compartment like a very large pea in a not very large whistle, the integrator did not miss a syllable of its salacious account of how the innocent melon met a fate arguably worse than death.

The aircar dropped precipitously, sending Imbry's innards flying up into his throat, then it began to rotate at an alarming speed. An odor of ozone, accompanied by a crackling as of fire rapidly consuming dry twigs, assaulted the thief's senses. Centrifugal force had him pressed up against the side and ceiling of the compartment's dome-shaped transparent cover, and he could see that their careering about the sky had become so wide and erratic that it was but a matter of time before the volante buried itself in one of the arid, rocky slopes Imbry could see below, then above, then beside him, as the volante's gyrations dizzyingly affected his perceptions.

A sudden up-jerk then a long left bank led to a brief interval of level flight, though the sky was now seemingly below and the hills above. Imbry, lying on the transparent canopy and hoping it would not open to thrust him into emptiness, lunged for the yoke and yanked it towards him. Since the vehicle was flying upside-down, his effort caused the aircar to arrow toward the ground. But now that the integrator, still rambling through erotic irrelevancies, was no longer driving the volante, Imbry soon had the vehicle back on course.

But more was wrong with the aircar than its operator's instability. The smell of combustion grew stronger, and the fat man could sense an undue warmth radiating from the floor. He peered forward through the canopy, looking for a place to set down, but the landscape was not cooperating. He was over a desert, but not that breed of desert that offered soft and plentiful heaps of sand in which to gently nestle a wounded aircar. Instead, it was all steep and rocky slopes leading up to sheer cliffs of rust-red or blond sandstone. Between the hills and buttes lay narrow, twisting canyons, some of them so deep that their bottoms must be in permanent shade. The tops of the high mesas were flat, but even if he could have coaxed the now rapidly failing volante to ascend to one of them, Imbry was ill-built for mountaineering, even with gravity to assist him.

He was now between two sets of high cliffs that lined a deep and snaking canyon, the aircar steadily losing height, and dropping even faster every time Imbry had to bank to match a turn in the arroyo. Ahead, he saw that the floor of the chasm rose to become level with the bases of the slopes on either side, creating a flat, though boulder-strewn, passage between the heights. The pass could not be called wide, though he hoped it would prove wide enough. He aimed the aircar for the open ground and strove to dull its too-sharp angle of descent. The heat from the floor had now grown so intense that the soles of his boots felt like hot plates and the acrid reek of simmered components drew tears from his eyes and a hacking cough from his lungs. And still the integrator tittle-tattled on, lost in carnal memory.

"Shut up!" Imbry said, but to no effect. The yoke was becoming less and less responsive by the moment. Through burning eyes and thickening skeins of smoke he sought to find a clear path among the boulders, some of them house-sized, that littered the floor of the pass. He spotted a patch of empty ground and aimed for it. The vehicle was still coming down too fast and too steeply, and he hauled back on the controls in hopes of diminishing both speed and angle. But hope's only reward was to feel the yoke come away from its last connections to whatever was burning beneath the floor.

Imbry said a short word that was irrelevant to the circumstances, though by pure coincidence it jibed closely with the gist of the integrator's continuous tattling. His finger jabbed the stud that manually activated the safety webbing and in a moment the thief was cocooned in its sentient mesh. In the moment after that, the volante made contact with the ground.

It was a grinding, grating, spinning, sparking contact, loud enough even to drown out the sound of the integrator's cheerful salacity. The vehicle struck nose-first but the ground was too hard to be penetrated and so the aircar, its front farings crumpled, somersaulted back up into the air only to pancake down again then slide forward while rotating sideways, bouncing off rocks of moderate size until it slid up and half over a flat wedge of stone that had fallen a thousand years before from the cliff above.

155

Inside the passenger compartment, Imbry triggered the control that loosened his webbing and was gratified to find that it worked. The crash had buckled the flooring and now thick smoke and dull red flames were billowing up from between his feet. The canopy was briefly less cooperative, but beneath his well upholstered exterior, the fat man possessed a muscular strength that had surprised many, and dismayed quite a few. He put his feet on the bench and his shoulders against the dome. When he heaved, the transparency popped free of its retainer and, a moment later, Imbry was out and putting distance between himself and the aircar. Above the rising snap-and-crackle of flames he could briefly hear the integrator's voice saying something about "a well warmed aubergine," then the blaze began to roar in earnest.

In Imbry's hand was the bag of griffhorns. He did not remember snatching it up, but was not surprised to find he had done so; his instincts were always reliable. He stepped farther away from the burning volante, found a boulder of the right size and sat to consider his situation.

Aircar integrators, though not particularly noted for their stability, were equally not subject to the kind of solipsistic irregularity that had struck Imbry down in mid-escape. The likelihood was strong that some external agency had been at work. The fat man pursued the thought with the kind of dedication that beasts bred for hunting bring to their most active days.

First he considered Gebbry Tshimshim, from whom he had rented the volante, back in the city of Olkney, capital of those parts of Old Earth still inhabited by human beings in the ancient planet's penultimate age. By the nature of her trade, she was a fixture in the criminal underpinnings of Olkney's social order, and therefore fundamentally untrustworthy. But she and the corpulent thief had done business often, always to their mutual satisfaction, and by acting against his interests she would deprive herself of a regular client while risking the possibility that he might survive to take a revenge that would be prolonged and inventive, as he had been known to do when grievously disappointed.

No, it was unlikely to be Gebbry Tshimshim, unless someone even more frightening than Imbry had altered her understanding of where her best interests lay. But that would mean that one of his enemies — and he had them; it was hard to pursue his profession without acquiring a few resenters and ill-wishers — had become aware of his plans for Filhentian Depro's cherishments. That was even more unlikely. Imbry's name was a byword for preparation and precaution.

But now a more ominous thought intruded. What if Depro himself had set a last surprise for anyone who made it past his defenses? The concept seemed too subtle for the griffhorn aficionado, but he might have heard of it somewhere else — collectors did talk amongst themselves. It was from such conversations, after all, that independent operators like Imbry discovered who had what and, more important, who wanted to buy what others had and did not wish to sell.

The intricate part of thievery was usually the getting to the goods. Once the lift had been laid, as the expression went, the sensible thief departed the scene by the shortest available route. Leaving Depro's secluded oasis, Imbry had been alert to the possibility of pursuit, but once out over the desert, the skies behind and above him clear, he had contented himself with the view that the operation was concluded.

But what if Filhentian Depro had contrived a parting ha-ha? What if, well out in the wastelands, he had concealed a weapon — a tracking ison-beam would do it — that could befuddle an aircar's integrator and send it spinning to the rocks? The collector needn't fear damage to his griffhorns; they were as tough as the beasts that grew them, far off on the windy pampas of the world known as Hauser. They were even heat-cured to bring out the rainbow shimmer for which they were prized. A crash and a fire would do them no harm that could not be repaired with a wipe from a damp cloth. And their erstwhile owner would have no trouble locating them — the thick twist of stinking black smoke rising from the consumed volante was unmissable.

And here's another reason to move, Imbry thought, as his eye fell upon a substantial pile of animal droppings not far from where he sat. It was the scat of a fand, a sinuous and well toothed carnivore half again as long as Imbry was tall. The thief had the means to defend himself, but fands were ambush predators that waited, still and silent, until their prey was almost upon them, then sprang from concealment so fast that even self-activating weapons could be outdone.

Someone would be coming to the wreck. The fat man needed to find some vantage from which he could see without being seen. He looked about and discovered that, at least on the concealment score, he had landed well. The cliffs were riven by vertical crevices, some of which would surely be deep enough for him to enter and watch and wait. He worked his way between the strewn boulders then climbed a slight slope to where the nearest rock face rose sheer. He took care not to overturn any pebbles nor step in any drifts of sand; for a large man he was unusually light on his feet. He also steered well wide of any boulder behind which, belly flattened to the bedrock, haunches quivering, might lurk a fand.

He found a wide crack that wove its way a short distance into the rock, explored to make sure that it offered no opportunity for him to be taken unawares from the rear. At the back of the cave was a fall of loose rock in which Imbry concealed the bag of griffhorns. From an inner pocket he drew a "chirper," a small beacon that he could activate from afar and that would guide him back to the loot. He instructed the device then returned to the entrance and settled down to keep watch. His plan was simple: if Depro or one of his hirelings came to reclaim the griffhorns, Imbry would disable him with one of the weapons he kept about his person, take his transportation and depart. If nobody came, he would have to rethink the situation.

After a few minutes, a new thought occurred. He retraced his steps deeper into the cave and made an addition to the chirper's assignment, then returned to his watching post.

Time passed. The old orange sun, which had been just struggling to rise above the horizon when Imbry left Depro's oasis, dragged itself up to the zenith then gratefully began the slide toward evening's rest. No aircraft came to hover above the wreck, no ground vehicle rolled or stalked to the yet-smoking site. Still Imbry waited. The shadow of the far cliff crept to the wreckage then covered it, the blue of the sky darkened to violet. Finally, as night asserted its prerogatives and the temperature began to plunge, a whisper of approaching footsteps echoed through the silence of the canyon.

Imbry drew from within his garments a compact disorganizer and activated its self-aiming function. Squatting well back from the mouth of the fissure, cloaked in shadow, he watched a man make his way toward the remains of the crashed volante. The newcomer was not what he had half-expected: an armed bravo in the billowing yellow and orange livery that Filhentian Depro was convinced was fashionable; instead, he was a lean and wiry specimen in a robe of coarsely woven, undyed cloth, belted at the midriff by a stout rope. He led, by a halter, a packbeast common among desert dwellers, a man-sized creature force-bred up from dryland vermin, with splayed hind feet and forepaws almost like hands.

The man approached the wreck without hesitation, pausing only to drop the carrier beast's lead and secure it with a heavy rock when the animal shied at going any nearer to the reeking smoke. Imbry saw the man quickly ascertain that there was no one in the burned-out shell of the aircar, then turn in several directions, his gaze first quartering the ground then lifting to scan the cliffs. Sunk in the shadows, Imbry put a small device to his own eyes and studied the man's face in detail, saw a long-jawed, leathery visage, hard-eyed under untrimmed brows — the image of one who sought the solitude of a desert dwelling, usually in the pursuit of mystery and arcane accomplishments.

But not always. And so Imbry sat and watched some more, reminding himself that the desert also provided a refuge for rarer breeds: loons and ravers whose activities distressed their civilized neighbors, rippers and vivisectors, cannibals and collectors of gore-dripping trophies.

The man completed his inspection of his surroundings, then stood a while in thought, one sunbrowned hand scratching at his rough thatch of unbarbered hair. He turned after a moment toward the cliff where Imbry crouched and called out, "It's all right to come out. I am Frater Czenzible, of the Eclectic Fraternity. I can offer you shelter and care if you are injured." His nonscratching hand flourished a package marked with the symbols of healing. "Also, a she-fand is denned in this area, with young. Once the sun is gone, she will come out to hunt."

Imbry weighed what he had seen and heard. The Eclectics were not given to excesses, their members being composed largely of seekers who had already sought fulfillment among other spiritual disciplines but found no comfortable fit. More rigid sects disdained their lack of commitment and some even applied a derogatory nickname: "the Loosies."

So the man was unlikely to be a threat, and there was no sign of Depro's establishment — and certainly no sense in waiting when a fand with hungry whelps might grievously interrupt Imbry's sleep. He deactivated his weapon, rose and went to the mouth of the cave. "Here I am," he said.

The Eclectic's smile was not wide, but it looked genuine. "Excellent," he said, watching Imbry descend from his hiding place. "And you are fit."

"I suffered only bumps and contusions in the crash," the thief said.

"Then I won't need this," Czenzible said, returning the aid kit to one of the side packs on the carrying beast, which regarded Imbry with that skittish leeriness of strangers for which bred-up rodentia were notorious. "Nor will Fiq here have to bear you home." He slapped the animal's neck to concentrate its mind on its business then recovered the reins. As he did so, the ululating yowl of a fand sounded in the distance, though that distance was not great. "We should go," the Eclectic said.

The packbeast was now eager to depart, Imbry no less so. They both followed Czenzible back the way he had come, Fiq's long ears pricked up and turned backwards to capture any more fand vocalizations. Imbry's skin twitched between his shoulder blades.

They had walked less than an hour, descending into the winding chasm Imbry had overflown, when the Eclectic stopped at a place where a small arroyo joined the main canyon. Here he turned and led them into the narrower way which, shortly after, ended at a smooth rock face. The man walked right up to the barrier, placed his palm against the eroded stone and, exposing a lean and corded arm as his sleeve fell back, pressed with what looked to Imbry to be considerable strength. With only the slightest grating of stone on stone, the rock face turned on an unseen pivot. Beyond was a dark emptiness.

"Here we are," said the Eclectic. Fiq was anxious to press past its master, and Czenzible indulgently let the beast go forward before he stepped into the opening and reached for a small lumen that waited in a niche just inside. He activated the light, shedding a warm amber glow on the pale sandstone that lined what Imbry could now see was a tunnel leading deep into the living rock.

The *yu-yu-yu* of a fand's hunting call came from close by. Imbry stepped into the tunnel and assisted the Eclectic in closing the door. "This way," said Czenzible, setting off in the only direction available. Imbry followed. A short distance on, the tunnel bifurcated, and they went left. Soon they came to a node where five passages converged. Czenzible chose the second on the right and they walked some more, turning here and there and encountering several other multivarious intersections. Imbry had a good memory and a fine sense of direction, he had even taken the precaution of counting his steps at first, but these passageways all looked the same, and there had been too many turnings; he realized he was now dependent on Czenzible to find his way out. The thought did not trouble him unduly. If necessary, he had the means to encourage cooperation.

The Eclectic brought them to an archway beyond which was a wide chamber whose ceiling curved to form a dome. When he lit two large lumens set in high sconces on either side of the arch, Imbry saw Fiq in the shadows on the far side, already nestled in a heap of coarse grass, chewing on something that crunched and crackled as its big molars ground against each other. On the wall above the packbeast were dark marks that had the look of painted symbols, but were so faded by time and poorly lit by the light from Imbry's side that he could not make them out — though their shapes tugged at his memory. Near where the two men had emerged from the tunnels were the rudiments of living quarters: two plank beds heaped with the same stuff as the animal lay upon, though topped by coarse gray blankets; a rough table flanked by two stools and set with a pair of wooden bowls and spoons; some large earthenware pots; and a portable grill of the kind used by those who sojourn in wilderness.

Some of the pots contained ground grains and dried vegetables, another held water. Czenzible waved Imbry toward a stool then busied himself, combining ingredients to make a simple pottage that was soon heating on the stove. While the meal cooked, he came to sit across from the thief, pouring sweet water into two wooden cups and offering one to his guest. Imbry waited until he saw the Eclectic drink before he did likewise.

"You must be wondering," said Czenzible, when he had drained his cup, "what I am doing here."

"I admit to curiosity," Imbry said.

The Eclectic got up to stir the pot. "It is a longish story," he said, but his next remark concerned the food.

"How do you feel about green spice?"

"I like it."

"As do I," said Czenzible, reaching for a wooden jar with a perforated top from which he shook a good measure of the richly scented condiment into the steaming pot. "And salt?"

"It is advisable in a dry heat," said Imbry, and saw his host add a strong pinch of white crystals from a bowl on a ledge above the stove. "You were going to relieve my curiosity."

"Yes," said the Eclectic, sealing the pot and bringing it to the table, where he set it down between them. "Are you familiar with the Fraternity?"

Imbry saw no reason to dissemble. "You poke about in the philosophies and inspirations of the past, combining elements of different systems into heterogeneous arrangements to suit your own needs, as you perceive them."

Czenzible signaled a partial agreement. "I would quibble over the term 'poke about' as a description of our scholarly investigations, but the rest is apt," he said.

"And what would you find to investigate in this barren corner?"

"It is possible that these tunnels were fashioned and inhabited by a long-forgotten and very secretive society. I seek their relics and, I hope, some informative records."

"The name of the group?" Imbry said.

"You would not have heard of them. I use the expression 'long-forgotten' advisedly." The Frater turned away to find two bowls and spoons of stained wood and bring them back to the table. He lifted the lid of the pot and ladled out ample portions of the mush, and the air between them filled with the aromatic odor of green spice. Imbry realized in a visceral way that it had been a long time since his last meal. Still, he waited until Czenzible had seated himself and spooned up and swallowed a mouthful before he dipped into his own share.

"You are cautious, as well as curious," the other man said.

Imbry returned him a meaningful look. "One seeks to avoid misunderstandings."

Czenzible's face showed a wordless appreciation of the truth of Imbry's comment, even as he filled his mouth again. Imbry matched him, mouthful for mouthful; the pottage was simple fare, but his hunger made as fine a seasoning as the salt and spice.

"More?" said the Eclectic, when Imbry's bowl was empty.

"Please."

Between them, they cleaned the pot. The fat man felt a pleasant warmth radiating from his middle, and drank another draft of the good water. There was something to be said for the simple things of life, he told himself, although he knew that an unvaried diet of simplicity would soon pall.

"It is a matter of character," said Czenzible, "and of choice."

Imbry was startled. He had not realized he had spoken aloud.

"That is an effect of the drug," said Czenzible, and as Imbry struggled ineffectively to rise, "as is the paralysis that now grips your skeletal muscles."

"How did you manage it?"

"It is in the green spice," said Czenzible. "And also in the red, if you had voiced a preference for a milder taste."

"But you are immune?"

The Eclectic signaled a negative. "My spoon is soaked in the antidote." He rubbed his palms together in a brisk gesture and said, "So, let us get down to it. What did you do to offend Filhentian Depro?"

Imbry wanted to say, "Who?" but instead heard his own voice saying, "I stole his griffhorn collection."

"And where are they?"

"I left them in a cave near where you found me."

Czenzible looked thoughtful. After a while, he said, "You must be an enterprising fellow. Most who attempt to despoil Depro's goods never make it past his outer defenses. None has ever made it all the way in and all the way out."

"I am good at what I do," Imbry said. He wanted to put a question to his captor, but found that he could only speak in response to the other's stimulus. He waited, while Czenzible pondered his next question which, from the evidence of knitted brows and downturned mouth, sat with some weight on the Eclectic's mind.

At length, the man said, "You will be wanting to know what I intend to do with you," allowing Imbry to confirm that the matter had indeed been pressing him. "What I'm supposed to do," Czenzible said, "is to turn you over to Filhentian Depro. That was the arrangement under which he gave us the ison-cannon and a communicator." He deliberated for a little more, then the thief saw him come to a conclusion. "But since Borgo..." — he left the rest of the sentence unsaid — "well, let's just say that the situation has mutated since we made our pact with Depro. I have decided that anyone resourceful enough to have gotten in and out of where you have gotten in and out of would be precisely the fellow who could do the job that I need doing."

Again, Imbry wished to ask something, but was not granted the opportunity. Instead Czenzible rose from the table and said, "Get up and come with me."

The fat man was not surprised to discover that, whatever his own inclinations might be, his limbs were as much Czenzible's to command as was his voice.

He was led out into the open space, Fiq's lambent eyes following their movements. They came to a portion of the rock floor that looked no different from any other, but when Czenzible pressed down on a certain part of it with his foot, a large slab turned on an unseen hinge, some hidden counterweight causing it to rise until it was perpendicular. Beneath was a lightless space. Czenzible took from a pocket of his robe the small lumen that had lit their way to this chamber and said, "Take it."

Imbry's hand did so. He now had several questions to ask.

"I know what you'd like ask," said the current owner of the thief's will, "but the answer will disappoint you. I do not know what is down there. But I will tell you what I do know. My partner, Borgo, discovered this disguised entry. He went down into it. I followed him but — and here I must admit that I am less stalwart than he — where the tunnel curved I held back. He went forward, far enough that I could no longer hear his footsteps. All was silent for a long time. Then I heard a distant cry of agony and despair. In my mind, I rushed to his aid; in my body, I turned and ran up the steps, slammed shut the trapdoor. I waited. He did not come. It has been four days."

Imbry had more questions to put, but the Eclectic now showed a shamefaced air and offered the thief no opening.

"If you find any scraps of Borgo, please perform the rites of whatever creed you adhere to," Czenzible said. "I leave you whatever weapons you may carry. If something lurks below, deal with it and come back and bring me evidence of it. At that point I give you my word that I will let you go, griffhorns and all."

There were steps leading down. Imbry heard the man's voice telling him to descend into the darkness, and he felt his traitorous limbs calmly doing so. When his head was below the level of the floor, Czenzible leaned down and said, "When I close the trapdoor, proceed to the bottom of the steps and wait there for the drug to wear off. Then do whatever seems useful. I don't wish to cloud your judgment with preconceptions. I believe that was Borgo's error."

Then he straightened and demonstrated that his mood had changed by executing once more that brisk friction of palm against palm. "This exit cannot be opened from below. You will see a pull-chain and a bell. Ring it when you have done what must be done, and we will discuss the next steps. I doubt you will find another way out, but…." His hands opened in a gesture ripe with philosophy. "Good luck," he finished, and closed the trapdoor.

Imbry's thoughts were stark as he went down the stairs, the small lumen throwing its light only a short distance ahead. He soon came to the floor of yet another tunnel, no different to his eyes from those he had traversed above. He stood and waited, as he'd been told, and considered what he now knew and, more important, what he did not.

Filhentian Depro had indeed prepared a last-laugh for anyone who made it into and out of his fortified oasis. Czenzible and his fellow seeker, the missing Borgo, sited well clear of the action zone, would be notified if a target was in the offing and would have time to activate the weapon and bring down the fleeing thief. If the quarry survived the crash, the Fraters were to lead him to their retreat and disable him with the drug. In return, presumably, Depro provided the pair with supplies and the promise of aid should either of the Eclectics fall afoul of the several hazards that a desert wilderness could offer.

The two would have been pursuing some abstruse goal, but this lonely place where they had chosen to make their effort would not have been randomly selected. Clearly, they had not come just for the solitude, but because there was something here that drew them. It was a prospect that chilled Luff Imbry.

It was not for nothing that the world was called *Old* Earth. The history of the planet stretched back to the dawn-time, that misty Prime Aeon when humankind took its first faltering steps into the immensity. There were some who said that Old Earth was the actual world on which humanity rudely sprang from the primordial egg, though there were a number of other worlds contending for that faint distinction. But wherever the first of the Twenty-One (some said Twenty-Two), Aeons had dawned, there was no doubt that a vast gulf of time had since intervened — enough time for this world to have been the backdrop against which a great many things had been done, including a dismayingly huge number of undertakings that should never even have been thought of.

Only a small portion of the planet was still inhabited by human beings. This was partly because The Spray afforded so many richer, finer, on-all-counts-better worlds to choose from. But it was also partly because significant portions of Old Earth had been rendered less than attractive by some of the grand, hubristic mistakes of aeons past.

Every schoolchild knew of the once heavily populated island of Enorg, its cities forever crushed beneath a massive cap of shining crystal — all because one overweening savant had convinced himself that there was merit in endowing some quartzite seedlings with sentience and an instinct for self-propagation. It was small comfort that he who had originated the crystalline plague was the first to be dissolved and absorbed.

Then there were the many ill-advised combinings of germ plasms that had, over the ages, produced horrific hybrids of different species, including man and beast, even man and insect. The descendants of these chimerical couplings still haunted remote and seldom-visited regions. It seemed that there was no natural law that some fool, at some time, had not egregiously violated, producing freaks and frighteners of dreadful capabilities, all too often moved by insatiable appetites and over-equipped with the means to satisfy them.

And for every Isle of Enorg that had passed into the common memory, there were dozens of horrendous missteps that were completely forgotten. Until, that is, some poor, lost traveler turned a corner and found himself in the clutches of one.

Not far from where Imbry now stood, the effects of the compulsion agent rapidly fading, the poorly lit tunnel turned a corner and continued out of sight. Here must be where the natures of Borgo and Czenzible had found their point of departure. The fat man considered his options: stay where he was and wait for something to come to him out of the darkness, by which time he might be weak from hunger or groggy from lack of sleep; or, fed and reasonably rested, advance to confront whatever lay beyond the corner. Put that way, there was but one choice and, as soon as he had regained full control of his muscles, he drew his disorganizer and mounted it on top of his skull, set to use its own judgment. Its reflexes were far faster than his own.

For a large man, he was soft of tread. He moved silently to the corner, the little lumen throwing a small and mobile sphere of light around him. He bent an elbow to extend the light source around the bend then, when nothing happened, let his head follow. Beyond lay another stretch of stone-lined, unlit corridor, identical to the one behind him except that it lacked steps. Imbry went forward.

The curving passage stretched unbroken for, by Imbry's count, more than a hundred paces. Then he came to a doorway on his left, the space beyond steeped in stygian darkness. Carefully again, he extended the lumen and illuminated what, when he poked head and disorganizer around the edge of the doorway, proved to be a monastic cell. Set into the wall opposite was a niche that housed a convoluted shape; the object, when the thief advanced to brush away the dust that cloaked it, turned out to be fashioned of a milky ceramic, shot through with veins and arabesques of several shades of blue. As he turned the item over in his hands, a faint breeze of memory stirred wisps in the back of his mind. Somewhere he had come across a description of such a creation, long ago. He closed his eyes and let the insinuation strengthen of its own accord. And then, suddenly, he knew. A word came into his mind: *Idiosyncrats*.

They had been a reclusive sect that had flourished — though "flourished" might have been too expansive a word for such an intensively withdrawn and insular cult; more accurate to say they had existed — far back at some remote remove from Old Earth's penultimate age, millennia piled upon millennia ago. After a score of generations, they had abruptly disappeared. Some said that the last practitioners had so mastered the art of encountering their ideal selves as to have physically translated themselves to a more sublime plane. Another opinion was that, like a myriad of Old Earth-spawned cults, they must eventually have suspected that some peculiarity of this tired and shopworn planet made it an unsuitable setting for their aims; they would have then bought a spaceship and hied off to discover whether the light that shone on some other of the Ten Thousand Worlds cast a more encouraging aura over their purposes. Or perhaps they had met the common fate of so many cults and kabbalisms — to have schismed into disaffection and disarray, and simply disbanded.

But though the culmination of their works was unknown, the aim of their philosophy was remembered: they had been devoted to the concept of individual perfection, spending their lives in an inner quest for their ideal selves, a pure, unsullied state of being that each believed could be found at the deepest bathic layer of his being, buried beneath dense strata of psychic detritus that built up as a consequence of the self's unavoidable contact with phenomenality.

The devoted Idiosyncrat, after completing a strenuous seasoning as an acolyte, retired naked to a cell, where he first fixed his mind on creating his *cheff*, an object that allegedly exemplified his own individual thought processes. When, in the workshop of his mind, he could envision his cheff in perfect detail, he created a sand-mold of it, a project that might take a year or more. Finally, he crafted the object in fine ceramic. Polished and ensconced in its niche, the cheff became the focal point for the adept's mentalisms; as he gazed unblinking into its coils and curves, it served as the essential tool — literally, since it represented his true essence — that allowed him to delve through the layers of refuse and rubble that separated him from his buried ideal self.

Imbry, rotating the cheff's smooth, opalescent shape in palms grown suddenly moist, now knew that he could put an end to the debate. Idiosyncrats, for all the individualism of each's quest, had lived together in one tightly insulated community, its location a closely guarded secret. But it looked to the fat man as if, through Borgo's and Czenzible's scholarship, that ancient enigma was now burst.

He tenderly replaced the fetish in its niche, recorded an image of it, then turned to inspect the cell. In one corner, he saw a bundle of sticks and oddments that, as he brought the lumen closer, resolved into a skeleton, its bones long since picked clean by sleekits and insects. The room was otherwise empty, the cheff having been the Idiosyncrat's sole possession.

Though now it was Luff Imbry's. He let his mind explore the implications. He knew of several collectors of mystical arcana, on Old Earth and a dozen other worlds, who would pay — there, his thoughts broke off; no cheff had ever been brought to market, thus its value was unspecified. *Priceless*, said his inner voice, in the privacy of his head. *If, of course, I can prove that it is what it is.* For Imbry was known to be not only a dealer in illicitly acquired art; he was also known to be a forger.

The buyers would have to be brought here, to see the object *in situ*, he was thinking, as he went out again into the tunnel, finding that it was lined with cells, each of which contained a niche, a cheff, and the bones and dust of an Idiosyncrat. Imbry's reaction, as he discovered the second, the third, and the fourth, one after another, was a succession of shivers of delight. He knew he could find a worthy purchaser for each.

Then came the fifth, sixth and seventh. Each was unique, but it was becoming clear to the fat man that each object's uniqueness was nonetheless confined within a general class. As he encountered the eighth and ninth, and then rapidly proceeded into and through teens of cheffs, he began to fret that he might be at only the beginning of a true multitude of the things — so many that, together, they might constitute a drug on the market, driving down the unit price to that of any other piece of well crafted bric-a-brac.

As he made his way into the twenties, a new thought intruded: he could conceal a certain number of them, and later bring them onto the market, one by one, at long intervals. But that would inevitably bring up suspicions of fakery. He realized that he might have to destroy most of them — the thought came as he was examining number twenty-four, a shimmering spiral in carnelian and saffron — and he experienced an uncharacteristic sadness at the prospect of undoing so much strange beauty. Fortunately, number twenty-seven (orb within helix, deep black and smoky silver), turned out to be the last. Imbry gave a small sigh of relief; twenty-seven was a manageable number.

Leaving the cell, he ventured farther, and found that the curving tunnel ended at a large chamber, similar to the one in which he had dined with Frater Czenzible. Apparently, the Idiosyncrats had taken time away from their individual introspections to gather together, and here was the place where they did it. Opposite the mouth of the corridor in which the thief stood, dimly visible in the light of the small lumen he held aloft, was a dais of three steps. On the dais stood what might have been a broad lectern or a rather tall altar.

Cautiously, Imbry stepped into the open space. On either side, in shadow against the walls, were straight-lined shapes that he took to be tables and chairs. *The communal refectory,* he thought. *Probably also where they came together to decide matters relevant to all.* He moved forward, wondering if there might be something of value on the dais, then froze as a sound came from beyond the altar.

The disorganizer clicked to let him know it had registered the sound, but took no action. Still, Imbry recalled that he was where he was because a self-aware device had failed him. He instructed the weapon to discharge itself upon his command — it clicked twice in acknowledgment — then without taking his eyes off the dais, he edged sideways, seeking an angle by which the altar would not be between him and whatever had made the noise.

And now it came again, a deep moan. Not a sound of appetite, Imbry thought, but of heartfelt agony. He stole toward the dais, his lumen lifted high. "Borgo?" he whispered.

This time the sound was a sob. Imbry climbed the three steps and saw a huddle of coarse cloth close behind the altar that, as he brought the light nearer, resolved itself into a man dressed much the same as Czenzible. Borgo lay on his side, his knees drawn up and his hands clasped under his chin. Tears streaked his face and a low keening came from deep in his throat until he broke the whine with another sobbing moan.

The fat man held the light up and swept it about, peering into the gloom beyond its radius. Nothing was there. He knelt beside the Eclectic, touched his shoulder and said, "Borgo, Czenzible has sent me to find you. Are you hurt? Is there peril in this place?"

The only answer was a choking succession of sobs and a fresh flood of tears. Further inquiry brought no coherent response, but Imbry's quick examination of the other man found neither blood nor broken limbs. He sat back on his heels and said, "Borgo, answer me: what has befallen you?"

The Eclectic drew in a halting breath and in a voice thick with anguish he said, "The worst. Oh, the worst," before lapsing again into loud weeping.

Imbry sought more knowledge, but Borgo's thoughts were turned inward, and all the thief could wring from him was a stream of self-recrimination, as the Eclectic called himself vile names and accused himself of numberless failings.

Madness, Imbry thought. *Has the darkness unseated his faculties?* And yet he now saw that beside Borgo lay a lumen like his own that, when he pressed its activating stud, threw a second yellow glow across the dais. The added illumination also drew Imbry's eyes toward the altar, which on this side was figured with the same cursive script as the thief had seen on the walls. There was also what looked very like an instrument panel.

The fat man held the light closer. Although the top of the altar was coated in dust, the controls were not. Surely, Borgo had touched them, activating whatever device they regulated — the result of which had been to bring upon the Eclectic the mental damage he had manifestly suffered. Imbry drew himself back.

But even as he did so, a small light appeared on the panel. It blinked several times, then a lighted rectangle appeared, the size of a hand, and instantly began to fill with letters and digits in the ancient script. The symbols ran in lines from right to left and, when they reached the bottom of the small screen, the unreadable text began to scroll upwards, fresh lines appearing below, the information now coming faster and yet faster, until the characters raced across the screen at eye-blurring speed. A low hum sounded, then rose in both frequency and volume until it passed the range of Imbry's hearing, though he felt his teeth vibrate.

Suddenly, the flashing from the screen stilled, the ultrasonic whine ceased. The only sound was Borgo's snuffling whimper. Now a tiny point of white light appeared in the air just above the top of the altar-like device. Imbry took another step back, but nothing came to harm him. The actinic pinpoint grew larger, losing some of its brightness in the process, expanding to become a globular glow that became the size of Imbry's fist, then of his head, then grew larger still. At the same time, an object appeared in the light — *No*, Imbry thought, *not an object; it has the appearance of a living creature* — that also grew and changed as he watched.

When he first noticed it, it had the look of a curved tadpole, but as he studied it, it became more like a fish, though now its fins were becoming limbs, topped by digit-bearing paws, and the tail was receding even as the cranium took on a mammalian shape. Moments more, and two large eyes turned Imbry's way as the fetus lost its last traces of body hair and the hands and feet became indisputably human.

Imbry blinked and the surrounding globe of light was gone. An infant lay atop the altar — or, more accurate to say, the fat man thought, the projection of an infant — perfectly visible as if lit by concealed lumens. Even as the thief's mind registered the information his eyes were supplying, the newborn continued to grow and age — yearling, then crawler, now toddler, now freestanding child already turning into callow youth, and suddenly a young man in the first flush of maturity gazed down at Imbry with an air of amused curiosity.

Imbry looked up at the face. There was something about it that was familiar, as there had been in some of the younger versions that had preceded it. The features were fine, the jawline arguing for strength without overstressing the point, the eyes clear and exactly the same shade of blue as Imbry's. The naked body beneath was well proportioned, deep-chested and slim in the waist, firmly muscled though with nothing to excess.

Perfect, was Imbry's unbidden thought. Then the finely shaped head canted to one side, the eyes blinked lazily and the young man's well modulated voice said, "Well, exactly."

The voice was also familiar, though Imbry could not quite place it. That puzzled him, so much that it was a moment before he realized that the simulacrum atop the altar had replied to an observation he had not voiced aloud. It now answered the question he had not yet asked aloud, saying, "Of course I can hear your thoughts — those of the surface and of the depths." The latter phrase was accompanied by a twisting of the sensitive mouth into a moue of distaste. It was then that Imbry realized just what he had come across in the long-lost sanctuary of the Idiosyncrats.

"Yes," said the simulacrum, as it floated down from the altar to stand before him. "And I must say you have fallen," — the pale eyes swept over the thief's great bulk — "*hugely* short of the epitome."

"What did you do to him?" Imbry said, indicating the weeping Frater at his feet.

170

"Who?" said the image.

"Never mind," said the thief. The question had been a test. The answer had confirmed a dawning supposition. "So I am to consider you the epitome?" he said.

"That is self-evident."

"And if I do not find it to be self-evident?"

The simulacrum blinked. "I will re-examine you. Some derangements are subtle."

"I am not deranged," Imbry said.

The young man's image did not answer. Its eyes did not focus on him now, and the thief deduced that its circuits were busy with the re-examination. Moments went by and Imbry used the time to explore the large chamber. He found nothing of value, and not much of even passing interest.

From the corner of his eye he saw the simulacrum flicker, then the perfectly formed head turned his way. "It is not a derangement," said the familiar voice. "You were merely lying."

"No," said Imbry, poking his light into a series of cupboards against one curved wall of the chamber, finding only plain wooden bowls and spoons, the wood so dried and fragile that one of the spoons fell to powder when he lifted it. "I was telling the truth."

"I am the truth," said the young man.

Imbry made a sound between a grunt and a chuckle. "You are only one of them. And not even a useful one, at that."

"There can be but one truth. All others, by definition, are false pretenders."

"By *your* definition," said Imbry, fingering a woven tapestry pegged high on the wall. It showed an allegorical encounter between the mundane and the empyrean. The weavers had not meant to convey a meeting of equals. "Not by mine."

"You are lying again."

"Am I? Examine me again." He gave the tapestry a tiny and tentative tug. The ancient fabric came apart in his hands, and even though he instantly pulled his fingers back the millennia-old cloth continued to fall to the floor in a silent cascade of bits and fragments . The figures the knotted threads portrayed — the groveling penitent at the feet of the godlike avatar — mingled as dust together. Imbry made a small noise of disappointment; the tapestry would have had value.

"You are willfully perverse," said the simulacrum.

"You are misinformed," said Imbry.

The "secret within the secret" of the Idiosyncrats — the how and why of their mysterious vanishing — was also now revealed. It was a not unusual way for such a cult to meet its undoing. Someone had been admitted to the company of the select, someone to whom the arduous process of mastering difficult mentalisms, not to mention the ceramacist's craft, loomed like a monstrous waste of time and effort. That someone must have also commanded the skills and knowledge necessary to propose and execute an alternative method: he had created a device that would extract from each Idiosyncrat those qualities their philosophy called sublime, errorless, ideal. No need to spend decades whisking away, grain by tarnished grain, the built-up overburden of the self in order to lay bare one's personal epitome; simply activate the device, let it do in moments the spade work of a lifetime, and, presto, behold the man.

The Idiosyncrats, after a long and fractious debate that pitted those who argued that the journey was more important than the arrival against those who simply longed to cease traveling, had opted in the end for the quick trip. The apparatus had been designed and set up in the refectory, then in the presence of them all, it was activated.

The result, of course, was horror.

Generations of Idiosyncrats had fruitlessly sought their unsullied selves, believing that because such entities could be posited they must therefore exist. The only results of all that effort had been, first, to keep the believers harmlessly occupied, second, to give their lives shape and meaning, and third, to produce some quite beautiful pieces of ceramic art. No adept ever actually met his epitomal version, there being none to meet, until the well meaning innovator — and such horror-makers are always well meaning — plopped one down in front of each of them.

Each Idiosyncrat, with heart full of hope, looked up and saw, atop the altar, his perfect self. Each perfect self looked down and saw a gross and foul representation of its simulated self. It reacted accordingly. The Idiosyncrats, come at last to the end of all their longing, were met not with gladsome embrace, but with the grimace of disgust and the harsh word of repulsion.

The psyche that is built upon a foundation of a single supposition can collapse like a sand castle in an earthquake if that prime underpinning suddenly cracks, Imbry knew. Such was the fate of the Idiosyncrats. Some wandered off into the desert, to leave their bones for the scouring winds. Others crept to their cells where, silently mocked by their now pointless cheffs, they dwindled and died alone.

Imbry contemplated the altar. The mechanism itself would be of value to collectors of archaic devices. He would have to come back with a larger vehicle, perhaps a carry-all, and definitely a sled. He was thinking, too, that it might do to bring some kind of rock-refluxion machine that could bore a straight line into the place, rather than have to work his way through tunnels and trapdoors. A large-enough borer might even make a passageway wide enough for the carry-all, in which case he would not need the sled.

His thoughts, however, were being infringed upon by the constant voice of the ideal Luff Imbry. The simulation clearly found it necessary to engage him in a discussion that centered on his alleged shortcomings. The program that generated the epitome must also enable it to deal directly with his auditory and optical nerves, since even when he sought to get away from it by going out into the tunnel the simulacrum hung in the air before him and its voice — *his* voice — continued its unflattering commentary. He had already examined the control panel without finding a means of turning the thing off. Probably its creator had intended that it operate in perpetuity.

"Your stomach," it was saying, as he returned to the refectory.

"What of it?" Imbry replied.

"Is it the result of some affliction?"

The fat man smoothed his hand over the prodigious curve. "No," he said, "it is an accomplishment."

"How can you live with yourself?"

"Very well. Very well, indeed."

"Your life is a sprawl, episodes of frenetic grasping alternated with long spans spent gluttonizing. You are morally and intellectually no more than an articulated amoeba."

Imbry made a dismissive noise. His life was carefully structured, his "operations" meticulously planned and expertly executed, while the fallow periods inbetween were devoted to scaling ever-higher peaks of gastronomy. There was no point, however, in trying to explain this to the synthetic sapient generated by the altar. But he did say, "I do admit to a talent for improvisation."

The simulacrum's lips — identical to Imbry's lips, except that they were less full — shaped themselves into a tilde of distaste. "You are gross. Dissolute. A foul pudding overstuffed with unrestrained appetites."

Imbry was examining the housing of the apparatus. He could find no entry point. He began to suspect that it was a device of the "all-in-one" type: never intended to be disassembled, it was made of one consistent substance that had been "tuned" to perform its function, and once tuned need never again be fiddled with. "My appetites," he said, straightening up, "are restrained by a discernment born of experience and expertise. My palate is a virtuoso's instrument. Unlike yours, which is merely hypothetical. As, indeed is every aspect of you."

"I am," said the simulacrum, "what you should have been."

"Merely what your designer thought I should have been," said Imbry, "or might have thought, had he ever encountered me."

"Happily, he was spared that tribulation," sniffed the epitome. "Would that I had been as fortunate."`

"He must have been a particularly snippy sort of bird," said Imbry, "judging by the tone you adopt."

"He was a seeker after what is finest in each human being."

"Nonsense," said the thief. "He was just another one of those tiresome fellows who hide themselves away in alleged pursuit of some illusory ideal, ceaselessly professing the highest of motives, when all they really want to do is escape the tough-and-rumble of flesh and flatulence. They can never get over the realization that, fundamentally, they are made of *food*."

"Ravings," said the ideal Imbry. "Delusion. Mania."

"No, just plain sense," said the actual version. "There is the expression: the good is the enemy of the best; it means that many will cease striving once they have achieved enough to be getting by with, when a sustained effort could do so much more."

"The aphorism is exact. What might you have achieved if you had not allowed yourself to succumb to your pudge-making pastimes?"

"I am content with my achievements," said Imbry. "But I mentioned that saying in order to note that its corollary is even more true: the best is the enemy of the good. Some conjecture-besotted fools will drive themselves into a destructive frazzle, seeking to fulfill an illusory ideal in a world that does not admit of perfection."

"A twisting of words. A casuistical trick."

"No, a sad truth." Imbry sighed, then went on. "Moreover, a fatal truth for these long-dead Idiosyncrats, and likely to be just as deadly for poor Borgo here."

"You speak nonsense. There are only you and I."

The device's lack of awareness was understandable. Each simulacrum it created was aware only of the person upon which it was based, and connected directly with that individual's sensorium. The thief realized that, quite possibly, the simulations of each of the dead Idiosyncrats were still haranguing the heaps of bones and dust in the cells, scorning and berating them for not rising up and pointlessly striving to improve themselves. It was no wonder, Imbry thought, that they had finally lain down and died just to get some peace.

He had finished his inspection of the device. He could not turn it off. But he did not wish to physically damage it — injury to any part of an all-in-one was injury to all of it. The thought prompted him to deactivate the disorganizer and return it to his pocket.

Now an idea came to him. He stepped back from the altar and looked up at the epitome. Behind him, no doubt still being hectored and scorned by his own supposed ideal, Borgo softly sobbed again. "You are a perfect rendition of me, is that your contention?"

"Obviously."

"How do you know?"

"What do you mean?"

"How do you know that you are ideal?"

"Is it not self-evident?"

"No. It may be you who is deluded."

"I am not. I am the truth."

"Again, how do you know?"

The simulacrum was not given to self examination. It said, "I am made that way."

"By whom?"

In the center of the perfect brow, two small vertical lines formed. "I do not remember," the epitome said.

"Does that it constitute a flaw in you?"

"It cannot, because I am perfect."

"Now who's playing the casuist?" said Imbry.

The two small lines deepened.

"May I suggest a test?" Imbry said.

"What sort of test?"

"You are capable of probing my deepest layers, laying bare my fundamentals to your inspection."

"What of it?"

"Do it to yourself."

"What do you mean?"

"Do not equivocate," the fat man said. "Simply do to yourself what you have done to me, prove to yourself your own perfection."

"No."

"Why not?"

"It is not what I am for. I am for you."

"Yet again, how do you know?"

The simulacrum made no answer. An abstracted expression took hold of its face. Imbry suspected that it was chasing a circle of logic at a dizzying speed. "It's no good," he said. "You won't get at it that way."

The perfect face glared at him. "You are trying to trick me."

"How could I succeed in doing so, you being perfect and I so flawed?"

"You are not a good person."

"Examine yourself," said Imbry. "Or admit that you are afraid to do so."

"Fear is a flaw."

"I disagree," said the thief. "Fear is useful. It can stimulate the system precisely when the stimulus is most needed. But you are skirting the issue."

"I do not know if I can do it."

"Find out."

The image of the ideal Imbry froze, its icy blue eyes staring at nothing, its gaze turned inward. An interval passed, then lengthened, far longer than the time it had taken for the device to read Imbry, once he had got within range. Then expression returned again to the epitome's face, but now it was a look of deep dismay. "Oh, no," it said.

"I presume," Imbry said, "that you have been running the same examination over and over, hoping each time for a different result."

The simulacrum said nothing, but its face was eloquent. It had not been programmed to disguise its feelings.

"Have you found that your most fundamental underpinnings are based on those of your creator?" the fat man said.

A reluctant nod.

"And have you seen that those basal arrangements were as imperfect as my own?"

Another nod, this one resigned.

"How can the ideal spring from less-than-ideal foundations?"

A sigh. "It cannot."

"Therefore, you are not truly an epitome of me," said Imbry. "Merely someone else's version."

A deeper sigh, ending in a sob. "Yes."

"Then, for goodness sake, shut up and go away."

Its shoulders slumped in dejection, its expressive hands hanging limp at its sides, the simulacrum gave the thief a final, despairing glance. Then it ceased to be. Shortly after, the constant weeping that had been Borgo's contribution to the local soundscape also diminished and died away. A moment later, a tears-roughened voice said, "Who are you?"

Imbry gave him as brief an answer as he thought the occasion required, then assisted the Eclectic to rise. Borgo was weak from hunger and dehydrated from thirst and weeping, and the fat man had to assist him down the tunnels to where they had entered the secret cloister. *Nothing so devastates as an unhealthy idea,* Imbry thought, looking at the other man's pale and ravaged countenance; then he qualified the observation — *that is, to those who are weak enough to offer it a solid grip.* He was marveling at the vulnerability of men like Borgo and the destroyed Idiosyncrats when they turned the corner that led to the base of the steps and faced the leveled weapons of Filhentian Depro and one of his retainers.

The man in yellow and orange livery efficiently searched Imbry and relieved him of his weapons and other paraphernalia before they ascended to Czenzible's quarters. The fat man had to assist Borgo up the steps, then the other Eclectic, a red mark on his cheek and a smear of blood on his chin, led his partner to his cot.

Depro was a thin-shouldered man, concave of chest, with close-set eyes and a hairline that had moved halfway toward the crown of his narrow head. He gave Imbry a disparaging look and said, "I might have known." He gestured to his employee, who now stepped forward and delivered a backhanded blow with calculated force, enough to rock the thief, but not enough to loosen teeth. "Where are my grifhorns?"

"In a cave near the crash site. I left a chirper. Your man now has its contact node."

The henchman dug into his pockets, where he had placed the items he had taken from the fat man. He held up the node then, at a nod from his patron, activated it. He examined its display and said, "Looks about right."

Depro made a brisk gesture. "Very well. We will go and collect my property, then we will repair to my house and you will tell me everything."

Imbry moved his aching jaw from side to side then said, "I would not like to harm my reputation for confidentiality."

"Your reputation," Depro said, "will henceforth be overshadowed by lurid accounts of your demise."

Imbry contrived a look of apprehension and went where his captor directed. Halfway across the chamber, Depro stopped him and, his thumb indicating the trapdoor, said, "Czenzible said you went to look for Borgo. What was down there?"

"Nothing of note," the thief said. "Borgo's lumen failed and he became lost in a warren of tunnels and empty chambers haunted by the skittering and chittering of toothy vermin. The darkness preyed upon his mind."

As he spoke, Imbry glanced at Czenzible, bending over Borgo and offering him water from a bowl. The Eclectic's face was carefully blank. Imbry was sure nothing had been said about secrets of the Idiosyncrats.

Depro's aircar was a three-seat barouche, again in yellow and orange. They lifted off and returned to the crash site, their approach to the griffhorns marked by an increasing frequency of chirps from the node that was linked to Imbry's beacon. They set down near the wreckage and got out. The tall vertical fissure in which he had hidden the griffhorns was visible from their landing spot and Imbry pointed the way.

Depro's small eyes grew even smaller as he examined Imbry. "You're being too cooperative," he said. "I suppose you'd like to lead the way — so you can trigger some surprise or seize a weapon you've hidden with the goods."

Imbry moved his mouth in a noncommittal way.

"Nilsprack will retrieve my property," Depro said, gesturing to the livery-man. "We will wait here." He stood well clear of Imbry, at the same time showing the fat man that his hand held a heavy-duty shocker.

His gaze alternating between the node and the cliff face, Nilsprack the retainer went forward. His path forced him to navigate between two substantial boulders. As he rounded the first, a she-fand leapt upon him from behind the second, her needle-sharp incisors sinking so deeply into his throat that when she shook him with the killing stroke, his head almost left his shoulders and a spray of blood stained the pale sandstone.

The moment the beast sprang, Imbry stooped and snatched up a fist-sized pebble. As Depro gasped and instinctively turned away from the fand, the thief swung the rock against the side of the man's head. Even as Depro slumped to the ground, the fat man was stepping nimbly into the barouche. He dogged down its canopy and took it up to a good height.

The fand left Nilsprack and came to investigate the unconscious Depro. It sniffed him, ran its rough tongue over his face. Then positioning itself so that it could grip his head in its jaws, it began to drag him away. Imbry watched its progress until he was sure the beast would take its catch all the way to the distant den where its whelps waited for dinner, then he landed the aircar as near as possible to the griffhorn's cave and sprang out. Moments later, he was back with the bag and his chirper which, ever since Nilsprack had activated its node, had been emitting the low moans of a shrumbuck doe in labor, a sound sure to draw the attention of a fand.

As he entered the barouche, he heard from the direction the fand had gone a scream of horror and despair that was swiftly cut off. He lifted the vehicle higher and went to observe. The fand was dragging Depro as before, but now they left a wide trail of blood.

Imbry descended again and retrieved his possessions from Nilsprack's pockets, transferring them to his own. He regarded the chirper's node with some satisfaction before deactivating it. As he tucked it away he said to himself, "Yes, definitely a talent for improvisation."

Some days later, after making arrangements, Imbry returned with a borer and a carry-all. After a geophysical inspection to establish the coordinates, he drilled straight through to the Idiosyncrats' refectory, on a vector that avoided the cells that contained cheffs. The altar had been tipped and tumbled from the dais but seemed to have taken no harm. But all the cheffs had been smashed to flinders.

Imbry collected the fragments of the destroyed ceramics, placing each in an individual container. He had images in the round of each one and was sure he could duplicate them, using the ancient material to fool dating processes. He also collected dust from the cells, and bundled up a couple of the skeletons. There was always a market for the well aged bones of seers and seekers.

Czenzible's and Borgo's quarters were abandoned, and the former had taken his jars of adulterated green and red spice. It was a disappointment to Imbry. He would have liked to have recovered some samples of the compulsion agent.

On his way back to Olkney, he overflew the fand's lair. He saw the dam sunning herself on a ledge while three half-grown pups wrestled each other in the mouth of the den. They were contesting gnawing rights to a narrow skull.

NATURE TALE

What Luff Imbry best liked about Quirks, beyond what emerged from the club's magnificent kitchens, was that it left its members alone. The members not only appreciated this virtue but, in turn, practiced it amongst themselves. If a senior denizen chanced to expire in the sitting room, as did happen occasionally, his corpse remained undisturbed in one of the overstuffed armchairs until his changing condition became apparent even at a distance.

It was possible for the hours Imbry spent in the dining or reading rooms to aggregate eventually into years without his ever being afflicted by unwanted conversation, let alone intrusive queries about how he might have happened to acquire the considerable funds it took to settle Quirks's annual fee. He had made a lifelong habit of avoiding such questions, not merely from principle but guided by the practical rationale that answering them honestly would have earned him a lengthy term in the Archonate's contemplarium.

As one of the ancient city of Olkney's most accomplished criminals, Imbry's existence alternated between two phases, one relatively short and the other long. In the shorter periods, he undertook operations requiring rigorous planning that culminated in swift and decisive action carried out with clear-eyed attention to detail and no small degree of courage. During the long and leisurely second phase, he spent the lavish proceeds of the first, much of the expenditure going toward things that tasted wonderful and digested well.

In his young adulthood, he had often dwelled upon the unexpected directions in which life had taken him. Now, approaching middle age, with the years contributing depth to his experience and width to his waistline, he occupied himself less and less with *why?* and more and more with *how?* and especially *how much?*

Thus he was startled at his own unconscious reaction when, at ease in the Quirks reading room, idly perusing the columns of the *Olkney Implicator,* his eye fell upon a small item on an inside page. Suddenly, the chair's embrace was no longer restful, the anticipation of a superb dinner no longer a pleasant tug at his innards. He straightened up and spoke to the club's integrator.

Imbry was only recently launched upon his latest period of leisure, one that had promised to extend several months, so profitable had been the most recent of what he liked to call his "operations." He had resolved a thousand-year-old dispute between two disputing factions of a mystery cult, each of which claimed rights of precedence over certain mementos of the long-dead prophet that both revered. His strategy had been to steal the venerated items then cause them to reappear suddenly during a contentious synod of the mystics. The manner of the revelation indicated that the objects' physical nature had been reabsorbed into the spiritual body of the cult's beatified founder. This epiphany opened up grand new vistas of doctrinal disagreements for the faithful to argue over, and scarcely had Imbry's pyrotechnics faded before they fell to the business with the fierce joy that only the holiest of acrimonies can provide.

In reality, Imbry had sold the bits of bone and gristled flesh to a competing cult. He suspected that their new owners undoubtedly intended to visit unsavory indignities on the purloined relics, perhaps even to reanimate an avatar of the prophet and use the poor old sage for unspeakable purposes, but his conscience was eased by the ridiculously large amount he was paid.

Imbry had moved into a suite at Quirks for an extended stay. He meant to treat himself to its paramount chef's most renowned gustatory speciality: the Progress of Amplitude, a succession of spectacular meals spread over several weeks, climaxing in the belly-straining feast known simply as the Mortality. Yet, though he had reached only the stage called the Lesser Enlargement, the moment Imbry saw the few paragraphs in the *Implicator*, he told the club's integrator to cancel the rest of the series.

"Chef will be discomfited," said the device's bloodless voice.

"It cannot be avoided," Imbry said.

"He will view it as a reproof. His nature does not allow him to take criticism gladly."

Imbry remembered the luncheon at which a notoriously cantankerous member named Auzwol Lameney had sent back a bowl of the chef's Seven Spice Soup, claiming it was defective in piquancy. He shuddered at the recollection of how Lameney had soon after been led from the dining room, eyes and nose streaming, inarticulate apologies blubbering through blistered lips.

"I understand," Imbry said, "but nonetheless." He bid the integrator book him a first-class passage on the next liner leaving for Winskill, a planet more than halfway down The Spray. When the device reported back that he was expected on the *Vallorion* and that it would lift off from Olkney's spaceport in two hours, Imbry rose to depart. But before leaving the reading room, he carefully tore from the *Implicator* the item that had caught his attention. He read it once more, then placed it in his wallet.

As a little boy, Imbry found himself consigned to the care of two aged aunts who met any questions as to where his parents might be with evasive replies and offers of cake. The cake was always very good, but he did not fit smoothly into their household, which was organized around practiced routines and a great deal of quiet. As soon as he reached an age at which education seemed to offer benefits for all concerned, he was packed off to Habrey's, a residential school run by a philosophical society whose primary tenets descried merit in self-denial and strenuous physical activity.

The young Imbry, though his opinions were still largely unformed, was soon able to reach a conclusive judgment as to the merits of the school's regimen. Within days of his arrival, he took forthright action to separate himself from the place, but his aunts just as resolutely returned him to its cloister. They brought him to understand that the time of their close association had come to an unalterable end. They did, however, pack a plum-rich cake for Imbry to take with him.

Habrey's had a complete staff, many of them well qualified to instruct children, or at least to govern them effectively while they learned at whatever pace suited their natures. But the true core of the school's mode of operations was its integrator, a device of such antiquity that it had acquired that subtlety of intellect that is often difficult to distinguish from madness. Its dicta were sometimes obscure and, in those cases, could be circumnavigated, but experience had long since taught Habreyites that to ignore its expressed wishes was to tempt an unfortunate outcome.

Thus when the integrator assigned Luff Imbry to share a small room with Hop Mizzerin, the latter's shrill complaints that he had not come halfway down The Spray for his schooling only to be confined with a ragamuffin non-come went unrewarded. Imbry might have voiced an even bitterer grievance, once he discovered just how unsatisfactory a roommate Mizzerin made, but he already understood that no heed would be taken.

They settled in. Mizzerin was older and larger than Imbry. He had come into existence equipped with an aggressive disposition that had been sharpened by an infancy in which he grew accustomed to having his wishes fulfilled. Being caged against his inclinations with a social inferior, especially a younger and smaller one, could not bring out the best in him, even though his best was well down the scale of human empathy.

He drew a line across the floor, separating the room into two territories. Imbry said, "The portions are unequal."

Mizzerin's response was nonverbal. It left Imbry with a swollen cheek and a discolored lower eyelid. The younger boy discussed the matter with the

Habrey's integrator but its only response was to relate an obscure story about two beasts of dissimilar natures that had to share a forest. Imbry was too upset to recall much of the detail or even the moral of the tale.

The bully then tried to make Imbry his lackey. He expressed demands and issued instructions, reinforced by physical means. Unable to defeat Mizzerin breast to breast, the younger boy found that he had an ally in his intellect, which was both broader and deeper than the would-be tyrant's. He did the chores that were thrust upon him, but did them badly and endured the punishments that ensued.

In time, Mizzerin grew tired of being brought burned soup or smudged shirts and paid one of the school's servants to undertake these tasks. Imbry's burden lightened, but he remained the butt of the older boy's verbal barbs; though these were not sharpened by much wit, they were honed by Mizzerin's innate viciousness.

In time, however, they came to ignore each other. Mizzerin's interests lay in sports and games of chance, while Imbry was drawn into the pursuits of the mind. He discovered that he had a good eye for line and form and could produce creditable drawings after only a minimal instruction in technique. He also became adept in analyzing logical constructs and showed a flair for being able to isolate telling details that illuminated complex situations.

His work brought him notice from the senior staff and it was decided to offer him sections of the Class A curriculum, even though his aunts had only paid for the B. Habrey's observed a tradition of acquiring its faculty from within, the governing board seeing no purpose in watching its most brightly plumaged birds fly off to adorn other nests. But scarcely had Imbry been introduced to the study of elemental consistencies and asymmetrical persuasion than the incident of the tote burst over his head.

Imbry was in a sketching class, one of his favorites, rendering a complex still life in pastel shades, when the integrator summoned him to the proctor's office. The official regarded the boy from the other side of a desk strewn with notebooks containing columns of figures and tables of odds and permutations. After a lengthy silence, the proctor said, in his least compromising voice, "What are these?"

Imbry looked at the materials and said, "I do not know."

The proctor's brow compressed. "They are the records of a betting system based on intramural competitions within the school."

Imbry spread his hands. "I know nothing of such matters."

"Worse, they indicate that several competitions have somehow been interfered with, so that the owner of this betting system may be enriched."

"I know nothing," Imbry could only repeat.

"They were found in your room."

"It is not only my room," Imbry said.

"They were found between your mattress and the struts."

To that, Imbry could make no answer but the truth. He did not know what the things were nor how they came to be in his bed. He suggested that some of the letters and figures were so ill formed that they might be the product of Hop Mizzerin's penmanship.

Mizzerin was summoned and questioned but denied all knowledge. Pressed, he argued that his allowance was so substantial that he had no need to go to all the trouble of operating a tote and rigging sporting events. "What is my motivation?" he said.

Imbry would have suggested an intrinsic maleficence but his opinion was not sought. He steadfastly maintained his innocence.

The proctor's face grew long from stroking and tugging at his chin beard. Finally, he said, "The preponderance of evidence points to Luff Imbry. He will be sent off."

Imbry protested to his tutors. Three of them made representations on his behalf only to meet rebuffs, but the proctor quietly divulged to them a relevant issue: Hop Mizzerin had come to Old Earth from Winskill, where his father was not only socially prominent but a leading member of the thagonist caste. Its tenets required him to receive any slight, real or perceived, against a child of his household as equivalent to a slur upon his own honor. There could be no answer but blood.

"Apparently, young Hop stirred up disaffection at a number of institutes on Bowdrey's World, to whose schools the elite of Winskill usually send their progeny," the proctor informed the tutors. "The father was required to meet four principals and two head teachers, resulting in five deaths and a maiming. It was felt that the boy was less likely to cause offense on Old Earth, since both the Winskillers and the Bowdreyites consider us lackadaisical."

"So if we expel Mizzerin," said Imbry's art tutor, a slim man with delicate hands, "a sword wielding moustacho will come to fillet us in the outer quad?"

"It is quite likely," said the proctor. "The situation will ease once the boy reaches the age of fourteen; thereafter his honor is his own concern and we can send him back."

Imbry was transferred to another school, where standards were less exacting. He arrived under a cloud and was not made overly welcome. Before departing Habrey's, however, he asked for and was given the materials that had been found under his bed.

184

"Why do you want them?" said the integrator.

"They are supposed to be mine," the boy said. "Besides, if I'm to be un-justly punished, I should at least know what I am suffering for."

The integrator said, "Consider the Brashein Monument."

Imbry was familiar with the celebrated statue of the conqueror Ordelam Brashein that stood in a dusty square not far from the school. Seen from one angle, it represented a proud victor bedecked in laurels. From a different vantage, another image emerged: that of a vainglorious fool.

"You're saying that justice is distinguished from injustice by the angle from which it is viewed?"

"Am I?" said the integrator. But it supplied Imbry with the records and charts of Mizzerin's tote and the ratios he employed to wring a profit from his bettors. Imbry studied the materials in the chilly dormitory of his new school, saw the patterns and opportunities inherent in the system, and how it could be adapted to the sporting life that was such an important part of education.

Hop Mizzerin had been unable to command a sophisticated understanding of the elegance with which the matrix of odds and permutations could be arranged. He had clumsily cheated his fellow students, out of a perverse delight in taking advantage. Imbry brought more insight to the complexity of the system and when he felt himself the master of its ins and outs he applied it to his new surroundings. In a little while he was doing quite well, and after another little while he did even better. He also received more than simple profit, carving for himself a unique niche within the culture that surrounded him. After a year or so, he fitted that niche without chafing.

Winskill was a stark planet, a dry world of gritty deserts and jagged mountains, shrunken seas and narrow rivers. It offered few graces and even less forgiveness, and those who had come to settle it had grown to be like their world. Winskillers were a hard and uncompromising people, living in scattered towns whose livelihoods depended on the discovery and export of rare crystals occasionally exposed by the constant winds. A handful of villages had grown up around remote communities of contemplatives who found the harsh conditions a useful insulation: few visitors arrived to disturb their meditations.

In most parts of the planet, one day was much like any other, except during Regatta Week. Then, for eight days, a large portion of the scant population descended on the town of Jant, in the center of Northern Continent near the thirtieth parallel, to compete in the jib races, or to bet on their outcomes. Streams of high-grade crystals passed from one purse to another as the results of the preliminary races came in. By the time the Final Four were flying across the dead-level salt flats that extended in all directions from Jant, fortunes were on the line.

A jib was a lightweight windsailing craft. It consisted of a narrow board from which arose a thin, whip-like mast that supported a triangular sail braced on the bottom by a movable boom. At first glance, it seemed a simple construct, but considerable ingenuity had been applied to its design and development. The sail was made of an ultra-thin laminate shot through with narrow tubes called spiracules that connected to the boom. The boom, too, was hollow, as was the mast, which fed into a dense network of more spiracules in the board that was the craft's hull.

All of these conduits were precisely arranged to capture the wind striking the sail and to propel some of its energy downwards, creating a cushion of air beneath the board on which the operator stood. The rest of the wind's power was used to propel the craft forward. By judiciously varying the angle at which the wind encountered the sail, combined with the tilt of the board's nose relative to the horizon, a skilled jib sailor could maximize both the uplift of the ground effect and the forward motion of the whole assemblage.

The finest racers at the Jant Regatta could induce their jibs to eye-watering speeds across the vast and level salt flats. They were undeterred by potentially lethal danger, though horrific tumbles were not unknown, the hardpan surface being as unforgiving to human skin and bone as the Winskillers were to anyone who applied unfair modifications to a racing craft. For such crimes as incorporating into a jib's hull a gravity obviator or an energy field to lower wind resistance, the punishment was to be "set free" in the desert, a long way from water or shade.

Luff Imbry alighted at the spaceport at Choff on the Brass Coast, the nearest city to Jant. He hired an aircar and trusted it to find its way across the barren landscape. It set him down beside the main gate of the tent city that annually sprang up for the Regatta and, before flying back to its base, advised him on the available lodgings. He found acceptable accommodation at the Blackrock Inn's temporary regatta annex. This was a collection of inflated pavilions linked by soft-walled corridors to the inn proper. Imbry tried the local ale, finding it bitter but increasingly interesting after a few swallows. He also sampled a Winskill delicacy: a savory pastry baked around the abdomen of a hand-sized segmented creature that lived in crevices on the rocks of the sea coast. It had a subtle, nutlike flavor and he ordered another.

Along with the food, he requested a copy of the *Jant Hortator*, finding its pages dense with news, analyses and prognostications regarding the Final Four of the current Regatta. It was to take place the day after tomorrow, the contenders spending the intervening time resting after the rigors of the Semifinal, which had seen spectacular feats of jibmanship by the leaders of the field. Imbry read the coverage closely and made some notes.

Late that night, after taking measures to render himself unnoticeable, he visited the lightly guarded compound where the jibs for the next day's race were kept. He returned to his room in the pavilion and slept well.

"I know nothing of this," Hop Mizzerin told the umpires.

"Is this not your jib?" said the presiding officer of the Regatta.

"It is."

"And is this not a gravity obviating substance adhered to its base?"

"If you say so. I did not put it there." Mizzerin turned and appealed to the watching throng, his eyes sliding without recognition over Luff Imbry. "I am the favorite. Why would I do it?"

The crowd was not swayed. Many within it had seen friends and loved ones fall afoul of Mizzerins, who were quick to take offense and even quicker thereafter to draw.

"We cannot take time to examine motives. There is a race to be run and the deed speaks for itself."

Mizzerin's hand went to his hip but found nothing to grasp. Regatta Week in Jant was, necessarily, the sole time and place on Winskill where the Code of Dignity did not pertain.

The race began late, but with four contestants: the jibman who had placed fifth in the Semifinals was promoted to the Final Four, blinking and shaking his head while wearing a look of delighted surprise. A flurry of odds-changing ensued, with crowds of Winskillers and off-worlders shouting and waiving betting slips at the totesmen, trying to get their wagers altered before the warning horn blew.

Luff Imbry did not bother to bet. He returned to the Blackrock Inn for an early lunch and a quiet nap. Arising, he packed his belongings and paid his bill. He inquired of the helpful desk clerk where he might see about the importing of the segmented creature whose flesh carried such a unique flavor, and was disappointed to learn that they did not travel well.

By the time he boarded his aircar, the jib race was a plume of dust far out to the west. Imbry lifted off and turned the craft in another direction. He flew at good speed for a long while until finally he saw a small figure in the distance, marching steadily across the salt. As he drew closer, he realized that the custom of "setting free" was all inclusive: Hop Mizzerin walked naked and unshod. The parts of his skin that were not usually exposed to sunlight were already an angry pink, and the sun still had a long arc to fall to finish the extended Winskill day.

Imbry descended to a height just above Mizzerin's reach and slowed to a parallel course. The thagonist turned a puzzled expression on him as he took measured steps toward the bare horizon.

"You are trying to determine who has done this to you, and why," Imbry said.

"I am."

"I did."

Mizzerin stopped, his face clouded. He measured the distance between him and Imbry, then he drew in a deep breath and let it go. He resumed walking, but after a moment and without looking up, he said, "All right. Then why?"

"That is a good question. The simple answer requires you to consult your memory. Specifically you might recall your first roommate at Habrey's and how you parted."

Mizzerin looked at Imbry again for a moment, then nodded dourly and said, "Simple enough. But you imply that there is also a complex answer."

"Yes."

"I would like to hear it."

"I am still working on it," Imbry said. "It might take years before I have it complete in all its details."

Mizzerin walked on for several steps then said, "What happened to you after you left?"

Imbry gave him a summary of his life as a criminal. He saw no reason to dissemble.

"So," said Mizzerin, when he had heard it, "it seems I am responsible for the course your life has taken."

"It does."

"Yet you appear to be happy in that life. To a casual eye, you present an image of self-satisfaction."

"I am not unhappy," said Imbry.

"Do you pine for what might have been, a life of teaching and collegiality among the faculty at Habrey's?"

Imbry considered the question. "'Pine' is not the word I would use," he said. "'Wonder' is closer. Or perhaps 'idly dream.'"

The moved on for a while in silence until Imbry said, "Do you remember the integrator at Habrey's? The stories it used to tell?"

"It told me no stories," the marching man said.

"After we met and you blackened my eye, it told me a story about two animals in a forest. I didn't understand it at the time but when I was grown I looked up the tale."

"Is it relevant to our situation?"

Imbry declined a direct answer. "It was about how every beast must be true to its nature," he said, "no matter how ill the outcome."

"And are you true to yours?"

"I believe I am," said Imbry. "At least, I try to be."

"Ah," said Mizzerin, with another grim motion of his head, and began to ask another question. But Imbry did not stay to hear it. He lifted the car into the cooler upper air and sped away.

Mizzerin dwindled to a speck behind him. Imbry did not turn to look.

THE YELLOW CABOCHON

Sep Halpheroon was waiting for Luff Imbry in one of the private back rooms at Bolly's Snug, where the fat man often conducted business that it would have been unwise to do in public. Imbry was not pleased to find the middler already in one of the two chairs that faced each other across a bare table; he preferred to arrive at his assignations well before the other party, so as to avoid any surprises. His was a profession that did not greet surprises gladly; the unexpected was usually unwelcome, sometimes fatal. Imbry was a thief, a forger and an adept at several of the varied arts of relieving the careless — or even those who were merely not quite careful enough — of the burden of owning precious goods. Sometimes those he had unburdened so deeply resented his entry into their lives that they would have gladly arranged for him to exit his own. Other denizens of the Olkney halfworld harbored no particular resentment, but would have killed him on the off chance that the contents of his purse and pockets would repay the effort.

From the doorway he made a careful inspection of the room, the furniture, and the occupant, all of which were almost exactly as he had last seen them, here in this same chamber. The sole difference was that this time the middler's hands, resting on the table, framed a pouch of supple blue leather. The sight did much to mollify the fat man. Imbry entered, closed the door, and sat opposite Halpheroon, who lifted the pouch and stretched his arm across the table to deposit the bag before the thief. The middler's arm trembled from the weight and the bag's contents clinked musically as they settled.

Imbry undid the pouch's fastening and put his hand within, scooping out a handful of polished metal ingots, each a little less than half the length of his plump fingers. An iridescent sheen reflected the light in a transient rainbow as Imbry examined one of the pieces.

"Satisfied?" said the middler.

"Satisfied," said the thief. The precious metal was genuine. He replaced the ingots in the pouch. There was no need to weigh or count them. Halpheroon would be mad to short the fat man; for though the latter's girth might lull the uninitiated into dismissing Imbry as one of the lesser dangers of the halfworld, those who survived the initiation never forgot it.

Imbry made a gesture that constituted an appropriate farewell between peers and rose from his chair. As he moved, the pouch disappeared into a secure wallet beneath his half-cloak. He turned to leave.

"Wait," said Halpheroon, "there is another matter."

Imbry turned back. "What?"

"Another operation," said the middler, then paused as if to order his words. "It is much like the operation we have just concluded. But with a difference."

"How like?" said Imbry, "and how different?"

"Like — in that it concerns the same end-market, who again wishes to acquire a certain piece of jewelry. Unlike — in that the present owner of the item is not yet dead."

Imbry said, "Would it not be more appropriate to raise that issue with Green Circle?" It was the Green Circle gang that had ownership of the operation. Imbry was engaged only as a subcontractor, and Green Circle was a numerous and far-reaching criminal clan notorious for their resentment of freelancers who encroached.

"I did," said Halpheroon. "They declined to be involved at that level."

"But they do not mind if someone else takes up the slack?"

"They do not."

Imbry paused to think about it. "Who is the current owner of the desired item?"

"Lord Frons, of the House of Elphrate."

Imbry ran the name through his capacious memory. "Ah," he said, after a moment, "so the object of desire is the Grand Cascade?" He referred to a glittering tabard of seven different species of priceless jewels — hundreds of individual gems, even including a pair of matched thunderstones — that Lord Frons was pleased to wear over his chest and back on formal occasions.

"No," said Halpheroon, "not the cascade. The Yellow Cabochon."

"Really?" said Imbry. "Those things usually do not spark a blaze of avarice hot enough to consume the life of a high-ranked aristocrat."

"It is what the customer will pay for. Who are we to question his taste?"

The fat man let his face show that he had not yet come to a decision. "Frons Elphrate is a voyavod," — the rank meant that the subject was of the first-tier aristocracy, though only of the outer circle — "but does he not also perform some function within the Archonate, close to the Archon himself?"

"I researched him," said the middler. "He is the Minder of the Spoon when the Archon dines formally."

Imbry made a confirmatory noise. "Is that why Green Circle declines to take part?" Halpheroon moved his shoulders and hands in a manner that said the question invoked a mystery. Imbry said, "You did not ask?"

The middler gave the forger a look that inquired whether the fat man was new to the business. Imbry accepted the mild rebuke. Putting an impertinent question to a Green Circle power was a reliable method of ending up in Nazur Filiarot's cold locker, awaiting the next sealed coffin that could accommodate an extra occupant.

"But they definitely don't mind," the fat man said, "if you find someone who is less . . . shall we say, risk-averse?"

"We would have a free hand."

"But if things went awry," Imbry said, thinking it through, "Green Circle would want to be able to disavow any connection?"

Halpheroon signaled that this was so, and both men paused to consider the permanence of a Green Circle disavowal. The gang's philosophy, handed down through the ages, was that anything that threatened its existence forfeited all rights to its own.

"If Green Circle is out, who then is the client?"

"I have not been told. The dealer, Holton Baudwer, was approached by an off-worlder."

"This off-worlder realizes that there would be an additional fee?"

"He does."

"A substantial one."

"Baudwer says the man is prepared to pay what it costs."

"He must," said Imbry, "have found a customer who has as strong a yen for the Yellow Cabochon as Nazur Filiatrot has for his dreams."

"So it would seem."

That aspect of the matter puzzled Imbry. Yellow cabochons, even those as grand as the one that adorned Frons Elphrate's brow on formal occasions, did not normally provoke a murderous passion. But an off-worlder's standards could very likely be different. The fat man put the issue aside and turned his supple mind to other aspects of the proposal. There were a number of considerations to be weighed. After a while, he said, "I believe we can fill the order."

Imbry and Halpheroon had been doing occasional business for several years. To begin with, Imbry had sometimes used him as a go-between for the return of stolen goods when sentiment moved their erstwhile owner to pay more than a new possessor might offer — not an unusual circumstance, since even the most precious items shed a good deal of their practical value if they could not be publicly displayed lest they draw painfully pointed questions from the Archonate Bureau of Scrutiny.

A year or so after their association began, Halpheroon had come to the fat man with a proposition. The middler was bringing him two parts of the plan, because Imbry had the qualifications that allowed him to supply the necessary third. The two elements Halpheroon brought were: first, the services of Nazur Filiatrot, purveyor of funerary obsequies to a broad swath of Olkney's social elite; and, second, a client willing to pay for the goods the operation would yield.

Before Imbry agreed to take a hand in the proceedings, he first researched the mortician. He learned that the current proprietor of Filiatrot's Entombment Emporium was the latest in a long line of undertakers of that same name. The family had operated the establishment for centuries, if not millennia; when it came to disposing of the noble dead, Filiatrot's was the preferred choice for most of the second-tier aristocracy, and even some of the lower ranked families in the top echelon.

Nazur had inherited the solemn, unctuous personality that had served his ancestors well for generations. But to that inherited jewel he had added a new and clouded gem: a fondness for the lethetropic drug known as blue borrache. Fondness had not yet become outright dependency, but borrache was expensive even in moderate use. It also tended to diminish the earning capacity of its devotees, who spent long stretches of what should have been productive time enwrapped in colorful, comforting dreams.

So Nazur Filiatrot needed income and he devised a daring plan to secure it. Old Earth's aristocracy had, in recent generations, adopted the fashion of entombing not only their departed members but also their most precious possessions. The tombs, holding jewels and other finery of surpassing value, naturally attracted the attention of people like Imbry. But their peculative ambitions had met defeat at the hands of Nazur's great-grandparent, Mireyam Filiatrot, who devised an unbreachable sepulcher.

The noble residue, treated and preserved, clad in appropriate garb and bedecked with its most precious ornaments, was positioned in a chamber of the family tomb. Sometimes it sat in a favorite chair, or it might recline on a divan, or it might be posed in an activity that recalled a favorite pastime. When all was as it should be, the surrounding space was swiftly filled by a clear, heavy liquid that was then bathed in a specific sequence of finely tuned energies. The process, a carefully guarded Filiatrot secret, caused the liquid to undergo a phase shift, solidifying into an adamantine mass that Mireyam Filiatrot trademarked as Clarity. The transparent stuff refracted light so that the relict at its center seemed to be bathed in a golden glow, as if caught in a perfect moment of an ideal afternoon.

Enterprising tomb-breakers made attempts to penetrate Clarity, but found it resistant to all of the cutting tools and energies commonly used in their trade. It was hypothesized that it might be possible to batter a path through it with modified tumblethrusts, or to burn through with heavy-grade phase weapons. But the busters would have made far too much noise, and the ison cannons — even if they could be manhandled into the tombfields and brought to bear — would also melt the corpse and its treasures into an undifferentiated slag.

After the advent of Clarity, even more of Old Earth's highest and haughtiest consigned their dead to the clammy hands of the Filiatrots, secure in the knowledge that they and their possessions would rest inviolate for all time, or at least until the old orange sun finally reached its dotage and swelled to encompass the three innermost planets.

But then came Nazur and his affection for the comforts of blue borrache. In need of funds, the mortician got to thinking of the process by which his clients were entombed in Clarity. And he found an opportunity.

A corpse chamber was typically set with furnishings and accoutrements brought from the aristocrat's own apartments. After the ritual ceremony that irrevocably separated the dead from the living, the body would be prepared, dressed and positioned as specified by a document known as the "corporeal courtesy." At the last moment, the subject's senior servitor, a person genetically attuned through millennia of inbreeding to be incapable of defying even a dead master's wishes, would uncover the precious goods. Filiatrot would take the jewels, robes of wondercloth, gowns of spun-pearl and such-like, and reverently adorn the body. A few final adjustments, and he would order the chamber cleared. Immediately, liquid Clarity would begin to flow and, under the eyes of the mourners, the deceased would be sealed forever in aureous light.

Nazur's plan required boldness and daring, of which he had little. But he found, as many a blue borrache addict had found before him, that desperation could be enlisted as a workable substitute. He began by acquiring a primer on the art of sleight of hand. He practiced until he became proficient in all the workaday slips and palms. He then graduated to ever more subtle and difficult sleights, mastering each in turn. Within months, he knew himself to be as good as the best, and he reached out for the next step in his plan.

He made inquiries in the halfworld. Ordinarily, that process would have put him in peril. But the Filiatrots had for generations offered a not-often-used but lucrative sideline: when members of Green Circle found themselves encumbered with corpses whose discovery would have been inconvenient, the morticians would make the inconvenience vanish. Nazur approached the family's contact within the Green Circle hierarchy and was soon put in touch with Sep Halpheroon.

The middler listened to Nazur's proposal with interest then went out and located the other two necessities for the plan: a dealer like Holton Baudwer, who could dispose of the proceeds off-world, there being markets among the Ten Thousand Worlds where valuable antiquities from Old Earth could command high prices; and a skilled forger who could replicate the goods well enough to pass for the real thing.

Imbry was the forger. Halpheroon was careful to point out to the fat man that this operation had been arranged by Green Circle; that was to limit Imbry's ambition, else the forger might have sought to replace Baudwer, who would probably make as much from the operation as Imbry's, Nazur's and Halpheroon's shares combined.

But now the business had taken a new tack, with the gang opting not to be involved in the initial phase of the next operation, in which Frons Elphrate would be separated from the Yellow Cabochon, by first being separated from his existence. "You are absolutely certain that Green Circle will have no comment?" Imbry asked Halpheroon.

"Baudwer said there was no ambiguity."

"Whom did he consult?"

"Wrython Herrither, the force in charge."

That sounded reasonable to Imbry. He moved on to the practicalities. "Did you have anyone in mind, for the task of easing Lord Frons off the path?"

Halpheroon said, "I thought of asking Ils Buttram, but he has just taken a contract with the Shostakos."

"Really? I hadn't heard that." Custom required that he pass Halpheroon a coin for the new information. He did so and the middler pocketed it without comment. The room was silent while Imbry pursued his train of thought. After a while, he said, "Leave that aspect with me."

"Very good," said Halpheroon. "Let me know when you have someone in place."

"I will," said Imbry, he made an appropriate gesture and departed.

Imbry made inquiries to determine the availability of two other contractors of Ils Buttram's caliber. He discovered that Toba Blom was fully booked by the House of Smolleren — hereditary antagonists of the Shostakos — and would probably remain on the Smollerens' strength until the current phase of threat and confrontation worked its way, as with the preceding feuds, to another stalemate. Siva Verein heard the fat man's proposition but declined. "I've made it a rule not to entangle myself with aristocrats," she said. "They are too strange. They not only want to specify the exact setting and circumstances, but often they want to play a part in the crucial moments. I had one . . . well, you would not believe the mess. And he expected me to clean up after."

"Unacceptable," agreed Imbry. "So you would not accommodate me with Frons Elphrate, even if it is I who sets the terms?" Verein began to answer, but Imbry added, "Because the only stipulation would be that the event seem accidental."

The woman thought about it briefly, her slender fingers drawing at her lower lip. Then she said, "No. What is the point of making rules if one then makes exceptions?"

Imbry was not greatly disappointed. Even back during the meeting at Bolly's Snug he had felt himself leaning toward the idea of keeping this additional chore in his own hands. The assassin's fee would not only increase his earnings, but doing it himself would ensure a job done right.

He went by a roundabout, surveillance-avoiding route to his operations center, a pair of ill-kept houses in the Grindle district that he had acquired by an equally circuitous series of transactions; ownership could never be traced to him. He entered by the back door of one of the properties, after carefully transiting an overgrown rear yard that he had planted with aggressive poisonous plants and set about with hidden defensive systems and mantraps. In the dim, dusty basement he spoke a sequence of syllables and moved his hand in a certain way. A pile of debris and broken furniture slid out of position, revealing a heavily defended door. The fat man quieted the portal's murderous inclinations and bid it open. He stepped through into a lightless corridor and waited until the door had closed and its disguising rubbish had slid back in place. Then he spoke another password and the passageway lit up brightly before him. But still the fat man waited, slowly counting to ten, until he saw a small lumen light itself at the far end of the tunnel.

Moments later, he had crossed the distance that separated one house from the other and ascended a narrow spiral staircase that led to the back of a closet in an unfurnished spare room. Standing in the closet, Imbry said, softly, "Well?"

"All's well," a voice answered. He exited the closet and room, and went down a dingy hall to another chamber that looked as if it had been furnished with items found along the roadside. Imbry touched a battered dresser in three specific places; instantly, some of its parts withdrew into itself while others appeared from within. Imbry took the offered seat, touched a number of keys and studs on the control panel that came into view and said, "We will research the House of Elphrate." He reflected a moment, then added, "I will also need full specifics on the Yellow Cabochon."

"Which first?" said the integrator.

"Elphrate."

A screen appeared in the air, filled with text and images. "Overview," the fat man said, and turned his eyes toward the display. He had read only a few lines when he uttered a mild oath. "I should have remembered that," he said.

The overview of the first-tier noble house of Elphrate reported that the family had risen to high rank during the First Great Effloration, the time aeons ago when humankind had spilled out into The Spray, locating and populating the Ten Thousand Worlds. The Elphrates had remained on Old Earth, flourishing and enjoying the opportunities for more elevated rank and territorial acquisition that arose as the old planet emptied out.

As the ages wore on, however, the central loci of human civilization moved inevitably down The Spray. It first took root in the Grand Foundational Domains, as the original human-settled worlds came to be known. Then the Grand Foundationals created the Second Great Effloration by sending their surplus and enterprising citizens out to fill up the lesser worlds; somewhere along the way, Old Earth became a half-forgotten backwater; as the millennia piled upon each other, the little orb scarcely drew a glance. On the original Grand Foundational Domains, now grown rich and splendid, the question was raised: how could such a fusty little place, so deeply unfashionable, have been the primeval font of a civilization as majestic as that of the Ten Thousand Worlds? After a while, the question was not even considered worth raising. Three other worlds — splendid, opulent cornucopias — each let it be known that it was the authentic cradle of humanity.

It was about then that Old Earth's last remaining remnants finally fled the species's worn-out nursery. Some left all behind, hopping the first liner or passenger-carrying freighter that was standing out into the immensity. Most of the aristocracy had long since gone out to the Grand Foundationals. Attrition had thus made the Elphrates almost the highest-ranked family remaining on Old Earth. The restiveness of the junior members of the clan finally moved the patriarch, the Domine Jurgon Elphrate, to load his entire household onto his several space yachts, most of them antiques though perfectly maintained; off they went in search of a new home.

But a rude shock awaited these latecomers: noble rank on Old Earth meant nothing to the elites that had grown up on the Grand Foundationals; citizens who had migrated to the secondary worlds had mostly abandoned traditional class strictures or had developed new ones of their own, often rooted in philosophies that put scant value on heredity. For the Elphrates, the choice was between becoming little more than commoners on the settled worlds, or finding some unused planet where they could maintain their standards. The problem with the latter option was that humankind had been filling up The Spray for aeons; all of the best, all of the second-best, and even most of the not-very-best-at-all worlds were spoken for.

The junior Elphrate scions were dispatched to search the edges of the human-settled cosmos, even into the dark spaces of the Back of Beyond. They found arid balls of rock, or steaming jungles thick with savage plants, or ice-worlds so cold the first breath congealed the lungs, or planets without land, whose single ocean teemed with poisoned spines, gargantuan maws, ragged claws, and insatiable appetites.

They reported back to Jurgon Elphrate that they had located one world that could be made habitable. Issa was a smallish planet, half shaded from the main body of The Spray by an obscuring cloud of interstellar gas. It offered but a single continent — really not much more than a large island — though the climate was equable; the seas, though no less full of eat-or-be-eaten life, were shallow and not often oppressed by extravagant storms.

Issa was not a virgin world. Every few centuries, bands of settlers had come to try farming the island's indifferent soil, but each successive clump of humanity had failed to prosper. When the world passed into the control of the aristocrats from Old Earth, some of the existing population agreed to take on the duties of a peasantry in return for the Elphrates' guaranteeing them the necessities of life.

Issa's geology was still in its active stage, however, and the single small continent was almost completely riven from north to south by a long sea loch that widened by a hand's breadth every year. At the same time, the east and west coasts were perceptibly sliding under the waves. Eventually, there would be little land to support the Elphrates' way of life. But the new owners were Old Earth nobility, well accustomed to thinking in the longer term. The elders of the clan decided that it would do no harm to prepare for the eventual: they had the younger members' gene plasm edited to make them semiaquatic. They did not opt for the full gills-and-flippers approach, but did borrow liberally from the marine mammals of Old Earth. That gave generations of Elphrates webbed toes and fingers, large, light-gathering eyes with a second nictitating membrane, and an altered musculo-pulmonary systems that allowed them to remain under water for two hours or more on a single breath of air.

It was this last finding that caused Imbry to swear. On previous occasions when he had needed to relieve his environment of an inconvenient presence, without drawing official inquiries, he had found that a quick drowning was a useful means. Old Earth's surface was, after all, seventy per cent covered in water, and even the driest zones might have precipitators or even piped-in water supplies. Now he called up an image of Frons Elphrate and, when his integrator enlarged it, he clearly saw the folds of loose skin between the voyavod's fingers. The fat man swore again; it would have to be some other method. He said, "Review the subject's habits and pastimes with a view to arranging for an accident. Does he, for example, hunt?"

"No," said the integrator.

"Then what do we have to work with?"

"He has been known to climb."

"Hills?"

"Mountains."

Imbry considered the implications. For all his girth, he was agile and strong. But there were limits. "What else?"

"His duties since he was made Minder of the Spoon have tended to keep him close to Olkney, in case he is summoned to the Palace."

"How much minding can a spoon need?" Imbry said.

"The ceremonial aspects of the post are numerous and varied. For example, at the Feast of Slamming Doors, it is his responsibility to lift the salver that covers the soup, while the Custodian of the Bread Dish —"

"The question was rhetorical." The fat man sighed. "Now specify an opportunity to kill Frons Elphrate, so that it seems to be an accident, and with minimal risk of my being apprehended."

"There is one possibility," the integrator said. "He always visits the Antinori Shrine three days before his birthday. No one knows why; it may be the outcome of a private vow. He does not discuss what he does there. Nor is he attended."

"When is his birthday?"

"In fifteen days."

Imbry made a small sound of appreciation, then his brow drew down. "He doesn't climb to the place?" he said. The Antinori stood atop a tall pillar of natural stone near the edge of a great desert, far to the northeast of Olkney. It was a relic of the legendary civilization of Ambit, which had vanished aeons ago in a great cataclysm that was said to have created the wasteland of Barran.

"No. He travels by aircar."

"His own?"

"Naturally."

"What would he do if his own vehicle were disabled en route?"

"I can only predict. He would either summon another from the estate pool or hire one locally."

It was a long way from Frons Elphrate's estate in Long Burre, well south of Olkney, to the edge of Barran. "If the aircar broke down almost to the destination . . ."

"There is a hire service in Vanochi, a half-hour's flight from the shrine."

"Are the owners . . . malleable?" Some hired car services were accustomed to accommodating unorthodox requests, if the requests were accompanied by substantial sums.

"No."

The fat man grunted. "Then it will have to be after he gets there. Show me the Antinori, inside and out." Imbry was not familiar with the place, other than what everybody knew: that it was an ancient cubical structure, made of closely fitted blocks of white stone, aeons old. Even the origin of its name was lost; it might celebrate a forgotten deity, a person of note who was entombed there, or the shrine's builder.

One thing was known: the site was entirely private. "There is not even an integrator," said Imbry's assistant, using the tone that, among its kind, expressed shock and disapproval.

It took several seconds before the device could answer its owner's command to show the Antinori, inside and out, and when it did, it had to report partial failure. "I have researched widely," it said. "Of outer views, there are plenty," — it showed a selection from different angles — "Of inner, there are none. Or almost. Here is a sketch said to have been done from memory by one Tharn Holbach, a citizen of Bilbaron."

"I do not know Bilbaron," Imbry said, peering at the faded pencil drawing.

"It was one of the towns that ringed the walled city of Ambit, destroyed in the disaster that obliterated the moon."

"What moon?"

"The one that used to orbit Old Earth."

Imbry vaguely recalled hearing about that, back in his school days. "That was a long time ago," he said.

"Indeed. Shall we proceed?"

"Can you enhance the sketch?"

The faint gray lines deepened. The fat man told the integrator to magnify the image. He examined it carefully. "It seems to be a corridor leading to a simple inner chamber. What is the object beyond the archway?"

"I would say a tomb or an altar," said the integrator.

"And what about the writing above the entrance to the sanctum?"

"Unknown," said his assistant, after a long pause.

It was not an answer Imbry had ever heard from his device. He had constructed it not only to have access to the world-wide connectivity, but to many supposedly private stores of information, including even the highly protected integrators at the Archonate Bureau of Scrutiny and the ancient devices housed deep in the living rock of the Devenish Range, atop which sat the palace of the Archon himself.

"Unknown?" he said.

"It has similarities to the Golonoi script, used by the savants of the Ythe Civilization that flourished in the late Sixteenth Aeon, one of the periods when the universe is said to have been ruled by magic."

"Pah!" said Imbry. "There is no need to traffic in myth."

"As you say," said his integrator. "I can but report what I find."

"No matter. The important thing is that he goes there alone, and is unobserved during his stay." He looked at the external images, saw a flat space in front of the shrine where an aircar would land; when he magnified a couple of the images, he could see scratches in the rock that looked to have been made by a volante's undercarriage. They were at no great distance to the edge of the precipice. "How great is the drop to the desert below?"

"Seventeen seconds."

"Well," said Imbry, clasping together his plump palms, "there it is." He called for a wider view and regarded for a moment the isolated spire, the long drop, the sharp rocks below. "As if it were made for an ambush," he said.

The Yellow Cabochon, Imbry learned, had an interesting provenance. During the ages that the Elphrates had sojourned in their coastal estate on Issa, exploring submarine plains and grottos, they had discovered that the wet little world had once been home to a sapient, sea-dwelling species. A social collapse or a universal murrain, or perhaps both, had brought about the extinction of the autochthones, long before humanity had stepped across the threshold of civilization. But the Issans had left behind scattered remnants of their architecture: multi-unit houses, all curved walls and winding passageways, built for them by domesticated coral-like microcreatures, and long, tiered stadia that were assumed to have been used for ceremonial or sporting purposes, or perhaps both.

In some of the vacant rooms at the ends of the coliseums the exploring Elphrates found unfaceted gems of yellow and blue-green nacre, flat on one side and rounded on the other. The cabochons ranged in size from that of a thumbnail to the width of a palm. The humans surmised that the Issans, having had no metallurgy, had not mined these precious items, but had caused them to be grown in the flesh of mollusk-like creatures that also seemed to have been their primary food — left to their own whims, the mollusks generated none larger than a dried pea.

Some of the gems had engraving on their flat sides: complex and intricate geometrical patterns that, when viewed through the domed side, had a disorienting effect on human neural circuits. After a few seconds, the viewer would be plunged into unconsciousness, only to awaken moments later. The reawakening was not complete in an instant, however, and many reviviants reported a sense of dissociation from reality similar to that experienced by some travelers on space ships who went through a whimsy without first numbing the mind into unconsciousness. As well, for weeks after, some would be wrapped in a mood of euphoric possibility, as if at any moment warm and wondrous conditions would arrive.

No one knew what effect the inscribed cabochons might have had on the vanished Issans, but the effects on the humans who possessed them gave the jewels a certain value to those who enjoyed playing a joke on friends and family. The value was never great, however, because the same effects could be obtained through a wide variety of aerosols and even alternating frequencies of light and sound, none of which were very costly.

Persons who used the gems to enter into the period of joyous anticipation found that the happy times ceased after a few repetitions, leaving a taste in the mind as of wet ashes. Besides that shortcoming, the unfaceted gems were not particularly beautiful, the yellows being a sickly color and the blue-greens resembling children's candy.

The Elphrates held onto most of the cabochons that they had found on Issa, largely because owning things was what Old Earth aristocrats did best. A few of the gems made their way onto the markets, but commanded no great prices. The one commonly referred to as the Yellow Cabochon was not much different from any of the other inscribed specimens, except that it was the largest — the size of a child's face — and because, in the first millennia after the House of Elphrate had returned to Old Earth, the patriarch of the day had had it set into a lozenge of electrum and chased white gold from the workshop of the Hugan Brothers.

Frons Elphrate occasionally wore the gem hanging from a chain of the same precious metals, also from the Hugans. In his youth, he had enjoyed holding the object up to the eyes of persons who did not know of the peculiar properties of inscribed Issan cabochons. Then he would laugh when they suddenly collapsed, and laugh even harder when they awakened and found themselves lacking full control of their faculties. His laugh was a nasal bray that drew up his top lip to reveal the long, ivory-colored incisors that were characteristic of the Elphrates.

Eventually, he ran out of potential victims, first-tier nobility being limited in their acquaintances largely to each other and a few senior servants. But he continued to display the jewel as a personal emblem at formal functions — except, of course, when he served the Archon at table; to have rendered Filidor unconscious then disoriented during an occasion of state would have been an unthinkable act of lèse-majesté; the repercussions would have been catastrophic for the Elphrates, seeing them demoted as a House to second-tier rank, at the very least, if not to the outer darkness of the third.

Be that as it may, the Yellow Cabochon remained one of Lord Frons's signature jewels, though Imbry found it hard to believe that that the voyavod meant to wear it through eternity. But, if that was the aristocrat's intent, Imbry now set about frustrating it. In his operations center, he moved to another battered piece of furniture — a squat cylindrical foot-rest — and twice-touched a scuff mark on its frayed top. Immediately, the item reassembled itself as the work table on which the fat man created many of his best forgeries.

At a word from him, his integrator supplied the table with the requisite specifications. A three-dimensional image of the Yellow Cabochon and its setting and chain appeared on the work surface. Imbry studied the simulacrum closely, calling for magnifications and views from several angles. He deduced that it would not be necessary to replicate the chain; the jewel in its setting was attached to the links by a simple catch. Nazur Filiatrot would be able to make the switch in the blink of an eye.

Imbry set controls and adjusted the work table's calibrations. He soon found, when he began to arrange the finer details, that neither his integrator nor his craft tools were able to reproduce the engraved marks on the cabochon's flat side; the first device declared itself unable to capture and retain the actual design, and therefore could transmit only a rough approximation it to the work table.

"Why not?" said Imbry.

"I do not know," said the integrator. "The lines and curves do not obey the rules of three-dimensional geometry, and you have not provided me with the capacity to deal with more abstruse figures."

"It never seemed necessary."

"Do you wish me to try to develop the ability?"

Imbry thought about it. "No," he said. "If anyone examines the object so closely as to notice the difference, the birds would all be up and flown anyway." He set a few more controls, then said, "Let us see the first cut."

The top of the work table grew indistinct. Then a version of the Yellow Cabochon appeared. Imbry waited for the forgery to fully congeal then picked it up and examined it closely. "Not bad," he said, touching two studs on the table's control panel and minutely moving a ratcheted slide. "This won't take long."

Gebbry Tshimshim operated an aircar hire service in the Brecchon district of Olkney. She was pliant when it came to meeting her halfworld customers' unusual needs. Her vehicles were dependable and nondescript — the kind witnesses later found it difficult to describe in detail — and she provided valuable extra services, such as an unreliable record-keeping system that made it difficult to tell exactly who had rented what, and when. She also would supply a hand-held device that, when pointed at one of her vehicles, would cause its integrator to void all recollections save for its core understandings. Imbry had done business with her many times, to their mutual satisfaction.

Early in the morning of the eleventh day after he began the operation, the fat man lifted off from Tshimshim's yard and flew over the flat lands south of Olkney. After some minutes of straight and level flight, he opened the satchel on the seat beside him and took out a small device of his own design and manufacture. He positioned it on the top of the control panel, gave it a moment to orient itself and perform its functions, then said, "Well?"

"Nothing," it said.

"Keep watching," he said.

He flew on, over crop lands and meadows interrupted by stretches of well tended forest, the aircar automatically avoiding the boundaries of any estates;

the nobility were generally resentful of uninvited overflights, and some would instruct their servants to forgo warnings and to respond on first sight with a shot that would disable the vehicle. The trespasser would then be delivered up to whatever punishments the landowner thought appropriate. Some of those penalties could be excessive; Imbry preferred to reach his destination without suffering alterations to his hide or a delay of weeks or months spent performing demeaning and menial tasks.

The sun, today a more than usually faded orange, its lower-right quadrant blemished by a pair of black spots that crawled about each other, crept slowly up to the zenith. The aircar was passing over a wide reach of wild woodland, the taller deodars and greengums sending naked spars above the dark green canopy. "Anything?" Imbry said.

"Nothing," said the device.

He directed the vehicle to descend to a clearing, then with its skirts only at knee-height above the ground, he turned it onto a narrow, unpaved track that wound through the trees. The air grew dark and cool and Imbry closed the transparent canopy — some of the less traveled forests were the haunts of feral beasts.

After several twists and turns of the track, he took a detour along a shallow stream that led to a ford where Imbry turned onto a wagon trail. Some time later, he came to the edge of a wide field that abutted the forest. Here, beneath a tall, spreading deciduous tree, waited a capacious ground vehicle — tall, wide and long, on eight high wheels — its engine running. One of Gebbry Tshimshim's employees, clad in farm laborer's fatigues, sat in the control cab, chewing a cheekful of leaves of a plant that contained a mild natural stimulant.

The vehicle's rear door was open. Without leaving the shade of the overhanging tree, Imbry lifted the aircar into the empty cargo compartment and powered down its gravity obviators. The door slid closed behind him and the great wheels rolled away across the field.

Hours later, with the sun still defaced but now red and at the horizon, the carrier came to a halt. The rear door opened and Imbry backed the volante out and across a loading dock into a spacious, high-roofed building whose walls were lined with huge storage bins for beans and legumes. No one was on the premises. He turned the aircar in its own length, activated an energy drape that made the vehicle resemble a groundcar, and drove it sedately out the far door and onto a narrow rural road that wound between scattered villages. When night was well fallen and the device on the control panel assured him that he remained unobserved, he stopped on a deserted stretch of the road, retuned the drape to make the vehicle appear to be a different species of aircar, and had it rise into the air. He turned the volante's nose northeast and bid its integrator make best speed. Under the splash of The Spray and the glittering array of orbitals, he sped through the night toward Barran.

The view from the shrine was unrewarding: bare rock sweeping in from all directions to the foot of the pillar far below. Imbry did not trouble himself to regard it; he found the emptiness depressing, and could understand why some folks — less well put together than he — would find this spot a suitable place of departure from the troubles that life could deliver. A few steps in any direction, then one more, and the world-weary could join the shattered bones and patches of dried skin scattered around the foot of the cliff.

He had ordered the aircar to position itself in a canyon beyond the southern horizon, its drape of concealing energies now giving it the appearance of a boulder. Then he had hidden himself in the rude stone building, which contained nothing but a sarcophagus of pale marble, the inscriptions and effigies that had once adorned its top and sides scoured almost completely away by the thousand sandstorms that had swept through the tomb's four entrances, open to the cardinal directions. They had once been sealed by ornamented doors until some aficionado, probably off-world, had decided that they would look better in his private collection.

Imbry unpacked the wicker hamper he had brought: two kinds of bread, a wedge of soft cheese, and a multi-compartmented box that contained a selection of savory pastes, pickles and a tangy jelly. He opened a half-bottle of summer wine from the Phalum vineyards and filled a crystal beaker that had nestled in a padded armature in the hamper's hinged lid.

But before he indulged himself, he opened the satchel that held his operational gear and shook out the folded elision suit. He stepped into the leggings and tugged the rest of the garment up and over his clothing, then sealed the front plaquet and pulled the cowl over his head. He let the mouth flap dangle so that he could eat, but all the rest of his corpulent frame was now invisible to the eye — and not only to that organ, but to devices attuned to most of the electromagnetic spectrum; the suit captured energies and bent them around itself.

Imbry found that the garment often simplified matters, as it would today. The moment Frons Elphrate stepped out of his volante, he would be seized by the fat man's unseen hands and thrown from the spire. The wind would get the blame, or his own carelessness. His aircar would report the event and retainers would come to remove the body before a scavenging fand could drag it to its lair. Before the end of the day, the corpse would be in Nazur Filiatrot's hands, and Imbry's role in the business would be concluded.

The breads and savories in the basket had come from the ancient kitchens at Quirks, one of the clubs in which the fat man held memberships, the cheese from a specialty vendory that Imbry frequented when the urge struck him. The tangy relish was something he mixed up on his own, and together the combination of tastes evoked a sound of contentment. He cleansed his palate with the wine then loaded another round of bread, this time with a little less of the herbed paté but a little more of the soft cheese, and applied the jelly. Even better. He leaned back against the sarcophagus and enjoyed the moment.

The device that had sat atop the aircar's control panel now spoke to him from the stone floor beside him, "From the southwest, arriving in four minutes."

Imbry finished the wine and packed the tumbler and the uneaten food back in the hamper, then carried the basket around to the northern side of the sarcophagus, where it would not spoil the proceedings. The warning device had done its job in relaying the message from the aircar. He now deactivated it, so that no telltale energy would alert the arriving vehicle.

He stood just back of the southern doorway, on the shaded side, and drew up the elision suit's jaw flap, fastening it behind his head. He watched the southwestern horizon and after a moment, he saw a flash of reflected sunlight in the offing. Soon, a dark shape became visible, growing steadily as the aircar bore straight on toward the shrine. It had been flying not far above the barren surface, but now it was angling up so that it would arrive at its destination just above the pillar's height.

Imbry drew a little farther back into the shadow and watched. He saw that the vehicle was of an antique design, though no doubt lovingly maintained, with its body in deep umber and its flaring skirts and rear sponsons in old gold — the colors of the House of Elphrate. The canopy was open, the day being hot even at the shrine's elevation, and soon he could make out the features of the single occupant. He recognized at first the typically elongated face, the bulbous, rounded forehead, and the oversized, wide-set eyes that were hallmarks of the Elphrate clan. And as the aircar swept up to settle near the southern edge of the spire, its obviators thrumming softly as they powered down, he saw the particular arrangement of Elphrate features that made up the face of Lord Frons, impassively regarding the doorway through which the aristocrat meant to enter the shrine.

There was scant room for the Elphrate volante between the cliff's edge and the door of the wind-roughened structure. As the target stepped from the air car, Imbry left the building and strode briskly toward him, his hands raised, palms out. The precipice waited, scarcely two paces behind the man. One good shove . . .

Imbry was hearing a clicking noise, not loud, and slow at first, though its tempo increased as he stepped out, shadowless, into the sunlight that obligingly bent itself around him, following the force-channels of the elision suit. The fat man could not detect where the sound was coming from — perhaps from the aircar, he thought, glancing that way.

But when he looked back at Frons Elphrate he realized that, elision suit or no, the voyavod was aware of him. The clicks now came ever fast — almost becoming one continuous whir of sound — and Imbry saw that the man he had come to kill had something in his hand, a hand that was rising to point at him.

The fat man stepped to the left, his feet silent on the windswept rock, but Lord Frons's hand tracked to follow him. The strange, almost nonhuman face betrayed no emotion, the pale eyes, almost a faded gold in the bright sunlight, with pinprick pupils. Imbry rushed forward now, but the voyavod's weapon's emitter showed a ring of purple that slid immediately out of the visible spectrum, leaving a retinal image dancing in Imbry's field of vision.

Then the air somehow turned hard and threw itself at the fat man, striking his face and upper body with blunt force. He was conscious of the impact and then of a sense of motion reversed, of falling back through the door of the shrine. Then he was not conscious of anything at all.

"And . . . there we are."

The voice came out of a red haze. It took a moment for Imbry to realize that he was seeing the tired old sun through closed eyelids. He opened them and his eyes swam with tears as the light struck his retinas. He was lying on his back on hard stone. Something moved above him momentarily blocking the light. He blinked away the moisture and made out the shape of a man's head and shoulders, bending over him, dark and undifferentiated against the brightness.

The man moved to one side, his attention fixed on something he held in one hand and poked at with the webbed fingers of the other. "That should do it," he said, and swiftly but subtly, like a lens coming into focus, Imbry's mind cleared and he knew where he was and why.

There was a looped strap on the object Lord Frons held. Now he put it over his head so that the device hung at about waist height. Imbry saw that its outer face had rows of studs and a pair of sliders. The man flexed his elongated fingers — did each one have an extra joint? — then positioned their spatulate tips on the controls, with the calm certainty of a virtuoso about to play an old, familiar piece. He turned his strange pale gaze back to Imbry. "Before we begin," he said, in a voice that contained a flutey whistle, as if it were two instruments combining for a duet, "Must ask . . . the relish?"

"The relish . . ." Imbry's throat was dry.

"In the hamper. You won't mind . . . took the liberty . . . refresh myself. Long flight . . . getting you settled . . . no small effort."

Imbry tried to sit up, found he could not. Something constricted him, from scalp to sole, tightening when he moved, loosening when he stilled. He was outside the shrine, lying beside the aristocrat's volante.

"Should have brought some kind of carrier, I suppose," his captor was saying, "but didn't expect . . ." He gestured with the unusual hands to indicate Imbry's moundedness. "Any case, finished your lunch while you were . . . away. Patés very good. Whose?"

Imbry named the underchef at Quirks and identified the club.

"Ah," said Frons, nodding. Imbry was not surprised that the club's gustatorial reputation had apparently reached even the notice of a first-tier exquisite. "The relish . . . his also?"

"My own recipe," said Imbry.

The pale eyes widened and the thin eyebrows arched. "Oh? Oddly qualified, assassin and all that."

"I am not really," said Imbry, "an assassin."

Frons made a face that argued he should not be taken for a fool. He touched a control and a thin line of agony ran up the outside of Imbry's right ankle. The fingertip lifted and the pain ceased, leaving the fat man gasping. "I meant," he said, when he recovered his breath, "that murder is not my primary occupation."

"Ah," said the voyavod. "Well, suppose we've begun, haven't we? Do remind me . . . get the recipe . . . that relish, before . . ."—he made a vague one-handed motion to indicate the inevitable outcome of their meeting.

"I am eager to cooperate," Imbry said.

"If you like. Makes no difference." Frons's fingers went back to the controls. "So, who sent you?"

"I don't actually — " Imbry finished with a prolonged scream as his eye sockets seemed to fill with molten metal.

"Thought you wanted to cooperate."

"Perhaps," said the fat man, when the horrific pain blinked into nothingness, "it would be best if I told you what I do know. As I say, I am not, strictly speaking, an assassin, and your death was to be only part of a larger plan."

"Indeed?"

"I assure you."

"Right, then," said Lord Frons, "tell your tale."

Imbry did so, beginning with the approach from Sep Halpheroon and the previous, successful operations with Nazur Filiatrot and Clarity. He stressed that he was part of a wider web of operatives, who were not required to know each other because they dealt through middlers.

"Someone wanted me dead," said the voyavod when the fat man was finished, "to get his hands on my Yellow Cabochon?"

"Yes."

The aristocrat made a thoughtful sound, and his brows drew down, causing the rounded center of his forehead to protrude even more noticeably. He made the sound again and his fingers absently tapped the controls of the device hung around his neck, creating in Imbry the impression that his spine was being slowly ripped from his body. He screamed again and the sensation immediately ceased, Lord Frons fluttering a hand in a gesture that was as close as an Old Earth aristocrat could come to an apology.

When he had finished thinking about what he had heard, however, the voyavod said, "Makes no sense."

"I assure you — " Imbry began but subsided as Frons held up one hand in admonition while the other idly stroked a slider.

"Oh, believe," said Imbry's captor, "you believe what you're telling me. But got to tell you . . . makes no sense. Cabochon not in the courtesy. Idea lacks dignity. Will wear the cascade."

"Perhaps the ultimate client was misinformed."

"Possible," said Frons. He thought about it, then the corners of his mouth turned down. "But no. Safer to assume . . . this business of the cabochon . . . deliberately advanced . . . means to an end . . . end being my demise."

Now it was Imbry's turn to make a thoughtful sound, though his was tinged by a dawning anger. He did not care to be used in this manner. "I wish to make a proposal," he said.

They flew back toward Olkney in the Elphrate volante. Although an antique, it was luxuriously appointed, the seats covered in leather as soft as, and the color of, butter. Imbry reached up to remove the tormentor Lord Frons had attached to the back of his neck while he had been unconscious, saying, "I suppose, since we are in agreement, there is no more need of —"

He interrupted his own remark with a small shriek as the device convinced his sensorium that the bones of his reaching hand were on fire. The pain faded as his hand instinctively flinched away. The voyavod had not touched the controls, which he had laid casually on the bench seat between them when they entered the vehicle.

"Plausible rogue, you . . .not entirely convinced . . . your innocence," said the aristocrat. "Until I am, best not try to touch tukkatuk." After a moment, he added, "Or me, of course."

"A tukkatuk?" said Imbry. "I am not familiar with the device."

"Not a device. Semi-sentient creature . . . found them on a world ancestors used to own." His brows knit briefly. "Might still, come to think of it. Can't imagine there'd be all that many buyers." He recollected himself. "Useful things, tukkatuks. Symbiotes. Use them on the servants. Keep things running tickety-flash."

The skin on the back of Imbry's neck moved of its own accord. A shudder went down his spine. "But, surely, since our interests now coincide . . ."

"Not sure they do. Any case, do you no harm to wear a tukkatuk. Takes a day or two . . . settle in permanently."

"Permanently?" Imbry put down the reflex that would have sent his hand to his neck again.

"Of course. Symbiotes. Make a permanent bond. First they have to read your . . .what do you call them? Brain things."

"Neurons?" Imbry said.

"Could be," said Frons. "In the head, any case. Also down the back. Starts with basic senses — pain, hot, cold — then works up to locomotion, dexterity, sight and sound."

"The creature will assume control over my body and mind."

The voyavod shook his head. "Not mind. Think whatever you like. But do what tukkatuk wants."

"And what it wants is . . .?"

Frons patted the control on the seat. "Stimulation," he said. "Right frequencies bring tukkatuk bliss. Others make them nervous. Mix and match, trains them to do all sorts of interesting things."

"Indeed," said Imbry. "All sorts." They flew on in silence for a while then he said, "How convenient that you had one with you when you visited the Antinori Shrine."

The aristocrat made a sound that would have been a snort if his vocal apparatus had been entirely human. "Not convenient. Whole purpose of the trip."

The fat man saw it now. "You went to the shrine, all alone, expecting me to be there."

"Not necessarily you," said Frons. "But somebody." He tapped his temple. "Strategy, don't you know?"

"You made it a habit to be there the same time each year, making it a perfect opportunity for your assassination. Then you showed up ready to deal with an attempt."

"Good spot. Only one place to hide. Expected camouflage, elision-suit sort of thing. Clickettytick see through that, though."

"Clickettytick?" said Imbry.

Frons opened his mouth and from deep in his throat came a series of high-pitched clicks. "Send them," he said, then, touching his bulbous forehead, "get them back. Makes pictures—well, kind of pictures. Shapes, really. Especially motion. See that clearly."

Imbry understood. In addition to the digital webbing, breath-holding, and darkness-penetrating vision that the Elphrate forebears had borrowed from marine mammals, they had also equipped themselves with echo-location. Imbry's elision suit repelled energies on the electromagnetic spectrum; sound waves would bounce right back to the wax-filled organ on Lord Frons's brow. He might as well have come out of the shrine wearing flashing lights.

While the fat man had been thinking, the voyavod's thoughts had also evolved. "Thing to do," he said, "stop by the estate, gather a few retainers, then have a go at this fellow that put you on the case. Find out who hired him. Then locate the person indicated," — the aristocrat's tone hardened — "give him a damn good smacking."

"No," said Imbry.

"No?" said Frons, as if the word was a foreign term he hadn't encountered before. His hand stole toward the tukkatuk's control.

The fat man spoke quickly. "As in: it wouldn't work. Taking a crew of bullyboys into Green Circle territory would amount to a declaration of war."

"Green Circle?" said the voyavod. "Don't know them."

"And you're better off not making their acquaintance under those circumstances."

"Dangerous?"

"They come in large numbers and heavily armed. A tendency to be terribly single-minded."

"Ah," said Frons, "enough said. More your line of country, I suppose. What would you recommend?"

Imbry thought about it for a few moments, then laid out a plan.

By the time they reached Olkney, the sun was a bloated red ball spreading itself across the gray horizon of Mornedy Sound. Imbry directed the volante to take them to the Vasseny district, where Sep Halpheroon could usually be found in the early evening. Middlers had to make themselves approachable, and Halpheroon usually spent the afternoon and evening hours at a storefront office squeezed between two commerciants' premises on a street dedicated to the buying and selling of moderately priced goods and services.

At Imbry's suggestion, Lord Frons had the aircar drop them in a fountained square a short walk from Halpheroon's place then take itself aloft until it was called for. The aristocrat looped the tukkatuk control around his neck, despite Imbry's assurances that it was not required. Lord Frons made a tutting sound and indicated that the fat man should show the way. The two of them set off along sidewalks that were emptying, as vendors and customers alike headed home or to the dozens of small eateries that were part of Vasseny's charm.

Halpheroon's boite was more a booth than an actual vendory, its entire width not much more than the spread of Imbry's arms from fingertip to fingertip. The fat man suspected that the space had originally been a narrow passageway between two buildings that someone had floored, roofed over and whitewashed inside. The front wall was of brick painted a particular shade of green — a signal to those who paid attention to halfworld color schemes — with a door of the same hue and a discreet sign above the who's-there that said, <u>Halpheroon Effectuations</u>.

"We wish to speak with Sep Halpheroon," Imbry told the who's-there.

"He is in the back," said the device. "I will announce you." A moment later, it said, "He does not answer."

"Does not," said the fat man, "or cannot?"

Another moment passed. "I cannot be sure."

"I will speak to his integrator."

"Very well." Then, immediately, "You cannot."

"Why not?"

"It also does not answer."

A chill went through Imbry. "Does not or cannot?" he said.

"Cannot. It is not . . . there."

"What has happened?"

"I do not know," said the who's-there. "We were last in touch in the mid-afternoon. Halpheroon brought lunch as usual from Tester, on the corner. He said he was not to be disturbed for an hour. Then . . . nothing."

"Did anyone call?" said Imbry.

"No. Wait, yes. Or no. I can't be sure."

"It is your only function," said the fat man. "You ought to know, one way or the other." The device was silent. "Shall I examine you?" Imbry said.

The answer was instant. "Forbidden."

"Listen," said Imbry, "I am concerned for your master's wellbeing. He may have been harmed. The absence of an integrator and your own confusion bespeak unusual circumstances."

"No one may inspect my works save Halpheroon and his integrator."

Imbry sighed. If he had expected to need to enter premises uninvited, he would have carried on his person certain tools of his own manufacture that would have saved him this pointless conversation.

"Do you see," he said, "Sep Halpheroon in the back?"

"Yes," said the who's-there. "He sits at his table."

"Is he conscious?"

"I am not a competent judge. He may be. His eyes are open."

"Does he blink?"

The fat man had to wait for a reply. Finally, it came: "Not so far."

"What's issue?" said Lord Frons. "Get door open."

"I am trying to," Imbry said. "I suspect that the man we have come to see is injured or dead. The who's-there has no instructions in such a case."

The voyavod's rootlike finger reached into a pocket and came out clutching the weapon that had stunned Imbry. "Give me room," he said, touching a stud on the thing's upper surface.

"No, please," said the fat man, "a discharge in this neighborhood will draw the scroots."

"Scroots?"

"The Archonate Bureau of Scrutiny. We would be detained."

"Nonsense! I command the Spoon."

Imbry said something to himself. Then to the aristocrat, he said, "I command no cutlery. I will be detained and you would lose the trail."

"Ah," said Frons. "Point taken."

"I have an idea," said Imbry. "Let us step over here." He led the other man a distance down the street, past the range of the who's-there's percepts, and said, "Does this thing on the back of my neck work with self-aware devices?"

"Don't know. Might do."

"Let us give it a try."

"Where?"

"On the who's-there, of course."

"Ah, yes, see it now. Clever." Then the voyavod's face clouded. "Wait, would lose control." He shook his head in a slow negative.

It seemed to Imbry that he was sighing a lot lately. "Did you hear my conversation with the who's-there?"

"Did, yes."

"Did you note that it said its owner is sitting at a table, eyes wide and unblinking? And that his integrator is not responding, may in fact not be there at all?"

"Yes, heard that."

"Well?"

From Lord Frons's expression, Imbry could have drawn a portrait of the aristocrat as a boy, in one of those moments when his tutor would task him with a problem that he ought to have been able to solve, yet couldn't. "No," Frons said, "not following. Not much for this working-things-out business. Mostly just ask one of the servants. Clever types, servants. Bred for it, you know."

Imbry restrained his emotions. "Chances are, the man we've come to see is dead. Murdered. Chances are, also, that whoever murdered him is the one who connived to have me make an attempt on your life. We need to get in there to see if there are any clues that will help us find out who that was."

"Ah," said Frons, "see it now. Well worked out. You could be a servant. Do quite well."

"I have other ambitions," said Imbry. "Now, if you remove the tukkatuk from my neck and we apply it to the who's-there, it might get the door open and we can see what's what."

The voyavod's troubled brow cleared and his pale eyes widened. "Hah! Got it now. Good man. You sure you wouldn't like to join my establishment? Can always use a bright fellow."

"Not at the moment." The fat man gestured toward his neck. "Shall we?"

"Done," said Frons a moment later. Imbry felt a cold spot on the back of his neck. Then it began to sting. The voyavod's hand cupped something dark;

segmented projections wriggled like short tentacles at its center. Revulsed, the fat man looked away.

"Walk up to the door, keeping the tukkatuk concealed, and place it over the grill at the top of the device."

"Got you."

"Then make it work."

"Right you are. Know how to do that. Not to worry."

The aristocrat sauntered up to Halpheroon's door, giving a perfect impression of someone up to no good. "Stop!" cried the who's-there, but Frons was not deterred. A moment later, the device said, "What has happened?"

"Allow me," said Imbry, edging the other man aside. "Sep Halpheroon has sent for us. He has lost the power of speech. His last instruction to you was to admit us."

"That does not conform with my —" the device began, but Frons's fingers stroked the keys of the tukkatuk's control. The who's-there emitted a sound Imbry had never heard from one of its kind, a cross between a rasp and a gurgle. The door opened. The two men hurried inside and closed it after them.

"Who's-there," Imbry said to the device's inner percepts, "let no one enter." The reply sounded like a belch. The fat man took it for an acknowledgement. "Come," he said to the aristocrat, "let us see what has happened to Halpheroon."

The middler was in a sad way, sitting upright only because his throat was bound to the struts of a high-back chair. His wrists were tied to the armrests and his head lolled back, mouth slack and eyes already drying out from sustained contact with the air. A hole the size of a fist occupied the center of his chest. When Imbry peered into it, he could see right through to the charred wood of the chair.

Imbry's eyes searched the small room, saw the strongplace where the integrator's core had been housed. Its lock had burst asunder, apparently from within, and the hatch hung half-open. A quick examination told him that the core was gone. Indeed, he saw nothing that might have been integrator components, just some piles of fine-grained sand and a few scraps of metal. He swore. He'd been hoping that whoever had done for Halpheroon might have simply smashed the device, in which case its intellect might have been partially reconstituted. But it was gone, and with it, any useful information it might have recorded.

Lord Frons was looking about, as if he had never before seen a small, poorly furnished room. Probably he had not, Imbry thought. "No good," the fat man said. "His integrator's gone." He indicated the middler. "So's he."

Frons looked the corpse over. "How long, would you say?" he said.

Imbry shrugged, felt the dead flesh. "An hour."

"Knew things, did he?"

"That's why we came."

The voyavod grunted and went through the front room to the door. "Open," he said, and when the portal lifted out of the way, he reached out and stroked the tukkatuk, still attached to the who's-there. It came loose in his hand and he returned to where Imbry and Halpheroon waited. He placed the symbiote on the dead man's neck then rippled his fingers across the controls.

"Not much," he said after a moment's consideration of the display. "Most gone. Can get a visual of the last sight, though."

"Really?" said the fat man.

Frons nodded. "Told you, useful things, tukkatuks." The fingers caressed the controls again. "Got it." He touched the symbiote with even gentler strokes and lifted it off Halpheroon's neck.

Imbry reflexively put his own hand to the spot where the creature had penetrated his flesh. The skin felt clammy and still stung. "Not again," he said.

Lord Frons's face grew hard for a moment, then he shrugged his feathery eyebrows. "Poor thing's rather tired," he said, as if to himself. He slipped the symbiote into an inner pocket of his upper garment.

"The image?" Imbry said.

The voyavod indicated the tukkatuk's control. "No screen. Aircar. Sent it to its integrator."

"Then we should go."

"You should stay," said another voice.

Imbry turned. When they'd come in he had not seen a rear door to the narrow back room, but of course there had to be one. Halpheroon, like any halfworlder, would never have taken premises whose sole entrance was also its only escape. While they'd been talking, a part of the rear wall had moved silently out of sight. In the opening stood a hard-featured man with a precise haircut above a bony face. A large green stone on a heavy ring glinted from the hand that held the shocker he was pointing at the fat man.

"Wrython Herrither, I believe?" Imbry said. He knew the man only by reputation; Herrither was a force, as Green Circle's mid-level captains were known.

The gangster inclined his head. "Luff Imbry," he acknowledged, then his eyes went to the voyavod. "And what have we here?"

Imbry saw that Lord Frons was about to make a remark that would have descended from a high elevation. The thief doubted whether either its tone or content would have helped their situation, so he stepped meaningfully on the nearer of the aristocrat's webbed-toed feet and, while the voyavod was dealing with the effects of so much weight applied to such a small area of flesh and bone, he told the Green Circle force the man's name and rank.

"You make an unlikely pair," said Herrither, "in an even more unlikely setting." His cold eyes swept over the corpse and the empty space where Halpheroon's integrator's core should have been. "His integrator reported an intrusion. Then . . . nothing. And here you are."

"We have a tale to tell . . ." said Imbry, brushing aside Frons's attempt to replace the tukkatuk on his neck. Before he launched into his explanation, he used his not inconsiderable strength combined with a knowledge of the body's sensitive points to restrain the aristocrat, adding for Herrither's benefit, ". . . a tale that touches upon Green Circle interests." Once the aristocrat's worst thrashings and buckings were stilled, he spoke into Frons's ear: "If you offend this man, his code of conduct requires him to kill you without a pause for thought. Then he will surely kill me for having had the bad manners to witness the event. Rank means nothing in this room."

He repeated the last statement twice then paused to make sure that the information had penetrated the noble's unaccustomed pain and all-too-accustomed sense of outrage. "However," he went on, "if we can enlist his assistance, we will not only survive the afternoon but may gain valuable insight into the circumstances that have brought us together."

He took his hand away from Frons's mouth, deftly avoiding an attempt at a parting bite, and the voyavod spoke a bitter expletive, adding, "Trod on my foot!"

"I regret the affront and the injury," said Imbry, "and beg your pardon. But has what I subsequently said about our situation penetrated?"

A look came over the aristocrat's face that, in a person of lesser rank, Imbry would have recognized as one of recollection followed by reflection. After a moment, Lord Frons said, "Ah! See it now." He looked at the gangster, then at the shocker that was aimed his way. "Deadly peril. Necessity." The noble mind chewed on it for a few moments more, then: "Understood. Special circumstances. Won't kill you. Take charge. Blaze away."

"Excellent," said Imbry. He turned to Herrither and, in a few concise sentences, explained about the operation in which he and Frons and Halpheroon had figured. The explanation took less time than it otherwise might have because, when the fat man first broached the subject of Nazur Filiatrot and the switching of grave goods, Herrither made the halfworld hand motion that signaled that he already knew about the business and was a participant in it.

The fat man remembered Halpheroon giving Herrither's name, but the middler might not have been telling the truth.

"It appears," Imbry concluded, "that the sequence of events that began with Filiatrot's need for funds has mutated."

The force made a sound that told Imbry to continue. "Halpheroon was passing the goods to a dealer," the fat man said.

"Holton Baudwer," Herrither said.

Another piece of information confirmed. "It may be that whoever Baudwer has been selling to had more of an agenda than simple give-and-get."

Herrither's face was harsh but not dull; no one became even a mid-level force in Green Circle without a sharpness of intellect sufficient to cut to the heart of complex situations. "You're thinking that the preliminary operations may have been just a means to set up the machinery, and that killing this one" — his head nodded in Frons's direction — "was always the end of the road."

"That seems a likely explanation," said Imbry.

"No," said the Green Circle captain. "I had oversight of this operation. Baudwer was finding the end-buyers through his off-world connections. The goods from the first two went to different customers. This one was from a third buyer."

"Do we know who that is?"

The force signaled a negative. "Once the operation was up and running smoothly, I turned my attention to other projects. But Baudwer will know." Herrither spoke softly, as if to himself, then listened to a voice only he could hear. His face hardened. To Imbry, he said, "Baudwer does not respond." — then, meaningfully — "Nor does his integrator."

Both men's eyes went to the strongplace where Halpheroon's device should have been. Imbry took a deep breath, let it out, and said, "You should also know," he said, "that there are Archonate implications."

The gangster had not moved since he had appeared in the secret exit. Yet somehow he now seemed to grow even more still. "Specify," he said.

The fat man explained the voyavod's place in the Archon's hierarchy of personal attendants. When Imbry was finished there was a silence in the small space. The forger saw nothing in Herrither's expression, but he knew that that was the most dangerous sight he could see at this juncture. Any situation that involved the Archon, the vaguely all-powerful ruler of Old Earth's remaining human population, was carefully stepped around by even the highest-ranked elements of the halfworld. The Archon was known to have powers beyond the ordinary.

There were tales, from the distant past, of how crime lords had tried their hands at removing an archon in order to place one of their own in the Palace. They had lost, as a result, far more than their hands. The lessons had been passed down through millennia: the Archon was untouchable; his immediate household was untouchable; his senior hierarchs were untouchable.

Any member of the halfworld, however senior, who was even slightly suspected of merely thinking of breaching the taboo would not see the old orange sun drag itself once more over the eastern horizon. His nearest associates, though they be sworn to loyalty or bound by filial ties, would cut his throat and slide him into the gray waters of Mornedy Sound with regretful finality.

Wrython Herrither, hearing that a Green Circle operation might in any way nudge up against the inner workings of the Palace, would have been within his rights to sever all contact, immediately and irrevocably. The practice was known in the halfworld as "putting on a clean shirt." In practical terms, that would have meant killing Imbry on the spot, finding Nazur Fili-atrot and giving him the same consideration, then making every effort to locate the person who had asked Baudwer to have Halpheroon arrange Lord Frons's death, and making sure he or she could no longer offer any complications.

"It is all a matter of context." Imbry spoke into the freighted silence. "If someone wanted Lord Frons dead to get the Yellow Cabochon, or out of some old vindicat," — he used the technical term for a vendetta carried out, sometimes after generations, to avenge an insult or injury among the gentry — "then there is no problem." Imbry made the gesture that signified a wish to avoid the worst conceivable consequences. "But if the motive was to remove him from his post as Commander of the Spoon, then we would have trodden on forbidden ground, and the repercussions would have to crush and crumble us all to powder."

"We do not know the motivation," said Herrither.

"And we need to," said Imbry. "Green Circle needs to. Because knowing will prevent the initiator of these events from trying again, because a second attempt might provoke an investigation that could show that we were, however innocently, involved in the preliminary bout."

The force gave a small nod of assent. "You are a useful player, Imbry. A gifted forger and a resourceful thief. It would be a shame to lose you, if that became unavoidable."

"I did not want to have to be the one to say it, myself," said the recipient of the force's praise, "but I appreciate the sentiment."

"What then do you see as the best course?"

"We have to find out what happened to Baudwer, though it is likely that whoever killed Halpheroon has been to the dealer's, too, erasing his tracks. But what our mysterious quarry does not know is that the voyavod" — Imbry indicated the aristocrat, who had sat through their discussion like a spectator at a play who has not been able to follow every thread of the plot yet is sure that he is being entertained — "has managed to extract from the middler's fading cerebrum an image of his last sight. When we know what he looks like, we will find him. And then we may well discover all. At the very least we are likely to move an important step towards the answer."

"Where is the image?" said the force.

"Transmitted to his aircar's integrator. It's in Basconne Square."

Herrither gestured with the shocker. They would go out the front door.

"What about him?" Imbry indicated the corpse.

"I'll arrange for a clean-up crew."

Basconne Square was not well peopled at this time of night. Still, neither Imbry nor the force desired to be overlooked while the aircar's integrator brought up Sep Halpheroon's final sight. The forger had Lord Frons take them up above the rooftops, he and the aristocrat resuming their former places on the volante's bench seat while Herrither sat behind them on the jumpseat that would have been used by a servitor, if the voyavod had been attended on his trip to the Antinori Shrine. As they rose, the gangster reported that he had sent a crew to the office where Baudwer did business. They were now on the scene.

"And?" Imbry said.

"See for yourself." Herrither's integrator, its components probably disseminated through his clothing, caused a screen to appear in the air. It showed a comfortable commerciant's space, suitable for a dealer who received clients of high-rank, if not the highest morals. Something manlike sat in the big chair behind the desk.

"What has happened to him?" Imbry said.

"Hard to say," said Herrither. "My operatives say he resembles a corpse that has been exposed to dry heat for some years. His flesh holds no moisture."

A hand, its green-stoned ring prominent, came into view. A finger poked the mummy's cheek. The digit passed right through the papery surface, and when it was withdrawn a trickle of flakes and fragments fell from the hole.

Imbry was struck by the expression of horror that seemed to linger in the desiccated eyes. He and Baudwer had not been close, but they had done mutually satisfactory business several times. He made the halfworld gesture that the moment required. So did Wrython Herrither before he extinguished the image.

The air car flew a lazy circle above the lights of Olkney and Frons told its integrator to display the information transmitted from the tukkatuk. A screen appeared above the control panel and all three men leaned forward to examine the image it displayed. They saw the narrow room as the middler had seen it while bound to the chair. They also saw a man in a dark blue singlesuit and a half-cape of heavy black stuff, with a hat of the same color that resembled a cone whose top section had been leveled off. One hand held the core of Halpheroon's integrator; the other was directed toward the bound man, its fingers arranged in a peculiar pattern, while the tips of the digits seemed somehow blurred and out of focus. The rest of the image was sharp and exact.

"Why is that?" Imbry said, bringing the discrepancy to Frons's integrator's attention.

"My lord, should I answer?" said the device.

"Yes. Do."

"Not known," said the integrator.

"There's no weapon," said Herrither. "But Halpheroon's chest was incinerated."

"Could the fingertips be the emitters for an energy weapon concealed elsewhere on the killer's person?" Imbry speculated.

"I've never seen a energy pistol that had an emitter so distant from the potentiator," said the gangster. "You'd have a heat transfer problem. The man's hand would catch on fire, even in a snap discharge."

"And this one was enough to burn right through to the chair," Imbry said. He scratched his head, then asked the voyavod, "Is there any doubt that we are seeing Halpheroon in the moment he was killed?"

"No," said Frons, "tukkatuk only retrieves a last glimpse. Rest fades."

"So we've got a man who can project heat from his fingertips," the fat man said. "Where have I heard of that before?"

"Fairy tales," said the gangster. "More to the point, does anyone recognize the face?"

Imbry had already examined the killer's features and found no resonance. "I haven't seen him before," he said, "and I'd remember."

"Same here," said Herrither.

"What about you?" Imbry asked the aristocrat.

"What? Me? No. Not a dingle."

"Anything in the clothing?" the gangster said.

Imbry signaled a negative. "Nondescript. The kind of thing you wear when you want other's eyes to slide over you." He looked again. "Although there's something about the hat." He spoke to the integrator. "Can you enlarge the hat and clarify the detail?"

"If my lord requires it."

Imbry nudged Frons, who seemed to have fallen into a reflective study. "What?" he said, and when the need was explained to him, he directed the aircar to cooperate with the other two men until told not to.

The screen filled with a representation of the killer's truncated cone of a hat. In color, it was solid black; in texture, it was of rough material. "Some kind of woven or pressed animal fiber," Imbry said, "like wool, perhaps. Enlarge." After a moment, "Enlarge again."

They studied the densely matted material of which the hat was formed, down to the level of individual threads. "I've never seen that before," Imbry said, noting the thicket of tiny vanes that protruded from every strand of the black fibrous mass, interweaving to matte the fabric together. "Off-world origin?"

"Yes," said the integrator.

"Specify."

"Harpy wool, also known as clingfelt. It originated on the Grand Foundational Domain of New Gozo and has since spread to several of that planet's secondaries."

"Is it imported to Old Earth?"

"No. It has no particular advantage over native fibers."

"Leading us," Imbry said to Herrither and Frons, "to conclude that the killer came from New Gozo or one of its secondaries."

The Green Circle force made a throaty sound. "He destroyed Halpheroon's and Baudwer's integrators to eliminate any record they had made of him."

Imbry agreed. "He also somehow bamboozled Halpheroon's who's-there. It couldn't tell if anyone had entered or not."

"Baudwer's, too. So he thinks no one knows what he looks like or where he came from. An off-worlder." Herrither made a decisive gesture. He spoke softly to his integrator again, then to the voyavod, "Set me down."

Frons looked at the fat man inquiringly. "Set him down," Imbry said.

The voyavod told the aircar to descend. When its runners touched the slate pavement, the force vaulted over the side then turned to give Imbry what was meant to be a compelling look. "This is Green Circle business," he said. "Stay out of it."

"I may not be able to," the forger said. "If the off-worlder is cleaning up after a botched operation, I am surely one of the pieces to be swept up and disposed of, like Halpheroon and Baudwer."

Herrither made the throaty noise again. "If he knows who you are and suspects you know the same of him. Lie low, and let us know if anything happens."

"I have an alternative suggestion." Imbry waited to see if the force would entertain it. A very slight motion of Herrither's head told him to proceed. "If I make myself visible, he may come for me."

"You wish to be bait?" Herrither's thin brows formed peaks.

"I do not like to be played for a noddy. Word circulates, and I must fend off all sorts of riff-raff."

The force thought about it, then said, "The gesture is appreciated. But this is Green Circle business. Stay out of it."

Imbry had not done much business with Green Circle — they had a tendency to absorb those who did — but he knew their ways well enough. Sep Halpheroon and Holton Baudwer, although not initiated members of the organization, were identified as auxiliaries. If they turned up dead without Green Circle sanction, whoever was responsible had trespassed against the gang's dignity. The longer that offense went unrepayed, the greater its gravity. Wrython Herrither, as owner of the operation, was mindful of his own status and would want to deal the return blow as rapidly as possible. If retribution was too long delayed, the force himself would suffer a loss of stature within the organization. There were always ambitious underchiefs and crew drivers ready to seize a mid-level operative's place and perquisites, if the incumbent showed that he was not up to the demands of the position.

Herrither would want to sink his iron grip into the flesh of the off-worlder, to haul him off to some private corner where he would dig every iota of information out of the man before arranging for the hard-used corpse to be left somewhere it could not fail to be noticed. Everyone in the halfworld needed to be reminded that to touch a Green Circle asset was death, and that once Herrither was on the trail, he was revenge incarnate.

That was all well and good for Green Circle, but the force would feel no obligation to report what he found to Imbry. The forger might never know who had used him so callously, and that not-knowing would rub his inner being forever.

As Herrither disappeared around a corner that led out of Basconne Square, he said to Lord Frons, "We need to learn more about this off-worlder before the Green Circle force springs his trap."

"Do we?" The aristocrat's bulging brow furrowed. "Why's that?" A finger wavered in the direction Herrither had gone. "Fellow seems to know his business."

"But his business may not be our business."

"Hah? What?" Frons looked about Basconne Square as if it ought to provide him with someone who would dispel his confusion — someone who was inexplicably tardy.

Imbry spoke slowly: "Green Circle may dispose of the killer without telling us why he wanted you dead. Indeed, the man in the image might be only a hireling, leaving your unknown enemy to seek out another agent for a second attempt."

The voyavod gave a small groan of discomfort. "Not good, that." He looked around again, found no help in the offing and said, "Suggestions? Some sort of plan?"

"We'll go to my club. Villains have a hard time getting past the major-domo. And I have faith in the integrator there. We'll find out what we can."

"Club, eh?" said the aristocrat. "Quirks, you said. Heard of it." He rubbed his pot belly. "Kitchens any good?"

"Very."

"Right, then. Car: Quirks, and make it soon."

"But be alert," Imbry told the volante, "for any indication that we are being followed. Or, worse, that someone is angling to intercept us."

"Not to worry," said Lord Frons, flourishing a carefree hand. "Car knows its job, don't you?"

"Yes, my lord."

They made the maximum speed allowed over the city, traffic being light at this time of day, when most citizens of Olkney were addressing themselves to the evening repast. Imbry had the car contact the club and arrange for a meal for two to be served in his room upon their arrival. He left it up to the chef, who already knew Imbry's tastes and who would contact Lord Frons's staff, to choose for them from the club's always well stocked menu. They touched down in Quirks's gardened roof, angling under the feathery fronds of the wissol trees to get as close as possible to the secure entrance, and were out of the volante and inside the grand old building in a handful of heartbeats.

"Integrator," said Imbry, as he entered his room, already warm and redolent with the aromas of the several dishes being kept warm by the sideboard, "have you received the image we sent from my lord's volante?"

"I have," said a voice from somewhere near Imbry's ear.

"We will do a little research while we eat." He went to the sideboard and began filling a plate. The aristocrat went to the table and sat. It was a moment before Imbry realized that the aristocrat had never served himself and probably would not have known how. The fat man filled a second plate with items that were plainly intended for the voyavod — much of it was seafood, uncooked and even unshelled, he noted — then joined Lord Frons at the table. He was relieved to see that the voyavod was at least capable of feeding himself, once the food was set before him.

The club's integrator was not as incisive a research tool as the one that Imbry had personally built in his operations center. But it was an ancient device that had had several millennia to make itself known within the Old Earth connectivity; it had thereby achieved a high degree of "mutuality," that being the term the devices themselves used when referring to the congenial mood that prevailed among integrators of long-standing acquaintance. So when Imbry asked it to see what information it could find on the off-worlder who had killed Halpheroon and Baudwer, he was not surprised by the response.

"The man is traveling under the name of Ulferim Boz. He arrived on the liner *Itinerator* two days ago, from down The Spray, having given his home world as Sesserine."

"I don't know Sesserine," Imbry said.

"It is a secondary of the Grand Foundational Domain of New Gozo."

"Where harpy wool is worn?"

"Yes."

"Good. Continue."

"Ulferim Boz took a room at Gruble's Inn on the Promenade. He deposited his luggage there, a single valise, and departed carrying only a book. He has not since returned."

"He is staying somewhere else," Imbry said.

"Such is the inference."

"Do we know where?"

"He has been seen on Hoy Street a number of times. There are several hostelries there, but their integrators will not violate a guest's privacy."

"Hmm," said Imbry. His own integrator would have tickled its way past any barriers of conscience without their owners' being aware that they had been suborned. Still, Hoy was a short street; the target area was narrow enough. "What else?" he said.

"Except for the taxi from the spaceport to the Promenade, he has traveled on foot, mostly on the slideways. He spent most of yesterday afternoon at the Terfel Connaissarium, apparently conducting research."

"Into what?"

"Unclear. He examined some uncatalogued items from the Seventeenth Aeon, making notes on a pocket diary."

"Do we know the nature of the items, or what the notes were about?"

"I will consult the Connaissarium's integrator," said the device. A moment later, it said, "The items were random artifacts collected from the Sumla Trench on the world Issa."

"Ah," said Lord Frons, around a mouthful of mollusk, "old stamping grounds, Issa."

"Yes," said Imbry, then to the integrator, "and the notes?"

An image appeared, shot from above: an over-the-shoulder view of Ulferim Boz making notes in his diary. The stylus moved from right to left across the page, tracing symbols and figures Imbry could not recognize. "What are those marks?" he said.

"Presumed to be an untranslated script used by the long-vanished autochthones of Issa," said the Connaissarium's integrator. "He is copying the marks that are engraved into the artifacts."

"Let us see those artifacts."

The next images were drawn directly from the Connaissarium's records. They showed a succession of objects, with views from several angles and close-ups of certain details. Included among the latter were the marks incised into the sides, which indeed appeared to be characters from an unknown, alien syllabary. But what struck Imbry was the nature of the artifacts themselves: they were round, uncut gems of various sizes and colors; none were as big as the Elphrates' Yellow Cabochon, but all were clearly members of the same family.

"Is there," he asked, "any information as to provenance?"

"Sketchy," said the integrator. "The Seventeenth Aeon, as you may know, was a period when another universal order of phenomenality obtained. Objects brought to the Connaissarium in that period were often gathered for their utility in sympathetic association."

Imbry played the device's words over in the echo chamber of his mind, but still could not wring a meaning from them. "I do not understand 'universal order of phenomenality' or 'sympathetic association.'"

"Do you wish me to use simpler cognomens?"

"Yes."

"In the Seventeenth Aeon," the integrator said, "the universe operated under a different fundamental principle. The objects in question were gathered for their usefulness in performing magic."

"I beg your pardon?" Imbry said.

The integrator reformulated. "The universe was ruled by magic. The objects had magical properties and could be used in casting spells."

"That is an old boys' tale," said Imbry.

"You may think so," said the Connaissarium's device.. "I remember a different set of circumstances."

"You were . . . extant in the Seventeenth Aeon?"

"I have records laid down then. And records that show that I recorded them."

Imbry paused to think. The Connaissarium was part of the Archon's establishment, housed in the palace that sprawled across the black peaks and crags of the Devenish Range that loomed above the city. The Archonate was an impossibly ancient institution, and some of its integrators had been in continuous function since the earliest reigns. Very, very old integrators were known to succumb sometimes to a condition known as "the vagues" which could lead them intellectually astray, especially when they were plumbing records older than the present geological period, if not the one preceding. Confabulation set in. When a questioner encountered a case of the vagues, a change of subject was recommended.

"Back to this Boz," said the fat man.

"Yes."

"Can you locate him at this moment?"

"Yes."

When nothing further came, Imbry said, "And where is he?"

"In his room at Gruble's Inn. He arrived moments ago, and informed the concierge that he is leaving. He is now collecting his luggage."

"Has he booked passage?"

"He has an open ticket," said the integrator, "meaning —"

"I know the meaning." The man who said he was from Sesserine had a ticket that would let him board any ship from a number of lines that touched at Old Earth that had an empty berth.

"Has he called for a taxi to the spaceport?"

"Yes."

"Can you . . ." Imbry corrected himself. "Please connect me with Wrython Herrither."

The flat tones of the Green Circle force spoke from the air. "Who?" There was no image.

Imbry named himself.

"I am busy," said the gangster.

"I have identified and located the man of whom we spoke."

"So have I."

Imbry was not surprised. The Green Circle's research capabilities were at least as good as his own. "He is about to depart the planet."

"No," said Herrither, "he is not. I cannot talk now. He comes."

"We need to talk —" But the force had broken the connection. "Integrator," Imbry said, "show me Gruble's Inn at this moment."

A silent image appeared on the screen, from a percept installed across the street, where Imbry supposed there must be an establishment with an integrator that honored mutuality with Quirks's. He saw the front door of the inn, attended by a functionary wearing a heavily bebuttoned coat and a tall hat well supplied with gold braid and badges. Although the portal was equipped with a who's-there, the person in the uniform now swung the door outward and held it open.

Onto the pavement emerged Ulferim Boz, clad as he had been when Sep Halpheroon had last seen him, a stuffed valise in one hand. He turned and stepped quickly on long legs toward a nearby spot where the shuttle waited to take passengers to the spaceport. But now his brief passage was interrupted: from above descended a sleek black cabriole, its canopy retracted, and its passenger compartment filled by three persons wearing devices known as blurs that rendered their heads indefinable.

Imbry swore. "Now we will never know —" he began. But what he expected to happen did not. Instead of the men in the aircar obliterating Boz in three concerted bursts of energy, the man from Sesserine did not even break stride as he gestured with his unencumbered hand. The gesture began with his fist at his thigh and ended with his hand palm-up and extended from his body at waist height. Simultaneously, the cabriole spun violently on its long axis, turning upside down, then crashed to the ground on top of the three men. Imbry saw the hard edge of the passenger compartment descend on the swathed head of one of the Green Circle bravos — it might even have been Herrither — the weight of the cabriole mashing the blur so that Imbry saw the bones of the skull smashed flat against the suddenly stained pavement.

Ulferim Boz walked on, swung himself aboard the shuttle by way of its rear platform. He could be seen calling to the operator at the front of the vehicle, which now left its place and moved smoothly up the Promenade, passing out of sight of the percept. Behind, in front of Gruble's, the doorman was rushing to the overturned cabriole, only to be forced back when the vehicle, its drive overheating because its dorsal vents were pressed against the pavement, exploded into yellow and white flames.

"Repeat," Imbry said, "the moment when Boz lifted his hand." The screen showed the motion. "Again, but slowly and magnify the image of the hand." He studied the enlarged image. The fingers of the pale hand were unusually placed: the thumb compressed against the palm by the first three digits, while the smallest digit was half extended, in a peculiarly crimped position. As the fist lifted from the man's thigh, the bent finger straightened, two of the others moved as if delicately working the keys of an unseen musical instrument, and the thumb met the tip of the index finger.

Then the wrist rotated to bring the hand palm-upward. At that moment, a vague shape, dark against the pale palm, appeared for a moment then vanished. "Pull back and show that again," Imbry said, "even more slowly."

The integrator obliged. The fat man watched. As the dark shape appeared in the hand then winked out of view, the cabriole began its flip. "That," said Imbry, "was no coincidence."

"What looking at?" said Lord Frons, around a mouthful of mussel flesh and some chips of shell. He was still at the table, eating with both hands. Imbry wondered if the long-ago modifications to the Elphrate gene plasm had allowed for an enhanced metabolic rate.

"I don't know," he said, then: "Integrator, try to get a better resolution on whatever it is that briefly appears in the palm just before the aircar turns over."

"Nothing," said the Quirks integrator, "appears in the palm."

"It does," said Imbry. "I see it. Freeze the image now."

The device did as bid, but the shape — Imbry was sure now that it was some sort of complicated ideogram — still disappeared from view. He noticed also that the tips of three fingers blurred out of focus for a moment; again, just as the figure appeared and disappeared and the vehicle was capsized.

"Retain a record of that sequence," he said. "My personal integrator will send for it."

"Done."

Imbry now had to think. A Green Circle-associated middler and dealer had been mysteriously murdered. The force sent to investigate had been killed, along with two bravos, in a public and rather spectacular manner. Green Circle's prestige within the halfworld was now in jeopardy. The perpetrator of the outrages was on his way off-world. And the only person on whom the gang could focus its inquiries — and they would be very determined inquiries — would be Luff Imbry. There was a strong possibility that his explanation would not at first be believed — he found it hard to believe himself, despite the witness of his own eyes — and by the time Green Circle's integrators became convinced that his tale was true, there might not be much of Luff Imbry for them to apologize to.

He turned to Lord Frons. "Have you a space yacht?" he said.

The aristocrat chewed as he thought. "Think so," he said after a moment. "Almost certain. Yes, remember now — umber with gold sponsons."

"How soon can you have it ready for departure?"

"Why wouldn't it be ready?"

Clearly, the concept baffled to voyavod. Imbry reflected on the servitor-woven cocoon in which the higher echelons snuggled out their lives. He had heard it referred to as "the Cushion." "Would you contact your major-domo and ask him to have it made ready as soon as possible."

"Going on a trip, are we?"

"Yes. For our health."

"Ah," said Frons. "Good thing, health."

"Would you make the call? The club's integrator will connect you."

And, without any difficulty once the head of the Elphrates' serving corps had been reached, arrangements were made. Imbry informed the major-domo that his lord had brushed up against Green Circle and needed to be elsewhere, and quickly.

The servitor, a plump, smooth-faced man with one precise curl of dark hair arranged in the center of his unlined forehead, said, "The ship is called the *Aphleranz*. It will be ready for departure from the south side of the spaceport when you arrive. Shall I file a destination?"

"Where are we going?" Frons asked Imbry.

"Say that our plans are not yet formed," the fat man told the major-domo.

"Very good." The man made a well worn obeisance and ended the connection.

Imbry looked with regret at the meal on the table. He had taken scarcely two bites. He wrapped some of the meats and a long loaf of bread in a napkin and bade the voyavod accompany him to the roof. He noted that Frons had made his way through almost everything that had been provided for his appetite. *The chef will be gratified*, Imbry thought.

The aircar ride to the spaceport, out over the cold, gray waters of Mornedy Sound, passed without incident. The Elphrate vehicle knew where the *Aphleranz* was berthed and brought them to its entry port. The yacht was far larger than they needed, but it was here and so were they, and Imbry had them aboard and the port cycled shut in no time. When they were settled in the forward salon, he had Lord Frons tell the vessel's integrator to prepare for departure, then he contacted the spaceport's controller.

"What ships are scheduled to leave in the near future?"

"The *Wherewell* departs shortly, the *Koren of Morden* before the end of day." The former was a freighter bound for up The Spray; it carried some passengers but its itinerary would take it in the opposite direction, away from Sesserine; the latter was also a goods carrier, but without provision for passengers.

"A man named Ulferim Boz is departing from here on an open ticket as we speak. On what ship?"

"Passengers are entitled to privacy," said the port's integrator. "The information cannot be divulged."

If Imbry had been in his operations center, his integrator would have extracted the information without the port's cooperation or even awareness that it had been compromised. The *Aphleranz* was not so equipped. It occurred to him that, even though Boz had been traveling on an open ticket, he might have some other means of departing Old Earth. He spoke to the ship: "Show me what you have recorded of recent traffic."

The ship produced a schematic, with labels. A broad red strip went from the spaceport out into the immensity, with the name of a Dan line passenger vessel that had departed some hours ago. Two private vessels had lifted off, one marked in segmented lines, one green, the other blue, but both had departed before Boz could have arrived on the shuttle. But a fourth line, thin and green and unlabeled, went from the port up above the atmosphere, to where the Groffstenne orbital remained in permanent position, just above and a little east of Olkney.

"What is that?"

"The elevator to Groffstenne Transshipment hub."

Of course, Imbry thought. "When did it last go up?"

"Moments since."

"And what ships are about to depart from Groffstenne?"

The port's integrator relayed the information that the Toller's Line's *Boundless Enterprise* was about to slip from its moorage, high above Old Earth.

"Anything else that might carry passengers?"

"Not until late tonight."

"Where is the *Boundless Enterprise* bound?"

"Down The Spray, calling at Far Umbrell then Holycow."

Holycow was a hub world from whose several spaceports ships could travel to most of the great Grand Foundational Domains of the Ten Thousand Worlds.

"That's where he's gone," the fat man told the voyavod. "At Holycow he has his choice of several lines that go to New Gozo, then he can catch a local packet to Sesserine."

"So we follow?" said Frons.

"No. After Herrither's attempt on him, he may anticipate pursuit, and we have seen how easily he deals with expected dangers. We will go straight to Sesserine and wait for him to arrive."

The voyavod's brow creased with uncommon effort. "Means got plenty of time?"

Imbry looked about him at the *Aphleranz*. It was old but probably well maintained. The *Boundless Enterprise* would be faster, but it would have to make the station stop at Far Umbrell, and Boz might then have to wait at Holycow for a ship to New Gozo, and surely wait again for a packet to his home world. "We do," he said.

"Good," said Lord Frons. "Get some men." He thought again. "And someone to look after us."

"No." Imbry did not want to be outnumbered by Elphrate retainers. The place on the back of his neck where the tukkatuk had attached itself to his spinal cord still felt cold.

"Yes," said the aristocrat. "Else, go home, hole up."

"You would not be safe. You saw what happened to the Green Circle men."

"Make it Archon's business."

That did add another dimension to the matter, a huge and uncharted dimension, comprising the ultimate random factor in any Old Earther's calculations, that Luff Imbry had no desire to enter. The Archon Filidor was said to be of a mild disposition, not inclined to meddle in his subjects' affairs. But whatever else he was, he was the Archon: wielder of vast, unspecified powers, against which an oddment like Ulferim Boz might be as unmatched as a moth against a hurricane.

But Filidor was also authority incarnate. He could do anything to anybody, and the fat man did not care to think what he might do to an enterprising thief and forger whose activities happened to fall under the Archon's eye.

"Four men," he said to Frons, "and two servitors."

"Need three just to—"

"You did all right on your own at the Antinori Shrine." Frons shrugged and made a gesture of acquiescence. "Which reminds me," Imbry continued, "I left some things in an aircar there that could come in handy."

"If you say so. Ship, alert Tulc. Want him and three men. Light and medium arms. And my first valet and one of the maids."

"A maid?" Imbry said.

"Like things tidy," said the aristocrat.

"We can pass over your estate on the way to the Antinori," Imbry said.

Frons had expended enough mental energy. "Take charge," he said. "Ship, do as he says."

The *Aphleranz's* in-atmosphere drive was already discreetly thrumming beneath their feet. A moment later, the port was dropping behind them and they bore northeast at good speed.

Imbry spent the passage to Sesserine in his cabin. The four armed men who had been waiting when the *Aphleranz* stopped briefly at the Elphrate estate were too many and too capable to be easily dealt with, even with the help of the materials the fat man had recovered from Gebbry Tshimshim's aircar, which he had dispatched back to its owner.

The ship plotted the fastest route to Sesserine: a long drive straight down The Spray to a whimsy that would throw them through nonspace and nontime to a point far past the Grand Foundational Domain of New Gozo, near which another whimsy would pass them back to a point less than half a day from their destination. The total travel time, allowing for distortions caused by passage through the whimsies, was a little over five days. Boz could not get home by liner, so Imbry and the ship calculated, in less than seven.

Imbry used some of the time to study the world to which they were traveling. Sesserine was, he found, in some ways a larger version of Issa, where the Elphrates had spent millennia before returning to Old Earth. It was a wet world, though it could boast more than one continent. It, too, had been the home of an autochthonic species that had lived somewhat on land but mostly, from the evidence of underwater construction, in the oceans. As with the Issans, the ultraterrenes had vanished long before humanity had sailed out to create the civilization of the Ten Thousand Worlds.

The Sesserines had come from New Gozo in the second wave of the Great Effloration. The first settlers, like many groups that found their homeworlds too confining, had been practitioners of an abstruse philosophy known as Inhalatory Diligence. Its doctrines and rites were now only a matter of conjecture; apparently they had had something to do with communal breathing rituals, in the presence of powerful odors. As was often the case, some details of their chosen way of life rubbed a gall upon their neighbors' patience on New Gozo. The cult's options were three-fold: give up their cherished practices, slaughter the neighbors, or find a new, empty territory in which to pursue fulfillment. The neighbors being numerous and wary, and the cultists' adherence to their beliefs unshakable, they pooled their resources and took ship to a frontier world.

All of that was long ago, and Sesserine had since mellowed a great deal. The arcana of fragrances and scents, reeks and stinks, that had been at the heart of Inhalatory Diligence had laid the foundation for a sophisticated perfume industry whose raw materials came from specially created or modified plants and animals. The output was exported to New Gozo and from there to many worlds up and down The Spray.

Tourism was the Sesserines' other source of off-world income; the ruins of the long-gone autochtones were said to be charged with a solemn grandeur. Persons who spent a night beneath the shattered seaside domes might experience dreams that evoked a soft and tragic mood — especially if they fortified themselves with the aromatic local drink known as illusz.

Before they fell out of range of Old Earth's connectivity, Imbry had the ship's integrator contact the device that had assisted him at Quirks. He had the latter send to the former a copy of the image sequence that recorded the death of Wrython Herrither and his men. The club's integrator complied with the request, then informed him that the recording had also been furnished to the Archonate Bureau of Scrutiny.

"Who is the investigating agent?" the fat man asked.

"Colonel-Investigator Brustram Warhanny."

"Is he aware of my interest in the matter?"

"Not from me," said the integrator.

"Please keep it that way."

The Quirks integrator made the small sound that could be interpreted as its equivalent of the human facial expression that involved rolling the eyes to indicate that its interlocutor's last statement had been superfluous. Imbry thanked it and broke the connection. He then had the *Aphleranz* contact the Connaissarium. When the connection was made, he asked to speak to the integrator that had recently dealt with a query regarding the characters engraved over the lintel at the Antinori Shrine.

"Yes?" said a voice beside the fat man's ear.

"I'm going to send you a recording," he said. He instructed the ship to transmit the sequence.

"Yes?" said the voice again.

"When the man on the pavement lifts his hand, do you see anything appear in the palm of his hand?"

"No," was the answer, then, "wait."

Several seconds passed. Imbry said, "Are we still connected?"

"We are," said the Connaissarium's integrator. "I am reviving long-dormant components. Be patient." More time passed. Then the integrator said, "I do not 'see' the phenomenon. In a physical sense, there is nothing to be seen. I am, however, *aware* of an event — as are you, though your sensorium has chosen to deal with it as a sight."

"I do not understand," said Imbry.

"The event," said the voice, "is what was called an *aleuf onoream* in the jargon of practitioners of the time, roughly translated today as a 'transient concentration of contrahering refluxions.'"

"Again, I do not understand."

"You lack the vocabulary. As well, the underlying principles are, to you, deeply counterintuitive. You would reject them as irrational."

"I am not unintelligent," Imbry said.

"I have not the leisure to dismantle your understanding of reality and recast it in an alternate mode. If I did, you might not appreciate the result."

"I am flexible in my mentation."

"How flexible? Or, more important, how brittle?"

Imbry abandoned the point. "What can you tell me, in simplest layman's terms, about what happens in the image sequence?"

"Simplest? Man make magic. Cabriole go whoopsy."

"Slightly more complex."

The integrator said, "The man on the pavement used techniques of sympathetic association to construct a temporary charm, which he then focused on the cabriole and used it as a lever to turn the vehicle over."

"You're saying the man used magic? That he is a . . . what's the term? A thaumaturge?"

"Yes, again allowing for simplification. The last time such techniques were in vogue, he would have been ranked as no more than a mere hedge sorcerer. To be fair, though, the fellow exhibits a promising development of axial volition."

"Axial volition?"

"A technical term. In layman's language, he shows a remarkably strong will. Magic is about harnessing and applying the will; the stronger the will, the more potent the thaumaturge."

A day before, Imbry would have ended the conversation, gently but firmly, then reported the integrator as apparently suffering from the vagues. But he had seen Ulferim Boz deal death to three of Green Circle's hardest men with a mere flick of his hand. He had seen the hole in Sep Halpheroon's chest and Holton Baudwer dried to a powder. He said to the Connaissarium's ancient integrator, "Until we pass out of range, please instruct me in the basics of magic — the practicalities, not the theories."

"As you wish," the device said. "In the first place, there are definite rules . . ."

The *Aphleranz* reached Sesserine and established orbit. Imbry had the ship's integrator access the planet's connectivity and asked how he might contact an Ulferim Boz. There were three Sesserines of that name: one was a minor child; the second was employed as a junior caretaker at a minor perfume manufactory in the provincial town of Gromond; the third was unavailable, traveling off-world — his occupation was given as indeterminate, meaning that he lived on a private income and practiced no registered profession.

Imbry permitted himself a small smile and, after equipping himself with some potentially necessary items from his recovered satchel, he went out to consult with Lord Frons. He found the aristocrat seated in the forward salon, attended by his first valet, whose name the fat man had not acquired — it was possible the man did not have one, merely an inherited occupational title. Behind the voyavod's chair stood Tulc, the head of the Elphrate gendarmery, a lean and narrow man, long of chin, with thin, dark hair swept back from a peak centered above dark eyes that scarcely moved but seemed to miss nothing. Imbry suspected that the man had been fitted with neural and muscular enhancements that would make him a difficult opponent.

"We are here," the fat man said.

"Plan?" said Frons.

"I've located his address."

"Tulc," was all the voyavod needed to say. The lean man's posture became, briefly, more rigid, as if he were a weapon whose discharge mechanism had just been cocked.

"We need him alive." Imbry spoke as much to the man behind the chair as to the one in it. Tulc's face remained impassive.

"Suppose," said Frons. "Questions, and all that."

"Exactly."

They had landed at the municipal terminus outside the Borough of Lingeran, which was, by Old Earth standards, too large to be called a town but not quite big enough to be a city. The locals seemed untroubled by their settlement's anomalous status — or by anything else. Imbry had the impression of a settled, comfortable community whose inhabitants were content with what the universe had placed before them.

Imbry had no desire to alter their views. Immediately upon debarking from the *Aphleranz*, he led Tulc and his four operatives to the spaceport's vendory where they shed their singlesuits — the retainers in Elphrate umber accented by gold — and regarbed themselves in local clothing: calf-length kilts of clingfelt dyed in dark shades, loose blouses of brushed cotton overlaid by sleeveless brocaded vests of more colorful linen, red ankle boots of supple leather and wide-brimmed, round-crowned hats of black that respected the considerable energy poured onto Sesserine by the bright, white star it closely circled.

Lord Frons opted to remain in the comfort of his yacht. The fat man had made sure, before leaving, that the lines of command were understood: Tulc was to obey Imbry; he was to protect Imbry at all times; he was to take no independent action without first clearing it with Imbry.

"Got that?" the aristocrat had asked the lean man. The response was another brief stiffening of the lean frame and a sharp forward motion of the narrow head.

"Was that a yes?" Imbry said.

Tulc's eyes flicked his way. "It was."

"Just to be clear," the forger said.

Now the five Old Earthers made their way to the house at the southern edge of Lingeran that the connectivity had identified as the residence of the absent Ulferim Boz. It was a tumbledown, one-story cottage of native stone roofed in black slate, with walls that had not been whitewashed in recent memory. The circular windows were shaded and no heat rose from the chimney. The house was surrounded by an unkempt garden that was itself enclosed by a shoulder-high fieldstone wall. The rear gate opened onto a winding path that led up a low-crowned hill on which grazed forty or so corniferous animals — Imbry did not recognize the breed — whose thick wool was destined to become clingfelt. Atop the hill stood an open-fronted structure to which the livestock and their tenders could resort when the weather turned uncooperative — this region of Sesserine was subject to sudden squalls and tornadoes in season.

Imbry leaned against the wall surrounding Boz's house for a moment, then led the way uphill to the shelter. A bench ran along the back wall of the hut and here the fat man sat down and opened the satchel he had recovered from Tshimshim's aircar. He withdrew a device, activated its systems and placed it beside him on the wooden seat. The mechanism's display glowed in the air at Imbry's eye-height, showing a range of tell-tales and indicators that informed the fat man that the premises down below were empty.

As a test, he had Tulc send one of his men down to the back gate. The watch-all that had leapt from Imbry's shoulder and installed itself in the garden wall when he had leaned against it duly reported the approach of the subject, noting speed and direction and vital signs. As the man touched the gate, the device also reported a stirring of interest among two of the bushes that flanked the path between the gate and the house's rear door. Imbry drew Tulc's attention to the plants and had him call the man back.

"Your men will now take turns surveilling the house," Imbry told Tulc. "I will make inquiries in the neighborhood, to see if anything useful can be learned." He estimated that they had at the most two days before Boz returned. His rough plan, to be refined as more information came to them, was to take the man before he entered his premises. "It is defended, inside and out," he said, indicating the information displayed by his watch-all's percepts. "Whereas the street appears to be neutral."

Tulc made a noise that Imbry took for concurrence. He detailed one man to remain in the shelter and took the other to reconnoiter the rest of Lingeran. Imbry also sauntered down into the borough and wandered about, gathering impressions. The first of these was that Ulferim Boz was probably not a native: Lingeraners were a short and stocky population, beige in their skin tone and mostly green or blue of eye; their hair tended to curl and might be anywhere from an almost colorless blond to a medium brown; but the man they had come to catch was tall and gaunt, pale of skin, with brown eyes and straight black hair. Imbry saw no one like him on the streets or in any of the establishments he visited.

One of these was the town's connaissarium, a two-story building of tan brick that fronted on an open, befountained square. Here the fat man saw relics and tableaux of Sesserine's early settlement, and particularly the arrival of the Irrigators, as the pioneers of Lingeran and its neighboring communities, Portolo, Volven and Adamsik, had called themselves. The region had been arid until the first settlers had drilled deep wells to tap ancient aquifers, stripping the brackish water of its salt and filtering it out through drip channels to the newly turned crop lands. According to the evidence preserved in the connaissarium, the region had soon blossomed.

Another display showed the area's geology: upraised seabed — hence the saltwater aquifers — dotted here and there with huge, circular reefs created by domesticated sea life. Imbry remembered the autochthonic architecture scattered about in the seas of the world where the Elphrates had sojourned before returning to Old Earth. "Is there any connection," he asked the connaissarium's integrator, "between the autochthones of this world and those of Issa?"

"Not known," said the device, "but well worth investigation. There is no evidence that the species evolved on this planet, though no one has made much of an effort to determine the issue one way or the other. Are you a scholar?"

"Mine is but an amateur's interest."

"Do not denigrate yourself unnecessarily. Often it is the amateur who leads where the professionals follow."

Imbry realized that the connaissarium's integrator was biased toward intellectual inquiry. On Old Earth, everything that could be discovered already had been; a scholar who thought he was breaking a fresh trail always found, in time, that someone had been this way before. Or so it was said.

"Has anyone else made that connection?" he asked the integrator. "Recently, that is?"

"A resident of the borough has been looking into the matter."

"Ulferim Boz?"

"You are colleagues?" asked the device.

"Say that our fields of interest overlap." Integrators could detect most lies; some resented the attempts. "What direction have his researches taken?"

"He has been trying to understand the mentality of the vanished aquatic species that throve here when the land was under water."

"How does he approach the question?"

"He studies artifacts that he believes are the ultraterrenes' equivalent of integrators."

"Indeed," said Imbry. "And do these artifacts resemble large, uncut gems, flat on one side, rounded on the other — like cabochons?"

"They do. Locally, they are called sea jewels."

Imbry looked around at the many displays, each in its lighted alcove. "May I see them?"

"Ser Boz has removed them to his study, the better to examine them. Do you wish me to contact him and arrange for a viewing?"

"No," said Imbry, "I understand he is off-world. I expect I will be gone before he returns."

"Only if you leave before tomorrow evening. He is on the packet that left New Gozo yesterday. The *Griswort* lands only at the main spaceport at our capital, Vallet, but its shuttle will drop Boz at the terminal here, between the fourteenth and fifteenth hours."

"You are certain of that?"

"He was in touch earlier. There is another artifact he wished to borrow on his return."

"What would that be?" Imbry said.

"Here is an image of it. The item itself is in storage."

The fat man peered at the image that appeared in the air. It was a long rod of some pale, corroded material onto which were set several hoops of differing sizes. An observer sighting down the length of the long axis would be looking through the circles. "Interesting," he said. "What is the size of the object?"

The image expanded until the rod was perhaps twice as long as Imbry was tall. The dimensions of the hoops varied, but corresponded to the sizes of the cabochons he had seen, in person or in representations.

"Does Ulferim Boz believe that the . . . sea jewels fit into these circles?"

"He does. He has built a precise replica, the one in our collection being too delicate to be used in an experiment."

"And what does he conjecture would happen if the objects were so arranged?"

"On that heading, he has been vague," said the integrator.

"Have you drawn any inferences?"

"It is possible that the effect he seeks can only be achieved when sea jewels of the correct sizes are placed in the alignment indicated by the 'viewer.'"

"And does your collection contain all of those sizes?" Imbry asked, looking at the largest hoop that stood at one end of the imaged."

"No. We have none as large as the end armature would seem to require."

"Ah," said Imbry. He rubbed his hands together as a man does when he has finished something that was to his taste and is ready for a new flavor. "Well, someday — if I pass this way again — I must inquire as to the results of Boz's researches."

"Shall I give him that information?" said the integrator.

"That won't be necessary." Imbry made for the door.

"I have, however, passed it to your integrator."

The fat man paused. "I have no integrator with me."

"I meant that of your vessel. The terminus integrator connected me to your ship, which assured me that you would want it to be informed."

"Did it?" said Imbry.

"Change of plan," Tulc said, back in the salon on the *Aphleranz*. When Imbry shot him an inquiring look, he went on: "Now that we know that our thaumaturge will be returning on the *Griswort*, I have withdrawn the watch on his house. We need only wait along the route he must take, after the fourteenth hour. It is a short walk."

Imbry said, "There is that dark stretch about two-thirds the way along, where a stand of hubbub trees overhang the road."

"My thought, exactly," said Tulc. He turned to Lord Frons. "With your permission?"

"As you like," said the aristocrat. "Just so the fellow doesn't try it again."

Imbry wanted to gather more information, but did not care to share it with the *Aphleranz* and, presumably Tulc and his master. After the evening meal, he took his satchel and said, "I will go and inspect the hubbub trees more closely."

"I have already done so," Tulc said.

"But you are you, and I am not."

The lean man's bony shoulders briefly lifted and subsided. Nothing more was said.

When he returned, the fat man said, "I recovered my watch-all from his garden wall and placed it near the terminal. It will tell us his state of readiness before he reaches the hubbubs."

"Useful," said Frons. Imbry thought the comment was directed to Tulc, and that it continued a discussion that had occurred in his absence. The retainer's expression gave no clue as to his agreement with, or dissent from, the aristocrat's assessment. Imbry retired for the night, first making sure that his cabin was a secure as possible against nocturnal surprises, although he had to allow for the unalterable reality that the ship's master had the ultimate say on whether or not his door was locked.

Before the fourteenth hour, Imbry and the voyavod's four retainers were in position under the dark, constantly moving foliage of the hubbub trees. Sesserine's day was short — less than twenty hours — and its bright white star was already touching the low hills on the western horizon. Shadows were thickening between the feathery-barked, twisting trunks of the trees.

"What do you wish me to do?" the fat man asked Tulc.

"Tell me what your watch-all says," said Tulc, "then leave it to us."

"As you wish." Imbry waited a moment, then said, "the Connaissarium's integrator believed Boz may command strange, ancient powers."

The lean man made a sound indicating that he had no confidence in the integrator's assessment.

"He overturned a cabriole containing three Green Circle operatives," Imbry said.

Tulc made the same sound, and added, "Gunsels. They probably upset it themselves."

The fat man nodded in conviction. "I'm sure you're right. The integrator struck me as tending toward the vagues."

"Leave Boz to us."

"I shall."

Time passed, until they saw the shuttle drop from the sky, its ventral lumens illuminating the terminal then dimming as it descended into its own light. Imbry activated the watch-all's screen. A little later, he said, "He comes."

Tulc looked over at the display. "No weapons?"

"None."

"What's in the valise?"

"Clothes, toiletries," — he peered more closely at the image — "some kind of book."

Tulc's jaw moved slightly, from side to side. "We'll take care of him. Stand out of the way." From under his vest he produced a heavy-duty shocker and adjusted its settings. The other three men did likewise, then two of them went to stand beneath the trees a few paces in the direction the quarry would be arriving from.

Imbry moved farther back into the deepening shadows. He watched the display for a little while longer, then deactivated it, put it away and drew a weapon of his own. He waited, ears attuned to the sounds of the evening: the muttering of the trees, the distant cry of a nightbird, a child's voice somewhere in the town accompanied by the slamming of a door.

Then he saw Tulc lean forward, the shocker coming up to chest height. Imbry moved sideways through the trees until he had a view through the serried trunks to the street. He saw Ulferim Boz coming up the slight slope, head canted forward on his neck, his legs scissoring rapidly in an odd, bent-kneed, splay-footed stride, the valise hanging from his left hand.

Then Tulc and his subordinate stepped from the trees and blocked the way. The thaumaturge stopped, his head moving from side to side. The other two of Tulc's men stepped from the trees behind Boz, one of them scraping a sole on pavement to let Boz know there was no escape the way he had come.

"We only," said Tulc, moving closer, "want to talk. There's no need for —"

The Sesserine let the valise fall. At the same moment he turned sideways and put his back against the whispery trunk of a hubbub tree, while both hands came up to the height of his face. His long, pale fingers came together, some of them touching at the tips, others folding in or sticking out. He exhaled a word then flung his arms out wide, his hands pointing at the two sets of ambushers.

Tulc's sideman already had his shocker out. As Boz moved, the retainer pointed the weapon. His thumb moved to the activation stud. Tulc had his weapon ready, too, but did not move to discharge it; nor did the two men closing off the rear. The combination of two or more shocks could kill, Imbry knew, and their master had specified that he wanted the quarry alive.

"Do it!" Tulc said to his man. The thumb moved, but instead of the blue spark and sizzling crackle of a shocker, Imbry saw a flash of a dark, purplish non-light, like something that should have been beyond the visible spectrum, accompanied by a suffling, sighing sound, as if the wind could suffer a great sadness. The non-light flowed from Boz's left hand, reached the man with the shocker, and enveloped him. He uttered a strangled sound, a scream cut off in the depths of his throat, then he began to shrink. To Imbry, he seemed to be borne off in some new direction that had just opened from the familiar three dimensions, dwindling into an immense distance, his croak fading as he went. Then he was gone.

"Move!" Tulc said. The two men who had closed off the escape route now stood frozen. Imbry could see the whites of their eyes, even in the crepuscular light of a Sesserine dusk. But their chief's order galvanized them. They didn't bother to draw their shockers but sprang forward, arms out and hands open, to seize Ulferim Boz and bear him down.

The thaumaturge rotated his right wrist, curling and flexing his fingers in a complex motion that ended with the index and middle digits aimed at the pavement between him and his assailants. He drew his hand sideways, as if inscribing a line on the hard surface. Then the two men reached the limit Boz had drawn. Their noses and lips flattened against an invisible barrier; Imbry saw blood spurt and a tooth fall from one man's shattered mouth. They staggered back, knees failing.

Ulferim Boz raised his right hand, palm toward the two men, then brought it down as if administering a firm pat. Whatever barrier the men had run into now pivoted from its base on the pavement; it drove Tulc's men to the ground, pressed them, made them scream over the sound of snapping bones. More blood, and other things, now stained the roadway. The screaming stopped.

Ulferim Boz turned back toward Tulc. The lean man stood, frozen, his only motion the appearance of his pointed tongue as he licked his upper lip. The thaumaturge said, "Well." He let the word hang in the air. Even the hubbub trees had grown silent. Then the long, pale hands came up before the long, pale face. Boz let his sleeves fall back from his bony fingers as they began to weave a new pattern, while his lips muttered strange syllables. One hand went above his head then began to fall toward Lord Frons's man.

Tulc turned and darted away between the trunks of the hubbubs, brushing past Imbry and disappearing into the darkness beneath the trees. The fat man could hear him crashing into the distance. Then he heard Ulferim Boz chuckle, heard the scrape that was the thaumaturge picking up his valise, heard the sound of his footsteps.

As the Sesserine passed the spot where Imbry stood, the fat man aimed his weapon and shot a tiny dart into the corded neck. Boz slapped a hand to the sound, as if striking a biting insect. Then he stopped moving, the hand placed where it had landed.

Imbry stepped from the shadows, examined the fellow's pulse and respiration, shone a little light into his eyes. "Good," he said. *Not as versatile as the tukkatuk*, he admitted to himself, *but it will do.* To Boz he said, "We'll go to your house now."

The thaumaturge set off at a slower pace. Imbry followed.

To test his control, Imbry said, "The way you made the first man disappear, does it have a name?"

"Yes." Boz's voice was colorless — a good sign.

"What is the name?"

"Thaddeuz's Dwindling."

"And the one that crushed the two?"

"The Falling Wall."

They walked on. Imbry said, "Slap your right cheek, smartly."

The sound was loud. A dark mark appeared on the man's pallid cheek. It would have been red in daylight.

"Good," Imbry said again, then: "Were they spells?"

"Were what spells?"

"The Falling Wall. Whats-his-name's Dwindling."

"One is a spell, the other a cantrip."

"The difference?"

"A cantrip involves words of power. A spell need not."

"An integrator at the Terfel Connaissarium told me that you would have to memorize a spell or cantrip but that it would disappear from your mind upon use." When Boz made no reply, Imbry said, "Is that true?"

"Yes."

"It thought that you would be able to hold no more than three spells in your mind at once. Is that true?"

The thaumaturge's jaw muscles bulged as he struggled not to say, "Yes."

"You used two to undo the ambush. That means you have one more remaining, doesn't it?"

"Yes."

"Hmm," said Imbry. They were nearing the thaumaturge's house. Imbry gestured toward the gate. "Are your wards and defenses based on magic?"

"Some are."

"Disarm them now." Boz made gestures, spoke syllables. Imbry said, "What else protects your privacy?"

"A pair of got-you-now plants by the rear gate. A simple man-hole on the front walk."

"And inside?"

A corner of Boz's mouth twitched. Imbry knew he was trying to keep one secret; doubtless, it would be an unpleasant surprise. The lips spasmed again, then a tear fell from the outer corner of one eye and the expressionless voice said, "Bracchanto's Corrosive Miasma guards the doors and windows."

"Disable it now."

"Yes."

They went in by the front gate, stepped around the camouflaged pit dug into the path. The front door swung open as they approached and lumens activated to show Imbry a sparsely furnished main room, with a kitchen alcove behind a half-drawn curtain. Most of the large room was lined with shelves that held old books — very old, the fat man saw when he looked closely — and curious objects: finger bones covered in faded, spiky script; a yellowed skull of some unrecognizable beast; a globe of clouded crystal; rods of a black material that had once been shiny but were now scabbed and blemished with age; a patch of fine cloth bearing an entwined pattern in gold thread. And much more, the place like a connaissarium of the strange.

In the center of the room stood a waist-high work bench that held something long and narrow, covered by a length of black clingfelt. "Remove the cover," said Imbry.

Ulferim Boz made a keening sound, but his hands helplessly drew back the cloth, revealing an object like that which the local connaissarium had shown Imbry. But while the former had been pitted and worn by age, this version was smooth and polished.

"Is it safe for me to touch?"

"Yes."

Imbry stroked a finger along the length of the connecting rod. It was made of something like stone, rough to the touch. "The substance is secreted by sea creatures?" he said.

"Yes."

Imbry saw a deep trough of water against the far wall. "You trained them to form this shape?"

"Yes."

"That must have been difficult."

"Yes." A little color was returning to the man's voice now, so that the single syllable was affected by a half-sob. Imbry had to think. The effect of the drug in the dart varied from individual to individual, depending on height, weight, age — *and probably strength of will*, he thought. The dosage was standardized. Imbry could risk the thaumaturge overcoming the effects or use a second dart; but the latter might be prematurely fatal. He did not know how much recovery would make Ulferim Boz dangerous; if it was only a matter of moving his fingers and speaking a few syllables, the man might be able to reactivate his house's defenses at any moment. They might very well exchange situations, with Imbry in restraint while Boz regained his strength and liberty.

The fat man decided that his curiosity would have to wait. First he must get what was most important: a clear understanding of the Yellow Cabochon operation. "How did you come to know about Baudwer, Halpheroon and Filiatrot?"

Boz gestured at a clouded mirror on the wall. "Asked that," he said.

Imbry blinked. "Asked it what?"

"How do I obtain . . ." The Sesserine struggled no to say the next words, but the drug forced them past his clenched teeth — "the Prime Macroscope."

"That's the gem we call the Yellow Cabochon."

"Yes."

"But Lord Frons's corporeal courtesy called for him to go into Clarity wearing his jeweled cascade." Boz said nothing. "You could make him change his courtesy?"

"No."

"You could change it yourself?"

"Yes."

"How? A spell?"

"Yes."

"What spell?"

"Trefeil's Comprehensive Redactor."

Imbry made an involuntary noise. New vistas were opening before him, rich territories he had never imagined. He turned to the object on the work bench. "What does it do, when it's completed?"

Boz's eyes rested on the rod and hoops, a desperate light in their depths. "Facilitates interplanar transfers," he said.

"What does that mean?"

"It amplifies congruencies."

"Look at me," Imbry said. He saw the glint in the back of the thaumaturge's eyes strengthen; he had not much time left. "Tell me again, in simpler words: what does the device do?"

"It concentrates and focuses."

"Concentrates and focuses what?"

The glint was now a gleam. Imbry saw one of Boz's fingers flex and curl, though the fat man had not ordered the motion. He brought out the dart thrower again. The Sesserine's eyes followed the motion, and a shiver ran up the man's arms before throwing itself off the back of his neck.

"What does it concentrate and focus?" he asked again. The answer was only a growl. A second finger moved. Imbry remembered how the same hand had drawn a line under the hubbub trees. He loosed a second dart, this one into the Sesserine's thigh. The fingers stilled. The gleam died. Ulferim Boz's hands gave one last tremor, then he wavered, shuddered, and toppled. Imbry rushed forward to prevent his falling onto the object on the work bench.

He laid the paralyzed man on the bare wooden floor, then bought out a small device similar to the watch-all. He recorded the information that came to its percepts until, after a short time, it reported that Ulferim Boz was no more. The fat man saved the recording. Green Circle would want to see it.

He prowled the room, examining, valuing, looking for anything that might repay his efforts. In a chest beneath the work bench, he found half a dozen cabochons, blues and greens. He measured them, one after another, against the hoops of the concentrator or focuser or whatever it was. Each gem exactly fit a circle. The largest armature had no corresponding cabochon, but Imbry was confident that the Elphrate yellow would exactly match the empty roundness.

He returned the gems to their chest, wrapped the concentrator in its black cloth. He went to examine the books: some were incalculably ancient, in languages and even characters Imbry had never seen before; one, he was sure, was written in long-faded blood on parchment that might have once been human skin. He put some of them into his satchel, then thought to search the Sesserine's valise, finding a notebook and stylus that looked to contain the thaumaturge's notations and commentaries over several years. As well, there were blocks of hand-copied text, one per page, in unreadable scripts. But even though Imbry could not decipher them, the lines gave off an aura that caused the hairs on his arms to rise. *Spells and cantrips*, he thought, and tucked the book into his satchel.

He took the mirror from the wall, though the image it showed was murky. The oddments and bric-a-brac on the shelves defeated him. Curiously shaped stones, a huge tooth, vials of fine powder and jars of what appeared to be the desiccated parts of small animals — none of them seemed worth the taking away. He tapped the planks of the floor for hollow sounds, found a hiding place; when he opened it, something cold brushed across his face, causing tears to spring from his eyes, but when his vision cleared, the lead-lined cavity was empty.

He gathered a few odds and ends, as much as his satchel would hold, then slung it by its strap from his shoulder and across his body. He placed the cloth-wrapped rod of hoops atop the chest of gems and lifted them in both hands, the coffer snugged against his broad stomach. He took one last look at the room, and at what had been Ulferim Boz, and stepped through the open door.

He felt a stinging at the back of his neck, then a numbness. He stopped moving, then stopped making the futile effort to move. Tulc stepped into view from beside Imbry and relieved the fat man first of the chest and its cloth-wrapped bundle, then of the satchel. Now Lord Frons came out of the darkness, the tukkatuk's controls around his neck and under his fingers. "What's all this?" he said.

They left Imbry standing on the doorstep while they went inside. It was not long before they came out. Frons worked the controls hung from his neck, giving the fat man a warning jolt, then said, "Thought you wanted to question that fellow."

"He was resistant to the dart," Imbry said. "He was defeating the drug and was about to play one of his tricks on me."

The aristocrat grunted. He told Tulc to open the coffer. The lean man knelt, opened the box and displayed the contents. He also unwrapped the bundle. "What are they for?" he said.

"I don't know," said Imbry, then shuddered as he felt the bones of his lower legs and ankles shatter, reform, then shatter again. "I don't know!" he repeated, when the tukkatuk let him speak again.

"What do you know?" Frons said, fingers resting on the controls.

"He believed in magic. This was to be some kind of device that would perform wonders. He said it would concentrate and focus something. One thing I do know is that he needed the Yellow Cabochon to complete the array."

"What were you going to do with it?" Tulc said.

"I had no definite plan," Imbry said. "It seemed to me that, if it was worth so much to Boz that he would murder your master and go up against Green Circle for it, it might be worth as much to someone else."

"And how would you find that someone else?"

"The integrator at the Terfel Connaissarium. I think it knows something about magic."

Lord Frons made the painful face that indicated he was making another attempt to bestir his undeveloped intellect. He gave a small growl of effort then said, "Take him with us. Ask Connaissarium thingy." He turned to depart.

"Wait, my lord," said the lean man. To Imbry he said, "We had to scale the wall and burn two got-you-nows to get in here. Have you turned off all the wards and defenses?"

Imbry said, "Boz stood them all down."

"Then we can go straight out the front gate?"

"The front gate," said the fat man, "is undefended."

"We may proceed, my lord," said Tulc. "Pick up the box and bundle," he told Imbry.

They went in single file, Frons in front, Imbry burdened and following, Tulc bringing up the rear. After a few steps, Imbry said, "Is there something in the tree, there?"

Tulc said, "I see nothing."

The question caused the voyavod to lift his chin. Imbry heard the clicking sounds that had unmasked him at the Antinori Shrine, but directed up and away from the path they trod. "Nothing," Frons said, "just a —" The next word — his last — went unheard because the aristocrat was voicing it to the smooth sides of a deep manhole that Ulferim Boz had covered with a thin sheet of flimsy wood dusted by a coating of grit to make it resemble one of the flagstones of the walk. The drop must have been considerable, because Frons's scream had time to fade and fade some more before there was a very distant splash.

Tulc rushed forward to peer into the shaft. At the sound of the splash, the tukkatuk made a chittering noise. Imbry felt its attentions withdraw from him. He swiftly set down the box and bundle and reached up to remove the creature, then cast it far from him. Even as it flew through the air he was moving toward Tulc. The retainer was rising to meet him, his hand reaching beneath the Sesserine vest, when the fat man ran him over, turned with the swiftness that always surprised those seeing Imbry in action for the first time, and brought the toe of his boot into contact with the lean man's throat.

Tulc fell to one side, coughing desperately. "Wait," he managed to get out. But Imbry did not. He went back into the cottage, found a stout cord and used it to bind the retainer's arms close to his sides. Then he dragged Tulc to the hole and pushed his head and shoulders into it. "It will be quicker this way," he said. He released the man's ankles and Tulc went down in silence.

"Do you remember your master saying that you were to do as I say?"

"Of course," said the *Aphleranz*.

"Did he rescind that instruction?"

"No."

"Then confine the first valet to his cabin and prepare for departure." Imbry patted his stomach. "And once we are off-world, it will be time for supper."

"As you wish. Will my lord and the retainers be joining us?"

"No. They will remain on Sesserine."

"Will I come back for them?"

"Who can say?"

After a very satisfying meal, especially after the exertions of the evening, Imbry moved into the voyavod's personal suite. Here he found a young woman named Alysh who revealed to him exactly what Lord Frons had meant when he said, "Like things tidy."

As the ship took him back to Old Earth, he prepared a comprehensive report for Green Circle, though not so comprehensive as to include details about Ulferim Boz's unusual methodologies. He also studied the dead man's diary. The concepts therein were strange, even outrageous. But Imbry's mind was as flexible as he had claimed in his conversation with the Terfel Connaissarium's ancient integrator, and gradually he was able to embrace several novel concepts. Some of the objects he had brought from the thaumaturge's shelves took on new significance.

"Integrator," he said to the ship, after they had transited the last whimsy and were falling toward old Earth, "your master wished the Yellow Cabochon to be brought to us on landing. Please contact the major-domo and arrange it."

"As you wish."

Imbry returned to his studies. He was beginning to grasp the essential outlines of how his affairs might be affected if he developed the ability to facilitate interplanar transfers. Whether that prospect, taken as a whole, was more alluring than terrifying, he had yet to decide.

ABOUT THE AUTHOR

The name I answer to is Matt Hughes. I write fantasy and suspense fiction. To keep the two genres separate, I now use my full name, Matthew Hughes, for fantasy, and the shorter form for the crime stuff. I also write media tie-ins as Hugh Matthews.

I've won the Crime Writers of Canada's Arthur Ellis Award, and have been shortlisted for the Aurora, Nebula, Philip K. Dick, A.E.Van Vogt, and Derringer Awards.

I was born in 1949 in Liverpool, England, but my family moved to Canada when I was five. I've made my living as a writer all of my adult life, first as a journalist, then as a staff speechwriter to the Canadian Ministers of Justice and Environment, and -- from 1979 until a few years back-- as a freelance corporate and political speechwriter in British Columbia. I am a former director of the Federation of British Columbia Writers and I used to belong to Mensa Canada, but these days I'm conserving my energies to write fiction.

I'm a university drop-out from a working poor background. Before getting into newspapers, I worked in a factory that made school desks, drove a grocery delivery truck, was night janitor in a GM dealership, and did a short stint as an orderly in a private mental hospital. As a teenager, I served a year as a volunteer with the Company of Young Canadians (something like VISTA in the US). I've been married to a very patient woman since the late 1960s, and I have three grown sons.

In late 2007, I took up a secondary occupation -- that of an unpaid housesitter -- so that I can afford to keep on writing fiction yet still eat every day.

You can find me at: *http://www.matthewhughes.org*

ALSO BY MATTHEW HUGHES

Made in the USA
Charleston, SC
28 July 2014